Scylla

&

Charybdis

Lindsey Duncan

Paperback ISBN 978-1-917435-04-8
Epub ISBN 978-1-917435-05-5

Cover art by Emma Sedgwick
Cover design by Ken Dawson
Typesetting by Book Polishers

Acknowledgements

Thank you to the magazine editors who read my original short story and said, "This should be a novel," until I finally listened.

Thank you to all the fellow writers who read pieces of the book and made suggestions.

Thank you to the Grimbold Books team, particularly Joanne Hall, acquisitions editor, who saw the diamond in the rough; Roz Clarke, my editor, who was immensely patient with my strange brain and made this a much better novel; and Creative Director Sammy Smith, who generally made the magic happen.

I also have to give a little shout-out to D'Aulaires' Book of Greek Myths, which is wholly responsible for my childhood obsession with Greek mythology, some of which wandered sidelong into this book. For those attempting to wrap their tongue around the title, both the "c" in Scylla and the "h" in Charybdis are silent (creating a hard k sound), as is the "c" in Themiscyra (seer-uh).

1

WAITING BEHIND THE AIRLOCK DOOR, ANAEA CARLISLE tried to wrap her mind around the nature of the refugees she might see on the other side. She clutched her medic's kit in twitching hands and flicked a glance to Valasca Braun, the angular woman who led the salvage team.

The door oozed open. Anemic grey light filtered in from the ship. Valasca gestured them forward. "Stay cautious," she said through her mask. "If anyone is alive, they won't be expecting rescue. Stun first, apologize later."

Anaea's breath quickened at the thought of the wrecked planets these people must have come from, how desperate they must be: hordes of pirates, clusters of refugees, scorched earth and ruined, abandoned cities. A far cry from the haven of Themiscyra Station, where every hand belonged to a friend. No wonder the ship hadn't responded to communications – if anyone was even in a state to do so.

Even through her mask's filter, the hall smelled like overstewed tomatoes. She moved gingerly, the maglocks in her suit keeping her grounded even without artificial gravity. Electronics hummed and then sputtered. Every time they cracked, she tensed, expecting someone to leap out. Though she was nearly the tallest of the six-woman team, Anaea felt overshadowed by the others: strong, broad, confident, even those without martial training. Would an attacker target her as the weak link? The ship had been adrift, no sign of response to the station broadcast. That didn't mean someone hadn't heard.

Braced, wary, Valasca led the way to a door that had melted open. The ship's hub, its central point for navigation, lay beyond, choked with broken girders. Anaea gasped as she saw the two bodies: one slumped across a console, the other sprawled on the floor, both in white-trimmed uniforms. She swallowed bile as she realized the console had staved in the side of the first figure's head. She had seen bodies before – well, a body – in her rotation training, but those had been clean, anonymous and peaceful, nothing like these two.

They were different in another way. Her eyes widened at the shapes, larger and more square than what she thought of as human norm. The one on the floor had a fringe of hair on the chin. Males.

"Grav system still functioning," Kyme said. "Probably because everything else is fried, so it has power to draw. Might be patchy elsewhere."

She squeezed Anaea's arm in reassurance as Valasca and Marpe inspected the bodies. Anaea managed a smile and returned to staring, the sickness in her stomach temporarily quelled by surprise. She had never seen a man before, not in person. A rare few had been rescued in salvage missions over the decades, but the men's compound was restricted to its caretakers and a few senior personnel. They were very much like the pictures she had studied and the figures in old holo movies, with no visible sign of the disease.

"They're gone," Valasca reported, voice cool. "Can't be more than six hours dead." That time-table meant they hadn't died in the hyperspace corridor, but after the anomaly had ripped them free. The salvage team might have been able to do something, if they had been faster. Anaea's stomach tightened.

"These bodies could still be carriers for Y-Poisoning, or something else," Valasca said. "Masks stay."

Anaea shuddered. In theory, she would be safe, but Y-Poisoning, a mysterious disease engineered by the alien Derithe, had been responsible for the collapse of order in the colonized planets.

The chief doctor pivoted to indicate sectors. "Marpe – top decks. Kyme – engineering. Anaea – mid-level aft. Call in if you find survivors."

Anaea tried to contain her disappointment, surprised it surfaced through her nerves. The preliminary scan of the ship had indicated her area was hit the worst. It was unlikely she would find anything. She clamped down on the thought, feeling a tang of guilt in her mouth. Selfish to make this a matter for excitement, but she had dreamed of such a meeting as a child.

She had to pry the door open, with help from the team's technician. Anaea stepped cautiously, feeling her way where the lights had died, stunner in her hand. She strained in the darkness, drawn taut by unformed hopes and fears of what she might see. The mask shielded her from contagion, but not attack. It also trapped a few strands of dark auburn hair in her field of vision; she puffed them away with a shallow breath.

Wrecks like this weren't common. Small ships, following the hyperspace corridor – to what end? To escape the ruins of civilization? The women of Themiscyra had fled here over a century ago, but they had done so in a colony ship, with the resources to build, to thrive, and to conceal themselves from the criminals that had survived the fall. For decades, isolation had been Themiscyra's only protection from greed and desperation.

Why come out here with nothing?

Anaea had thought she was prepared for her first salvage mission, but training in a simulation when she knew friendly faces waited just beyond the door was nothing like trying to navigate the unfamiliar corridor. She had applied for the salvage team five months ago and been surprised when she was accepted. They must have needed people. She was even more surprised that a wreck had been spotted during her posting.

She tried to picture the ship from the outside, imagine how long this corridor was and how much further she had to travel. She remembered seeing it swell on the shuttle's viewscreen, as dull and pitted as an asteroid. The scroll of diagnostics, too much information and not enough, including the ship manifest and roster.

There had been nineteen people on this ship, the White Hound. That left seven women and ten men who might be alive. Any of the men could be mad with the disease, lashing out at anyone who neared. Anaea reached the dining room door and checked the panel, breath quivering in her throat. It had sealed itself: the chamber was vented to space. She moved on.

The door of the recreation area opened as she approached, releasing a smell that made her choke. It wasn't biological, she realized; it was the stale bread odor of burnt electronics.

Beyond that, she was almost blind. The chamber's far wall must have staved inward, knocking over equipment and supports. She started to climb over the hillock of metal, then hesitated. Surely no one could have survived this.

She spotted a human-sized silver tube, battered, but intact. Half a label indicated it was a virtual reality chamber. She guessed it was sealed to prevent the user from distracting others in the room – but what could keep out could also keep in.

She climbed, slid, pushed her way to the tube. A weights apparatus lay across the tube door. She laid her hip against it and pushed. The shrieking of metal made her flinch.

The sound almost masked the rhythmic thump from within the tube. Anaea gasped and redoubled her efforts, jamming her body against the piece of equipment. It slid free, knocking her back.

The person inside the tube must have shoved against the door.

It swung open, and someone tumbled on top of her, muscle, flesh and weight.

Anaea screamed and jerked her wrist up, firing the stunner by instinct. The energy discharged above her, a spangle of starlight in the wreckage.

The person rocked forward as detritus rained down. She realized that, without thinking, whoever it was had tried to protect her.

The figure fell to one side, gasping . . . and she realized it was a man, closer than she had ever expected one to be. His complexion was wan, sweat plastering a few blonde curls to his brow.

The aural link in her ear buzzed. "Anaea? Are you all right?" Valasca asked.

She studied him, fingers hovering by the link as she fought to catch her breath. He was slender, his face gaunt, but strong shoulders and a flat jaw offset his frailty. His eyes were not so much brown as amber, lit by something that flickered and refused to settle.

She wondered if he was more than frightened, if he was sick. The thought he might have Y-Poisoning choked her. The virus was only supposed to affect men, but what if it had mutated in the century since the Derithe had introduced it?

His eyes tried to focus. "Sophie?" he whispered.

"You're going to be fine," Anaea said in what she hoped was a soothing tone, though her jaw quivered with adrenaline. "Your ship was damaged and dropped out of the corridor. I'm an intern with the rescue team."

"Are you with the Empire?" he asked. He was obviously confused, half delirious. He squinted in the darkness, scanning her face. "You can't arrest us. We're on a legitimate exploration mission. I'm . . ." He fell silent.

His words washed over her, an incomprehensible jumble. She had been taught that there was no surviving Y-Poisoning; whatever their reasons, the aliens had designed the disease too well. Civilization had dissolved, a pit of anarchy, its days numbered. Would there even be law enforcers to arrest him?

"Anaea!" Valasca's voice called, echoing down the corridor.

"I'm here!" she returned. "I've found one. She's – I mean he. I found a male. He's alive."

The chief doctor's response came through the aural link. "What? How . . ." She stopped, started again. "Don't talk to him. He's probably half-mad with being cooped up on a dead ship. I'm coming."

The young man hauled himself into a seated position. "Who are you?" he asked. "Where are we?"

"I . . ." Anaea fumbled, caught between the order she had been given and the urge to reassure him.

Valasca's arrival saved her from decision. The doctor threaded through the rubble, each step sure. "This him?" she asked. Before either could reply, she bent and pressed a sedative patch to the young man's arm. He slipped out of consciousness without a sound.

Anaea's head flooded with questions like a sea of stars, each flaring with airless light. She helped Valasca when the automated stretcher arrived.

The doctor paused as they wrestled the stretcher over the threshold. "Did he say anything?"

Anaea hesitated. During the briefing, Valasca had made a point of insisting anything the crew said would be nonsense. In everything she had learned about the old colony planets, there had never been a word about an Empire that could oppose or approve explorers. It was strange enough she could finally put a face – his face – to that forgotten place. Maybe he was only rambling; she cringed at the idea of eliciting Valasca's scorn.

"Nothing," she said.

"Good you found him," Valasca said briskly. "He's the only survivor. Finish your survey."

Though reluctance ached in her limbs, Anaea retreated into the storage hold. Half-buried, she found a food storage unit, scuffed and battered, but almost full. Despite her disquiet, Anaea found herself intrigued by the flavors of ice cream.

The others spoke through the aural link, summing up their discoveries. Anaea read off a few labels.

"Mint Condition? Ellisflower Delight?" Hazy memories of botany lessons reminded her the spicy seeds were native to Solomon, the first colony planet.

"Crew must have had a sweet-tooth," Marpe observed.

"If I had to follow a hyperspace corridor into the unknown," Kyme said, "I would pack all the ice cream I could find."

"Be practical," Marpe said. "I would pack seeds."

"The obvious answer is seed cakes," Anaea pointed out. Their laughter made her feel as if she had passed some kind of social test, and she smiled.

But the smile didn't remain long. As they loaded the stretcher, she looked down at the man's quiet face. His words jumbled in her mind with thoughts of how quick Valasca had been to dismiss anything he might have said. And who was Sophie? The name had not appeared on the crew roster.

Anaea watched the viewscreen as they approached the station. Themiscyra had been built as a cube, three sectors in each dimension. Its core had been cobbled together from a colony ship, and even though the nearby asteroid belt had provided ample material to build its present form, there were still artifacts of the original ship visible inside the station, little monuments of the past. Embedded in the ceiling of one of the shrines were the labyrinthine coils of the outdated propulsion system. As a child, Anaea had tilted her head every which way and seen faces and fantasies in its curves.

The station was neither ornate nor elegant from space, but it didn't need to be. It was a haven from a fallen universe; it was home. Today was the first time Anaea had touched anything not part of the station, and that was supposed to be the end of it until the next salvage mission. But with their mysterious passenger, it no longer felt so simple.

*

By the time they reached Themiscyra, Anaea's speculations seemed silly and her worries unfounded. She lingered near the landing crew as the young women laughed and chatted, not really part of the conversation, but content with the illusion.

She saw the refugee only briefly as Valasca whisked him away to the infirmary. She felt a pang of sympathy. He couldn't be much older than she – early twenties? It was hard to guess.

She left the docks only to be pounced upon by a blur of cherry hair and inexplicable grease marks. "How did it go?"

"Ori!" Anaea returned the hug and pecked her friend on the cheek. "It was – eventful," she said. An artificial skylight let in the imitation of vibrant afternoon. "I found a survivor. He was so vulnerable."

"Did he have the disease?" Orithia Roslin watched her, wide-eyed.

"No," Anaea said. "At least, he didn't have physical symptoms: the rash or jaundice. He said some things, though."

Orithia cocked her head. "What kind of things?"

"Snatches about where he came from." Anaea found herself keeping her voice low. "He thought we were coming to arrest him."

Orithia leaned forward, hazel eyes bright. "Why would he think that?"

"I don't know," Anaea said. "I didn't have a chance to speak with him before he was sedated—"

"Oh!" It was an exclamation of triumph. "I can bypass the security system so you can sneak in if—"

Anaea laughed. She had known Orithia too long, first as a lover and then as a friend, to take her too seriously, even if she revelled in showing off her skills at system manipulation.

"No need for that," Anaea said. "I just . . . need to talk to someone about it. Not Valasca." Even as she ruled out the chief doctor, she thought of Thalestris. She had worked under the obstetrician's guidance a few times and instinctively trusted her. Besides, as one of the colony's leaders, she was one of the few women with access to the men's compound.

Orithia crinkled her nose. "Not Valasca," she agreed. "What was he like?"

"He was . . ." Anaea found the words difficult to locate, as if she had left them in the darkness of the ship. "He didn't seem stronger than us. Not physically, at least. He was pale and battered." She frowned. "He tried to protect me. From falling debris."

Orithia recoiled to stare. "Are you all right?"

"Of course," Anaea said, a little surprised. "A few scratches, maybe." A covert glance at her knuckles showed a thin line of blood she hadn't noticed in the climbing and scrambling.

"Not as if you'd say anything even if you had a gaping hole in your side," Orithia said.

"It isn't a gaping hole," Anaea said. Orithia canted her head to one side and made such a show of ogling that Anaea laughed.

"If you're not mortally wounded," Orithia said, "you could come star-dancing with me this weekend?"

Star-dancing was a Themiscyran pastime Anaea loved: a zero-gravity chamber within a perfect holographic star-field, planets spinning to the music and the music itself shifted by the dancers. Now, though, the weekend seemed very far away.

"Maybe," she said.

"Make a girl feel special, hmm?"

Even though Orithia was teasing, Anaea flushed. "I just have a lot on my mind," she said. "I would love to."

"Sure, you say that now. Too late." But Orithia grinned. "Oh, fine. I'll call you up that morning and see how you feel. I'm on shift in fifteen. Go pamper yourself." She smothered Anaea in a farewell hug and scampered away.

Anaea headed for the nearest elevation pad. The transparent tube sent her floating up through the space station to the third level. Life bustled around her, women mingling or rushing on their way through pristine halls. Courtyards invited conversation and contemplation: some framed in fractal stained glass, others mimicking nature. A tow-headed child flitted past, barefoot, in merry pursuit of one of her peers.

Anaea passed the lace-filigree windows of an artisan depot, a place where anyone might requisition a work of art for their quarters. This one specialized in vases and glass flowers. She could never resist slowing down when she passed by the depot: the flowers, a frozen moment in time, fascinated her. How the station leaders figured out the worth of things, how this type of painting was somehow less valuable than another and easier to requisition, she had no idea, but it all seemed to work out.

She lived in sector eleven, designated for girls who had left their homes but had yet to choose a profession. Six years of intern rotation, going on seven, and still no career seemed right: not food production, station design, or electronics repair . . . and certainly not mediator, her last position, where she had found every way possible to trip over her own tongue. Sometimes it felt as if she wasn't designed to fit Themiscyra's efficient system, that she was a part engineered for some other structure, and no amount of rewiring or retooling would make her fit in.

Mentally, she compiled a list of questions about the refugee. Before she decided who to ask for answers, she intended to return to her room, decompress, and take advantage of the true-water shower credited to her account for joining the salvage mission. But her steps slowed as she passed through a courtyard, the synthesized smell of flowers tickling her nose. There was one question she knew no station resident would be able to answer.

Who was Sophie? Why had he seen her face in Anaea's, and why had he looked for it? The unknown woman was part of his world. It made him real, and because he was real, because she had saved him, and maybe because he had tried to save her, she wanted to know how he was doing.

Her sensible plan started to fade under the light of her curiosity. There was so much she couldn't learn, or might only be able to get pieces of, if she spoke to anyone else. Anaea knew better than to ask Valasca's permission. A mere intern would not be allowed access. That barrier should have been the end of it, turned her aside. She argued inwardly: She shouldn't take the risk, shouldn't make a nuisance of herself. But they would transfer him to the men's compound when he was well, and that might as well be another planet. Slowly, then certainly, that led her to a bolder idea.

Randomized bird-song faded as she left the courtyard in a different direction to the one she'd intended. She tucked herself inside the transport car, a half-cup chair with a bar restraint. She kneaded her hands on her lap. Calm. She wasn't doing anything wrong. But would the doctors see it that way if they caught her?

The car swerved through residential corridors. It halted outside the soothing cream façade of the infirmary. Anaea palmed the door panel. It chirped, an inquiry scrolling.

"Logging in," she said.

The door eased aside, admitting her into the infirmary foyer. A brunette with a coffee complexion worked the desk, though her glazed expression and the virtual link tucked behind her ear made it obvious that "work" was a loose word for it.

Anaea didn't blame her. It was best to have a human presence in case someone arrived frightened or shaken, but the rest of the job could have been automated. "Trainee," she explained. "Not on shift, just doing research." She was sure her voice vibrated with nerves, and was surprised when the words came out casual.

"Go ahead," the brunette said. "They've got the refugee settled in, so everything is quiet."

Anaea bobbed her head. There was a high security door between the main infirmary and the isolation area, but when people were involved, security was only as good as the individuals passing through it.

She felt predatory as she sought out one of her mentors: Derinoe, an older woman who specialized in immune system deficiencies and spent most of her time assigned to isolation.

Anaea lingered around the corner, listening to conversations.

". . . check on the progress of my patients," the woman said. "Should I look in on the . . . boy?"

"You don't need to act like he's an alien," said another doctor. "No. Valasca is handling him personally."

Anaea breathed an inward prayer to the divine presence. As long as the rest of her mission went this well, no one would ever need to know. She scuttled forward, trying to look natural as she hastened to meet up with her mentor. "Doctor?"

"Anaea?" Derinoe smiled vaguely, not looking up. Her association with reality was one of convenience, and it was never convenient when she was working. "What can I do for you?"

"I have some questions about Y-Poisoning," she said, her mouth drying out at the pretext. "Things I thought of on salvage. Do you have some time?"

"Walk with me," Derinoe said, starting toward the isolation area. "What do you want to know?"

"Are there times when certain symptoms don't display?"

"Very rarely. The disease is quite regular, a clear sign the Derithe engineered it." She sighed. "False positives are more frequent than an individual being asymptomatic, with the exception of female carriers, of course."

Anaea tensed as they reached the main door. What if her mentor noticed their course? "Has there ever been a carrier on the station?"

Derinoe palmed open the door without thought. "Not for a long time. Close to seventy years."

Anaea relaxed as they passed into the isolation chamber, a series of transparent rooms. First obstacle crossed, but she was now in areas forbidden to an intern, with unknown punishment if she were caught. Her mentor walked with absent purpose, consulting her datapad.

"Does that mean it's possible the disease might have disappeared?" Anaea asked. "Or been cured?"

"Quite impossible, but even if the disease faded, its social symptoms – the death of law and decency – would still threaten us."

"Why?" Anaea pressed. She had meant mostly to keep Derinoe talking, but this one begged an answer.

"To which?" Derinoe slowed, but to Anaea's relief, she picked up pace a moment later. "My predecessors studied the disease. Their notes indicate it can lie dormant for decades. And society is an odd and fragile thing, much like the human body."

Anaea wanted to push on the second part, but she was afraid to direct Derinoe's attention to something outside her work. She scrambled for a different question. "What diseases would give a false positive?"

"Four, including the common cold," her mentor began. She returned her attention to the datapad, narrating more to space than to Anaea. "Wait out here." She let herself into her patient's chamber, the decontamination protocols soundless. "Seeing as it starts with fever and mild psychological symptoms that could simply be a side effect of not feeling well . . ." The lecture continued; the walls didn't block sound unless locked. As Derinoe became absorbed in her subject, her tone became a droning patter, thinned by distance.

Anaea backed up a step, then another, before daring to turn. Her footsteps sounded like torquing metal to her ear. She could tell his room from the others: it was the only one darkened. She slid to the door. She held her breath, wishing she had taken Orithia up on her offer of help.

It palmed open. No security lock. Anyone who had made it through the main door was supposed to be here. Presumably. She smiled, triumphant, momentarily forgetting the risks.

He was sleeping: half-curled to the right, head tucked. They must have sedated him . . . she hesitated. Had she come this far for nothing?

One amber eye opened. "Miss!" he said, propping himself up on one elbow. "I never got to thank you."

She hurried to his side. "How are you feeling?" she asked.

"Confused. But okay – thanks to all of you. I can't believe the others are dead." He let out a shuddering sigh, then pushed up the rest of the way and offered a hand. "Gwydion Mallory."

"Anaea Carlisle," she said, taking his hand. His grip was weak, fingers cool. "Pleased to meet you."

"Thank you for rescuing me," he said. Some question hovered on his lips, but he didn't seem to know how to voice it. Anaea tensed, frightened of what he might ask. "Are you a doctor, then?"

The simple question left her relieved and a bit disappointed. "No," she said, "just an intern. Every woman on this station takes rotations to try out professions. I happened to be on salvage."

"What about the men?"

Valasca either hadn't told him, or he hadn't believed her. "There are no men," she said.

"What am I, then?" he asked. He smiled, though it was too anxious to be humor.

"Rarely, a ship wrecks itself in the hyperspace corridor that intersects this system. We rescue the survivors," she said. "Women join the station. Men – if they don't have the disease – stay in isolation." It sounded unfair, when she put it that way. "Because of Y-Poisoning. Dormant strains, or new engineering. Who knows if the Derithe are done with us?"

He stared, breath quickening. "You don't let us go home?"

She returned the look, feeling dizzy. In the back of her mind, she sensed the digital click of seconds passing, even as they spun in their separate worlds. "Why would you want to?" she asked. "A civilization in ruins, a fatal disease that causes madness, and aliens lurking out there, waiting . . ."

"It's not in ruins," he said softly. "Sometimes, I'm not sure it's much better, and that's the Collective, never mind the Empire, but there are places out there I could never leave or forget." In his voice was the sound of home, wistful, carried across light years. "And there hasn't been a case of Y-Poisoning in decades."

Decades? How could that be? There was no time to delve

into everything he implied, and if she tried, she would drown. "I can't stay," she said. "I'll come back. I promise."

"Wait!" he said, jerking in the bed. He reached for her. "Are we on a diurnal cycle here?"

Anaea blinked at the non-sequitor. "Yes, but—"

"How long?"

"Twenty-five hours," she answered. "It's about sixteen-twenty now."

"You're on galactic standard time. So I haven't missed evening prayers." Gwydion pulled at his collar self-consciously.

More mystery, this hint of ritual. Anaea had been taught that the divine presence had no form or consciousness the mind could grasp, and the women of Themiscyra each worshipped however they chose.

"If you need to leave, go," he said. "I don't want to get you in trouble."

Too late, Anaea thought. Even if she wasn't caught, she sensed this conversation leading her to an inevitable collision. "We'll meet again, Gwydion," she said. "I promise." She spun, palming the door open.

She pulled up before she could slam into her mentor Derinoe. "Anaea?" the doctor asked. "What are you doing in here?"

2

ANAEA STOOD FROZEN LONG ENOUGH SHE WAS SURE SHE'D confirmed her guilt. "I'm sorry," she said, "I just wanted to see him. To look."

Derinoe tipped her head and chuckled. "He's sleeping like a babe, isn't he?"

Anaea managed not to jerk in surprise. She turned her head and saw him curled up. Because she was looking for it, she noticed his breathing indicated he was faking it. It surprised her he had realized their conversation was clandestine and acted so quickly. Thank you, Gwydion, she thought.

Derinoe shook her head. "He wasn't going to explode when you weren't looking, girl. If nothing else, Valasca probably sedated him enough it will be hours before he stirs."

Or not, Anaea thought. "We don't need to tell anyone about this, do we?" she asked – hoping the quaver in her voice was anxious rather than panicked. "All I did was look."

Derinoe paused, lips twitching. She was clearly thinking over the amount of deskwork required and did not find it to her taste. "No need to mention it," she said. "Come along. I have other duties."

Anaea remained tense, her thoughts quivering under her skin. Her mentor left her at the entrance to the isolation ward, already lost in another case.

She hurried out of the infirmary and palmed into a hovercar at the entrance. She studied the inside of her eyelids, thinking. The team had not expected someone to be found in her section of the White Hound. Just now, Gwydion should have been asleep. She had not been meant to speak to him, but she had.

Civilisation was not in ruins, he had said. Easy to explain – he was in shock, delirious – but he seemed so steady. Something in her wanted to believe he knew what he was talking about. Was it only the lure of possibility? That there might be a universe worth discovering, more than isolated pockets, savage and haunted by pirates?

The conundrum kept her chewing until the hovercar stopped outside her residence block. The main courtyard was dark and cool; a waterfall garden overhung with willows.

Her quarters consisted of one room and a necessary closet. The furnishings were simple and sparse, as befitted her status; the plainness of the walls had been a personal choice, though not a deliberate one. She simply had never gotten around to designing a wall space.

Anaea plopped on the bed, hands on her knees. She turned to her terminal to call a search on Orithia's location, then paused. She trusted her friend, but it was too soon, when she knew less than she had before. The prudent thing would be to give it time to settle, to see if the matter was easily answered.

She hadn't expected to fall asleep, but the excitement of the rescue mission on top of her investigation left her wrung out. A hundred more questions followed her into slumber.

*

Anaea slept through dinner and awoke in the early evening with the vague nausea that accompanied too deep a sleep. She had blankets bunched around her for comfort rather than need. Temperatures in Themiscyra remained within two degrees of twenty-four Celsius.

She called out a search query for Thalestris Fenyang. The query came back: Thalestris was off-shift, retired to her quarters, but not asleep. Anaea hesitated, then opened a voice channel. It went live as Thalestris accepted the message.

"Dr. Fenyang?" she said. "I was wondering if I could speak to you."

"Anaea? What is this regarding?" Thalestris' voice was a soothing, raspy thrum.

"My participation in the rescue mission yesterday."

"Ah." A soft exhalation. "Come see me, child, and we'll talk."

Anaea didn't mind being labeled a child by Thalestris: one of the original colonists, she was ancient, though well-preserved by the aging treatment. "Thank you." She switched off and changed her tunic. After combing through her hair, she headed out.

Thalestris lived amongst the other station leaders. The hovercar took the shortest route from sector eleven to sector fourteen, through grey utility corridors.

The hovercar drifted down an elevation tube within the central hub. It halted at the gate of a private courtyard, and Anaea alighted. The gate looked wrought-iron, though it was plastic, and had an antique call box; Anaea pressed the button. "Dr. Fenyang?"

"Come in, child."

The gate opened, and Anaea stepped through. She drew a sharp breath. She stood on a moor dominated by a cold and cloudy sky. A full moon provided illumination, no hint of the line between walls and hologram. The door was disguised in a gnarled apple tree.

Thalestris met her and showed her inside. Her chamber was not large, but it boasted multiple rooms and high-level requisitions of furniture and artwork: rich mahogany, snowflake lace, and two Neo-Pointillism starscapes, each dot a miniature depiction of genetic code.

"Sit down," Thalestris said, guiding her to the couch. "What has you so troubled?"

Anaea resisted sinking back into the plush lure of the couch, clutching her hands on her knee as she sat straight and braced. "The refugee said a few things before we took him off the White Hound," she said. "They don't fit."

"You didn't mention this to Valasca, I assume." Thalestris was calm, without judgement, though her eyes, more black than brown, pierced. She was a stately woman with a patrician nose and mocha skin, and despite her advanced years her curls still held a trace of youth's black. Anaea had always been a little in awe of her, but she was consistently encouraging and open.

"No." Anaea felt she should offer some explanation. "She frightens me?"

Thalestris chuckled. "You are not alone in that. What did this young man say?"

Where could she start? "He said something about a Collective and an Empire," Anaea said. "They sounded like governments."

"Those specific labels I am not familiar with," Thalestris allowed, "but I do know there are many names for the clans, if you will, into which humanity has gathered itself. Not a few of those names are grandiose beyond the powers they represent."

It was almost as if Thalestris had read her mind, but Anaea knew hypermental abilities had not survived the station's first generation. Something didn't transfer in genetic splicing, only in live breeding.

"He said something about being arrested," she added. "That has the implication . . ."

"Of a larger organization?" Thalestris shrugged. "Are you familiar with the evolution of language, Anaea? Words often change in their use and meaning. Historically, the word 'cool' referred only to temperature. It was then applied to a state of personality – cool under pressure – and then it became an exclamation of something impressive. Now it's more often used to mean someone who is too reserved.

"Much the same could have happened with a verb such as arrested. It could describe a more informal assault."

"Is that part of why men aren't allowed out of isolation? The language barrier?"

The question hadn't seemed so foolish in her head. Unable to meet Thalestris' gaze, Anaea focused on the twin planet painting behind the older woman's head. She had done a three-month rotation as an artist apprentice, but she hadn't felt creative enough to stay. She enjoyed the tactile rush of making something with her hands, but the question of what she should create always seemed to intrude on her bliss.

Thalestris chuckled. "A trifle, perhaps. A larger reason is how durable Y-Poisoning is: it can stay dormant on surfaces for a long time. Bring it in with a salvage, expose a male who happens to be wandering the station, and you have a madman on the loose."

Anaea bit her lip and said nothing.

"You're thinking that seems tenuous. Remember this disease shattered everything we know, and we only survived it through Asteria's leadership and decisive action." Thalestris closed her eyes, added mildly, "There is, of course, the social element: reintroducing men would be disruptive. Technological advances recently have made it possible to consider the idea, but it will be a long debate."

Anaea tried to imagine living side by side with someone like Gwydion, wondered why it was so hard to picture. Was he so different from her, apart from the physical element? And she had seen women, not many, but a few, who were larger and more muscular than he was, even if the shape and distribution of the muscles were different.

"You're saying that men are disruptive?" she asked.

"No more or less than we would be, in the reverse situation," Thalestris said. "Men and women are strangely designed. They do not fit together with ease."

Yet people had lived as such for far longer than they had not. Anaea swallowed. These questions made her uncomfortable. Surely Thalestris had a better understanding than she of the oddities of gender.

"He wants to go back," she said. "I don't think he understands where he is, but it's the last thing he said."

"Why would you find that hard to reconcile, Anaea?" Thalestris asked. "We all have friends and family. We all are cradled by our surroundings, and they become the only world we can imagine. In the face of that, no one would prefer the unknown, however superior."

She was wrong. Anaea tightened her toes inside her shoes. It was the only way she could express her tension. She couldn't imagine facing an unfamiliar world and turning away merely because it was strange to her. Indeed, the idea fascinated her.

Everything Thalestris had said made sense, save for those last words. She let the security of home and Thalestris' reassuring presence warm her, but it did not entirely dispel the chill of uncertainty.

"This place is a refuge," Anaea said. "Maybe he has one of his own."

Thalestris spread her hands in a gesture of concession. "Of that, I cannot say. I would doubt it: the greatest thing that protects Themiscyra is its secrecy."

Against pirates, madmen, aliens. Anaea listed them off in her head, and wondered again what drew Gwydion back. Curiosity tingled inside her.

"I hope I have done something to quiet your fears," Thalestris said.

Anaea smiled wryly. The obstetrician had done perhaps as much as anyone could. She rose, inclining her head in a respectful gesture. "It does help, Dr. Fenyang," she said. "Thank you for your time."

*

Anaea had a little time to herself, and she needed to escape from her buzzing thoughts. Any other day, she might have headed for a communal sphere to play games. She preferred the puzzles; the older women liked to gather around virtual versions of antique card games. She might even join a basketball team; she might not be the best player, but it never mattered. Friendly laughter was the worst consequence she would face.

Not today: she needed to be alone. She closed her door behind her and called up the entertainment console. She scrolled to fiction, but found herself torn between old holomovies from before Y-Poisoning had struck, and new inventions filmed in Themiscyra's empty sectors. Buried in a category within a category were also a few examples of written word fiction. It was never popular: when holographic technology could simulate the full range of imagination, there was no need to tax the individual.

Anaea paused, sighed. Certainly, her range of imagination felt too small, right now. She had seen Themiscyra's small collection of physical books on a student tour, but only through glass. The books were kept in sterile isolation and one could only read the covers: mostly non-fiction about metaphysics, but a few had enticingly romantic titles and there had been one about motorcycle repair. Anaea had looked up a description of the contents later and had not been enlightened.

She ended up choosing an old favorite, *Landfall*, a retelling of the arrival of the Promise expedition in Tau Ceti and its landing on the planet that would be named Solomon. It was one of the only older holomovies that had a historical basis, though she had no doubt it was dressed up in roses and tears, every aspect of human drama magnified. And it was all tied up neatly, which couldn't possibly be accurate.

Landfall's holographic world surrounded her, the sights and sounds forming a bubble around her. The action flowed around her, deceptively real, though she had only to lift her hand to break that illusion. The actors bickered and laughed and shouted, their lives on imaginary display. Eighteen years after departing Earth, these figments of history kicked off shoes to savor the loam of a new world.

Anaea sprawled back at the end of the movie, staring at the ceiling. Absently, she called up meditation music. It flowed through the space; pentatonic melody, the time signature matching her heartbeat.

Briefly, she imagined she felt the station moving around her, the blood of hidden electronics pouring through metal veins, rushing to the low sectors to sustain food production and humming within sector seventeen, the starship bay.

Her mother had been more at home with machines than people, and often left her daughter to the care of the rest of her engineering team. Anaea's play-spaces had been the ducts and access tunnels that threaded through the sectors. She had imagined entire worlds behind grates and portals. Asteria and the other founders of Themiscyra had created a living being, or nearly so, and it sheltered her.

Anaea exhaled, rising. The thought had hovered in the back of her mind throughout the movie, and would not be ignored. There was, indeed, more out there, and she had to seek it. The ground, artificial or not, was steady beneath her feet.

She pressed the activation button on her aural link and queried Orithia's location. The link informed her the programmer was at the Preserve. She considered waiting until her friend was off-shift, but the doctors could move Gwydion at any time.

The air on the lowest level of Themiscyra smelled clean and organic. It swelled into her lungs with a power of its own. She palmed through the Preserve gate.

The habitats of the Preserve dominated one of the largest open spaces on the station. Lush jungle crowded against open plain; grey cliffs seemed to disappear into an invisible statrosphere above. Cloudy plastic alloy divided the ecosystems. The numerous animal species that populated the Preserve had once run wild, and here had their own small world.

She found Orithia by a reptile habitat, speaking to a keeper.

A six-limbed reptile from Perica eyed them glumly from the other side of the barrier.

Anaea was surprised to see Penelope clinging to Orithia's shoulders. The kearl's tail was tucked around her human's arm. She purred happily when she saw Anaea, pulling her owner's curls to get her attention. The genetically engineered beasts were the only pets on the station; every other animal was a preserved specimen or food.

Orithia swatted at the paws. "Penelope, would you—" She turned, beaming when she saw the reason's for the creature's excitement. "Ann! Good to see you." She held up a hand for patience and turned back to the keeper. "So you need the code checked on the atmosphere variables?"

"Yes – the creatures aren't reacting well . . ."

Anaea stood aside until the conversation finished. Penelope squirmed, but remained obedient on her owner's shoulder, grooming one golden-furred paw.

"The Preserve has a protected core," Orithia explained. "Have to make modifications on-site – plus, it's nifty to come down here. Penelope loves it. What's going on, Anaea?"

Anaea scritched the kearl behind the ears. The creature cooed. "Can we talk?"

"If we walk as we do it." Orithia waved for her to follow. "Is this about your mystery man?"

"Even more mysterious than I thought." Anaea explained what he had said, keeping her voice low. They moved past habitats, including one that housed Earth zebras.

Orithia whistled. "So do you think he makes blood sacrifices and worships idols?"

"Ori!" Anaea protested.

The young woman giggled as she palmed them into the computer room, then sobered. "All this and he wants to go home?"

"He seemed very sure." Anaea sat in the room's other chair as Orithia flipped out her kit. Like most programmers, she backed up the vocal commands with a spatial relay cube; unlike most, she also had an old-fashioned keyboard. Anaea had always found it endearing and a little hypnotic: she enjoyed watching the flurry of Orithia's fingers.

"How will that go, I wonder?" Orithia spoke half to herself. "I didn't think we let people do that."

"We don't." Anaea jumped as Penelope hopped over and crawled onto her shoulder, burrowing against her neck.

Orithia chewed her lip, anxious. "I can't imagine leaving Themiscyra and never seeing it again. So how can I help?"

"I need to meet with him again," Anaea said, stroking the kearl. Penelope rubbed her side against the touch. "I know you were joking before . . ."

"I was," Orithia said, "but I can still bypass security for you. Let's check on him first, shall we?" Her hands flitted over the keys.

Anaea blinked. "You just said the core—"

"With a little creativity, I can work from here," Orithia said. "Anyhow, we have this great viewscreen." She waved to a monitor that cycled through the habitats, then concentrated on her work. She made a worried sound. "Anaea, they have your friend in for surgery. You didn't tell me he was that badly injured."

Surgery? What could have happened? Confusion twisted at her. "He wasn't."

Orithia frowned. "Let me tap in."

Anaea knew she should have protested and couldn't, her mind twitching with scenarios that wouldn't have occurred to her a few days ago. She didn't want to consider them now, and it left her stomach sour. She stroked Penelope and felt the creature's hum through her hand. Kearls had been engineered as companion animals, and the pattern of Penelope's breath soothed her, even though she half-knew the science.

"Ori," she said, "if this is risky, I don't want you to do it."

Orithia paused, swiveling in her chair. Hazel eyes fixed on Anaea's face. "We've known each other forever, Ann. You've always had a steady head on your shoulders – better than mine. If you want to do something, I trust you."

Anaea felt a twinge. They had split, almost three years ago, not because of any lack of feeling, but due to a dozen small things that had been fine for friends, but awkward in a couple. She still half-sensed the failing had been hers.

"The record is blank," Orithia reported. "No procedure logged. That means – I have no idea what that means. They're not supposed to do that." She flicked a pensive look sideways at Anaea. "Do you want a feed?"

"Can you do that?"

"No cameras in the chamber, and their links are bound to be off," Orithia said, "but some of the other equipment – I can extrapolate, at least with audio." She drew a puffy breath. "I haven't had this much of a challenge since I was first in training."

Since she had been in training ,and since she had astonished instructors two decades older than she. Anaea nodded, waiting in tense silence. She realized she was squeezing Penelope when the kearl nibbled her hand in protest.

"—not working, Dr. Braun." The voice that came through the speakers was thin and static-laden.

"That's impossible," Valasca said.

"The neural readings are—" incomprehensible.

Orithia made a face. "I'm running it through an enhancement program."

"—not a mistake."

"—tested and worked on others—" Valasca snapped, which made it harder to discern the words. "This shouldn't be happening."

"The facts are as they are, Valasca." The relay evened out as Thalestris' calm tones came through. "For whatever reason, his memories are immutable."

Orithia mouthed the words, "Memories?" Anaea bit her lip, remembering part of her conversation with Thalestris. Technological advances, she had said, would make it possible for men to join Themiscyran society. Gwydion might be the first.

As long as he – they – didn't remember where they had come from?

"He's waking up," someone reported.

Anaea's body went cold. Was it possible to remove an individual's memories? Who would allow it? The people she knew and looked up to were not capable of such a thing.

"Not possible," Valasca repeated. "I confirmed the doses myself."

"Valasca, look at the brainwave readings."

"Cancer on hyperspace," the chief doctor swore.

"Oh, come on, tell us!" Orithia burst out. "Or I'll have to hack the readings."

"Those are hypermental levels," another doctor said.

"Thank you," Orithia muttered. Despite the tension pouring through her, Anaea had to fight the urge to smile.

"His shipboard records said nothing about this," Valasca said. "Why would they send someone with his gifts out into the middle of nowhere? Does someone suspect . . ."

"Easy, Valasca," Thalestris said.

"What do we do with him if this won't work?"

Valasca didn't hesitate. "We have to—"

The voices cut out to the accompaniment of Orithia's typing. She jerked her hands back as if she had been burned.

"Security program was about to find us out," she said, her face pale and strained.

Anaea sat in silence, fingers clenched into the kearl's fur. Penelope chittered, but did not otherwise protest. What would they do with him, and what were they destroying as they did it?

Themiscyra was a place of harmony, of finding the right path, and it left space for those like her who had yet to find theirs. She had to believe, if Gwydion knew what he was talking about, that the doctors were unaware of the truth of his world.

"Thank you, Ori," Anaea said, rising in a rush. She scooped Penelope onto the chair. "I have to go before they make a mistake."

"Ann . . ."

Anaea had reached the doorway, the scents of the Preserve swirling around her, rich and earthy. She turned back to Orithia's strained face.

"Please stay," Orithia said. "Just trust them." It had been a game to her minutes before, but now she looked frightened. Her hands twitched as if she wanted to grab Anaea and hold her back, putting her whole body into it.

Anaea was acutely conscious this was the first important thing Orithia had asked of her in three years. The realization burned, but it had no chance of changing her mind, and that made her feel worse. Not only was she failing Orithia, she couldn't even try. "I'm sorry," she said, and spun out the door.

3

Heart snapping against her ribcage, Anaea rushed out of the Preserve to the hovercar hub. "Infirmary, emergency code," she said, throwing herself into the car. Once she was in motion and the shaking in her hands started to subside, she continued, "Page Valasca Braun."

"Paging," the system acknowledged – then silence as the station rushed by, at a pace the dampeners couldn't neutralize. There was no response. Had she expected one?

Even with worries the size of stars, she couldn't keep her mind off Orithia's face. She had failed Orithia, in some way she couldn't fully understand. Turn around, close her eyes, leave it be. The easiest thing anyone could do. Orithia had begged her, but she had known her decision before the words were spoken. She felt cold, ruthless. A machine, not a woman loyal to a dear friend.

The hovercar halted. Anaea tumbled out and palmed her way into the infirmary. The girl behind the desk met her with a doctor, both rigid with alarm. The false use of an emergency code was almost unheard of, and Anaea felt a prickle of guilt . . . yet it might be an emergency for Gwydion.

"Valasca," she said. "I need to speak to Valasca."

"What is this regarding?" the doctor asked.

"The male refugee. I brought him in."

It was the only chip she had to play, and she was surprised when it worked. The doctor nodded. "Wait here."

She couldn't make herself sit, so she lurked and stared down corridors she already knew, after three months on rotation. Was she too late?

Valasca strode into view, manner agitated. She paused, harsh features smoothing over, with limited success. Anaea found herself relieved. She hoped it meant they hadn't succeeded in altering Gwydion's memories.

"Dr. Braun," she said, "I need to talk to you about the refugee. I think he—"

"Not out here," Valasca snapped. She latched her fingers onto Anaea's arm and pulled her along. She didn't speak again until they steamed to a halt in her office. "Did you speak to him, Anaea?"

Her mouth moved, but nothing came out. She had expected to stammer through the confession, trying to reach the important part. "Yes," she said. "How—"

"There is some logic as to who is recruited for salvage missions," Valasca said. "Tell me what he said."

Anaea couldn't read the doctor's expression. She spoke as calmly as she could. "I thought he must be awake by now," she finished. "I needed to know. Before you moved him."

"Do you believe him to be mad?" Valasca asked.

"No. I believe some part of his story is true." She met the doctor's eyes. "Perhaps more of it than we know."

"Why is this your affair, Anaea? You are neither doctor nor psychologist, tasked with fitting this individual into his new home."

Anaea flinched, but did not look away. "I found him. His life is important to me. I can't turn away without an answer." She was out of words, waiting for the response. To hear her world had not changed, that she had misunderstood Gwydion and there was another explanation.

Valasca's lips thinned. She measured her words carefully before she spoke. "What would you say if I told you it was true?"

The question stunned Anaea. She couldn't see. Themiscyra seemed unreal, its pulse a dream. The sense of betrayal pulled her down. Had her whole existence been an illusion, maintained by the people she had thought were there to protect her? "How could they keep something like that from us?" she said. "We could go back—"

Valasca snorted. "What is out there may not be ruin, but it is not worth saving. This – here – is the best refuge for civilization."

Thoughts chased around Anaea's head, making her nauseous. Was she more shocked because the station leaders had concealed it, spun a century of orchestrated lies, one tale leading to another, such as the persistence of Y-Poisoning . . . or was it the concept of this universe unknown, many times larger than she had ever imagined?

She snatched instinctively for other explanations: that Valasca was mad, that she was mistaken, that this was a test. Somewhere at the top of the chasm, the doctor waited for her reaction.

"What would be the harm if someone wanted to leave?" Anaea asked. She felt as if she was reading a script, numbly asking the questions expected of her. Nothing about Valasca's response changed that impression.

"Anyone who left could, by their very presence, give indication we are out here," Valasca said. "Secrecy is our only defense. Even if a man remembered nothing of this place, his return from nowhere would raise questions. Have you seen weapons lying around, Anaea? We have none. We couldn't keep them out."

Anaea knew she wasn't supposed to know about the memory wipe, but a man with a gap in his recollection would be almost as suspicious as one spouting stories of a hermetic space station.

"You were not supposed to hear what you did," Valasca continued. "He should have been sedated. Nor should there have been anyone in that section of the White Hound to start with. That part of the ship was worst hit."

Calculated risk, Anaea thought, but why? There must be enough people who knew the truth to comprise a salvage mission.

Valasca quirked an eyebrow at whatever she saw in Anaea's expression. "Not everyone who protects our secret saw the devastation from which we fled: myself, for instance. We regularly assess interns with a view to bringing in new blood.

"Those who have dealt with you on previous rotations, Anaea, have been impressed with your steadiness, obedience and attention to detail. You were recommended to the mission to gauge the possibility of bringing you in . . . eventually." Anyone else might have showed a hint of humor; Valasca's expression didn't change. "Now it seems the timeline has been altered. Will you aid us in guarding the secret that keeps Themiscyra intact?"

Their confidence in her was a compliment, Anaea realized: they thought she was sensible and clever . . . and that she didn't question orders. She wasn't flattered; she wasn't sure how to interpret the roiling in her stomach. It drew her in like a black hole, and every part of her ached with the pain of resistance.

She managed to find her tongue. "I'm grateful for the chance," she said. "What happens if I say no?"

"You won't have to worry about any of this." Valasca shrugged. "We don't put unwanted burdens on the shoulders of our residents."

They could wipe memories, Anaea thought, and was stunned by the rush of warmth she felt. She could go home and never worry about this again, be comforted by the harmony of her world, stay with Orithia and earn back the loyalty she had lost.

She closed her eyes, her heart clenching at how tempting it was. It didn't feel right, wanting to hide away, but it would be so much easier, so much simpler.

"Anaea?"

There was more at stake than her comfort. She opened her eyes and offered a confident smile, even if she didn't feel it.

"I can't know such a thing and ignore it," she said. This was her opportunity to find answers, and a way to help Gwydion. "I'm . . . yes."

Valasca's nostrils flared. "Good." Anaea had the sense she was surprised. "This doesn't obligate you to remain in the medical rotation, of course. You can be of help to us in several areas. Our last recruit was in engineering."

She didn't want to seem too anxious, but she had to know. "What will happen to Gwydion?"

"That's an open question," Valasca said. "He obviously feels strongly about his situation. We've learned he has hypermental abilities, so he could be problematic."

Anaea had had so much to think about, but now she had time to break the problem down into smaller pieces, to decide if she could lie to everyone in the colony. At some point, would it stop feeling wrong? She had a mission now: find out as much as she could and do what she needed to protect Gwydion.

She shouldn't have to protect him. The station leaders should never hurt a refugee unless he acted maliciously, and she couldn't believe he would, not even though she knew he could reach into her mind and make her feel that way.

"What could he do?" she asked.

"One thought could put us in a precarious position." Valasca sighed. "But it would damage his brain to keep him sedated for too long."

That was more familiar to Anaea, that desire not to harm, and she centered herself on it. "I could speak to him?" she offered.

"And tell him what?"

"Maybe I can convince him to hear me out," she said. "He seems to trust me." She had little to base that on, except perhaps that she wanted him to.

Valasca frowned. "I'll have to consult," she said, rising. "Stay here." She speared Anaea with a look, then stepped out.

Just the fact the chief doctor, who was militant about controlling everything in the infirmary, deferred to someone else told Anaea how serious things were. She kept her eyes focused on the wall, as if looking around could incriminate her or show her something she didn't want to see.

She wondered what stories the other men in the compound had. There were only a handful, a wide spread of ages, said to be grateful for escape from the chaos of the old planets. She wondered about that now. Was every trace of the outside universe now locked in Gwydion's mind? What of the people who mourned them for lost? She had never thought about the personal things the confined men had left behind. Gwydion had left Sophie.

Valasca returned. "Once he's out of surgery and awake, you can speak with him," she said.

"Could we be unmonitored?" When Valasca shot her a sharp look, she hurried on, "You said he had special abilities. What if he knows he's being watched?"

The doctor considered. "Very well, but the focus of the conversation is to convince him to stay, and that doesn't need to involve any discussion of where he came from."

Anaea wanted to point out that comparing where he had come from with where he was might be useful, but bit her tongue. She had no intention of sticking to the program. "I think he's a good person, at heart."

"I very much doubt that. Not with the environment that raised him," Valasca said.

*

IT WAS ALMOST two hours before Anaea could see Gwydion. Anaea spent it trying vainly to think. Every time she tried to come up with a strategy as to what she would say, her mind derailed into a maze of implications and unknowns. She didn't know what she could promise. She didn't know how she would answer his questions.

What did he have to go home to? What would he do to reach it? Why come so far, if home was that dear to him?

No . . . the last wasn't so strange. If peering beyond the familiar wasn't a human impulse, what was she doing here?

She wished she could check on Orithia, though she had no idea what she would say. Thank you, everything is all right? But it wasn't.

Valasca put her on menial data duties. Occasionally, she saw the chief doctor pass. Once, Valasca and Thalestris stood in the corridor, the latter soft as kearl's fur, the other agitated and staccato.

Finally, Valasca rapped on the console. "Are you ready?" she said brusquely.

The only change in the isolation chamber was the lingering scent of fresh bread. Gwydion started upright when she entered. There were hollows under his eyes, and a nervous flit that rippled through his body, but his first comment was, "It's good to see you again."

Guilt flared. He wouldn't feel that way when she explained. "You, too." It was a simple response, but it surprised her to realize how much she meant it.

"You grow candim here?" he asked.

"It's an easy crop to grow," she said. "And sweet enough it gets children to eat their vegetables."

Gwydion chuckled. "My father used to dye the rest of my food blue to match."

Anaea laughed. They both laughed, and she wondered at it. They had different backgrounds, and yet they shared something both could understand.

But then he disturbed the moment. "You're Anaea. The doctor tending to me earlier was named Valasca, and I think I heard reference to an Asteria?"

"Our founder," Anaea said. "She risked her life on an experimental aging treatment."

"Well, I'm curious . . ." He colored. "They're strange names, I mean."

"The first generation of babies born here were named after

the mythological Amazons," Anaea said. "Greek warrior-women. We're on the fourth generation. It's tradition by now." She pushed on before he could ask more questions, before they could become enveloped in conversation, and maybe she lost her nerve. "We need to talk," she said. "I know you want to leave here—"

"No," he said, then frowned. "Yes. But not until I've had a chance to speak with your leaders. We heard rumors of an expedition that took hyperspace corridors to this part of space, but many things sound like legends and dreams these days."

"We?" she asked.

Gwydion cleared his throat. "I'm part of a resistance – no, not a resistance," he amended. "We live apart by choice. Not outlaws, just a group of people who want to live by older traditions. We've made our home in a place called the Sanctum."

"The White Hound flew for your group?"

"No," he said, "but I had approval to speak for them. Have approval," he corrected himself, his face drawn with hope.

Then it had already happened: someone suspected Themiscyra existed. What Valasca and the others feared was a reality. The thought made Anaea dizzy; she wasn't sure whether to be glad or fearful.

"What do you want to speak about?" she asked.

"We were hoping for an alliance," Gwydion said. "But that isn't likely, is it? I sense . . ." He hesitated.

"I know you have hypermental talents," Anaea said gently.

"Oh." He seemed to lose the starch in his spine. "I've sensed the alarm my presence has caused in the people taking care of me. I know they had me sedated. I represent a threat, don't I?"

"I wouldn't say a threat," Anaea said, feeling a flush of guilt on behalf of the station leaders. "Did you read their minds?"

"No." He recoiled, eyes widening. "I wouldn't without permission, not unless it was a matter of life or death. I'm afraid, but . . ."

Impulsively, she leaned forward and squeezed his hand. She was surprised when his fingers felt not at all unfamiliar. "I can ask if they will speak with you," she said, "but being isolated out here is our defense." Wasn't it? she wondered.

"If they won't – or don't – agree to an alliance, I'll just have to go home empty-handed." He smiled ruefully.

She had to tell him, though she dreaded his reaction. "You can't go home."

"I have to," he said. "There are things I still have to do. People waiting for me."

"Sophie?" she asked.

He jumped, a hint of red rising in his cheeks. There went the myth that men didn't blush, Anaea thought. "How do you know about her?"

"You said her name when you were delirious. Who is she?"

"My brother's wife." The flush remained, deepening as he fumbled with the words. "I – she's been a great friend. She's a doctor," he continued, his voice stronger. "I guess she's the person I would turn to if I were in pain."

What did that awkwardness mean? But Anaea couldn't ask. At least she knew what a wife was, though she was unclear on exactly how marriage functioned, except it was similar to a life-tie. "I'm sorry for prying."

"It's all right." Gwydion's amber eyes sought hers; she couldn't look away. "Anaea, I promise I would never breathe a word this place existed, make up whatever story necessary to explain the White Hound's return and the fate of the others, and never deviate from it for anything. I understand why someone would want to keep themselves apart from the world. I would be as silent as the grave."

"I believe you," she said, and she did.

"That won't be enough?" he asked.

"I don't know." She feared she did, that the best he could hope for was confinement. He might be released into the station, if they could find a way to remove his memories and if the women decided that was the right move, but she kept returning to

Valasca's words. One traveler could jeopardize the security of the station. How much was it worth to protect that?

"I promise you," she said, feeling as if this was a dream, "that if it comes to it . . ." She suspended on a ledge. She let herself fall. "I'll help you leave."

His eyes flew wide. "Should you – are you allowed to do that?"

"No," she said, "but I will. Not much in this makes sense, but I do know this. You have a home. You should be there."

"Not if it puts someone else in danger," he protested.

"We'll see," she said, with more bravery than she felt. Yet it was the one certainty she had in this spinning mass, and now that she had voiced it, she was determined to see it through. "I should talk to someone about your meeting." It was more important than the host of questions she wanted to ask. One way or another, there would be time for those.

Anxiety prickled through her, dancing across her skin in search of release. She offered him a reassuring smile and stepped out.

Valasca swooped down. "Well?"

"Can I speak to Thalestris? About a request he made." Of the two women she knew were involved in the secret – she didn't want to term it a conspiracy – Thalestris was more open-minded. If there was any chance that Gwydion would be heard, it would come from her. Anaea rested her hopes on that.

Valasca looked suspicious, then shrugged. "We don't grant concessions, but I understand it is impossible to lie to him. Whatever makes the process easier. She's in her office."

When Anaea stopped at the door, she could hear the harmonious hum of a meditation program. She laid her hand on the panel and waited for a response.

"Anaea? Please come in."

Anaea was reassured, despite everything, by the woman's tranquil smile. "I have a request from Gwydion," she said.

Thalestris spread her hands. "Please. Sit and explain."

Anaea described his Sanctum and their desire for a meeting, trying not to sound too invested. The obstetrician's gently arched brow implied she could sense whose side Anaea was on, but she did not interrupt.

"We could benefit from what they have to say," Anaea finished. "Maybe – some day – go back."

Thalestris chuckled. "You think that's a good thing?"

"It's our birthplace. The universe that created us." Anaea tried not to clench her fingers. "Yes."

"Created us? So, too, did the Dark Ages, and all three World Wars." Thalestris' voice was soft as dappled light in the enclosed gardens, sympathetic. "We would not return to those times. What the boy offers is a fall into barbarism."

Anaea stiffened. "He wouldn't—" she stopped herself, feeling the flush burn her cheeks.

"I never said it was intentional, on his part or that of his allies," Thalestris said, "but the result is the same."

"Wouldn't it be worth speaking to him?" Anaea said. "Maybe there is some kind of compromise . . ."

Thalestris sighed. "Anaea," she said, "let it go. Let him go. He won't be harmed. He will have much the same life as anyone on this station. Freed from whatever worries drove him so far into space."

No one knew Anaea had learned about the memory wipe, though she felt it must be etched in her face. There it was again: the idea that ignorance was a small price to pay for safety . It should have been so easy to accept, and she couldn't.

"What about the people waiting for him?" she asked.

"No one waits forever. It will pass." Thalestris laid a hand over hers. "These are weighty things, Anaea, and there is no good answer. What we have to concentrate on is the safest option, the one that offers the least risk to Themiscyra."

Perhaps Thalestris was right, but Anaea trusted him. It was unjust to hold him for something outside of his control.

"This boy seems a good person," Thalestris said. "Tell him what his presence here means. I believe he will understand."

"I will," Anaea said.

But she had already made up her mind.

4

He might understand, Anaea thought as she returned to the isolation chamber. Perhaps better than she did: he knew what Themiscyra was hiding from.

She palmed the door without thought and was surprised when it opened. Breathe, Anaea, she told herself. Valasca and the others believed she was on their side. Were they right? She couldn't believe lying to everyone taking the decision from their hands, was the right course of action, but the leaders of Themiscyra had made it and continued to support it. Who was she to second-guess them?

Anaea composed herself before she entered Gwydion's room. Conscious of his ability, she tried to think calmly.

He was fiddling with a holographic blocks puzzle when she entered. He pushed the projection plate aside. "Bad news?" he asked.

She managed a grave smile. "They won't let you speak to anyone. It was like shouting into the stars. I wouldn't get anywhere, not before both of us were old and gray."

Gwydion laughed, though the sound was taut, a nervous

hiccough. "I had to hope." He sighed. "You think hiraeth is a myth until you feel it."

"Hiraeth?" she asked.

"It's an old word in a dead language. It means – not exactly homesickness, something a little darker."

She leaned forward as if to take his hands, but stopped. They might be observed now, and this had to be said in secret. She lowered her voice and murmured, "Speak into my mind."

His eyes widened. She could have fallen into their depths. She nodded and braced herself.

Anaea had only half-ideas as to what mental contact would feel like. She had not expected the impression of words written on a backdrop of stars.

Think at the front of your mind, they-he said, *and I can speak with you.*

She watched the after-image fade. Thinking had never seemed so difficult. She focused, or thought she did, but sensed only silence in answer. A prickle of reassurance moved through her. The foreign feeling made her shiver. She tried again, imagining the words as a shout. *I thought I would hear your voice.*

He winced, and she realized it must have been just that – a shout. *I don't know how you're receiving me,* he admitted. *They taught me in the Academy that the mind interprets telepathy the same way you subconsciously process language.*

She tried to think more quietly. *Academy?*

She felt his embarrassment, not quite as if it were her own. *I was a junior cop,* he said.

How old are you? She was surprised at how natural thinking this way seemed. Then, she considered she might be doing it wrong and he was being polite.

Twenty-four.

That made him five years older than she. She couldn't guess where she might be in five years, any more. *I still want to help you leave the station. I believe you when you say you wouldn't betray us.*

She felt no anxiety or protest, but she knew he withheld it

from his surface thoughts, because she could see it in his eyes and the catch in his jaw. He didn't want to put her in danger, but what choice did he have? *Thank you. I think I could break out of your infirmary, but without access to a ship and knowing where to go . . .*

It won't be right away, she said. *They're too nervous and watchful now. They're a little frightened of you, I think. If you say you want to talk to me, we can keep meeting.* She must be doing something right – or wrong – for her skull itched after putting that lengthy phrase together.

Gwydion closed his eyes; she thought he was going to shrink on himself again. *If you're trying to hide this conversation, we should speak out loud, as well.*

Anaea started to nod, then caught herself. "Is there anything I can get you?"

"Do you have a tailor here?"

"We have prefabricated clothing, and some women who do custom work," she said. She took his hand as she went back to thinking at him, hoping he would take it as a sign to read. *I also hope I can learn more about where you've come from.* The idea of this outside universe, so different from the one she had learned about, fascinated her.

I'll answer as many questions as I can, he replied, and then, without skipping a beat, "I'm feeling naked without my *tallit.*"

She paused. "Your what?"

He blinked. "What?"

They sat, mutually paralyzed by bewilderment. "I'm sorry," he said, "just surprised. I know that before the *Promise* expedition, we weren't the dominant religion, but that's—"

"—ancient history," Anaea finished for him. The *Promise* had been the ship, before hyperspace corridors, before Y-Poisoning, that carried humanity from the arms of Earth and colonized Solomon. She opened her mouth to ask a question, then shut it. She wasn't ready to find out what had happened to the mother planet. She searched her memory for a term she had heard in history class. "You're Jewish?"

"I am," he said, then added with ginger curiosity, "What are you, then?"

"I'm . . ." Anaea faltered. She had been raised with a belief in the divine spirit, and if that needed no name, neither did the belief. "I'm a believer."

Gwydion ducked his head, mumbling an apology. He explained without looking up, "Prayer shawl. I'm supposed to wear it during the diurnal part of the station cycle."

"I'll ask," she said.

"Thank you. I know belief evolved in multiple directions since the *Promise*, but this is mine." He lifted his gaze to hers. *I was the junior security officer on the White Hound. I have codes to the logs. If you want to read them.*

Yes.

She must have thought too fiercely, for he winced before providing her with the sequences. They etched into her mind, and she knew she wouldn't forget them.

"So you have decided you'll stay here?" she asked out loud, playing the role she had set for herself.

"I don't know." He offered a lopsided smile. "The only thing I've seen of your station is this infirmary bed. I hope that isn't what the rest of it looks like."

Her laugh was fake. "We try to make the living spaces seem like a slice of planetfall," she said. "I suppose I wouldn't know how well we succeeded." Why had she never thought of that before? She had always assumed that every image was accurate, that a clear sky was blue and the scent of autumn leaves – stop. No reason to assume everything was a lie.

Gwydion nodded. "What about money?"

"You won't have to worry about that," she said. "The station provides everything you need. If you were working, you'd have an allotment according to your performance, but—"

"I don't work," he said. "I don't see anyone, do I?"

Anaea faltered. "It's not like that—"

The door opened and a small blonde entered, maybe a decade

older than Anaea. She carried a covered tray. "Intern?" she said. "You're free to go."

She tried not to stare too hard at the other girl, who must have known the truth. What did she believe about their situation? She hopped to her feet. "Thank you," she said. She flashed Gwydion a smile from the doorway.

Lost in thought, she approached the entrance to the infirmary with no clear memory of the walk. The first thing she had to do was reassure Orithia.

That thought made her slow until each step hurt. What was she going to say? Orithia had begged her not to investigate, to leave alone even the hint of the things she had learned were true. Yet Anaea had to say something, offer some explanation.

She shook herself. It was not fair to draw out the wait, even if she wasn't sure what to say. She quickened her step.

Once in the hovercar, she put a call through to Orithia. One ring, two—

"Anaea!" Orithia squealed. "You're all right?"

"Of course I am." The words came out without thought. "I wasn't in danger."

"And him?" Her voice throbbed with nerves.

"He's fine. They weren't going to kill him." Not yet, she thought. "Can you come to my quarters? I think we should talk."

"I'll be there."

Anaea ended the call and told the hypercar to travel to the nearest dining station. This would go better with food.

Her first instinct was to lie, let Orithia believe what she wanted to – needed to? She had already shaken the other's world with hints and whispers, and wasn't that bad enough? How would she react to the rest? Anaea knew if Orithia heard more, she would want to help, no matter how she hated the situation. How could she let her friend take risks for something she had never wanted to learn?

The combination of aromas in the dining station overwhelmed her: tingling spices, fresh bread that made her lungs expand with every breath. A handful of people ate, seated in clusters, conversational hum mingling with the scents. It was home, distilled and poured into an invisible glass, and it almost soothed her.

She slipped into line. Lying, however much it might have been the easy, kinder solution, was not an option. She couldn't betray Orithia's trust . . . and if she did, she was no different than the leaders of Themiscyra.

The truth seemed equally impossible, and she tried not to squirm, trapped by the wires of thought. Could Orithia deal with this and ever have faith in her surroundings again? Anaea couldn't see how it was fair to make the choice for her. She had pursued Gwydion, even committed to help him escape; Orithia had not.

"What would you like, miss?" the server inquired.

"Sandwiches, the turkey ones; kandim souffle—" a flash to her conversation with Gwydion "—fruit cups and . . ." She hesitated, focusing on the menu screen. "Two firecream sodas and packages of baklava." Orithia's favorites.

The server keyed it in. "That will use up your special rations until—"

"That's all right," Anaea said.

The hovercar stopped in the courtyard outside her quarters. Orithia lingered by her door.

"Ori!" she called.

Orithia smothered her in a hug. "I'm so glad it was bother for nothing," she said, then tipped her head to the basket. "What's that?"

"Picked us up some sweets," she said, "and I missed dinner, so sandwiches, but I thought you might—"

Orithia blinked. "Oh, that's what I forgot to do: eat."

Anaea palmed them in. After a few bites of meal which Anaea could scarcely taste, Gwydion's words scuttling under her tongue, Orithia broke the silence.

"What happened?"

"I sent an emergency call for Valasca," Anaea said. "I said I was concerned about him. She let me see him, make sure he was all right." She rolled away from the table and pulled up her personal files. "I'm going back to the White Hound," she said.

Orithia paused, a bit of lettuce tucked in the corner of her mouth. "Why? And what are you doing?"

"My mother had an interest in pre-isolation ships," she said. "I figured the schematics would help me. Gwydion said there was proof for where he came from on the ship."

Orithia swallowed. "Oh."

"I don't know if that proof exists," Anaea said, feeling a small twinge of guilt. That was technically true, but her doubts were few and growing fainter. "I can get in and out of the hold without help. But if you want to see for yourself, I wouldn't mind the company." She thought she managed not to sound hopeful, if only because she wasn't sure which way to hope. Would Orithia stand with her? Turn away?

Orithia looked down at her hands. The silence extended. If she said no, was this the end of their friendship? Anaea desperately wanted to grab those hands, as if holding on would help. "I don't know," Orithia said, exhaling a sigh. She smiled tentatively. "Let me think, hmm? Everything's easier on a full stomach."

The delay made her heart lurch in relief. "I'll drink to that," Anaea agreed, raising her soda.

"You didn't see Evadne while you were there, did you?" Orithia said, changing the subject. "Seems she's been in the infirmary constantly and it's always something silly. Meanwhile, she leaves strings of unfinished code around like so much pasta."

"Preparing for carrying a child, maybe?" Anaea guessed. "Aren't she and her partner planning to request one?"

"Her partner is." Orithia leaned forward. "I think she's trying to make sure they don't get approval, without it being her fault . . ."

It was gossip, but it was normal, something she could hold onto. They drifted into other topics, chattering and laughing, an evening that could have been any other.

"My fingers are going to be sticky for days," Orithia complained around a mouthful of dessert.

"I could take the rest," Anaea offered.

Hazel eyes narrowed. "Oh, no, you don't."

Anaea watched the last bites of the meal disappear with dread. No matter what happened, she should be able to tell if the White Hound would fly again, the part of her mission she hadn't told Orithia about. She had to focus on getting Gwydion home. But was righting that wrong more important than her friendship?

It had to be. It was his life and his world. For Anaea . . . she would survive.

Orithia exhaled a sigh. "You know what?" she said. "I'm coming with you. You'll need company when you find out your refugee is crazy."

She believed it, Anaea thought. "All right," she said. "I need to look at the hold schematics to be sure we can get in."

"While you're doing that, give me your link," Orithia said.

Anaea flipped it to her and issued commands to the terminal. "What are you doing?"

"Locking the frequency. If you call me, no one else can horn in."

Anaea discovered the hold was connected to an engineer quickway she had played in as a child. The White Hound was slated for deconstruction. Hopefully, they hadn't done anything permanent yet.

"Thanks," she said, "how much longer do you need—"

"Done." Orithia tossed her the link.

Anaea blinked in surprise, even as she ran her mother's schematics into the link. "That was fast."

"I'm that good." Orithia made a face, then sobered. "So we ready?"

"We are now," Anaea said. There it was, she thought – lying despite her best intentions.

*

"I didn't realize we'd have to crouch through here," Orithia said from behind her.

"Neither did I," Anaea answered. When she had last entered the corridors, the ceiling had been well above her head. Her mother had left her in the quickway tunnel above the hanger for hours, content to play in the darkness and imagine she was on a ship to a new world.

She and her mother had never been close, but Tereis encouraged her flights of fancy. "The universe is as wide as you can imagine it, Ann," she had said, yet narrowed her own world to the next circuit board or broken machine. They had hardly spoken since Anaea decided engineering was not her path.

The station hummed beneath her as she opened the access panel. Darkness curved around the White Hound's frame. Anaea pulled herself up into the crawlspace beneath the wing. No sound of motion – good. The engineering crews were off-duty. If they were caught, she would have no explanation, nowhere to go but a memory wipe.

"This way," she whispered. She felt her way along the underside of the ship; she could feel more than see the seam where the access ramp extended. She wanted light, and all she would have to do was step away from the ship to activate the sensors, but that could draw attention. She edged closer until her hand found the panel housing the emergency release.

Orithia hiccoughed as the access ramp moaned to life. "Yikes! That's loud."

Anaea winced at the echo of her voice. "If we get caught, Ori—"

"More than detention." It wasn't a question.

Anaea entered the White Hound and noticed how small and quiet it seemed. It felt dead in a way it had not been when adrift in space.

"Core?" Orithia asked.

Anaea nodded. The salvage crew had cleared a crude path to the control room, a shattered wall beaten out of the way.

She picked her way carefully, anxious not to leave a trace of her passing. The consoles looked lumpish, angular, with protrusions that might have been children's toys, but they hummed to life at a touch and brought up a sequence of displays.

She set the White Hound's systems to diagnostics and called up the database. She started to speak the codes, then paused.

"Ori? Are you all right?"

The programmer smiled weakly. "Everyone looks bad in console light. It's a universal law. I'm fine."

Anaea was surprised to realize her jaw twitched as she finished the last code. A calendar popped up, comforting in its familiarity: ten months, each composed of three and a half ten-day weeks. It had stopped recording last Lachday, one of the three days added to the archaic seven-day week.

"Pull up red-flagged entry," she said.

A booming male voice filled the core, startling her with its depth. "We encountered pirates just outside our calculated entry point for the corridor. They were well-armed, but the Hound is fast, and we didn't linger for chit-chat."

"Pirates," Orithia said. "Of course. That's what we were told was out there."

"I have reason to believe," the narrator continued, "they were not hunting us. We passed close to their base of operations. I have stored a message for relay to the warlords of Annwyn upon our return to known space."

"Warlords?" Orithia wondered.

Anaea shook her head. Annwyn she knew – the massive moon was the last "planet" to be colonized, at least until her knowledge of history stopped – but she had no more idea what a warlord was than Orithia did, except in pre-space historical context. Probably a leader of pirates, but that didn't make sense with the narrator's comments.

"Another entry," Orithia said, searching the list.

The diagnostics uttered a preliminary beep. Anaea frowned, looking at the lines of red. Her attention was drawn away as the voice launched into his next account.

"Despite clearing customs after we crossed the Bridge, the Hound was ordered into lockdown by a warlord from the station. His police force boarded us." The speaker sighed. "They were rather cruel to Gwydion, I suppose because he looked small and meek. I am just thankful there wasn't more trouble on that count." It was obvious he wasn't saying something, or was it only because Anaea knew what the omission was? The security senior must know about his junior's abilities.

"Turns out they were looking for smugglers dealing in Earth antiquities," the voice continued. "The warlord thought our exploration mission was a cover story. A thorough search of the ship and they sent us on our way. Without so much as an apology, I might add."

Customs, police forces, Earth antiquities. In Anaea's mind, these were features of a universe in better shape than they had been led to believe. She glanced at Orithia.

"An isolated warlord laying down the law on whoever enters his turf," the programmer said, sounding nervous. "That's basically – I mean, that's what I thought I was going to hear."

Anaea didn't answer, studying the readouts. She pressed her link and called up her mother's diagrams.

"Ann? What are you doing?" Orithia scuttled over. Anaea fought the urge to cover the screens. "What does this say?"

"The White Hound is no longer capable of space flight," she said, hearing her voice quaver. "It's not going anywhere."

Orithia's eyes flicked to her face, accusing. "You were going to help him go home."

Anaea bit her lip. "Yes."

"You couldn't tell me?" Her voice rose, echoing in the empty core. "You think you're going to do this all by yourself? What happens if things go wrong?"

Anaea winced, fearing someone would hear them. "What happens if things go wrong?" she countered. "Ori, I made a promise that means flouting station law. I need to do this, but

I don't have any right to pull someone else down with me." She massaged the bridge of her nose. "I believe him," she said softly. "That there is something worth going back to. That can be true even for a world in ruins."

"Your fights are my fights," Orithia said curtly. "They always will be."

Anaea slumped against the nearest panel. "I was trying to protect you."

Orithia stiffened, then she laughed, a weak trill. "I don't need protection, Ann. There's nothing here."

Maybe there wasn't. Anaea wavered, feeling numb. She looked at the list of entries. Every moment they spent here increased the risk of being caught.

"One more," she said. "From the departure date." She selected the one entitled Clearances.

Instead of the deep voice, a hologram materialized. Even though it had been centuries since paper was in use for records, the image imitated a stack of sheets with labeled tabs. The first page certified the engine was within operation specs. It bore the electronic prints of three individuals: a shipyard overseer, a bureaucrat with an endless title, and the security senior.

Anaea tabbed back. Other forms for the ship's frame, the shields for hyperspace, a sworn statement the Hound was unarmed; some of the same names showed up, but there were others, and different titles. The infrastructure implied behind the deskwork was extensive. Anaea tried to imagine the reams of regulations, the personnel needed for so many batteries of tests.

"Could it be forged?" Orithia whispered.

Why go to that trouble? "Go ahead and check," Anaea said. As the programmer inched forward to better access the unfamiliar interface, Anaea clicked on the tab labeled Mission Statement.

Text scrolled. "Primary Purpose: scout for systems rich in rare or new materials that could host a ground base. Human habitable ideal but not necessary if resources have the potential to outweigh the construction costs for hermetic environment.

Suitable locations will be reviewed for a future cooperative colony between the Galactive Collective and the Pinnacle Empire.

"Secondary Purpose: Any discovery of the following resources should be recorded for—"

Anaea stopped reading. The blood rushed in her ears . . . and then whispered out, leaving her calm and content. All the pieces fit: she couldn't question it any more.

5

"ORI?" ANAEA ASKED QUIETLY. SHE WISHED SHE COULD be absolved of showing her friend the truth.

Orithia's head snapped up. She scanned the text and looked quizzical. "What's this about mining rights?"

"Scroll up," Anaea directed.

She thought at first the White Hound's computers had failed. But it scrolled: she was simply too aware of the space between seconds. Orithia read, lips moving, then her hands dropped from the panel.

"It's forged, it's forged—" her voice rose, high-pitched and panicked, then finally softened. "It's not forged," she concluded. "This is real, isn't it? We're hidden in a tiny corner of something impossibly big—"

Anaea caught her friend by the shoulders. "We're protected in this tiny corner," she said. "We don't have to face the rest." She felt Orithia shaking; slid one hand under her elbow to hold her up. "This doesn't have to change anything."

"It does," Orithia said in a strained voice. "I know now. You can't fix that."

The station leaders could, Anaea thought. "I'm sorry," she said. "I had to know—"

Orithia shook her head. "Send him away. Then none of this will matter."

For Anaea, it would still matter: she was part of the conspiracy, though that might be short-lived after they found Gwydion had disappeared . . . and that was another thing she had kept to herself. She couldn't seem to stop lying. She wondered if this was how a simple measure of protection came to last a century, with no indication the leaders had any thought of ending it. One small concealment, then another.

Orithia quivered against her, drew swooping breaths that hovered on the edge of tears. "Take me out of here," she whispered. "The lights are – I feel as if they're going to taint me, Ann, make me part of this other world."

Anaea hadn't seen enough, had found more questions than answers, but she couldn't ignore that plea. "We'll go," she said. "It's okay, Ori."

They retreated from the hold, through the engineer quickways, drained and quiet. They returned to Anaea's quarters, where Orithia burrowed into her and cried.

Anaea held her, murmuring reassurance. Despite her own fear and disbelief, her reaction hadn't been tears. She didn't have any urge to shed them.

Orithia calmed, with a sigh that swept all the breath from her body. She plopped onto the couch. "I've always broken the rules," she said, "but only the ones that don't matter. I should have left this alone. Trusted Asteria and her council."

Anaea studied her. "You're not angry?"

"Why would I be? We weren't there." Orithia shook her head. "They thought about it. They knew things we can't. This is – this is our world, Anaea. I wouldn't trade it away."

Anaea squeezed her shoulder. "Then keep it."

The other narrowed her eyes. "You don't feel the same way, do you? You want to know what's out there, you want to taste the dust of a planet, and you don't mind what could happen. Themiscyra is controlled, Ann. I complain about that all the time, but . . ." Her voice faded away. "It means we're safe."

"I want—" Anaea stopped. "I can't put this aside. But I promise I'll do everything I can to let you do so."

Orithia's lips twitched. "I hate this."

"I'm sorry I brought you—"

"No, not that," she interrupted, then grimaced. "All right, that, but more, I hate feeling like an alien to you. It hurts . . ." she trailed off again.

Anaea hugged her with one arm, a futile gesture. "I feel the same way." That had always been their story: wanting it to work and not quite making it. "We can talk—"

"I just want to sit," Orithia said, "and not say anything. Can we do that?"

"Of course." Anaea slid next to her on the couch. There was no awkwardness; that had passed a long time ago. The thoughts that had consumed her gave up their pacing.

Orithia fell asleep, slumping with her head against Anaea's shoulder. In that position, Anaea could see only a fraction of her face. She still thought it was beautiful, though others might have called it childish; deceptive in a woman seven months her senior, almost twenty. Beautiful or not, though, she no longer felt the longing she once had. Instead, she remembered another face, sleeping, or feigning sleep.

Carefully, she inched off the couch, letting Orithia slip to the pillows. She took a blanket from the bed and tucked it around her friend, then curled up herself. She sent a silent good night to Gwydion and drifted.

*

In the morning, Orithia was gone. Anaea's stomach tightened, but she knew her friend would find her if she needed to talk.

She pushed through breakfast, head bowed. Younger girls

giggled and flirted; an older pair argued about ambient lighting hues as if it were a life-or-death topic. After finishing the synthetic sausage, Anaea's enthusiasm picked up. Another conversation with Thalestris or Valasca – preferably the former – was overdue; the White Hound waited with its secrets only brushed; and she looked forward to more dialogue with Gwydion.

She wolfed the last bites and hurried to the infirmary. More practical considerations began to assert themselves. The White Hound, crippled, would not provide the escape route. Could she let him take one of the shuttles? That would be theft on a grand scale, and it might be different enough from the ships in his Collective to raise suspicion.

Anaea felt warm and even giddy as she walked through the infirmary. The people she passed had no idea she had a secret. There was nothing more heady than knowing what no one else did.

She spent two hours assisting the doctor on rounds. With few diseases left to fight and violence rare, the bulk of the cases were minor accidents and mishaps. She had never been especially interested in medical routine, and now it was difficult to focus.

Her aural link chirped – Valasca. "Anaea, my office, please."

Anaea made her excuses and peeked into the chief doctor's office. Valasca, Thalestris and a woman she didn't recognize with an enforcement insignia waited inside. She hesitated, panic bubbling within her. Had she been caught? But she couldn't bolt. She calmed herself. Perhaps there was some signature to be witnessed.

"Dr. Braun," she said, bowing her head. "Dr. Fenyang. Ma'am."

"Sit down." Valasca's voice was cold, her eyes pinched, but that was normal for her. Anaea settled herself, hands in her lap. "Your friend called for you."

A leap of eagerness surfaced; she held it down. "Oh. I guess we must have made a connection. Is there something specific I need to talk to him about?" She glanced sideways at Thalestris, hunting for a cue, hoping for reassurance.

"We monitor the activity of new recruits," Valasca said briskly. "It helps to prevent cold feet or rash declarations, and contain them when they occur."

Orithia! She felt a chill flush of panic. She had palmed open the doors for them – hadn't she? Orithia could be imprisoned or put on menial duty for the hacking she had done.

"I don't have cold feet," she said.

"Anaea Carlisle," the officer said, "why did you research the technical specs of the White Hound and other archaic ships?"

That was easy, wasn't it? "I was curious about his world," she said. "It was research, nothing more."

"Coincidence, then, that someone ran a diagnostic on the Hound?"

"I—" She hadn't expected anyone would check the logs. Why had she assumed they wouldn't watch her, as long as she acted as if she believed?

"Anaea, dear," Thalestris said, "it would be better if you didn't lie."

"Miss Carlisle," the officer said, "I can put you under oath wherein the penalty for giving false witness—"

Valasca cut her off with an irritated look. "What were you doing on Mallory's ship?"

Anaea's head throbbed. She should have thought of this. How could she have hidden it without involving Orithia more deeply? What else had she done that might still be traced? She had to make them believe her.

She focused on the chief doctor, though her stomach curled in. "My mother used to work on ships like these. It was her hobby." Her voice sounded thin to her own ears. "I was curious."

"Curious enough to break the regulations, when you could have simply asked for permission?" Thalestris shook her head. "I'm sorry, Anaea. That doesn't fit what we know about you. I hoped you would have a reasonable explanation."

"Your friends and work colleagues will be cross-examined if we aren't satisfied," the officer said briskly. "It would be better for all concerned if you explain yourself."

Ori! She had to keep her out of this. It was obvious they didn't believe her. The truth was there to be taken, and she had to surrender it.

"I was looking to see if he could fly out with the Hound," she said in a small voice. "I discovered it won't fly. I felt sorry for him and he so desperately wants to go home and—" She swallowed. The taste in her mouth was sour and stale.

"That's enough, Anaea." Thalestris' voice hadn't changed; it seemed she wasn't surprised, but she was gentle, sympathetic.

"More than enough." Valasca's lips pressed into an angry line. "It seems I was wrong about you."

"I made a mistake, Anaea said, "but—"

"A mistake that betrayed this station," the officer said. "Do you understand what you could have jeopardized?"

"It's over, Anaea." Thalestris rose, interposing herself between the intern and the others. It seemed almost protective. "I'm afraid we can't allow you to work with us. In view of the fact it stopped at the stage of harmless inquiry—"

Valasca shot her an irritable look. Thalestris smiled ever so slightly. Anaea sensed an argument that had gone in her favor and tried to breathe.

"—you won't be punished," the obstetrician continued. "But you won't remember any of this. Come with us."

Anaea reminded herself this was supposed to be the first she had heard of the memory wipe, tried to look confused, even as a raw, cold sensation rose up her throat. She couldn't let her new knowledge be erased. Valasca hadn't moved from her desk; she didn't intend to follow. It would be easier to escape from two than three, easier to run in a corridor than an office.

Anaea stood, feeling her ankles wobble. Run to where? And what about *him*?

Gwydion, she thought as hard as she could, hoping he could hear her. *We need to get out of here. Break out of your room.* Her anxiety pushed over her attempts at projecting. He had told her he could break out, only needed somewhere to go. She hoped he was right.

Thalestris put a hand on her arm and guided her out of the office. The door whispered shut. The legal officer fell in step behind them; Anaea could feel her watchful eyes on the back of her neck. She hesitated. If she continued towards the entrance of the infirmary, she had a better chance of evading them, but Gwydion was in the other direction. What would happen if she left him?

There was no voice to help her make the decision. The two women walked her down the hall.

"Dr. Fenyang?" A new intern perched nervously in one of the doorways. She looked twelve or thirteen. "May I ask you a question?"

Thalestris turned, perhaps to refer her to another doctor. Anaea never heard. As the hand slipped from her arm, she twisted on her heel and dove. The officer grabbed for her; she felt a tug on her sleeve before she pulled free. The unexpected weight made her stumble, but quivering ankles firmed under her, and she ran.

She headed for the isolation ward, no response from Gwydion, no retreat planned, no guarantee she would reach him. Somehow, she was moving too fast for the madness to catch up with her.

"Carlisle," the officer called, her voice sharp but unconcerned. She knew there was nowhere to go. "Stop this foolishness. Otherwise, I will be obliged to stun you. This is your only warning."

Anaea reached the end of the hall and the isolation ward. She palmed the panel without hope, and wasn't surprised when it blared red.

Anaea?

Upon seeing those words written in starlight in her mind, she felt a surge of relief. *Join me. Quickly.*

What's going on? he asked. *I sensed a burst of alarm and realized it was you.*

Not her frantic attempts to attract his attention, then, but the reactions she hadn't been able to control. *We don't have time.* She was dimly aware this conversation moved fast as thought, of course, and the exchange had taken a fraction of a second. *I can't get to the ward, they've locked me out. They'll lock you in. If you want to leave, it has to be now.*

The officer lifted her closed fist; the stunner was a dull sheath of interlocked metal bands on her index finger. Anaea pressed against the wall.

A shuddering bang echoed in her ears. The door frame warped under unseen force. The metal screeched. Thalestris gasped; the officer paled.

When Anaea saw the woman open her hand to fire, she dropped. Her body smacked the floor – and a boom flooded the space above her. She rolled to one side, wondering how one could be jarred so badly by a simple fall. The door-frame had come away from the wall, a split just large enough to push through.

She dove to her feet and shoved, squeezing through. The warped material dragged along her skin. The officer shouted after. She heard the staccato patter of argument between the woman and Thalestris.

Anaea stumbled, turning towards Gwydion's room. She palmed the door, holding her breath, hoping she hadn't been excluded from locks meant only to keep the patients in. It opened; he stepped out to take hold of her arm, the other hand clenched about a sedative patch and his breath coming fast. The patches were kept handy in occupied rooms.

"Are you all right?" he asked.

She nodded. "They realized I was going to help you," she said, rapid, whispering. "They're going to remove my memories of this. They'll do the same to you. If they can't, then—" Then what? It still seemed fantasy to imagine they would kill him. They were protectors, not murderers.

Valasca bulled out of her office. The other two explained, to a hiss of fury from the chief doctor.

"They're staying where they are," Gwydion said, sounding uncertain. He looked as if he wanted to duck behind Anaea.

"I'm not sure the door can open again like that," she pointed out.

He flushed. "Sorry."

"There's nowhere to go from the isolation ward." Anaea tried to think. "If we can get out of isolation, the infirmary will be locked down, but not the quickways."

"What's a – no, don't explain," he said. "As long as they can get us out. Do you really want to do this? You must be breaking every law this place has."

She swallowed, the words fire on her face. She hadn't had time to think, to realize the sum of her actions could put her in confinement for a long time: decades, if they weighed the risk of Gwydion revealing the station to the universe. But to go back to knowing nothing, to abandon him? She had the strange feeling the choice was out of her hands.

"Yes, I do." Her eyes fell on the patch in his hand. "I have an idea."

The hand on her arm squeezed. *Tell me.*

Valasca stepped forward. "How dare you cause this kind of commotion on my turf?" she said. "I can make your lives a misery—"

"Dr. Braun," the legal officer interceded. "That is not helpful."

Anaea held up a hand in a gesture of surrender. "We're not going to cause any more trouble." With the other hand, behind her back, she took the patch from Gwydion. "Just get this over with."

The women advanced. Valasca frowned, looking dubious as she examined the broken door. Her shoulder twitched in an angry shrug, and she laid her hand on the palm-panel. Mechanisms growled in protest, but the door slid open, though it stuck at the last inches. Anaea and Gwydion squeezed through.

The officer stopped them. "Please step apart," she said. She turned her attention to Valasca. "I need a sedative that will work on him."

Now, Gwydion said.

She wasn't ready. *But—*

No time to think! He didn't move, didn't blink, but the stunner jerked in the officer's hand, sliding free. Anaea scrambled forward, pressing the patch against Valasca's arm as the weapon pinged off the floor. The doctor stumbled, and Gwydion shoved past the officer. Then they were running, the corridor clear and a dozen confused faces staring after. Security alarms blared, cutting the light with striations of purple.

Left turn, right, again, hopefully fast enough to lose the women, if only briefly. The officer's voice echoed through the overhead, commanding a response from security.

"Over here!" Anaea hauled him into a supply room. She pushed aside a shelf covering the quickway grate. She looked back to find him scanning the shelves. "What are you doing?"

"Looking for a Karan class drug," he replied. She realized he was panting, breathing far harder than their exertions could explain. The color had drained out of his face.

"What?" She knew they were a reflex-enhancing synthetic, named after their creator. He couldn't be thinking of fighting their way out?

"Hypermental stimulants." His smile was hard, and he looked much older than before. "Just in case."

Anaea pulled on the grate handle and froze. "It's sealed."

He hurried over. "I thought you said it wouldn't be locked down."

"It's not closed because of the alarms. It was welded shut. Maybe months ago." Distress twisted Anaea's stomach. These were *her* tunnels, and now was not the time to be orphaned from them.

"You must know others." Despite the panic in his face, his voice tried to reassure.

"Yes," she said, "but security personnel will be between us and them. They're not going to hurt us, but they will stop us and erase our memories. Or at least mine. I won't even remember you exist." That seemed impossible to imagine.

Gwydion hovered in silence, then winced as voices shrilled questions outside. "I can think of a way to get us out of here," he said.

"How?" As he explained his plan, her eyes widened. "Are you sure you want to do that? It would make you look like—"

"Your people already seem to think I'm a menace," he said. "Let's play to it. Do you trust me?"

Strange how easy a question that was to answer. "Yes, I do."

"Then let's get out of here."

6

GWYDION POCKETED THREE VIALS AND INSERTED A syringe into the fourth. Most medicines were administered by patch or aerosol, so Anaea was grateful this one used a more primitive method. Best to rely on a method that was harder to apply accidentally.

She was still nervous, even as she pocketed sedative patches and hoped she wouldn't need the trick again. "If you inject me with that—"

"It won't hurt you," he said. "You might hyperventilate a bit, nothing more. But they're not going to know that's what I have." His face crinkled up. "I'm going to grab you now."

His dismay would have been comical, in other circumstances. A weird, awkward dance ensued before they ended up with him clutching her elbow, the other arm pinning hers to her side and the syringe against her neck. It felt so ludicrous, so staged to Anaea she was sure anyone would see through it.

". . . into the supply room," a voice said.

Gwydion darted through the doorway, jerking her along. She sucked in a breath as the needlepoint scraped her skin; she didn't need to fake the surge of adrenaline. She clutched at his arm, trying to make it look as if she was trying to hold him off rather than keeping him steady.

Two officers pivoted to face them. A frightened intern shrank back, hiding behind two white-haired doctors. Anaea recognized her: a classmate a year younger than she who had decided to go into pediatrics. The officer on the left raised her hand, then hesitated.

"Whatever you're thinking, don't do it," Gwydion said. She could feel the quaver in his voice through her backbone. "If my hand tenses, it will depress the syringe."

"Don't be dramatic," the lead officer said. "There's no cause to make this unpleasant. Miss, are you all right?"

Anaea froze. How did someone answer in these situations? She hadn't been hurt, but she couldn't say she was fine. She wouldn't have been if the threat were real. "I—"

"Hush." Gwydion's voice was soft. "You've made me a prisoner here. If it's unpleasant, I didn't start it."

That, Anaea realized with an inward shiver, was genuine anger. She also noticed his hand shook, and not with nerves. They had to hurry.

"You are not a prisoner," the other officer said, "just—"

"Stay where you are," Gwydion said. "Don't move."

The officers had almost certainly never seen a man before, and they held back, obviously trying to figure out how best to approach. Hesitation became stasis, and Gwydion backed up the hall. Anaea scrambled to keep her feet in line with his.

Where are we going? he asked.

She turned her head as far as she dared. *Take the second corridor. Third door.*

A pair of interns shrieked as they saw the young man. They fled. Gwydion backed up a few more steps, then released her shoulder and spun her around.

They ducked together into a testing chamber. Anaea ran to the back; the grate was on the ceiling, allowing drop-down access to the equipment. She bounced futilely on her toes once before using the white arm of the scanner to push herself up.

His hands rested on one hip and boosted her. She felt the tremor in his arm. She pulled the grate handle; it swung free. Adrenaline sent spots prickling at the back of her eyes. She grabbed the edge and scrambled up.

He followed. She yanked the grate up and looked over at him. "Can you—"

"Get back," he said. He stared hard at the grate.

A low crunch as the metal shifted, bending against the frame. Even brute force might have trouble opening it. Gwydion rose, almost pitching into her. She caught his arm and guided him down the quickway.

One turn, then another. Only then did she risk asking the question. "What's wrong?"

"I just applied more pressure and moved more weight in the past five minutes than I have in almost a year," he said. "I'm not that strong."

Anaea guided him away from the infirmary and the station core with no clear destination. A shuttle-launch would attract immediate attention, even assuming she could get him that far.

"Where are we going?" he asked.

She shook her head. "I'm thinking. There has to be a way you can still leave the station."

"I'm sorry," he said. "I didn't intend to force you to leave your home."

She opened her mouth to protest . . . and then it hit her. By assaulting a doctor, engineering the escape from isolation and planning to steal a shuttle, against the warnings of her superiors, that was exactly the situation she was in, the alternative being ignorance and imprisonment. She had already decided that wasn't an option.

She was leaving Themiscyra . . . if she and Gwydion could escape.

"It wasn't your fault," she said. In the wake of the realization, her mind went numb and still while the universe careened around her.

Gwydion moved his hand as if he wanted to squeeze her arm, then dropped it. "Are we safe through here?"

She forced her thoughts into motion. "We should be. They're only passages between points. You could go anywhere, but you'll still be on the station."

"And it's not as if you can cross a border, sneak out on a ship, or get a Tweaker to change your identity," Gwydion said, mostly to himself. He tapped behind his ear. "What about that?"

Anaea was too busy stumbling over the cryptic descriptions to realize what he meant at first. "The link? I don't know if they can track it; Orithia only isolated . . ."

Ori. Would the officers recruit her, tell her that Gwydion had kidnapped her? It was easy to think Orithia would believe it. She hesitated, then put a call through.

"Ann?" Orithia's voice was tight and anxious. "My system has been blaring with emergency codes. Is that you?"

"Yes." Anaea bit her lip. "Ori, things have gone crazy. I got Gwydion out of the isolation ward. I broke him out," she corrected herself. "I just didn't want you to believe whatever they're going to tell you."

Silence. "Where do we meet?"

"Ori, this isn't—"

"Of course it's my fight," Orithia said. "You're my friend, and how else am I going to get an opportunity to ogle a man? Give me five minutes, I'm going to put a masking pattern on your link. Stay careful."

Anaea grinned despite herself; a good thing Gwydion couldn't hear Orithia. "I will," she said, gave her a location, and ended the call.

*

A WARREN OF quickways ran beneath the arctic regions of the Preserve, allowing access to the temperature controls. Anaea knew it was a good place to hide. The travel system in the quickways was automated and rudimentary, but it worked, though with none of the inertial dampening of the system in surface corridors. Gwydion wobbled into a crouch when they climbed off, clutching his knees.

He waved her off. "I'm fine."

The storage room, shaped on the outside to look like a glacier, was not monitored. It was, however, frigid enough to make her toes curl through her shoes.

The door opened. Orithia squawked at the cold. "Are you trying to kill us?" But then she gawped at Gwydion. "I thought you'd be taller," she said.

Gwydion nodded to her awkwardly. "Miss Roslin, thank you in advance for any help you can give."

Introductions seemed unnecessary. Anaea let out a breath, watching the ice crystals form. "They know I was trying to release the White Hound for him," she said.

"What does that mean?" Orithia asked in a small voice.

Anaea swallowed hard. "It means," she said, "we have to get him out of here."

Penelope oozed up Orithia's shoulder and then hopped to Anaea's. She chittered and rubbed her face against Anaea's in greeting. Anaea rubbed the fur behind her ears.

Gwydion looked wary. "Is that a cat or a monkey?" he asked.

"Neither. Both," Orithia volunteered. "She's a kearl, genetically engineered to be a companion. Which means they're shameless for attention and they purr in harmony."

"Engineered. You can do that?" He extended a tentative hand towards Penelope. Anaea turned so he could brush the kearl's golden flank with his fingertips.

"Some basic blends, that's all," Orithia said. "I skipped the rotation in theoretical genetics."

The kearl had eased the tension, but Anaea knew she had to push onwards. "We need to leave the station," she said.

Orithia bit her lip. "I don't see how it's possible," she said. "Any shuttle launched can be traced, and a practiced pilot is going to beat out the two days you and I spent in a simulator."

Anaea's thoughts whirled. "The aural link."

"What about it?" Orithia asked. Gwydion scritched the kearl under the chin while he listened.

"You said you put a masking pattern on mine," Anaea said. "That means they think I'm somewhere else, right? Can we send an empty shuttle out and make them think I'm on it?"

"Yes, but . . ." Orithia's protest turned thoughtful. "If we disguised your real departure as a routine functions check, it would buy time. Maybe."

Maybe was more than Anaea had expected. "I can get us to the docking bay."

Gwydion cleared his throat uneasily. "Are you sure?"

"We've come this far," Anaea said. "We can't go back now." She reached out and gave his arm a tentative squeeze. Penelope chittered, flicking her tail.

Orithia laughed, an anxious chirp. "I guess that's her way of agreeing."

*

BY THE TIME they reached the quickways running parallel to the docking bay, Anaea's back hurt from crouching. The three slumped into individual heaps as Orithia made the programming changes with her portable kit.

"I like typing," she said defensively.

Gwydion held up his hands. "I didn't say anything. It's a Tweaker trademark where I come from, actually."

Orithia looked puzzled, but ducked her head over her work. Anaea could see the firmness in her refusal to ask. "Soon as I'm done," she said, "you'll need to drop the link aboard the decoy and then get to other shuttle as quickly as possible."

They fell silent again, though Anaea's head was loud enough for three conversations. How was she going to explain she would be leaving with Gwydion, and there was no question of return?

Penelope perched on anyone who would give her attention. She finally settled in Gwydion's lap, paws tucked underneath her.

"I'm done," Orithia announced, holding out the link. She gave Gwydion a stern look as she rose. "You take care of her, you hear? Make sure she stays safe out there."

Anaea swallowed the lump in her throat. Orithia had already guessed. "Ori—" she tried.

Gwydion smiled wryly. "So far, it's been the other way around, but I'll try."

"I was speaking to Penelope," Orithia said, her voice tight. "She's going with you. You need something familiar out there. A piece of home." She jerked her gaze away. The tension and pain vibrated in her, too intense to put into words. "You shouldn't wait."

"You could come with us," Anaea said. She knew better, but she still hoped. Had she really had any other friends? Certainly none so close.

Orithia shook her head. "This is home, Ann. I couldn't give this up for whatever's out there. Penelope will look after you for me."

Anaea swallowed, the pain scratching at her throat. "Tell them we tricked you or forced you."

Orithia smiled nervously. "Oh, Ann, I'm even worse at lying than you are. It wouldn't work."

That stung a little. Anaea ducked her head. "I just—"

"There's a way to make it more authentic," Gwydion said softly.

Orithia folded her arms, chin tilted. "Hit me with it."

"If you allow me, if you really want to believe it, I can make you think that's what happened."

"You can change someone's mind like that?" Anaea asked. Maybe the doctors were right to be frightened of him.

"Only if the mind wants to be changed," Gwydion said. "It's – the brain is too complex to force in a foreign direction."

"I don't want to think of you as a villain, Anaea," Orithia said, fingers tapping with the words. "What can they really do to me?"

"You've broken a lot of laws helping us, Ori." Please. Don't make me worry about what I'm leaving you to face."

Orithia closed her eyes. "All right."

"You should sedate her as soon as I'm done." Gwydion looked anxious, rolling the link in his fingers.

Anaea crushed her in a hug. Orithia whimpered against her ear, then kissed her cheek.

"Good luck out there," she said. "Remember I'm always your friend – even if I don't."

Anaea wanted to protest, but she feared another word would break Orithia's resolve and her own. She hovered, patch in hand, as Gwydion touched his fingers to Orithia's temples. Her eyelids fluttered.

Orithia's spine jerked, and she recoiled. Anaea froze at the film of hatred that passed over those hazel eyes. She reminded herself that if the station leaders believed Orithia had been forced, it would spare her friend from imprisonment . . . and if they wiped her memory, it would all go back to normal, at least for Ori. This was the only gift Anaea could give.

"Use the whole station to your own ends, fine," Orithia said, "but why me?"

Her voice throbbed with hurt. The tone slammed into Anaea's heart. She thought she had been ready for this; she was wrong. She stared, hunting for some hint of the telepathic sleight of hand, terrified somewhere Orithia had simply changed her mind, no trick, no intervention. "Ori?"

"Anaea!" Gwydion hissed.

Instinct hit her muscles. She wobbled forward and pressed the patch to her friend's arm. Orithia's eyes widened and flashed one last look of betrayal. She oozed against the wall. Her eyes fluttered shut as she fought to keep them open. Anaea prayed, silently, compulsively.

Gwydion grabbed her arm. "We have to go."

He was right. She nodded, turned, tears escaping her self-control. Penelope bumped against her ankle and chirred; blindly, she scooped up the kearl with one hand. Even the purring couldn't ease the jagged edge in her heart. She jerked open the quickway grate and tumbled out into the docking bay.

*

The shuttle they had chosen was large, but paired cargo holds filled most of it. The controls squeezed into the curved bow and left little space for a razor-thin cot. Gwydion gave it a dubious look.

"We'll have to trade off watching the controls anyhow," Anaea said, inspecting the panel. Her voice sounded hollow. Soft hisses seemed to fill the cabin with serpents as the automatic launch sequence Orithia had programmed began.

"I'm surprised you have vessels capable of hyperspace." His voice was soft. Perhaps he was trying to distract her as much as he was curious. "Where do you go?"

"This is a mineral-rich system, but there are other things we need." Anaea felt as if she were reciting her childhood lessons; the words were no more alive on her tongue. "We've sounded out two corridors from the system and go there for gathering."

The precise nature of hyperspace remained a question mark, but corridors provided a way of cheating around speed-of-light limitations. Distances simply weren't the same in hyperspace. Corridors formed between certain gravity wells; that same celestial pressure weakened the boundary between hyperspace and real space enough for a ship to breach it. Each corridor had a finite number of end points. Regions unconnected by a hyperspace corridor had to be reached at slower than light speeds. It was part of why Earth had fallen out of humanity's network.

The mention of connected corridors caught Gwydion's interest. "Where—"

She shook her head. She might trust him, might not believe in the secrecy, but Themiscyra's resources were its own. Penelope chittered and rubbed her face against Anaea's ear.

Anaea called up the viewscreen, and space surrounded them. In front, the trailing debris of the asteroid belt. Behind, the silvery arch of the station. She said nothing, trying to multiply the sight in her mind and imagine how big the rest of the universe must be. She failed.

An atonal voice informed them manual control had been engaged. Anaea leaned over to center herself over the console. Gwydion put a hand over hers, pushing it gently away. "Let me do that," he said.

She surrendered, grateful even though she knew he was too tired to do so for long. "We have to enter the hyperspace corridor past the point where the White Hound was buffeted free," she said. "Avoid the turbulence." She stood, shifting the view with a hand. This point – here—" a red dot appeared "—is where you came out."

"Got it," Gwydion said. "Can we be sure we'll pass it?"

"No."

She fell silent, watching the dark masses grow near and stroking the kearl, who, oblivious to the tension, fell asleep. Navigating an asteroid field wasn't as difficult as it sounded, given the distance between objects, but mistakes were still possible. Gwydion focused on the controls, his expression strained.

The hyperspace console beeped and came to life, indicating their proximity to the corridor. Gwydion flicked a look up to the marker and shook his head. Anaea watched him, bursting with questions and yet glad she couldn't ask them. She had the excuse she might distract him. Now, when it came to it, did she not want to know?

They passed the marked coordinates on the outer fringe. Gwydion gave the console calibration instructions.

It blared red. "Parameters outside safe space. Aborting."

Anaea's heart leapt in her throat, but before she could panic, the warning message faded, and the console resumed calculations. She let out a sigh.

"Coordinates resolved and egress set," the console announced. "Shields are in place."

Gwydion glanced at her. "Ready?"

"Where are we going?"

"We only have one choice for the first jump," he said. "We'll arrive on the fringe of the Dinifour system – err, that's DN-48 on a system map. From there, I should send a report to the group that commissioned the White Hound, but I have nothing to explain." His smile might have been meant to be reassuring, but it was equal parts nervous and weary. "So we head to the Sanctum. You'll be safe there. Three jumps. Are we good for that?"

"I hope so." Anaea shuddered, thinking of what happened to unshielded vessels. Hyperspace was unexplored and undefined. She had been taught it was the soul of the universe, but that didn't make it less frightening. The soul was immortal and mysterious, and it drove the body to do things it didn't understand.

Nineteen people on the White Hound, and only Gwydion survived.

"I'm ready," she said.

Gwydion bit his lip. "Engage hyperspace engines," he said.

The view of space faded to blank walls as the ship hummed. Vibrating force poured down the walls, surged through the floor, played a rhythm through her body. Anaea gasped, bracing against the sensation. Penelope shrieked, claws digging into her stomach and cutting through her shirt. The flare of pain oscillated with the ship. For an instant, everything hit the same pitch and she thought she might fuse into the vessel.

The ship went still, so suddenly she slid from her perch, clutching her stomach to keep from heaving. Once the initial shock wore off, she felt curiously light, as if her body had converted to bubbles. Penelope made a startled sound and launched out of her lap, doing more damage to her abdomen. Anaea winced and made a mental note to find the medkit.

She looked around and had the disconcerting impression of an imperfect hologram. The consoles, the cot, even Gwydion's face quivered with the diaphanous quality of an image interrupted. She shook her head to clear it.

"Is it always like this?" she asked.

"I've only done this a couple times, but yes." Gwydion leaned forward, putting his head in his hands. "Can you watch the console? I just – it's more than the hyperspace. Everything is blurring. Changing Orithia's thoughts took a lot out of me." In his voice was implicit apology.

"I will." Anaea frowned. "But I don't know what we're headed into."

"When I wake up, I'll give you basic orientation." He smiled wryly. "I did spend some time thinking about how best to present it, should your people have wanted to hear."

Just one more plan that had gone awry. She nodded, swallowing the frantic pitch of her worries. "Go rest."

He slumped more than stood, easing onto the cot. "Anaea? Thank you. I have a debt towards you I can't ever repay."

"I'm not asking you to," she said. "That's not why I did this."

"I still mean it." He glanced towards the back of the ship. "What if you want to go back some day?"

"I don't know if that will ever be possible."

He didn't respond, and when the silence stretched, she realized he had fallen asleep. Blinking hard to clear the after-image of hyperspace, and never quite succeeding, Anaea settled at the console.

7

THE SCRATCHES PENELOPE HAD LEFT STUNG, RUBBING against Anaea's shirt whenever she moved. The pain cut across her consciousness, slicing through a haze of loss and confusion. She couldn't yet grasp the transformation that knifed through her. She half-expected to hear the rustle and whisper of voices, to find that the shuttle was only a simulation and she was still in training.

After four hours in weightless holographic silence, she decided it was safe to leave the console. The shuttle clock ticked, keeping time mechanically; the galactic positioning that standard clocks relied upon didn't work in hyperspace.

Even her footsteps were muted and strange, melodic. She found the medical kit on the wall of the left hold and returned. She set aside the sedative patches and picked out the weakest healing gel. It would do to numb the scratches and seal them. She rolled up her shirt so she could reach the spot.

Penelope chittered, flitting up the back of the chair to peer at Anaea's handiwork. "This is your fault, you know," she said. Though the kearl couldn't understand, her features drooped into such a pathetic expression that Anaea laughed and scritched her forehead. "I think Orithia was just looking for a reason to give you up."

Anguish, cold, metallic and real, even in the dreamy state of hyperspace. Everything coalesced, a puzzle with jagged edges. She stung herself on the pieces: she loved her friend; she had been safe and content in Themiscyra; she knew nothing about this outside universe; she had no idea if her scant skills had any value. She managed a smile that tugged on the aches inside. She no longer had to worry about the pressure of choosing a station profession, but there were a hundred other problems.

She tried to apply the gel, but the rolled-up shirt kept getting in her way. She pulled it over her head and set it aside. She followed the scratches to their corners, then capped the gel. Her stomach felt cold, but it no longer bothered her.

A low mumble from the cot. Anaea turned, startled. Gwydion jerked upright, brown eyes widened almost out of their orbits. It took a half second for her to understand his reaction, and then she gasped, clutching for the shirt and holding it to her chest as he averted his eyes.

The heat of embarrassment trickled down from the top of her head. Even in Themiscyra, she had been somewhat body-shy, and those were women, who had the same parts she did. She wished she could melt into the ship and the hum of hyperspace beyond.

He broke the silence first. "Sorry. I didn't expect—"

"I should have gone into one of the holds." Anaea huddled against the chair's frame. She was suddenly tempted to ask him any number of questions that made her want to blush harder.

Gwydion swung his leg around so he faced the wall. "Please, change. I didn't mean to see – erm."

"It's – fine." She yanked the shirt back on hastily. "How are you feeling? You can turn," she added.

He did. "Still a little dragged out, but refreshed enough I can take the controls while you rest." He offered an anxious smile, cheeks pink.

"I'd like to know what I'll wake up to," Anaea said quietly. "The Collective and the Empire."

"That's fair." He jumped as Penelope hopped up next to him, then ran fingers through her fur. "One civilization on each side of the Bridge: the only known corridor connecting them. I guess it fell out that way because it was a natural barrier. We'll exit hyperspace on the Pinnacle Empire's turf: two planets, Independence and Annwyn, and a handful of stations and colonies. It's controlled by a few hundred fiercely territorial warlords. They, and the people vying for positions beneath them, live by challenge and competition."

Anaea blinked. "That sounds like anarchy." Which was what she had been told.

"Not quite." Gwydion smiled wryly. "It has rules, like a game, which keeps some order in the chaos. But no one is denying the emperor has more pomp than power."

She rubbed reflexively at her stomach, though it no longer hurt. "How did it get to that? We used to have representative councils . . ."

"It fell out in the wake of Y-Poisoning. I'm not much of a historian." He looked apologetic. "It would be better to talk to someone in the Sanctum or read the databases for yourself."

She nodded. "And the Collective?"

"The Galactic Collective is ruled by an over-class of matriarchs," Gwydion said. "There's a lot more of them, but most don't have much power. Still, it's an influential community, and the social weight of their approval alone keeps their world in check. Neither government," he added with a hint of wryness, "holds as broad an expanse as the names might imply. The Collective controls Solomon, Elysium and Perica."

"So there hasn't been any new planetary landfall since the epidemic." She tried to be comforted by that, but the scope of it still defeated her. She reached for the one concrete piece she knew. "The Collective is where your Sanctum is?" she asked.

"Yes, on Elysium. A comitissa offered to appoint Dr. Anders

her successor, but she asked for the land grant for the Sanctum instead." Gwydion seemed to relax, though he wouldn't meet her eyes. "If it weren't for her, I would never have flown on the White Hound."

"How so?" she prompted.

"Most of the Sanctum's supporters live there, but we have some itinerant members. I – needed to leave for a while . . ." Gwydion flushed, awkward, defensive, with remembered embarrassment. "We've always known there was a group of women who fled known space in the early years of Y-Poisoning. Dr. Anders requested that I and a few others apply to exploration missions, to report if we found you."

Anaea didn't want to feel the unease trickling up from her stomach, much less voice it, but she needed to. "I can't be your proof," she said. "I have no right to make the decision for Themiscyra."

"I know," he said. "You saved me: the least I can do is keep your secret. But the Sanctum is still home, and it's the safest place I know. I'll teach you as much as can, but right now, you look exhausted. You rest, I'll take the console?"

Anaea's head buzzed, but she nodded. "Though I'm only going to curl up for a minute," she said as they traded places. "I have so many other questions, and I don't feel tired . . ."

*

ANAEA AWOKE FEELING as if someone had stuffed pillows into her head. She also noticed immediately the world had returned to single vision and was heavy, solid. They were no longer in hyperspace.

She swung upright, hunting for the clock. Seven hours had passed. "You shouldn't have let me sleep so long," she said, then realized his head was bent forward, his posture still.

He looked up, his face beatific; then it faded into a smile. "No need to wake you," he said. "Everything was fine."

"You looked as if you were asleep."

"Morning prayers," he said. "Thanking God for how far we've come."

"Isn't your God a man?"

"Don't wrinkle your nose," he said. She blinked; she hadn't been aware of doing it. "No. God is beyond gender. There are two common names for . . . it—" he obviously wasn't happy with the choice of pronoun "—one masculine, one feminine. He is just a convenient neutral pronoun. Even the matriarchs use it without thought, though there is a splinter sect . . ." he trailed off.

She still found the concept of a personified creator strange, but didn't want to offend him. "The sect calls it a She?"

"Does that make any more sense to you?" he asked, lips twitching.

She chuckled, relieved he could find amusement in it. "No," she admitted. "Can you pull up the star screen? I want to see."

He nodded and waved up the viewscreen. Excitement rushed through her as the stars surrounded them, followed by disappointment; it looked little different from the view outside Themiscyra, save for the mass of an approaching planet and the distant spheres of its sisters.

"Dinifour's fifth planet," Gwydion said. "We stay this close to the fringe, we should be fine."

Anaea leaned forward, as if being a few inches closer could possibly make a difference with the view. She picked out the dull silver of the third planet, Avalon, and its massive moon, Annwyn. Avalon was uninhabitable, but Annwyn had been colonized a little under two centuries ago. The last landfall of humanity before the Derithe, as far as she knew . . . and it was warlord territory now.

"We'll reach the other corridor in about nine – seven hours?" Gwydion rubbed his eyes, squinting at the console. "My math must be off somehow."

"Seventy-five percent lightspeed?" Anaea prompted.

He blinked. "Holy – err." He cut off the profanity with a sheepish look. "No, I was figuring sixty-six. That's what the navigator said the Hound did."

"Oh." Not for the first time, she had misgivings about the conditions she might be entering. But a little technological backslide didn't mean the culture was similarly depressed, old-fashioned monotheism or not.

She popped to her feet. "Going to get us food," she said. What she found troubled her. She returned with two pre-packaged meals. "How long are we going to be traveling?" she asked. "There's only two more. I guess they don't expect the double crew that usually flies this craft to need more."

"We had better split the meals," Gwydion said, "and we still . . . no. I don't think we can get across the Bridge with that."

She bit her lip. "It's not absolutely crucial we eat, is it?"

He gave her a wry look. "Well, no, but it's usually recommended . . ." He rubbed his temples. "You're right. I'd rather not stop in warlord territory unless we have to. Can Penelope eat this?"

Anaea hadn't even thought of the kearl and felt guilty for forgetting. "Most of it, yes." She put one meal aside and tore open the other package. Divided two and a half ways, it seemed very small, but they didn't need much energy aboard ship.

They ate in silence and their own thoughts. After the meal, he coached her on which signals meant pirates, which came from warlord scouting, and what to do if hailed. Then he took the cot and left her alone, on course for a new universe.

*

THEY TRADED OFF again after the next hyperspace jump. Anaea felt peculiar leaving Dinifour behind; it seemed as if she should have absorbed some truth from their brief passage. They had decided to tackle the subject of the new world she was entering once they dropped back into normal space. By then, probably a necessary distraction from growling stomachs.

Eight hours in the corridor, Gwydion at the front; Anaea tried to brush a restless Penelope, whose long fur was already tangled.

She tried not to be as nervous as the kearl, reminding herself that even though the physical distance was much shorter than their last jump, time and space were strange in . . .

The shuttle seemed to flip over. Anaea yelped; she planted her feet in a subconscious effort not to fall to the ceiling. The world shuddered and went triple.

"Gwydion . . . ?" Orange lights blazed on the consoles.

"I don't know," he said. "There's a strain on the shields. Something hit them? We're all right, though . . . they're holding . . ."

She could hear what he wasn't saying out loud: for now. "Get us out," she pleaded. If the shield fell in hyperspace, the shuttle would be ripped open to a vastness more inhospitable than the void of space.

"Distances," he said. "We don't know where we'd come out of hyperspace. Or if we could get back. A good navigator could bring us out easily, but . . . we don't have that. We're maybe forty minutes from the exit point. We've got to wait."

She closed her eyes and felt Penelope press against her stomach. She clutched the kearl hard, subconsciously trying to meld her fear into the small body. "You're right."

They waited, staring at the clock and watching the hands tick. The three-fold sensation did not return, but that didn't stop Anaea from waiting for it – and what might come after. Gwydion puffed out little breaths. Every noise boomed. She tried to speak, but was afraid of the sound of her own voice. She imagined the shield disintegrating like metal under acid . . .

"We're there," he said finally. "I can pull us out."

It was all Anaea could do to keep herself from jumping in and issuing the commands herself. It didn't matter if they had reached the right point if he couldn't extract them fast enough. The consoles flared in a fractal profusion of colors and readings, then flicked dark one by one.

The sensation of hyperspace faded, like water settling after a spill. Anaea's chest hurt as she let out the breath she'd been holding.

Gwydion slumped. "Check the engines—"

Her mother's diagrams danced through her head, but how much help would they be? Anaea darted to the hold and pulled up the grate that exposed the shuttle's inner workings. It was easier to assess than she had feared.

"Shield is damaged and the engine is strained," she said. "Both might make another jump. Might not." She had basic training in spacesuit operation, but that would help not at all stranded in space, or dashed into attendant molecules by hyperspace flux. The memory of the White Hound's dead trickled through her mind, faces she thought she had forgotten in the chaos of the past few days.

Gwydion studied her. They both stood on the edge of the obvious, yet it took a long time for him to take the lead. "Then we have a new destination," he said. "Eastwood."

"The mining colony?"

"Best place to get repairs from someone who won't tell tales about what they find," he said. "I hope there was a data-burst across the Bridge recently, though, or my coins from working the White Hound won't have registered."

Anaea wished for Orithia's intervention and ached. "Eastwood it is."

*

THERE WERE SEVEN planets in the UL-50 system, Gwydion reminded her, none habitable. Blackore, second from the sun, housed the artificial expanse of the colony.

"Small, insular and independent," he said, pulling up the viewscreen. "Four warlords run the colony; each one has his own quadrant, with is own shield generator. None of them could trust the others to maintain a colony-wide generator. They only cooperate when it comes to affairs outside the colony."

She remembered the size he had mentioned; one hundred and twenty miles at the widest point; and couldn't reconcile that with small. The colony was many times the diameter of Themiscyra, much bigger even considering the station was built in a cube. Anxiously, she thought of everything they had not discussed . . . but could any primer prepare her for landfall? As they neared the planet, she could see the shield, a structure half holographic, half gaseous meant to serve as a buffer and safe zone in case one of the smaller domes were breached.

They broke through the atmosphere smoothly, with only a slight shudder; here, Gwydion did not seem surprised by the shuttle's capabilities. The four quadrants lay below. Anaea could not see the microscopic details, but she swore she could sense their presence, the swelling build of humanity around nerve-points.

The planet's surface appeared flat black; only dusted ash suggested contour and terrain. They crossed a line in their descent, and those traces of silver abruptly leapt into peaks and valleys, rough-cut mountains all but invisible from space.

The shuttle approached a group of colored beacons. Anaea shot Gwydion a questioning look as she stroked Penelope.

"We want light blue," he said. "Southeast quadrant. The warlord's more laidback there, with little knowledge of novelty. That means his people have a freer hand, but still the best idea."

The markers flashed into view at regular intervals. The trapped gas prevented a clear view of the colony below, but occasionally she saw a flash of metal.

The console buzzed for incoming communication. Gwydion waved it in.

"What is your business at Eastwood, shuttle?" said a sharp, nasal female voice.

"Repairs," Gwydion said, "we—"

"Your troubles aren't my concern. Docking clearance. Bay fourteen." The console went dead.

Gwydion shrugged. "I guess it saves explaining?"

A corridor appeared in the gas, formed by white energy. Gwydion waved away the viewscreen as they descended. Moments later, the shuttle touched down.

Landfall on a planet. A week ago, it would have seemed an impossible fantasy, a child's dream. Could it live up to what she had imagined?

"Anaea?" Gwydion touched her shoulder. "Are you all right?"

She jumped, upsetting the kearl from her lap. "I'm fine," she said. "What now?"

"Customs, currency, a place to stay," he said. He studied her, frowning. "You should keep your head down. Don't attract anyone's attention. Let me take Penelope."

Anaea murmured nonsense syllables to the kearl, depositing her on Gwydion's shoulder. "Why?"

He flushed a little, but replied, "The warlords and their retainers, sometimes they take a fancy to pretty women. It's better if she doesn't draw attention to you."

She was puzzled, though the implicit compliment warmed her. She lacked the visible tranquility so much prized in Themiscyra: her face was thin, marred with angles and anxiety. No woman could be pretty who looked as she did.

"Lead the way," she said.

They descended the ramp into a docking bay similar to the one in Themiscyra, though it was dark and smelled of grease. The bay door opened into a corridor; she counted ten bays to each side. A menial robot whisked down the passage, its click providing the only sound in miserly light.

Gwydion walked briskly, spine stiff. He was nervous, she could tell, but he forced a confidence that seemed too brash. The corridor ended in a octagon-shaped room. Half the walls opened onto manned counters.

The brightest of these was marked Customs and tended by a man part muscle, part mass, rolling heavily in the latter direction. He grunted when he saw the pair, barely looking up from a monitor screen. "Put your hand over the scanner."

He was only the second male she had seen in person, and she puzzled over him. He scarcely seemed to even have a shape. Was he more usual, or was it Gwydion's type? There was still a squareness, a foreignness to both she found unsettling.

Gwydion waved his hand over the silver plate. The monitor scrolled with data. Anaea leaned forward, saw his name, occupation, a list of travel permits . . .

Something the attendant saw made him cough. He looked up, studying the young man at a squint. He nodded; his voice came out softer. "The woman, please."

Anaea flicked a look to Gwydion. She wouldn't be in the system; what then? But he nodded, and she extended her fingers over the plate.

The monitor shrilled. The attendant scowled. "Says here you don't exist."

Anaea swallowed, waiting for security to descend. "I—"

"She doesn't," Gwydion said. "At least, not to anyone who can touch her here." His lips twitched; he was trying not to show his nerves. "Are we clear?"

Something about those words was magic to the attendant. He relaxed. "Purpose and length of your visit?"

"Repairs. A few days at most . . ."

The man shoved two thin bracelets across the counter. "Welcome to Eastwood Mining Colony," he said, thumping the words out by rote. "Any attempt to travel without the visitor bands will result in immediate deportation. Enjoy your stay." He flicked a penetrating look over Anaea, then returned to his work.

Gwydion held out a band. Plastic, dull grey, with no distinguishing marks. Dubious, she slid it over her wrist, and jumped when it grew prickers that dug into her skin. Instinctively, she moved to tear it off.

He stopped her. "You can't. Not without a technician – or leaving Eastwood. They keep track of transients."

She glanced over to make sure the attendant paid them no mind, and whispered, "Why did he clear me?"

Gwydion's voice came as mental starlight. *In some places, poor workers with beautiful daughters avoid registering them in the system. It's difficult, but it can be done – it means a face can't be marked or its owner tracked.*

Feeling disquieted, Anaea buried her next question. *Oh.*

He let us pass because I implied I had pulled you out of somewhere in a hurry. He'll put word out, to see if anyone is looking for you. Hoping for a reward from an interested patron. He sounded frightened, unsure, and she remembered this place was new to him as well.

He secured the tube on the bracelet and led them to the counter labeled exchange office. A woman worked there, Anaea was relieved to see. She was framed by a horde of lights and signs that warned of the consequences of violence.

"Currency of exchange?" The clerk was, Anaea realized then, quite homely: a lopsided face, overthrust jaw, eyes too small.

"Collective coins," Gwydion said.

The clerk grunted. "You look the type. Wave in and I'll check your account." After he did, she quoted a number that made him sigh with relief. "You can exchange for an amount not to exceed twenty percent of your reserve."

Gwydion nodded. "Twenty percent it is, then." Would they need so much? Anaea had no idea of the meaning of the numbers or the exchange rate.

The clerk eyed the display, then moved a few figures with her finger. Penelope canted forward, watching this process with undue interest. Anaea supposed the clerk, and everything else, must have smelled unusual and exotic to the kearl, if not appealing.

"Nice monkey," the clerk said.

"Do you think you could recommend some place to look for repairs?" Gwydion asked.

"Do I look like a tour guide to entertain you?" Her tone was more accusatory than her question seemed to merit. "Go. You're holding me up."

There was no one else in the octagon. Gwydion got as far as clearing his throat before he seemed to think better of it. He turned, gesturing Anaea to follow. She did, staying close.

He approached the far wall of the octagon. A synthesized

voice chimed, "Welcome to Eastwood Mining Colony." The wall dissolved into dust and revealed blue skies beyond.

Together, they stepped into the colony.

8

WHITEHILL ROAD WAS WIDER THAN A DINING HALL on Themiscyra, the street an expanse of tawny brown with copper sidewalks. Three lines marked the route for heavy, nondescript vehicles as they trundled past. Two holographic black lines scored the air as well, but the purpose of those, Anaea couldn't discern.

This must be a business district, built up and looming over. The walls were like the crowd, angry, jutting into each other and shoving for purchase. Most of the buildings were dark, hoarding the light until the sky suddenly burst in with buoyant blue, more vivid than Anaea remembered from holograms. To her eyes, it seemed artificial in its intensity, and she realized she had only ever seen an echo. One neon shack welcomed visitors and offered an array of toys, accessories and bric-a-brac stamped with an Eastwood logo.

Gwydion pulled her back as a pair of hip-heavy older women waddled past. Anaea realized the outer part of the sidewalk moved, an almost imperceptible blur ferrying people along until they neared their destination. She was fascinated by the ease with which they stepped on and off.

"Nearest callport is on the other side," he said. "Follow me." He threaded through the crowd and crossed the moving walkway. Anaea hastened after. She landed on the shivering strip, felt it pull it at her foot before she was past it. She stumbled into Gwydion; he steadied her with a hand.

They waited until two vehicles zipped past. He gave her a tug and started across the street. She meant to follow, but a flicker of darkness in the sky caught her attention. She tipped her head back and stared. Was that a bird? Not penned up in a sanctuary to keep it safe, but spent casually in the air? It was black-winged, large, ungraceful.

She was losing her guide. She hurried forward, though she kept half an eye upwards. A faint vibration passed through her, setting her teeth on edge.

"Anaea!" Gwydion shouted. "Down!"

His words, and the dim impression of something massive approaching, made her drop. A jet-black shape roared over her close enough she could feel the whine of the energy propelling it. She rolled onto her side as it passed, heart hammering. What had just happened?

The red-headed man who rode the vehicle flashed her a look of disgust and called down, "There are ways to take yourself out that don't leave an ugly corpse." The conveyance rose, following the black line.

A herd of faces watched, caught by the drama. A man spat in her direction. "Stupid cow, didn't you feel the signal?"

Anaea remembered the ripple of sickness. She tried to catch her breath. "I—"

Gwydion waited until a ground vehicle passed, then darted forward to help her up. They hurried across the street. Penelope crawled from his shoulder to hers and stroked her hair, chittering in a search for reassurance. Anaea stroked her fur, conscious of people watching the kearl.

"I'm sorry," she said, her heart still twitching with delayed fear. "Don't be." He smiled weakly.

Anaea glanced over her shoulder, feeling the shivers subside. Calm. She hadn't been hurt, and now she knew how to avoid it. "That vehicle – it looked a lot like a horse."

A brawny woman strutting out of the nearest business pushed herself into the dialogue. "Of course it does," she said. "Regal black stallion, untamed beast, so on, so on. That's the way of the warlords and their men."

Anaea jumped, surprised to be addressed. "Err, thank you."

"It's part of the mystique of Eastwood." The woman rolled her eyes and continued down the street.

"I'm not really sure I'm less confused," Anaea murmured.

Gwydion shrugged. "Don't look at me. Here – this way." He led them to a niche set against the wall. "Stand close." He laid his palm on the plate in the center. White light flowed around them, providing an opaque barrier from the rest of the street. It also swallowed sound; the silence buzzed in Anaea's ears.

"Welcome, transient," a honeyed female voice said. "What assistance do you need?"

"Spaceship repair listings in the vicinity," Gwydion said. A list of five names materialized. He tapped one and watched information scroll past, shook his head and went to the next. "Roswell Repairs. That should do it."

"Do you wish a location imprint?" the voice inquired.

Gwydion started to respond, then caught her hand and exchanged it for his on the plate. "Yes."

Anaea instinctively held still as the metal warmed under her fingers. Something wet brushed her palm.

"Imprint complete. What other assistance do you need?"

"I thought it would be better if you had the map, in case we get separated." Gwydion took Anaea's hand gently – his were a little too hot – and turned it over. "Open it. Index finger to thumb."

As she obeyed, a three dimensional image of the colony streets appeared. She gasped, then considered. "I see," she said, "the ink is the basis, the linking of fingers makes a circuit. It must fade when it dries?"

"You're brilliant," he said.

She blushed. "Indecisive," she corrected him. "On Themiscyra, we take rotations with every profession until we find the right one. I never did."

"Nothing wrong with that." The niche was small, and being so close to him should have been uncomfortable, but she felt no awkwardness. Maybe it was Penelope's cooing. "Let's go," he said, "End session."

The white light faded, and the clamor of Whitehill Road pounded in to meet them. Gwydion started towards the moving sidewalk while Anaea snuck another curious look around her. The people varied in coloration, build and manner, though they shared in common that giving ground was a last resort. Priority of movement went to the person most willing to bull forward. There seemed to be no set uniform or style, though most were dressed simply, the garb similar for men and women.

The walkway moved like a hovercar, with little nausea of motion despite the speed at which they moved. Gwydion let her lead, following the map imprinted on her palm. Finally, he helped her off the accelerated strip.

This was a narrow street with flat, identical entrances. It was less crowded than the main street. As she studied a group moving away, she realized with a start the delicate shape on the right was a man. It was a strange concept to wrap her mind around, but in the population of Eastwood, there was sometimes less distinction between a man and a woman than between two people of the same gender.

A shadow passed overhead, and it grew colder. Anaea shivered, glancing up at the – clouds, she realized.

Gwydion followed her gaze and made a face. "Might even rain. Why it does when they could localize the effects over the crops . . ." he trailed off.

But Anaea understood the need to make an imitation as real

as possible, even with a little inconvenience. She glanced at her hand. "A third of the way down," she said.

As they passed three men wearing spaceport uniforms, Gwydion bumped into the stout figure on the left. He mumbled an apology, head ducked.

"Hey!" The man grabbed his shoulder and pushed him back. "What's the matter, too good to watch where you're going?"

Gwydion blinked in confusion. "I . . . err . . ." Penelope hissed from the other shoulder, her tail snapping up like a flag.

The other two paused. Gwydion's assailant addressed them. "Won't even look me in the eye like a man." His voice went harsh and loud. "Limp-limbed outworlder, too concerned with being infected by our low class germs."

"Wonder how much that exotic beast of his cost?" The second man snorted as he moved about to flank. The three stood tense, ready to strike.

Anaea swallowed dizziness. It was about the game, she thought, not the jostle that had been the pretext. "Leave him be," she said. "Look elsewhere for your entertainment."

The stout man jerked his head back and swiveled to regard her. He seemed surprised, his brows flicking downwards. Then he smirked. "And just where should we look?"

Anaea knew there was an implication she missed. The flitted looks of the other two men set off warning bells in her mind. Gwydion cupped her elbow; she felt his tension in the touch. She risked a glance past the trio, seeking other passers by. Somehow, the street had become a desert. The few people walking by fixed their eyes assiduously elsewhere.

That made her more nervous, but also surprised her. In Themiscyra, physical disputes were rare and quickly disrupted. No one stood for such things.

"Anywhere but here," she said.

"You're wasting your time, gentleman," Gwydion said. His soft tone had steel beneath it.

The leader sized them up. Anaea felt that if she breathed

wrong, she would tilt the scale against them.

Then the man snorted. "Maybe you're right. Not worth the time. But you, girl – you should come with us. You need a real man."

"He seems perfectly real to me," she said.

This, apparently, was the height of wit. Their laughter, though contemptuous, broke the tension. He gestured, and the trio dissolved, weaving down the street.

Anaea held her breath until they turned a corner. Her sigh hurt her chest. "That was unnerving."

Gwydion hurried them on, flicking an anxious look back. "It could have been worse if you hadn't showed them you had fight. I forget the way things work here, sometimes."

"Surely someone would have stepped in . . ." she trailed off when he shook his head. "Oh." She turned her face up to the sky, searching for the blue, but it was a thin, comfortless stripe. She opened her hand, checking the diagram again. "We're almost there."

They reached a nondescript door, distinguished only by a white-lit sign stating, "Roswell Repairs." It was a dim space smelling of grease, electrical char and something stale but beyond identifying. The masses of metal that dominated the space put Anaea in mind of the interior of the White Hound after the hyperspace accident. Engines and parts in various degrees of assembly made up the maze and she couldn't discern which belonged to ships and which to ground vehicles.

The store's owner seemed a natural part of this landscape. He eased to his feet and flashed a grin as they entered. "Good afternoon," he said. "How can I help two travelers?"

"Our hyperspace engine and shields need repair," Gwydion said. "They were strained by the last jump."

"Hmm? I always recommend gambling with it, myself – see if the equipment holds or abandons you in the vastness of space." He flashed a good-natured grin. "What model, year and specs?"

Gwydion coughed. "It's – err, a custom design. It was a loan from an asteroid prospector. We got stranded."

The man clapped his hands. He had a round, open face and a fuzz of scarlet beard. Anaea tried not to stare openly at the facial hair. Wasn't it uncomfortable? Certainly it had to be unsanitary. "Excellent! A challenge. Of course, I can't quote a rate without a look at the complexity and the condition, mister . . . ?" He looked for a name.

"Mallory. And this is Ann Carlisle," Gwydion said. They had already decided not to use her full name.

The man engulfed her hand in a meaty grip. "Janek Roswell. Good to meet you, miss," he said. "I can look over your problem for a modest fee and then give you a call wherever you're staying."

"We hadn't gotten that far," Gwydion said, "but—"

"Can we reach you at your personal connection once we're settled?" Anaea asked. She hadn't seen anyone wearing an aural link, but she knew the technology pre-dated Themiscyra.

Janek stared, then burst out laughing. "Do I seem like someone of importance, a public servant or a warlord's man? Why would I bind myself to the grid and tracking by anyone who wants to know? Privacy is a man's first right, miss Carlisle, whatever the other side of the Bridge would say about it. I prefer to be found when I want to be."

"Oh," she said in a small voice, and glanced her apology at Gwydion.

"As to the question of lodgings, though, I believe I can help with that," Janek continued. "The Dusty Rose Inn is two blocks down. Not as kitschy or expensive as the tourist hotels, and the hostess welcomes transients. I'll be happy to contact you there."

"That sounds reasonable," Gwydion said.

Janek grinned. "Good. How about you link me into your docking bay and I'll get started?"

*

THEY CONCLUDED THE transaction and stepped outside into mist. Anaea turned her face up, reveling in the soft and dewy air.

They crossed two intersections; the sweet smell of roses floated down the street. Startled, she tried to track it and saw a trail of holographic petals leading up to a front door. It stood out from its neighbors without being gaudy, an elevated threshold of cream and blue.

To the right of the door hung a carved wooden cylinder, and this brought a small sigh from Gwydion. "The proprietor is observant," he said. "I feel reassured."

It seemed to Anaea that with how much of the population followed his religion, many questionable people must be devout. Perhaps even the toughs they had bumped into earlier. She said nothing.

A flash caught the corner of her eye. She turned to see an equine vehicle swooping down. It was the same one that had nearly run her over earlier, the pole-thin redhead lounging against the front column with a look of aggressive boredom on his features.

A tiny woman hurried out from the shop next to the hotel, two bags on either arm and a fifth clutched precariously by the bend of her neck. She wove towards the vehicle, unable to course-correct for passers by. She pitched forward as someone cut in front of her.

Anaea leapt for the top package as it slid free. It hovered, suspended in air, and she caught the handle. She and the girl collided; she barely caught one of the other bags and heard a clatter of breaking glass. Gwydion winced.

Wide eyes stared into hers. The girl was freckled, gawky. "Oh, I'm so sorry."

"What's this?" The redhead leapt from the simulated beast and landed with a casual ease that still managed to be showy. His fury bubbled over as he continued, "You clumsy shrew! Ten paces you had to travel! And do you usually help servants break things, you—" He stopped, staring. "You're the one who almost wrecked my stallion."

That was an odd way to describe the encounter, Anaea thought. "I was only trying to help," she said.

He snorted. "Well, don't." He whirled back towards the servant. "You!" He snapped a look at the girl, who flinched and almost dropped the packages again, but rather than resume his tirade, all he said was, "Load the remnants. I'll deal with it."

His gaze raked over Gwydion, dismissed him with a scornful cut, then returned to her. "The universe is harsh and chaotic," he said. "Even in a place ruled by such a stern hand, unweakened by feminine flutter." Anaea jerked at the unflattering use of the adjective "feminine." He continued, "A pretty little thing like you should have no problem finding a protector. Do it before you get someone else hurt."

Anaea's first instinct was to scramble to her own defense, even though she had never felt particularly capable, now least of all. Then she realized the warlord expected no response, his body already half pivoted for retreat. He expected obedience, not debate.

"I was an officer of the law on Elysium," Gwydion said. "I can protect her if I must."

Strange that he had felt the need to put a verbal shield around her. It was even odder to be discussed as if she had to be in someone's keeping, but before she could say as much, the warlord roared laughter. "Among the women and their niggling laws of courtesy, where a mischance sneeze is a vile offense? You learned nothing there, man."

Catching the mood of the dialogue, Penelope bared her teeth and hissed.

The warlord frowned at the kearl. "And put your beast on a leash." He whirled. "Move it!" This last was snapped at his servant, who had managed to right herself, as he retreated to his vehicle.

Anaea stepped forward to steady the last of the hanging bags. She wanted to ask why the girl would put up with such treatment, but didn't want to get her into further trouble. "Take care," she said.

The girl offered a faltering smile and hurried away. Gwydion took Anaea's arm and urged her into the hotel.

The lobby was a homey room carpeted in green with over-stuffed chairs. Gwydion frowned in puzzlement. "Check-in panel must be integrated into the counter – ack!"

"Don't look so surprised to see me," said a reedy voice.

Anaea hastened to join him and found that seated behind the counter was a tiny wisp of a woman with auburn curls. She had the look of experience without age.

"Automation is all very well and good," she said, "but I prefer to look my customers in the eye. Say what you will, it makes my place one of the safest in Eastwood. Now, what brings you to the colony? I hope this isn't your honeymoon," she continued briskly, "the meteor showers don't start for another week and if you ask me there's nothing at all romantic about flaming rock."

Anaea wondered why Gwydion started to blush midway through the speech, and picked up on the gist by the end. "We're friends," she said firmly, "not lovers."

The woman's brows flew up, and Gwydion made a soft choking sound. "A very forthright way to put matters," she said in a dry voice. "What brings you to Eastwood?"

Gwydion explained, sounding a bit strained.

When he mentioned the recommendation, she laughed. "Ah, Janek – a good sort, but too boisterous. What kind of animal is that?"

"It's a kearl," Anaea said, "they're native to—"

"The third planet of JF-9," Gwydion interjected.

The woman nodded judiciously. "Very well. There's a standard pet deposit. Names, please?" As she input them into her system, she continued, "I assume two beds? Rooms are linked to the colony database and the entertainment hubs. Dinner is served here at additional charge: nothing fancy, home cooking, by hand."

"Kosher?" he asked.

She looked vaguely irritated. "Of course." She directed them upstairs to the third room on the left.

Anaea laid her hand on the balcony as they climbed and was surprised to discover it was real wood, not synth. She marveled at the sensation, fingers lingering until Gwydion called her on.

The room was carpeted in plush blue, the beds and mounded pillows in lighter tones. The array of details struck her, from a genuine archaic fireplace to porcelain cats on the dresser. White lace curtains framed a window overlooking the colony.

"We'll go down for dinner after Janek calls, then I should make a trip and get some food," Gwydion said, then paused, looking awkward. "If that's all right with you, of course. I don't mean to take charge."

She laid a hand on his arm. "You're not the warlord's man."

This drew a smile from him. "I still – Penelope!" He tried to snatch the figurine from her grip.

"Penelope! Put that down." The kearl leapt onto the fireplace and from there to the chandelier. Anaea finally coaxed her down and removed the trinket. She turned it over in her fingers, relishing the small thing that would have been a privilege for an intern at home.

The call came through. Janek's holographic face hovered in front of the fireplace. "My compliments to whoever designed your system," he said. "Very smart, very efficient. I should be able to tack it up and get you headed home in half a rotation."

Gwydion frowned. "Err—"

"Ah, blast." He quirked a grin. "That's a little over a standard day. Been on Eastwood all my life. Nuisance when trying to live by the schedules of the rest of the universe. Anyhow, as to the rate . . ."

Gwydion blanched when he heard the price, but nodded firmly. "We can arrange that."

"Good doing business with you and Miss Carlisle," came the reply. The face vanished.

Gwydion dropped, head in his hands. "The Sanctum will

reimburse me for the shuttle, even if they can't make much of it," he said to his palms. "It will be fine."

"I'm sorry," Anaea said, squeezing his shoulder. "If there's any way I can help—" Guilt tugged at her. She had no resources, no way to share the burden of paying for the repairs. She had given him the method of escape, but wasn't it her fault he had to escape? Her fault and the fault of the women of Themiscyra, and it was not an easy distinction to make.

He looked up and smiled weakly. "No. This is the easy part." He chuckled as Penelope crawled into his lap and bumped her head under his chin. He rubbed her fur. "I'll work better on a full stomach, I think."

The meal the proprietor provided them with was as good as a week's worth of special rations, a hearty stew with rich white bread. Anaea ate fit to bursting and took a portion up for Penelope even as Gwydion headed into the colony.

She shouldn't have worried: what danger was there in walking a street? Yet Anaea remembered that until recently, she had thought the populated universe was anarchy and pirates, and Eastwood seemed uncomfortably close to that vision. A law for certain, but one where strength ruled. She rubbed at the visitor band, wishing it would come off.

To distract herself, she entered the database and pulled up the colony's history. The section on the Y-Poisoning Epidemic drew her. She played the record, confronted with images of riots in the streets, and then—

Breath left her, as if she had been punched. To minimize the impact, the colony had dumped early sufferers onto the planet's surface. Oxygen deprivation killed most before the cold set in. The neutral feminine narrator praised it as a harsh but necessary step which had contributed to the minimal impact of the pandemic on Eastwood.

It was the tone of the narration more than its content that left her chilled. She caught herself shifting, thinking to get off the bed and check the lock, but it was electronic and automatic, nothing to secure.

She pulled Penelope onto her lap. Out the window, she noticed the slow twilight darkening of an artificial sky, color splashed on Eastwood's protective shield.

9

THE REST OF THE SECTION ON THE PANDEMIC WAS, IF NOT more relaxing, informative and interesting enough that Anaea watched it to the end.

Widespread panic from the belief the alien Derithe were trying to destroy humanity, combined with the disease's psychological symptoms, had thrown the colony into disorder. Many who died did so not from the disease itself, but from madness and panic. Four individuals, future warlords, had led efforts to shore up the shield generator plants as bases of operation, islands of order in the chaos.

One of those leaders had been what the database called an overloaded hypermental; someone who had survived Y-Poisoning and, due to the effects of the antibodies, come through with stronger abilities. Anaea wondered uneasily if there had been people exposed deliberately.

She swung to her feet and moved to the window, watching the paint-splash descent of evening.

The door hummed open. Anaea whirled, body tensing; the motion disturbed Penelope, and the kearl shrieked protest.

"Anaea?" Gwydion said. "It's just me."

"It's you," she said with a sheepish smile. She reached for Penelope, but the creature was having none of it. She hopped onto the mantle and curled up, tail perilously close to knocking off the trinkets.

Gwydion had three containers. He showed her the contents: packaged meals, purified water and an antique tin for cookies. For Penelope, there was cat food.

"I hope she can eat it," he said.

They tried. Penelope sniffed the tin disdainfully, but took a few bites and seemed satisfied.

It wasn't early enough to sleep, so Gwydion found a holo-movie, a classic from the days directly after the pandemic. Anaea thought the storyline was as illuminating as the database: the warlords like archaic kings, arbitrary laws turned against a pilot and his sister, and the love interest a damsel waiting to be rescued. She found the actress' proportions exaggerated and unrealistic, and there was no tranquility in the copper-skinned face.

She turned to Gwydion at the end of the movie, only to find him asleep in the chair. He had rolled to the right, his head tucked in, face sweet and childish.

Anaea felt a surge of maternal feeling, a strange sensation; it was something she'd had to work for even when attending the newborn ward on Themiscyra. Certainly, she had watched Orithia sleep more than once, and never felt that urge to gather her close and protect her. Was it a particular quality of men, that she somehow responded to?

Rather than wake him, she removed the top blanket from his bed and tucked it around him. "Good night," she whispered.

She retreated to her bed to chase sleep and half-formed hopes. There was still so much more to see.

*

Breakfast was a communal buffet reigned over by the proprietor. She hovered between tables, checking as to each guest's tastes.

"Everything good, hot, how are the eggs, miss? How did you sleep?"

Anaea shifted thoughts with an effort. "Fine, thank you. We—" She was speaking to the woman's animated back, and abandoned the sentence.

"We have the day. Do you want to go out into the colony?" Gwydion asked. "Take in the sights?"

She offered a smile. A day in this place seemed like an adventure, as long as he was there. "I'd love that."

They found a sporting event open to the public: gladiator chess. The stadium buzzed and roared as two teams faced off over a grid of black and red. Each man brandished a menacing melee weapon. Anaea blanched until she realized they were replicas, blunted, but not – one resounding impact told – any less heavy.

"So much more interesting with real weapons," said a man behind them.

"Yeah, but that's the pro leagues," another said. "These lunks would hack each other up."

Anaea winced, trying not to picture that.

The action dissolved into darting, leaping, sprinting chaos, then abruptly resolved into one-on-one bouts. Opponents switched whenever the whistle blew or opportunity arose, each combination of weapons, from quarterstaff to curved blade, demanding new tactics.

The noise deafened: dull clanging and the oddly delicate squeak of footwear against the board. The teams hurled insults at each other. The crowd roared approval.

Gwydion tried to explain the scoring system in an undertone, though he nearly had to shout to be heard; a loud fan to their right butted in with corrections until he looked as confused as she. They snuck out after the third round. She caught her breath; the comparative quiet swelled into her ears.

Gwydion guided them along the walkways to a strip mall,

store-fronts spreading out in all directions, including up. The faux-wood facades hovered like buzzards with no apparent support, reached by elevation platforms.

Three-dimensional signs offered pricing, but as far as Anaea could see, most were suggestions. People haggled with gusto. Some of the rates in exclusive shops were non-negotiable, and the merchants shouted would-be hagglers out of range, driving them off by sheer force of words. Somehow, the shoppers seemed to be able to tell the difference between genuine rage and bargaining ploy. It left her bewildered, cringing at slapped counters and roared responses.

Anaea ducked out of the way of airborne carts and whirling, singing, exploding displays. There seemed to be no plan to the design, the store-fronts and signs clashing, sometimes overlapping, and fighting for dominance. An adorable moppet of a holographic dog sat incongruously amidst a ring of fire.

Gwydion angled them towards a pet store and made the clerk suspicious when he paid the price on the label for a leash and collar. "Not that Penelope seems to need it," he said, "but it will help her blend."

Anaea picked up a turquoise coat in small-dog size. "What about this?"

"Do you think you could get her to wear it?"

"Point," she admitted.

As they walked back, he filled her in on some imperial customs. "You have to take it with a grain of salt, of course," he said. "Everything looks different from the other side. Not to mention this is Eastwood. It's different from here to Independence to Annwyn . . . different planet-side to far-side of Annwyn, for that matter. So what I know is a jumble of averages and specifics."

"It's very helpful," she assured him.

A few businesses had the same doorpost ornament as the hotel; what Gwydion called a mezuzah. One flickered, a bad hologram.

Gwydion laughed. "My parents would be horrified," he said. "Real case – real Torah, for the matter of that. It's the most requested of the hundred-some books still printed on Elysium."

Anaea's only encounter with real books had been from the other side of glass, the tiny, and static, library on her station. She remembered it in a vivid splash, spines of burnished leather and lime-green plastic alike. "They print new books?"

"Some," Gwydion said. "Mostly for collectors and historians. The Sanctum has a full library, though."

Anaea wondered what would be considered a full library and started to ask. Penelope dove after a red robot that bobbed between two street stalls.

"That's mine!" wailed a toddler. She thought it was a boy, though it was surprisingly hard to tell, at that age.

"It's all right, you can have it back – Penelope, stop chewing . . ." She disentangled kearl from contraptation.

She never did get back to the question.

The call came from Janek after dinner. "I've got your beast working," he reported. "Purrs like new. That's a very slick system you have. Prototype design?"

"Exactly," Gwydion said, his voice weak.

The proprietor of the Dusty Rose saw them out with advice and a biscuit for Penelope. They passed exchange and customs without incident. A new woman was on duty, a sallow, drippy creature who wished them a safe journey. When the visitor band popped off, Anaea was startled to realize she'd forgotten about it in the explorations of the day.

Twenty minutes later, they received permission to depart. The guidance systems took them aloft, and first Eastwood, then Blackore, dwindled into nothing. Anaea was relieved to be away, sorry not to spend more time exploring, but most of all she felt a sense of triumph. She had faced this universe and survived it . . . or at least, a small piece of it.

*

The Bridge, the stable hyperspace corridor that now divided the two civilizations, was in the UL-50 system, near the outer edge. It meant a long stretch of slower than light travel before the final jump.

The two travelers played a few holographic games that had been loaded into the shuttle, but mostly, they talked. She told him about Themiscyra, about Orithia, about the intimidating presence of Valasca, and the religion he labeled as Lightsoul. He answered with traditions of his own beliefs, tales of his family, and in particular warm praise for his brother.

"Adrian is the warrior of the family," he said, "and he makes sense as a soldier. He's more devout than I am – more certain than I am. He has no doubt that any children he raises will be the best they can be." He faltered, a little wistful. "Sophie will make a perfect mother."

She wanted to ask, but it seemed as if any pressure would cause him to shatter. He rallied, changing the subject to his hypermental training and the police force.

"What should be a simple examination of the truth turned out to be an examination of what was proper to say and how things should be presented so people would accept them." He shook his head. "I couldn't take it, and I'm not ashamed of that." His voiced wavered, then steadied. "I quit when they asked me to bury a kidnapping investigation because the suspect was an important matriarch in the midst of a social campaign. Progress over justice."

"Sounds as if you did what you had to," she said. The words ran through her brain: progress over justice. Security over truth.

Gwydion smiled wryly. "Maybe. Still, it brought me to the Sanctum. I was at loose ends until I volunteered for the White Hound."

He demonstrated telekinetic tricks used by students to entertain themselves. He gave Penelope a scritch from a distance, which caused the kearl to hiss and flee into the cargo hold. All their coaxing and apologies would not bring her back out.

Time and distance passed; Gwydion took his turn to rest. Anaea didn't disturb him until an artificial monster grew on the horizon, silver and black.

She tapped him awake, barely let him blink before she pointed to the viewscreen. "What is that?"

"Mmph?" he said blearily. He rubbed at his eyes. "Centurion Station," he said. "The warlord military outpost. Watches the Bridge."

Anaea made a nervous sound.

"No, it's all right," he said. "Their scanners will pick up the marker put on the shuttle at Eastwood. Foreigners leaving their space aren't of much concern. Unless . . ."

She nodded and held the silence, waiting. Would the warlords accost them for some anomaly in the shuttle, or for no reason at all?

As they neared the station, two white-fire structures stretched beyond it. Anaea knew what they were from history lessons: the Gates marked the optimal entrance point to the Bridge, the only hyperspace corridor with no record of casualty.

They passed close enough to Centurion Station that it was the size of Anaea's torso in the viewscreen. She leaned closer until the image zoomed, sweeping outwards to fill the cabin. Unlike Themiscyra, which was built as a cube, Centurion was an endless flat expanse, interrupted only by spearing towers. Anaea guessed by the dimensions they must be a mile wide, but they still looked flimsy.

The shuttle signaled the presence of the corridor when they were still shy of the Gates. Gwydion shook his head, hand hovering until the massive brackets surrounded them. A ship stamped with a crimson insignia materialized above, bound on its own journey.

Anaea felt a sick knot in her stomach as Gwydion engaged the hyperspace sequence. She closed her eyes, breathed a two-measure melody of prayer—

Then she was air and thought, and she opened her eyes with

a sigh of relief. She felt childish, silly. Did she imagine everyone was out to cheat them?

The dream of hyperspace surrounded them. During the journey, they coaxed Penelope out of the cargo hold and soon, she arched her back pointedly for long-distance scratches. She fought the collar, but by the time they emerged hours later, she settled down to tugging at it.

As soon as they passed the Gates on the other side, Gwydion summoned the viewscreen. A planet rose into view, a stunning expanse of cloud-drizzled blue and green.

"Elysium," Gwydion said, his voice touched with the warmth of home. "We'll put down in New Athens and take transport to the Sanctum, and there I'll file my report." His expression darkened. "I did everything I could for the White Hound and its crew."

Two moons hovered on the far side of the planet, just shy of its curvature. Anaea vaguely recalled they were an orbital pair, dancing around each other and toying with the tides below.

As they descended, rolling planes of color stretched out, intermittently broken by topological thrust. Cities were the most prominent landmarks, high, white and precisely ordered. As the jarring of their descent leveled, the shuttle banked towards one of these. Its satellites skipped out for miles: villages, homes, farms?

Soft blue light infused the view, guiding the ship. Seconds later, the communications console buzzed. Gwydion activated it.

"Welcome to New Athens," said a neutral male voice. "What is your purpose here?"

"Homecoming," Gwydion said. "The Sanctum."

"Oh, really?" A hint of confederacy entered the man's tone; then he cleared his throat. The next words came out flat, as if he were embarrassed. "Follow the navigation line. Welcome to New Athens."

Merchant ships and two planet-bound vacation cruisers populated the airspace, but their route was straightforward. Still, Gwydion breathed a shaky sigh when they touched down. He pulled his hands from the console with an air of finality.

"Ready?" he asked. "Remember, you're from a remote warlord colony. We met when my escape pod crashed there."

"I'm ready," she said. Her ears hummed with excitement. The Galactic Collective, ruled by the matriarchs – she hoped these would be people not unlike those of her home, the presence of men notwithstanding. "Come on, Penelope." She picked up the end of the leash to a disgruntled chitter from the kearl.

They descended the shuttle ramp into luminous white light. Anaea blinked, trying to adjust.

Two uniformed figures seemed to leap out as the glow turned bearable. One performed a perfunctory bow. "Mr. Mallory? Spaceport security. You'll have to come with us."

10

Anaea flicked Gwydion a worried look and saw the whiteness of his face. "What is this is about?" he said.

"The voyage of the White Hound," the woman on the left said, "and why you've returned alone and without reporting."

Gwydion's thoughts tapped Anaea's, clouds covering the starlight. *This is what I wanted to avoid: questions on their turf. They might ask another hypermental to interrogate me.*

She knew what that would lead to: revelation, Themiscyra exposed, herself under a microscope, all in the hands of a government she knew nothing about. *Can't you block them?*

I might be able to.

"I intend to file a full report," he said, "but—"

"Come with us. Now." The other turned to Anaea. "Your companion must wait for you in our offices. We'll need to speak with her."

Gwydion placed a hand on her arm. "Everything will be fine." But then he added in a rush, belying his calm, "When you get a guestlink, call Sophie Rianna Mallory. Tell her—" His face went still. Anaea sympathized: how could anyone summarize what had happened to them?

"Mr. Mallory." The guard's voice dropped half an octave, tightened. Penelope retreated behind Anaea's limb, hissing.

"Lead on," he said.

Security whisked them away in opposite directions. Anaea's protests went numb in the brightness, the warm glow of the corridor.

The guard led her into a circular white chamber, where she was met by a tiny man with a vapid smile and a handheld device. "Welcome to New Athens, miss—"

A subtle prickle moved through Anaea. She jumped, looking up sharply.

"—she doesn't have a record." The man addressed the guard.

That sensation had been so subtle. What else had it discerned about her? Disconcerted, Anaea wrapped her arms about herself. Penelope pushed up against her.

"If I may explain?" she said, her voice sounding thin and false. "I'm from star-side Annwyn. My family declined to have me recorded." Why did the lie sound better coming from Gwydion?

The guard and the official exchanged looks. "Imperials," she muttered.

He shrugged. "I will need your name, miss. It will be stamped on your transient record along with your vitals and other relevant information."

Anaea wished there were none of that. It made her feel exposed, vulnerable. "My name is Anaea Carlisle."

The official mumbled commands over the datapad, then looked up, depthless cheer back in force. "Here is your guestlink," he said, offering her a device the size of a button. "It will monitor your health, guide you should you go astray and otherwise facilitate your stay in New Athens. You'll be as safe as in a mother's womb."

Anaea took it uncertainly. She sympathized with what the ship mechanic had said back on Eastwood: there was virtue in disconnection, in anonymity. "Where do I put it?" she asked.

"Against your heart," he directed.

She placed it on her collarbone. It flushed hot; when she pulled her hand away, it stuck to the skin. She hoped she and Gwydion would not have to run. Criminals for a second time?

"This way, miss Carlisle," the guard directed. She led the way into a hall of windows. A white and amber city fell away to one side, built upwards with symmetrical, fractal precision. Anaea tried to identify landmarks and gave up. It was gorgeous, but the structures were indistinguishable.

Penelope capered along, fascinated with the view. Anaea turned her head and faltered. The trees, she realized, with their faint yellow under the green: they were real, and more than that, had grown there, had stretched out their wiry branches with little help from human hands.

She stopped, resisting the child's impulse to run up to the glass. She made herself breathe. Silly to feel so stunned: had she really imagined it was all gone, that every faithful imitation was nothing more than that? The colors of the trees were unrealistic, too bright, like a hallucination.

"Miss Carlisle." The guard's voice cut through her daze. A denizen of Annwyn would be conversant with nature, even if it was a different panorama.

She turned, giving the leash a tug to provide herself with an alibi. "Come along, Penelope." The kearl made an irritated sound and peeled away from the window.

The hall closed up, vanishing into white. They passed people in uniforms with different patches. Anaea assumed they worked in other parts of the space port. The ceiling rose to frame an edifice criss-crossed with grey lines. Angular letters announced the building's purpose: Spaceport Security – New Athens.

The guard stepped over a mark on the floor. It lit with a hum, and the puzzle formed by the lines disassembled itself to reveal a lobby. Seated on the bench were men with plastic and glass piercings, a husky woman with an ugly scar, and a handful of others who fragmented the serenity with grime and anxiety.

The guard grabbed her as Anaea drifted in their direction. "They're under a light aerial sedative," she said. "You don't want to get too close."

Anaea flicked a look around her, at the polished desk with its functions hidden under translucent glass; at the other uniformed figures passing through, their weapons discreetly concealed in matching fabric and utterly harmless at a glance. She understood she should underestimate none of it.

"Sorry," she said.

Three turns away from the lobby, the guard showed her into a holding room. The furnishings were taupe, the carpet plain, and the one adornment a wall-hanging that pulsed through a soothing pattern of colors.

"If you need anything, you have only to step outside," the guard said. "Your presence will be noted." It was perfect courtesy; it was also warning wrapped within politeness. With that, she shut the door.

Anaea sighed, draping herself in the chair. That dazzling view played on the interior of her mind, accompanied by disbelief. Might it only be a projection for the tourists?

Penelope climbed onto her lap. She scritched the kearl's neck as her tail thumped against her side. Could they blame Gwydion for what happened to the White Hound? It seemed incredible, but with no other evidence, what conclusion would they draw? She tapped on the device on her chest.

"Request?"

Anaea jumped. The voice vibrated in her collarbone. "Err, place a call," she said, "to Sophie Rianna Mallory." The name struck her as odd. Did women in the matriarch territory take the names of their husbands? Or was it some kind of personal declaration? Children in Themiscyra were automatically given the surname of their birth mother.

"Seeking . . . multiple entries found. Request list or provide further information."

That was new. In Themiscyra, there were no duplicate names. "Husband Adrian," she said. "Residence: the Sanctum."

"Cross-checking – connecting. Save this individual as default?"

"Yes."

A grey holographic globe appeared in front of her. It vibrated once, twice . . . then resolved into the image of a heart-shaped face framed by golden hair. The woman's eyes were the same shade as the sky outside and just as much a hallucination.

"Good afternoon," she said. It was a sweet voice, inviting. "May I ask who is calling?"

"Anaea Carlisle. I'm a friend of Gwydion's."

"Gwydion!" Her tone was affectionate, but it dropped into concern. "Is he well? I've heard nothing about the return voyage . . ."

"The White Hound—" Anaea stopped herself. She was coming at it the wrong way. "Gwydion is fine," she said. "But he was the only one to survive."

"What happened?" The lovely face paled.

"A hyperspace crash," Anaea said.

Sophie inhaled sharply. "Terrible news."

"I may need your help," Anaea continued. "Security is crawling down his throat."

"He could have no fault in what happened to the ship. I cannot believe that of my little brother."

Anaea felt a surge of empathy for the woman. "I know for a fact he did nothing wrong," she said, "but my knowing doesn't do any good."

"How did this come to pass?" Sophie leaned forward anxiously.

It felt wrong to lie to this woman. Anaea shifted, hoping it wasn't visible. "He was . . . stranded. I happened to be in a position where—"

"You rescued him?" Her voice warmed. "You have my sincere thanks."

"No, I didn't. I—" It was too complicated to invent herself the right amount of credit. "He told me about the Sanctum. He seemed to think there was something you could do."

"Where is my head?" Sophie said. "I should be concentrating on a solution. I can make some calls, pull some strings . . . I'm sorry for your involvement."

Anaea shook her head. "Gwydion is my friend," she said. "I owe him just as much as he owes me. Anything I can do to help, I will."

"Thank you." The smile warmed; it was like music. Even when she was troubled, serenity burnished Sophie from within. Anaea could see why Gwydion was attracted to her, felt a little of it herself. "If anything changes, contact me?"

"I will," she said.

"Good luck." The image faded out, and the globe dispersed.

Anaea leaned back in the chair and tried to stave off the gnawing of her stomach. Would they connect the shuttle with an old mystery? Would they turn to another hypermental, who would rip the story from Gwydion's mind? Would he resist, and what would be the consequences?

To distract herself, she tuned the guestlink into the local network – or what was allowed, for it flashed warnings under her eyelids when she tried to call up specific sections.

It allowed her into the history archives, and she found herself drawn to the same place she had begun on Eastwood. Y-Poisoning had decimated New Athens, but the account emphasized that no one was given up for lost. Ordinary citizens went out of their way to help and restrain even violently hallucinating victims. The gentle hands of the first matriarchs restored order. It was a gloss, too easy, but she wanted to believe it.

She was about to explore further when the door opened. She jumped, sitting upright in a flurry that could not help but be guilty, even though she hadn't been doing anything untoward. Penelope chirred angrily and scampered off her lap under the desk.

Anaea tapped the link off. "You startled me."

The guard who had escorted her from the docking bay

sketched a bow in greeting. "We have some questions for you, miss Carlisle. Keep in mind you're being recorded." Her tone was identical: absolute courtesy, revealing nothing.

Anaea smiled, felt it quiver with nerves. "I'm happy to help."

The guard seated herself. "What is the nature of your relationship with Mr. Mallory?"

"We met about a week ago when he was stranded," she said. "I asked to accompany him."

"Why?" The gaze was piercing.

Why was that her business? But Anaea figured the more she said and the closer to the truth she stayed, the less suspicious it would seem. "I wanted to leave home, and he needed a right-hand person."

"And you had no previous association with him?"

She flinched at the sharpness in the woman's voice. "None."

The guard folded her hands. "Miss Carlisle, are you romantically involved with him?"

Anaea balked, feeling as if the woman were trying to peer under her skin. "That's none of your business."

"Everything is my business in this matter," came the brisk reply. "I am seeking to ascertain why someone who had just met a man would throw out everything she knew to follow him, provide him with a ship and ask what in return?"

"I—" Anaea started, but it was apparently rhetorical, for the guard continued to talk.

"If I decide I need to know what you ate for breakfast to create a clear picture of the situation, I will ask," she said. "If I want to investigate your animal's pedigree five generations back, you will provide the relevant information."

Anaea's stomach sloshed. "The ship is mine. He took berth on it and paid for the repairs." There could be nothing to indicate, she thought with a flush of relief, that the damage had been done to the shuttle during the journey rather than before. "It's a fair exchange. There's nothing wrong with it."

She must have sounded too defensive, for the guard narrowed

her eyes. "Nothing wrong? You saw nothing strange about taking on a refugee?"

"Why would I assume there was anything sinister – especially in warlord space?" Anaea was proud of that addition. "Many disasters can befall a ship."

"What did he say had happened to the White Hound?"

"Hyperspace accident. No particulars." She twined her hands together under the desk.

"How did you come by a ship?"

Anaea twitched at the swerve in questions. She and Gwydion had talked about this. Stay calm. "I – it's my family's," she said. "My – father—" Had she hesitated too much on the strange word? The guard's expression tensed. What had she seen? "—passed it down to me. Always said I should leave when I had the chance."

"And this was your chance."

The flatness in the guard's voice made her cringe inside. She could feel her story unraveling. "I could never have paid for the repairs myself," she said. "We managed to jury-rig the ship to get to Eastwood." There would be a records trail, though would it have been transmitted across the Bridge yet?

The silence extended. The guard contemplated her next question, eyes too thoughtful. "Another topic. You clearly trust him, but what are your other impressions of him?"

"I think he has a calm head and a tender heart," she said.

"Might that be an act?"

How had she been cornered into that question? Was it some lack in her skill? She was no trained investigator, nor even a social butterfly, to make a study of people. She took a heartbeat for the answer, trying to find a way to minimize further attack – and it felt like an attack – in this vein.

"I don't think so," she said, "and I can only act from my best judgement."

She was relieved when the guard swerved to another question. "What is his final goal here?"

"To go home. Isn't that everyone's goal?"

"Including yours?"

The guard could have no idea just how complex a question that was. Anaea smiled wryly. "I've got a lot to see first."

It was the truest answer she had given.

The interrogation marched on, things she could not be sure matched Gwydion's answers. Finally left alone, Anaea leaned forward on the desk, head in her hands. Penelope crawled up and bumped her head under her chin. Anaea smiled weakly and rubbed the kearl's neck.

"Gwydion," she said softly, "contact me. We have to talk." She closed her eyes and willed it, and imagined Penelope's determined animal thoughts joined her – but there was nothing. She did not have his ability, and he must be too consumed to seek her.

She sighed. "If nothing else, Penelope, we have time for something else to happen."

*

THE GUARD RETURNED a few hours later. Anaea tensed, though her muscles barely obeyed her from weariness.

"Miss Carlisle," the woman said briskly, "you're free to go."

Anaea inhaled. "What happened with—"

"Mr. Mallory will meet you outside," she interrupted. "I suggest you depart before the wind changes."

Anaea needed no more encouragement, moving so fast her hand yanked the leash. Penelope yelped in protest.

In the lobby, Gwydion stood with folded arms and more grey than pink in his face. She hurried to him. He crossed the distance in three steps and hugged her, and she felt as if the whole planet was on her side.

"Let's go," he said. Penelope chirped a greeting, and he bent to scratch her head.

They left the security station and descended a translucent glass elevator towards the city. "What happened?" she asked.

"I told the story as truthfully as I could," he said. "I was even able to explain the reason I was separated from the rest of the crew: trapped in the virtual training unit." His eyes were anxious, never settling on their surroundings. "Someone on the outside intervened. The chief being a matriarch, I suppose it was a political matter."

Anaea told him about her dialogue with Sophie. The nerves sloughed off him. "That would explain it," he said. "Dr. Anders has a lot of connections, or the Sanctum wouldn't exist. That she invoked them for me, though!"

"Why not?" she asked. "You were sent out to find allies."

He shook his head. "I found you – but that's not enough."

Anaea swallowed, her mouth tasting sour. They said nothing as the elevator finished its descent and admitted them into a pristine antechamber with the same cloudy glass walls. Gwydion rushed forward; she followed. Part of the wall folded up and away in diamond sections.

She hesitated, trying to find her breath. Gwydion turned back, brow furrowed. "Anaea? Are you all right?"

She nodded, not speaking, and stepped into the sunlight – real sunlight, a glow she instinctively knew. People on Themiscyra spoke about it like a gift from the divine presence, an impossibility, a dream . . . and now she stood in that dream. She tried not to make a fool of herself with tears, but she could barely hold it in.

He took her elbow and guided her away from the flow of people, a polite, fixed row of walking figures. He tipped his head, studying her. "I think I understand now."

"What?" She blinked at him.

"Why Eastwood simulates the weather. I see it in your face." He smiled, then turned on his heel. "We should go. Unless we get very lucky with the red hololines, we'll be here overnight while the spaceport clears the shuttle for transfer to the Sanctum."

As the sun blindness, literal and figurative, wore off, she turned her attention to the crowds. As in Eastwood, a flurry of color and style surrounded her, but everyone seemed to know, as if there had been a signal, that collars should be v-neck and pants fitted below the knee.

Gwydion started down the street. She followed, wondering, "Don't you need a link?"

"I have one," he said. "My parents paid for implants."

New Athens offered an accelerated sidewalk, but there the resemblances with Eastwood ceased. The center of the street was populated by aerial platforms, most with several people aboard. They milled, chattered and paid no attention to the path the platforms took.

The uniform white facades of the buildings appeared to be marble. Every fourth building, to enhance the appearance, a carved pillar fronted the corners.

Anaea's link hummed on her collarbone. "You do not seem to be availing yourself of public transport. Do you require assistance?" it inquired.

"Tell it to turn guidance mode off," Gwydion said.

The link buzzed when she repeated the command. "This function not available for guestlinks."

He made a face. "Ignore it, then."

The platforms swerved off at marked pillars to exchange passengers. She and Gwydion climbed aboard one and whisked through the city. She closed her eyes and felt the breeze of passage.

"Here is as good a place as any," he said when it stopped in front of a line of restaurants. "I just didn't want to make this call on the steps of the spaceport."

They entered the Sisyphus Café. The interior reminded her, with a faint twinge, of the dining halls on Themiscyra, except for splashed-purple walls and the matching uniform the girl on duty wore. She commanded a fleet of robots that handled tidying tables, preparing trays and otherwise allowing their keeper to do little more than smile at customers.

Anaea found three ingredients on the menu she had never heard of and promptly ordered something with each. Gwydion settled for a shake and guided them to a table, where he tapped his link. While Anaea tried to discern the taste of bruitseeds from ellisflower, which she knew, and whether or not she liked it, the image of a blonde woman appeared.

"Rightway Shipping and Transit! I hope you're having a pleasant day?"

"Very much, thank you," Gwydion said. Anaea was somewhat bemused by the polite lie. "And yourself?"

"Quite well. I hope you like our fair city?"

Three or four more exchanges of this nature occurred before it seemed it was permissible to discuss business. In the meantime, Anaea sipped her drink and studied the other patrons.

A dowdy older woman with blotched pink cheeks nibbled on a muffin. Two teenagers with thrice-pierced ears flirted with each other. They were of opposite genders, and Anaea watched the give and take with interest. There was an old saying that in love, one person offered the kiss, and the other the cheek, but few couples in Themiscyra seemed to hold to that without at least switching roles now and then. Here it was almost textbook, the young woman accepting courtship as her due.

They were not the only romantic couple in the café. The other pair were boys a little older than Gwydion. Anaea realized she was gawking just before one of them looked over. She dropped her sandwich off its plate as she tried to focus somewhere else.

They whispered to each other. Embarrassed, she kept her eyes down. It did not help that her brain was trying, without her cooperation, to figure out the biological mechanics of such an arrangement.

"The extra cost is for placating the bureaucrats," the blonde holograph said.

A hoarse, rasping sound caught Anaea's attention. She looked up to see that the older woman was fighting to breathe.

11

IT TOOK ANAEA ONLY A SECOND TO RECOGNIZE THE SIGNS OF allergic reaction. She pushed out of her chair to help, then pulled up in bewilderment when she realized supportive hands already swarmed the woman, patting her back, setting water before her.

"Is someone a doctor?" Anaea asked.

Four blank looks answered her. "We're just trying to help," said the café clerk.

A grey-haired man at a window-side table rolled his eyes. "They just want the social credits," he muttered. "Harpies."

"I've had some training," Anaea said, taking charge. "Get her off the chair – ma'am, you need to lie down. Feet above your head – it will help blood get to your brain."

"It's not the food, is it?" the clerk asked anxiously.

"Does anyone have a kit?" Anaea had no idea what the average person here did for the aches, pains and sniffles that no medical development could entirely excise. On Themiscyra, convenience medicines flowed readily from common stock, but that would surely fall apart among such a massive population.

"I have a comfort bag," one of the women volunteered.

"Hand it over," Anaea said. The speaker gave her a fuschia case full of patches, gels and gadgets of purpose unknown. Anaea rooted through, trying to make sense of a maze of drug names. Had they gotten even stranger in the intervening decades? She squinted at labels, skimming as fast as she could, acutely conscious of the seconds that passed.

The older woman gasped for air. The color had not left her cheeks, but from the sounds, her throat was trying to close over.

There! Anaea fumbled an antihistamine patch out of the kit. She pressed it against the woman's neck.

The woman's breathing leveled, and the harsh burn in her cheeks faded. She moved to sit up; Anaea halted her with a hand. "Easy," she said. "Just lay there for a moment." The other patrons fluttered and offered soothing commentary, but dispersed when the woman wobbled into a seated position.

"Ma'am?" Gwydion stood by the table, offering his hand and a smile. He helped her up, then did the same for Anaea.

"Thank you," the woman said with an awkward tremor of dignity. "I'll file this for social credits, if I can have your name?"

"It's really not necessary—" Anaea began.

Let her, Gwydion interjected gently. *It's expected. Social credits help the world move.*

Though uncomfortable, she smiled and answered, then excused them as quickly as possible.

"What exactly can I use social credits for?" she wondered in a low voice as they returned to their table.

"Licenses and permits, legal concessions, school passes, child-rearing rights." Gwydion rattled it off, then looked sheepish. "Nothing too relevant to our current situation, I suppose."

Except that they had almost been in trouble with the law. Could this regulated karma have protected them? "Will someone investigate?" she asked. "Make sure that it's valid?" Her skin prickled. She didn't want more attention.

"Not for something like this," Gwydion reassured her. "They'll just award the credits."

Anaea sipped at her drink. "So the others were hoping to earn a share of the credits?" When he nodded, she frowned. "If you do something in the hope of reward, is it really a good deed?"

"No system is perfect," he hedged. "I finished with Rightway. The shuttle will be on its way tomorrow morning."

"Should we call Sophie and let her know everything is all right?"

"That's a good idea," he said. "I'll find a place for us to stay and you can call her. Thank her for everything she did."

Before she could question him, he stood and made his way outside. Following, Anaea tapped the link on her breastbone and requested a connection with Sophie. The hologram formed before the first ring ended. "Miss Carlisle?" she said, her voice clipped and anxious.

"Whatever you did, it worked," Anaea said. "We're free now. Thank you from both of us."

"May I speak to Gwydion?" Sophie asked. "I haven't seen him for months."

As Anaea caught up with him, she opened her mouth to relay the offer. He shook his head and pretended to be intent on what he was reading.

She didn't know how to transfer a call, so she had no options even if she had wanted to. "He can't talk right now," she said, "but we're headed to the Sanctum. You'll see him soon."

"I see." Sophie's lips lilted into a pensive smile. Anaea wondered if Gwydion's secret was as well-hidden as he believed. "Give him my love. I look forward to meeting you face to face."

Anaea tapped the link off and turned to her traveling companion. He was so absorbed in the listings that she had to grab his elbow to steer him out of the way of two girls in pink. They stared after them as if an oblivious bump were criminal.

"Found us a place," he said. "The Ivory Tower."

*

Anaea turned her face to the clouds as the vehicle flashed through the teeth-like rows of the city. From her perspective, the atmospheric wanderers moved slower than the platform beneath them.

She looked down when Gwydion nudged her, pointing out city-sponsored works of art: crystal mandalas, abstract splashes of colors, a massive painting, of an old school known as surrealism. Everything was beautiful, but it seemed somehow unsurprising, though she had never seen this place before.

The Ivory Tower came by its name honestly, though its base was obscured by greenery. Glass shields hovered over the plants, dispensing mist. Anaea stretched onto her toes, peering into the tangled beds.

The lobby was a luxurious expanse of peacock blue minded by two boys who scurried about on the whims of guests. One greeted them with a smile that tried not to look harried. "Welcome to the Ivory Tower," he said, disappearing below the counter with his bow. "We only just received your reservation . . ."

"I only just made it," Gwydion said.

The boy looked flustered, as if he felt that he should have foreseen the future. "This way."

The corridors wound in an oblique spiral. Their room was ten floors up via float elevators. The boy assured them earnestly that if they tapped the wall, a light would appear for them to follow. He disappeared about his duties, still panting for breath.

The room was pale cream with translucent panels, the two beds round and the furnishings simple but distinguished by their continuous curve, one blending into the next; even when they were physically separate, they followed the same line. When Gwydion entered, the walls faded to blue, then warmed to mauve as she followed.

"Psych panels," he explained. "They pick up subliminal body signals and adjust accordingly."

"Penelope, stop trying to chew the door-frame," Anaea said with a tug on the leash. As the kearl allowed herself to be dragged inside, the panels lightened a few shades.

"The listing said there was an arboretum," Gwydion said. "Did you want to see it?"

"I'd love that," Anaea said.

"Have the wall guide you and I'll join you soon." He made a face. "There's a few things I need to take care of."

She felt a twinge of disappointment, but the scenery could be no less beautiful for seeing it alone. She retreated into the hall.

At her direction, a pulse of mauve chased down the wall. It seemed to take her by the most roundabout route possible, but maybe there was no direct path. Other guests passed in twos and threes. She felt strange under their regard, as if they could sense she was more foreign than they knew. Or perhaps it was the fact they didn't seem to see anything odd that made her skin itch.

She smelled the perfume of fresh flowers before she turned the corner and saw the wrought iron arch into the arboretum. Precise rows of roses, pansies and sampsonias greeted her, their colors playing along the arc of a rainbow. White wings flashed: butterflies flitting from plant to plant. Penelope watched intently, but stayed close, leaping for the insects only when they drew near. Anaea took a deep breath and walked into paradise.

Placards described the flowers and provided more information at a tap. Anaea wandered through local flowers, Earth transplants, and exotics from other planets, including a few from planets that did not support human habitat.

Some of these were trapped under domes or filtered lights to recreate their native environment. Silver-leafed plants from Avalon, the planet around which Annwyn circled; massive scarlet blossoms from one of Perica's inner neighbors, its petals large enough to sit on; and a hermetically sealed climbing vine whose buds were teal and black.

The faint stench of lilies drew Anaea onwards. She loved them, had even requisitioned artwork involving their blossoms, but on Themiscyra they were a luxury, a single bed of Daylilies and Calla lilies in the Preserve. Here there was an astonishing variety: Stargazers, bright yellow Windblowns, Checkered Lilies with mottled pink and white, and hybrids proudly bearing the names of their creators.

She seemed to be alone. Her head turned when she heard voices, but she lingered with the lilies. Someone walked with hasty stride.

"Stop there," an alto voice said. "I was speaking to you."

Anaea paused by a hanging shrub native to Elysium, its bluish leaves concealing her from view. She saw Gwydion as he halted, spine stiff.

"Sorry," he said, "I didn't hear."

The woman came closer. She was tall and broad of shoulder, gold hair falling in loose waves. "Aren't you officer Mallory?"

"No, ma'am." His eyes hunted for a reason to break off the dialogue. Anaea wondered why he looked so nervous.

"Are you sure? Gwydion Mallory of New Troy?" She circled to face him, clicked her tongue. "Oh, I know you. Why are you evading me, Mallory?"

"Not evading," he said. "I'm no longer with the police, and it was a painful parting."

"They let you leave?" Her voice lilted up in surprise. "Well, perhaps their loss is my gain. Do you remember me?"

"I do, Ms. Dennison," he said. "I didn't realize you were here."Penelope's leash jerked in Anaea's hand. She twisted to regain her balance and tugged the kearl out from under the bench. Mulch dangled from her mouth.

"Don't eat that, it could be bad for your physiology," she whispered, but her attention was half-hearted.

"Morgan, please," the woman said. "Have I ever made anyone stand on ceremony? I dare say you will never find a more egalitarian matriarch."

Gwydion smiled weakly. "Perhaps not."

"Which brings us to you," Morgan continued. "Your skills are still sharp, I trust? Have you considered a role in private security? This place is much in need of such an addition."

Anaea could feel the tension building and decided she had to step in. She threaded her way out from the lilies. "Gwydion?"

"Anaea." He crossed to her and squeezed her arm, relief palpable in his face. "How do you like Ms. Dennison's arboretum?"

"It's lovely," she said, but the compliment did not remove the crinkle of displeasure from the woman's lips. If anything, it deepened.

Gwydion hurried to provide the introductions. "This is baronissa Morgan Dennison," he said. "Ms. Dennison, this is my friend Anaea Carlisle."

Morgan smiled, a cloying expression. "A pleasure to make your acquaintance. Gwydion and I were just discussing his potential in private security."

Conscious of his anxiety, Anaea spoke more hastily than she had intended. "I don't think that would be a good idea."

Morgan's eyes took on a glint. "And who are you to design his life?"

She did not need the tightening of Gwydion's fingers to know she had misstepped. "No one of any wisdom," she said, "just a friend to—"

Her brain played out scenarios. Could she make some claim on him without raising the woman's hackles? "—a man who has had much sorrow in recent times," she concluded. "As friend and observer, I'm not sure he's—"

Stop, Gwydion advised. *What's unsaid is more powerful.*

She did, her lips hanging on the rest of the words. She spread her hands.

The glint in Morgan's eyes did not lessen, but she let her shoulders drop. "I am glad to see he has a supportive hand on him," she said. "Perhaps we will have something to speak of later."

Anaea dared not disagree. "Perhaps," she said. She puffed out a breath as Morgan strode away, gown fluttering behind her, a little disconcerted by the relief that flowed through her. "She's not going to barge in on us in the middle of the night, is she?"

Gwydion bit down a laugh. "I doubt it." His expression sobered. He frowned, scuffing his foot. "Thank you. That could have been awkward."

It had seemed plenty awkward to her. "What was that about?" she asked.

"Morgan Dennison is a second generation matriarch," Gwydion said. "She assisted the marchionissa for the district of New Troy where I was assigned. She always admired me; she must have seen my name on the guest roster. I wouldn't have thought she would remember me."

What did that say about the way he saw himself? Anaea wondered. The conclusion saddened her. It was clear her interest had gone beyond admiration, and she flitted a look back to make sure the baronissa – the word had an odd, ancient weight – had not lingered.

They wandered, conversation confined to botanical wonders, then returned to the room to find a lavish meal set out and a series of luxury fragrance settings available.

"Goodness," Anaea said, selecting the herbal garden and closing her eyes as the aroma flooded around her. Her eyes popped open when the uneasy thought intruded. "Is this – should we accept this?"

"You mean is it a bribe from Morgan?" Gwydion asked. "I don't think so. She might want to put you in a good mood for negotiations, maybe."

"She'll be talking to the wrong person," Anaea said wryly.

Gwydion chuckled. "You're a woman, and you spoke as if you had some oversight over me. That's the natural assumption."

Anaea nodded, processing this. It was strange to see the role gender played. In Themiscyra, it might as well not have existed, except as a myth. As an unassigned intern, she drifted further into stigma the older she became. Everyone around her expected her to find a purpose, to join the harmony of the whole. She had felt all thumbs – or in the case of mediator, thick-tongued – everywhere she went. It meant a broad, basic knowledge of skills, but little depth.

Maybe she had felt like an outcast because the occupation ideally suited to her only existed in this part of the universe. She entertained this whimsy with a small smile.

"So you're sure there's no harm in eating this?" she asked.

He spread his hands. "I don't see any," he said.

He sounded a little less sure than she would have liked, but the pungent scent of almond and lavender drew her to a golden souffle. She cut out a piece of pillowy meringue, and then there was no point in going back.

There was more than they could have possibly eaten and things Anaea had never seen before: pheasant and architectural pastries pioneered in the last twenty years by the luxury chefs at the Twin Fires space station. Gwydion talked about the vacation his parents had taken there.

"It's not exactly a den of sin," he said, "but it might be the foyer."

Anaea laughed and threw a sweet-nut at him. He ducked; it rolled across the carpet. Penelope pounced on it and scuttled off under one of the beds to eat it.

Anaea hadn't expected to be tired, but the meal and the anxieties of the day weighed her down. Gwydion said he wanted to look at files. She curled up for a nap, Penelope climbing into the curve of her arm. They had the rest of the evening in New Athens; a good while, with the luxury of Elysium's longer day; at twenty-seven hours, two more than galactic standard. That meant . . .

*

SHE AWOKE WITH sunlight on her face. A light breeze rustled through the curtains, carrying the putty scent of industry.

She sat up, realizing the patio door to the balcony was open.

She assumed Gwydion was there and leaned forward furtively, hoping to catch a glimpse of him.

She saw nothing, which might only mean he was at the edge. She pulled back and couldn't keep her balance, sliding onto the sheets with a thump.

"Anaea?" he called. "Are you awake?"

She gathered a blanket around her and went out to the balcony. She had been perfectly comfortable in night-clothes with Orithia, even after their relationship had ended and everything was still sore, but the idea of being around a man in a nightshirt made her want to hide. She wasn't sure why.

The view, however, was worth it. The city glowed with after-images of dawn, facets sometimes gold, sometimes streaked with rosebud pink.

From here, she could see the layout of the streets, but she could hardly make out one region from the next. Sometimes, there were fancy buildings such as a government dome or a theatre, but if there were other differences, they vanished at distance.

The absence of a rail alarmed her, yet Gwydion's body inclined over the edge with no sign of fear. She resisted the urge to pluck at his arm. "There haven't been any calls from staff or security," he said.

She blinked, then realized she was stiff and hunched; he had misread her discomfiture. She found it oddly comforting he could be wrong. "Were you expecting one?" she asked. "I thought you said she wanted to negotiate."

"I said that might be it," he said. "Maybe she's waiting for you."

Anaea shook her head, vaguely bemused. "Then she'll be waiting a long time. Would you please come away from the edge before you fall?"

He laughed as he retreated. "Sorry."

They dressed separately and headed out. Anaea half-expected the wall-lights to lead them in an endless circle, preventing their departure, and chided herself when they reached the lobby. She had to stop jumping at shadows.

Another bubbly boy checked them out. "Oh! Wait one moment."

Anaea wouldn't have thought anything of it, but Gwydion tensed. She flashed him a questioning look. Morgan?

"Baronissa Dennison offers her heartfelt wishes for a safe trip," the boy continued. "She prays that you consult her, miss Carlisle, should you have need of her advice."

Anaea's chest twinged in relief. She tipped her head in acknowledgement. "Err . . . send her back my thanks."

"Of course, madam."

Anaea turned and nodded to the main doors. "Let's go."

They stepped out into the brilliant, heady sunshine. She celebrated it once again. The guestlink offered her guidance; she silenced it.

A transport platform took them to the station, a plain building with rows of padded benches. When sat upon, they offered a series of entertainments, which Anaea declined in favor of watching the comings and goings. A shuttle from the other side of the planet disgorged a group of businesswomen, tourists and students. Again, their attire was in perfect sync, following fashion.

Gwydion, more accustomed to his surroundings, watched a news program and soothed Penelope. He stood as his bench gave a chime. "That's ours."

The shuttle had deep white plush chairs and privacy screens. It had enough room for twenty, but there were only three other passengers: a middle-aged male couple and a teenaged girl with silver ornaments glinting under her chin and studded in her eyebrow. Anaea stared.

The roof slid aside to allow their egress upwards. The shuttle obtained an altitude of several thousand feet in a few seconds and then shot forward, skimming the landscape so quickly her starved eyes couldn't hold the details below. She uttered a little cry.

Gwydion shot her an alarmed look. "What?"

She blushed. "I didn't know it would go so fast."

She pressed to the window, wholly observed as the world flashed by, an impression of unlikely green rising into hills. It dropped away into a rocky valley, and in the center glinted silver and glass, threads woven on a metal loom: another settlement. Anaea had just become accustomed to their dizzying pace of travel when they descended.

Gwydion let out a breath as if he had been holding it since he boarded the White Hound. "Home," he said.

12

G WYDION PLACED A HAND ON ANAEA'S SHOULDER AND
held her back as the others exited, then guided her into
a station identical to the one they had left. A figure wove
through the crowds and drew Gwydion into a warm embrace.

"It's so good to see you, my brother," she said.

Though she had recognized the face, Anaea was still surprised.
She had expected a woman whose size matched her presence,
not someone so short and slender. She felt awkward and coltish
in comparison.

Gwydion dropped one arm out of the hug and turned to face
her. "Anaea, this is my—"

"Gwydion!"

The second voice boomed in the baritone ranges; the bizarre
timbre made her jump. The speaker was six feet and more,
broad-shouldered, squared off.

"Adrian? I didn't know you had come home." The brothers
exchanged a strange greeting, not really a hug: a clasp of hands
and a pounding of shoulders. Adrian expended more force,
eliciting a wince from Gwydion.

"A few days ago," Adrian answered. "Had some bad news at my post, but—" he cast a fond look to his wife "—everything has a good side."

"Adrian, Sophie, this is my friend Anaea," Gwydion said. The change in his manner was marked: deferential, a little anxious. They exchanged bows; Anaea managed to keep hers from being too awkward. "I wouldn't be here without her."

"Or I without him," Anaea said loyally. Penelope chittered, tugging at her leg. "And this is Penelope."

Sophie half-crouched, holding out a hand. "What an adorable creature." Penelope pressed up into her hand, purring fervently.

They exited the station. Anaea yelped as a soft shock went through her body. Remembering what had happened in Eastwood, she rocked forward to throw herself onto the ground. Gwydion caught her.

"Scramble signal," he said. "Prevents anyone from outside the Sanctum from tracking your guestlink and finding out where you are. Limits the functionality inside, too. Works just as well without making everything about you public knowledge." His voice was quick, proud.

"This from a boy who could pry about in any of our brains," Adrian said lightly.

Gwydion looked pained. "I wouldn't."

"Hypermental's curse, hmm? So much to do, so many reasons not to do it." Adrian ruffled his hair, almost ruffled his whole head; rough but playful.

Anaea glanced around her. The Sanctum was laid out in rounds, curved streets with buildings predominantly in rose and blue. They looked similar, puzzle pieces arranged in different combinations with tamed garden patches out front. Most of the doors had mezuzahs. People shouted and waved, conversing as friends, never passing without a smile. She remembered Gwydion's estimate that the community was smaller than Themiscyra's.

The air smelled fresh, clean . . . and deep, as if she could taste the layers of the planet beneath rising up to meet her. The sheer expanse of space dizzied her. She had never seen such limitless tumble without barrier or simulation, except for the expanse of space.

She realized she had fallen behind and hurried to catch up. Gwydion was relating the invented story of their journey.

"Phailin wants to hear the account from your lips as soon as possible," Adrian said.

"But she won't have you until you're rested," Sophie said firmly. "Of course, you—" she slid Anaea into the conversation "—will be welcome to stay with us as long as you like. It wouldn't be proper for a young woman to stay at a bachelor's apartment."

The meaning there coursed over Anaea's head. Enough other mysteries presented themselves that she let this one go.

For instance: the Mallories spoke of the founder of the Sanctum with such casualness it astonished her. As if she were a friend to chat up for breakfast, to tease, to scold. Asteria and the other founders of Themiscyra were legends, but then again, the station had been founded decades before this place. The Sanctum showed no signs of its youth, however: it seemed rooted deep in the hills.

Anaea realized what she was looking for and didn't see. "What about transportation?" she asked.

"Long distance only," Sophie said. "The street layout is designed so it takes no more than seven minutes to reach any point on foot. If you can't spare that, you aren't planning correctly."

Adrian snagged an arm around her, a gesture which emphasized the differences in their heights. Then Anaea noticed the taut line in Gwydion's chin. She focused elsewhere.

Gwydion served as tour-guide, pointing out a business with glass front windows and rainbow confections; an open-air stadium for amateur musicians and actors; a nook down which cozy blue houses lay. His manner was possessive of the place, and also somehow pleading. He kept scanning her face for her reactions.

She became aware slowly that he half-expected, or at least wanted, her to stay in the Sanctum. The uncomfortable feeling rose inside her and would not settle. She wondered what else her plan should be. She had wanted to explore, but there was too much universe to know where to start. She could pick places at random and never be finished.

They turned down a cul-de-sac and headed for the second house, white paneled with a porch and birch wood steps. Sophie quickened her stride to the door. It opened as she approached. "Welcome to our home," she said, with a proprietary hum.

The house was built over three levels with hover-steps instead of stairs, the dominant colors intervals between cream and canary yellow. The décor was artful: accents, end-tables and artwork arranged so the eye flowed from one to the next. With generous windows and skylights, and few inner walls, the house was filled with light and air, so much that Anaea felt weightless and a little disconcerted.

"That vase is new, isn't it?" Gwydion asked. It was a slender yellow spindle painted with birds, opening like a flower at the top.

Sophie's smile expanded. "Less than a week. Eight days, to be exact. I still haven't figured out where to put it."

"Near the window, maybe?" he suggested. From his expression, Anaea guessed he had no idea how these things were supposed to go, but he was determined to be helpful.

Adrian laughed. "I can't believe you notice these things, little brother. Sure you're not thinking of taking a bachelor under your wing?"

Gwydion pinked. "I'm not—"

"Stop teasing him," Sophie said. "If you would pay more heed to residential details, you'd earn more respect from the commanders."

Adrian snorted. "Not going to develop a skill I have no use for," he said. "Come on, Gwydion, I have a tactical question."

Sophie led Anaea to a saffron-gold guest room,. "Is this all right for you? I just want you to be comfortable."

Like the rest of the house, it was warm and bright. Lace curtains framed the window and the sunlit expanse of the Sanctum.

"It's lovely. Thank you," Anaea said. Penelope sniffed the mound of blankets intended for her with a dubious air, then burrowed inside, disappearing all but for the flick of her tail-tip. "For this, and for helping us back at New Athens."

"Thank you," Sophie said firmly, "for bringing my brother home." She glanced down the hall, then continued, "Is there anything I should know? Something two women would concern themselves with, but not their men?"

Anaea stood tongue-tied. She had only a slight idea what sort of things might belong to one gender or another, and none of the secrets were hers to tell. "I . . ." Her eyes lit on the mezuzah outside the guest door. "I'm not Jewish," she said.

Sophie laughed. "That's all right, dear. Everyone needs some flaw. Gwydion is a dear boy, isn't he? I'm lucky to have gained a brother along with a husband."

She led Anaea onto the porch where the men stood, then excused herself. "Cooking isn't the same unless you're doing it by hand," she said.

Anaea tried to follow their conversation, something about disclosure laws for hypermentals, but the view was too absorbing. She leaned on the rail and watched the surreal dash of blue seeping down from the ceiling of the world. In places, the clouds blotted it away.

The forest that rose into rocky mountainside at first looked uniform green, but she soon detected lighter shades and dark, moss and emerald, sage and leaves that approached teal. The vastness of the landscape hurt her head. She had the urge to draw it all to her chest and hold it, except there was too much.

She heard Sophie singing inside, a bright soprano. The men broke off their conversation to listen and Anaea was struck by the similarity of their expressions, though the younger kept his head down. They picked up the conversation again with more ferocity than before.

Sophie was one of those, a nesting woman. In Themiscyra, couples traded off household duties with work, by the week or sometimes the day. Someone who wanted only the single role was an oddity, but not unheard of. What left Anaea flummoxed was trying to figure out how a woman like that fit into society in New Athens or the Sanctum.

Was that what the Mallory brothers saw in Sophie? The thought made her uneasy. She wasn't sure what she thought of her new friend favoring a nesting woman. What did that say about him? And why did it matter to her?

Sophie called them in for a simple but hearty meal. The story of their journey dominated the conversation. Gwydion discussed his time aboard the White Hound and how he had taken shelter in the virtual reality unit. Anaea tensed, but neither seemed to notice the abrupt jump from disaster to their damaged drive and landing on Eastwood.

"Barbarous place," Adrian said.

Sophie diverted the conversation onto Penelope. "I would love to have such creatures for some of my patients," she said. "Companion animals have a wonderful effect on the spirit, and they're healthier than stimulation treatment or medication. Where did you say they originated from?"

Gwydion jumped in, changing the subject again. The dialogue circled back to their travels. He looked discomfited as he related the meeting with Morgan Dennison.

Adrian snorted. "I remember her. Poison with a smile."

His wife headed him off. "Did you get to see any of the new fixtures? They've been renovating that quarter for three months, I hear." Few hostile remarks seemed to get past Sophie Mallory.

After lunch, Gwydion ushered Anaea out with vague excuses. Penelope seemed to have attached herself to their hosts, so they left her.

As soon as they were on the street, Gwydion explained, "I thought you might want to see the library. The custodian specializes in the social history of the Y-Poisoning era."

Anaea glanced up, startled. It seemed ages since she had asked bewildered questions about how the history of her world had become his. "I'd like that," she said.

The library was an austere rose-marble building with a dome ceiling and two abstract figure sculptures for front pillars. Pulses of light passed through their glass limbs, mimicking features. Inside, two doors led into massive chambers on either side. Anaea's attention was drawn to the central dome and the encased pillar.

"Central terminal," Gwydion explained. "More comprehensive and faster than using the link." The other rooms were for group holographs, school programs and tours. Past the terminal lay a series of isolation doors.

Anaea pressed herself up against the isolation doors with a little cry of astonishment. In that sealed, regulated environment stood shelves upon shelves of real books: massive hardbounds, some with plastic, others velvet or vineskin, paperbacks staggering in untidy lines, and everything in between. Far more than the three bookcases in Themiscyra, these swept away in rows.

Labels on the shelves divided them by subject and origin. She could see two sections that dated to before landfall on Elysium.

"Oh," she said, warmed by some ancestral feeling of ownership. Her hand uncurled against the glass.

"I feel the same way," he said. "It's silly, I know, old-fashioned, but something about the fact they don't change, that every word is permanent, speaks to me."

"They're a world to themselves," Anaea said. Like home, she thought, and felt a twinge of regret.

To assuage that sickness, she pondered the idea of working here, the meticulous attention to detail and the constant guard against decay. New books, he had said, were printed for collectors or historians, but the originals were priceless. The idea charmed her, but perhaps only because it was unfamiliar.

Gwydion had moved away, speaking in soft tones to his link. He smiled ruefully when she turned to him. "The officer I report to wants to speak with me," he said. "I think it would be better if he didn't meet you just yet. Will you—"

"I don't need to be chaperoned," she assured him. "I can find my way back."

He slipped out. Apart from a few voices in one viewing room, she seemed to be alone. She studied the labels on the bookshelves, noticing the preponderance of fiction. The soft light blurred too much detail to read more than a few of the covers: *Drinking The Stars,* a battered vintage copy of *Zombie Tales,* ethnographic studies.

The directions next to the door admonished that visitors must be accompanied, clean, free of food, beverage and disease, and that the decontamination protocols took two minutes during which it was crucial the visitor remain still. She wandered away. She glanced around for the custodian, but when no one seemed to be in evidence, she slipped into a chair at the terminal and put her palm on the activation panel.

A holographic corridor stretched out before her. On the periphery of her vision, she could still make out her surroundings. The terminal database had the façade of the book-room times a hundred, shelves stretching out into blissful infinity.

A thought took her forward. There was scent, too, a deep, pungent aroma that could have been unpleasant in larger doses and yet invited inhalation. Anaea did so, savoring the aroma, even knowing it was just an illusion.

She jumped to the local shelves and studied information on book preservation and the issuance of new volumes. A voice in the back of her head whispered she had to keep moving, had to focus, had to finalize her bearings. When she stopped to consider, she wondered why. Was there a rush? Surely there was more out there than she could ever grasp. It was a matter for the heart, not the head.

She had never been particularly good with that.

Anaea stretched out her hand on the plate and felt the illusion of tactile sensation, her fingers rubbing over leather and then cheap plastic.

"You're a new face." The voice startled her: the slim figure had glided into the corner of her vision like a mote of dust. She had dirty blonde hair, pinned back into half a ponytail, the rest going wherever in an untidy mop. "Is there anything I can do for you?"

She had to be the custodian. Anaea moved her palm off the panel so she could focus on the other woman, dipping her head for greeting. The book display faded.

"I was told you knew a lot about the Y-Poisoning era, and how things developed," she said. "I am interested—" she bit her lip, feeling the careless flow of logic from those words: the why, the how, the confusions that even the most sheltered colonist should not have.

Dark eyes pierced from a coffee au lait face. "When the past is too close," the woman said, "people tend to bury it. Antiquity is the only way to get perspective, and by then, we've lost things."

"That's a gloomy view," Anaea said.

"Maybe, maybe not. The human mind may be better off when it can't over-analyze its failings." The woman flashed a smile, too high on one side and showing a few teeth. "But what did you want to know?"

"The matriarchs," Anaea said. "How did it come to be women in control over here?"

"If you ask some people, it's because the natural order of things finally won out." The smile broadened. It wasn't unpleasant, Anaea decided: it just looked askew. "The way I understand it, it was a perfect storm. The first female-dominated council had a five-year hold on the planet Solomon, and where Solomon goes, we on this side of the Bridge tend to follow. We had more men immune to the disease and fewer who survived it stronger—"

"Why?" she cut in.

The custodian shrugged. "Doctors think it's linked to testosterone, but it wasn't a one-to-one correlation, even though milder men tended to be the ones immune. Anyhow, women took charge because that's what it looked like at the top, and because we needed cooperation and coordination to bring us together. No one had the time or strength to buck the status quo."

"Oh." Anaea hoped she sounded more as if she were only being reminded.

The custodian arched an eyebrow. "The warlords—"

"I know," she said, anxious to sound knowledgeable. "The planet of Independence is where hypermentals got their start. And they had overloaded hypermentals."

"That's a big part of it," the woman said. "Any survivor got a boost to aggression. Don't know why the Derithe would've designed it that way, or maybe they don't understand us any better than we do." The smile was back, with edge: a gallows grin. "Put those kind of people in a broken world and they push their way to the top."

And why, Anaea wondered, asking the question she suspected no one had answered: why had the Derithe attacked and then vanished? Why leave the job undone, or was the purpose something other than destruction? Yet even Earth, theoretically isolated from the empires it had spawned, had felt the weight of Y-Poisoning, as far as she had learned on Themiscyra.

"I've always been inclined to think the founders and their influence on cultural mindset had something to do with it." The custodian seemed deep in her own thoughts at this juncture. "The expedition that landed on Solomon was supposed to be a jewel of achievement for Earth, but the colonists refused to be toys. Those sent to Independence were undesirables and misfits, and they found found new life in their banishment.

"There was a third group, when Y-Poisoning struck," she continued, "who had the sense to flee. Women all, so there was no risk of sickness. When you think about it, the long odds are on their survival. More likely than not, they were destroyed by the ripples of hyperspace, ran out of fuel, got picked off by a hostile force or went mad out there in isolation. What do you think?"

Anaea felt a chill, but told herself she had started the discussion. "I think you're probably right," she said. "If a settlement is going to fail, it's usually in the first forty years, isn't it?"

A light of – approval? – in the custodian's eyes. "That's true. I don't recognize your face. Are you new? Who told you to speak with me?"

"Gwydion Mallory," she said.

"Mallory?" The woman was interested, but not surprised. She shifted to face Anaea fully. "I thought he was off-planet on some mission."

Anaea hesitated. "I'm not sure it's my story to tell . . ."

The custodian leaned back and spread her hands. "I would never pry," she said.

Those words reminded Anaea that whatever Gwydion had to say would be filed officially. What did it matter if she talked about it? "Well, I can share my part," she said. The custodian interrupted her in places with questions. They seemed purposeful rather than curious, surgical in their precision.

"What made you decide to leave?"

She was glad she had rehearsed. It wasn't even a lie. "My mother used to say, 'The universe is as wide as you can imagine it, Ann.' I realized my imagination needed fuel."

"Ann? Is that your name, then?" the woman probed.

"Oh!" She blushed in apology and offered a hand. "Anaea Carlisle."

The woman accepted it in a firm grip but did not immediately reply. The smile surfaced, canine. "I suppose I should introduce myself."

The nuances in the statement brought Anaea's head up. "You're not the custodian, are you?" she asked.

The woman dipped her head. "No."

"Then who are you?"

13

DR. PHAILIN ANDERS." THE WOMAN'S SMILE DISCON-certed Anaea, even though her body language was relaxed and the crinkle in her eyes apologetic. "At your service."

Anaea stiffened. She had been wasting the time of the community leader, the legend, with history lessons? What might she have said by accident? Her brain whirred. "Oh."

"I apologize for abusing my position to track you down," Phailin continued. "When Mallory answered the call, I checked the position of the nearest guestlink."

Anaea blinked. "You hardly need to apologize for—"

"Something commonplace on the rest of Elysium? I brought people here to escape. Hypocritical of me to ignore my own rules."

"You were that curious about me?"

Phailin snorted. The smile disappeared, but she spoke conversationally. "I find it unusual that one of my agents would go out on an exploration mission with instructions to look for signs of a lost colony. That he would come back from the wreckage with a girl from nowhere. One might think it was too convenient, even wonder if he had been successful."

Anaea swallowed, but there was no menace in the words. The tone was a gentle touch, asking nothing, but open . . . and Phailin suspected, she must, might even decide in the privacy of her mind that she *knew*.

Anaea was afraid the truth was written beneath the glass of her face. "If such a place existed, would they send one lone girl as their envoy?"

Phailin's chin tilted. "It would only be an envoy if my messenger succeeded. If they want an alliance."

"I am no envoy. But even a girl from a minor colony would have secrets that weren't hers to share," Anaea said, watching her palms – or she tried. Her eyes flicked up involuntarily to track the other's reaction.

Phailin arched her brows. "Who is entitled to keep secrets for whom, and from whom? That's a question that has baffled philosophers and toppled regimes."

Some uncomfortable part of Anaea agreed. It still felt like a betrayal, even as she found out the extent of the lie she had been told. Her face heated. "Dr. Anders, you wouldn't – that is . . ." She struggled with how to say it without making an admission.

"Ann," Phailin said, tone level, "I've worked the last several years to build a community apart from the world. It would be against everything I stand for to jeopardize that for anyone else."

Anaea didn't say what she wanted to: her thanks would have been too transparent. Her chest eased, though the uncertainty continued to gnaw. If it was not her secret to share, did she have a right to keep it? By whose reckoning? "This is a lovely place," she said.

"I hope you feel at home here," Phailin said. "If you have any more history questions, I'm open. Any good psychologist knows that people are the product of their pasts." Her lips quirked, a shadow of a smile.

Anaea took the plunge. "What happened to Earth?"

Phailin shook her head, mood darkening. "No one knows."

She blinked. "What?"

"You heard me. Earth tried to quarantine, but too late, or so the evidence suggests." Phailin shrugged. "There's no hyperspace corridor aligned with Sol. The journey from Proxima Centauri, the closest corridor, is what, six years? When the old world went quiet and dark, there wasn't any time to investigate. Now . . . I'm not sure anyone wants to spend twelve years to find out that it's empty and dead. We've moved on from the homeland."

Anaea found it hard to credit. Earth was the birthplace of humanity. Who could simply let it go? "Do you think we will find out?" she asked.

"I'm sure," Phailin said, "but there's also the flip side. What if there are survivors and they need us? Do we bring them back? What if there are more than the ship can carry? Send for supplies? The travel time is almost insurmountable for any mission of mercy. For all we know, that was what the Derithe wanted, they're hived up there and content to leave us to the other planets."

Anaea laughed nervously. "Oh."

"It makes for good holofiction. I had better head out, though," Phailin continued. "I need to be present for the end of the dialogue with Mallory. I don't want to worry that sister of his by keeping him too long."

"You know them personally?" Anaea asked, surprised.

"Of course. I know as much about my people as a baronissa does, just with less supervision." She rose, a graceful spring of muscles. "I'll make sure you have a social credit allotment added."

Anaea blinked. "For what?"

"For nothing," Phailin said, lips twitching. "I don't hold with instilling false altruism through bells and whistles. I get an allotment direct from the Imperatrix for my discretion, and I simply choose not to have any." She shrugged. "Good day, Ann. Welcome to the Sanctum."

"Thank you, Dr. Anders," Anaea said, and watched a legend walk away. The link against her breastbone buzzed, warning her a thunderstorm was inbound, but she wanted to take one last look at the real books through the glass. The march of spines mesmerized her, from the commercial sheen of plastic to sturdy paper and archaic leather.

The sky cleared its throat and practiced bass scales. The thunder made her hurry; perched in the doorway, she strained, waited, watched for an incandescent handful of lightning. It splattered across the grey-green mounds of clouds and disappeared.

The door beeped at the human who stood impertinently in its path, but Anaea did not move. She listened and watched until the sixth strike, then shimmied out into the rainfall and let it play on her skin.

Soaked and content, she wandered back to the Mallory residence.

*

"Come in this instant," Sophie said, invoking a tradition of countless generations, "You're going to catch your death of cold."

"There is no direct correlation between germs and rainwater," Anaea pointed out.

Sophie pierced her with a look. "It lowers resistance. Don't argue with a doctor."

It was definitely her nesting side, not her doctor side, that got Anaea inside, changed, and bundled in warming blankets with cinnamon hot chocolate. Penelope plopped on her lap.

Sophie stood before her, hands on hips. "Are we feeling better?"

"Much, thank you." She sipped as the other woman disappeared into the kitchen.

"I'm so glad Adrian and I were both able to take the day. I feel like I can be a proper hostess, and there are three days of weekend ahead."

"I thought you worked at home." Anaea chewed on her tongue as soon as the words were out. It had sounded different in her head.

"At home?" Sophie appeared in the doorway with a plate of treats. "I'm a doctor, dear. They don't come to me. Would you like something?"

It was not a question, then, of trading duties as nesting women did: Sophie managed both, and it did not seem as if Adrian had much hand in the household. Bewildered, Anaea shook her head. It did not seem like something that would work in a female-dominated society, but Gwydion had indicated the Sanctum was unconventional.

"They're here if you want them," Sophie said, misinterpreting the head shake. She placed the tray on the lace-glass table. "Where did you go?"

Anaea told her about the library and the books, leading to a pleasant conversation of the feel of spines and Sophie's intention to start a library. What books would be best to own if one were making a show of it? For the tactile pleasure of reading? For the sprawling stories or the intellectual enlightenment?

"They don't print technical knowledge," Sophie said, "that would be redundant, but there is still wisdom in old philosophy and history written by those who are now history themselves. In a database, it would have been updated and corrected into oblivion."

Sorrow tugged at Anaea. Those were pieces of this world she would never see, unless she found them in an old book.

The door opened, and the Mallory brothers entered. Anaea darted to her feet, upsetting the kearl, who applied teeth to her ankle without biting. Sophie flurried over to hug them both. Gwydion pulled out of the embrace; Anaea thought she was the only one who saw the strain in his face.

When their eyes met, the tension melted out of his expression. "Enjoy your outing?"

"It was . . . illuminating," she said. "What happened at the briefing?"

Gwydion relayed that he had told their rehearsed story. If he suspected Phailin had seen through his explanation, he gave no sign of it.

"There's a puzzle tourney tonight," Adrian said, after it had been settled all was well on the official front. "A four-dimensional history crossword. Thought our visitor might enjoy spectating."

Gwydion had explained this: with the links allowing access to a virtual domain, most puzzles were cooperative or built for team competition. They went planet-wide.

"We could play?" she suggested.

"Can't," he said. "Because the Sanctum blocks location tracking, we can't grid into the official games. We could play a local round—"

Adrian snorted. "Oh, that would be slightly more exciting than watching grass grow."

"Really, love, that's a bit mean," Sophie said.

"I'd like to see it," Anaea said. "We don't have such things at home." She was relieved when they accepted that as something that might be possible.

The rest of the day was idyllic, spent in conversation, impromptu meteorology lessons, and virtual entertainment. She slipped into its unaccustomed length more easily than she had expected, apart from being truly tired when nightfall came.

The next day, Gwydion lured her out for a walking tour of the Sanctum. People bustled and occasionally jostled, but seemed good-natured enough about it. In place of standing artwork, gardens perched in the center of streets, not orderly gatherings of flowers, but tumultuous wildflower tapestry. The town was not otherwise aesthetic, but it was efficient, a short walk to some variation of any service.

Midway through morning, Gwydion received a call on his link. When it ended, he said, "They've sold off your shuttle, for a very good price. It will be broken down into parts."

Anaea felt a rush of relief. That would mean no questions about the advanced technology, no way of tracking down the source if there were. It didn't mean she was stuck: she could buy passage on any number of ships out. "I thought it would take longer," she said.

"There's always a need for parts," Gwydion said. "Couriers, trading vessels, transports, even an exploration mission or two like the White Hound. We've healed from Y-Poisoning," he continued, his tone earnest but not quite steady, "and now it's time to broaden our horizons."

"Do you think you'll go back to doing that?" she said.

He hesitated, releasing a swirl of breath. "Not yet. I just want to be home for a bit. Even if I do feel like a third wheel around my brother and his wife."

Anaea wasn't quite sure what to say. She was embarrassed for him, but she had no wise words. He seemed displaced, almost as unsettled as she.

The Sanctum held a single museum in Greek temple style, devoted to local talent. The first exhibit was still photographs, altered to display lower and higher spectra of light as saturated color. Their rainbow auras showed distant mountains and berry bushes, the majestic and the minute side by side. Anaea had trouble believing so many vistas could exist, much less, as the placards claimed, within a hundred miles of the Sanctum.

The second exhibit showcased collaborative light-painting: three-dimensional spheres "painted" with projected color, different from each angle. Each artist, male or female, had worked on it in turn until they felt their part was done, passing it on to the next. Mood, mannerism, and technique blended into a single whole.

Something about the massive displays and their reverent care made Anaea feel dizzy, sucked down , as if the rest of the universe had disappeared inside the walls. The only concession to life beyond the Sanctum was an immersive exhibit of Earth music, concerts captured in time and preserved exactly as they had been played up to four hundred years ago.

Anaea entered the booth for the Meridean Minuet, a neo-Baroque symphony that interspersed synthesized bird-song with traditional instruments. Closing her eyes, it was easy to drift back in time.

After she stepped out, another call interrupted: central wanted Gwydion's advice on an investigation.

Anaea tilted her head. "I thought you were no longer official."

"I'm not." He smiled wryly. "But hypermentals with my talent for a psychometric read are in short supply, so if the physical evidence could tell a story the witnesses don't, I'm there as a consultant. You'll be in good hands with Sophie?" The words came out a little halting, a little wistful.

Woman's work, Anaea thought, and wondered why it irritated her. In this place, some older memory clashed with how people had been raised and what they were trying to become. It disconcerted her.

Themiscyra had escaped the baggage, she thought, then dismissed the idea. Solving the dynamic by removing one gender was somehow cheating.

Maybe it was Sophie that bothered her, Gwydion's perfect woman. Anaea wished she knew why it kept sticking in her mind.

On her way back to the Mallory residence, she detoured into the library. This time, she did not let the decontamination protocols deter her: she stood patiently in the airlock as sterile air puffed over her skin, then stepped into the company of the books.

The smell washed over her first. The simulation had been accurate, but somehow incomplete: it did not capture the full complexity of the musk, the almost dusty aroma that flirted with the edge of unpleasant. She drifted to the fiction section and was attracted to a velvet-covered copy of *Falling Stars,* the science fiction novel which had given the planet Perica its name.

The story had been required reading for history class. Anaea shimmied the book off the shelf. The cover tickled her fingers as she cradled it; the embossed letters shimmered even in the protective low light.

The pages murmured as she turned to the first chapter and the opening description of sunset from a moon sea. She recognized the words; had not realized she remembered the novel so well; but the plain black text made them feel different, more weighty, more real. It was the gravity of permanence, though the book could be destroyed by a single flame.

At length, she returned it to the shelf and continued to browse. In another section, a songbook caught her attention. The simple cover, little more than cardboard, protected a bewildering profusion of dark marks flurrying across the pages. It was another language all to itself which only a musician could read.

She meandered through the shelves for a while longer before making her retreat. She felt somehow more whole, as if she had somehow drawn the aura of the books in with her breath.

Sophie was working on a report when Anaea entered the house. She disconnected from her link, crinkling her nose. "How much training did you receive in medicine?" At the answer, she said, "I could use someone to bounce some thoughts off. I'm going in circles."

"What's going on?"

"The issue is mostly theoretical, but in a closed community like the Sanctum, disease mutation is—" Sophie paused, flushing. "I am sorry! You're a guest here, and don't need to be subjected to my professional concerns – unless you are thinking about applying here?"

"I don't mind," Anaea said. "It makes me feel useful."

"Let me help you in turn," Sophie said. "I notice you brought almost nothing with you. May I help you put together a suitable wardrobe?"

On Themiscyra, Anaea had sometimes browsed alternate clothing, cloned from Earth and early Solomon styles, but she never got beyond browsing. She had seen only occasional glimpses here that reminded her of station wear. Obviously, fashion was a complex science.

"I would appreciate that," she said.

They set out, talking over issues of medical containment and disease transmission. Anaea was nothing close to a full-fledged doctor, but she was able to grasp the Sanctum's problems.

They entered a mall and wandered elevation corridors. Anaea

kept one ear on the bubble of conversation and heard none of the haggling that had characterized Eastwood's markets. At least her buying power wouldn't be measured by the loudness of her voice.

She stopped, entranced by a peacock blue dress in a store-front window. It fell off the shoulder on one side, with layered skirts and a translucent back. Even knowing little about the construction of clothes, she could see it was meant for someone tall.

"You want to try that on?" Sophie said.

"Where in the world would I wear it?"

"When does that ever matter?" Humor played at Sophie's lips. "You should at least try it on, dear."

People stopped them as they moved through the mall, full of news. Sophie laughed and gossiped and glimmered with each. A dozen small worlds opened up, those of the doctor, the neighbor, the military wife, the member of the faith, and those that had no apparent connection except they fell within Sanctum boundaries, children thriving, restaurants adding to their menu, construction on new avenues.

There was an entire world compressed in this space, fleshed out so fully no one would need more. Certainly Sophie was comfortable, the center of her sphere and eminently in control. Most of those who stopped to talk seemed in awe of her.

Anaea slowed at the homesick lurch in the pit of her stomach. This place reminded her of all the good in Themiscyra, the trust and connection she had sometimes struggled to be part of, a small sphere of existence where no path was barred. One could be involved in everything.

Sophie paused. "Are you all right?"

There was no explaining this. "Close enough," she said. She ignored the skepticism in the other's face; Sophie was too gentle to pry.

They returned to the Mallory residence fifteen minutes before Gwydion entered, looking wan; he mumbled something about a messy homicide. Sophie pulled him in and smothered him with sympathy.

Dinner was a home affair again. Sophie chivvied Anaea into her room and insisted she change into one of her acquisitions. "Comb your hair back, pin it out of your eyes, and wear these shoes," she directed. Having been raised in an environment where the desired elements of beauty were serenity and simplicity, Anaea let her work. "There. Just lovely." Sophie directed her charge to the mirror.

The outfit was a split-skirt in midnight blue with diagonal white threads at the waist and a black cap-sleeve shirt with lace cut-outs. Against white skin, the striking contrast made her eyes seem impossibly bright.

It surprised her to realize she was buying into a foreign standard of beauty, and she even saw it – no. There was no call for vanity, particularly unearned. She did not have that air of inner harmony; how could she? She turned to thank her hostess, but Sophie had flurried out like a flock of birds.

"Gwydion," Anaea said as she entered the living room, "what is the investigator program like for regular people?"

"Two weeks shorter, with different focus," he said. "I'm not sure the Sanctum program is—" He lifted his eyes to her and seemed to lose his train of thought.

"Gwydion?" she prompted.

Adrian interrupted with a low bark of laughter. "Stop ogling, little brother. Remind me how you put up with such a Neanderthal, Anaea?"

Gwydion flushed. Anaea was sure the color rose in her cheeks, if only in sympathy. "He's not," she said. "He's—" She had no word for it.

"A gentleman," Sophie said from the doorway. "An archaic word, but appropriate."

Adrian spent most of the meal discussing sports. Gwydion smiled automatically whenever addressed, but did not comment much. Anaea caught him feeding Penelope under the table and shook her head. Then, she noticed Sophie had set aside a tidy portion as well.

She thought Orithia would be furious at her for fattening up the kearl, then remembered her friend would never know. She ducked her head over the wine, swallowing tears. She did not dare look up until she could control the squeeze in her heart.

Afterwards, Gwydion arrowed to the patio. Anaea lingered to ask Adrian a question, then followed.

He glanced over with a tentative smile as she leaned against the railing. There was a crisp, fresh scent to the air; it changed every time she inhaled.

"You look beautiful," he said.

She couldn't contradict him, but couldn't control the color in her cheeks, either. "Thank you."

His lips moved around words without reaching them. She waited it out, conscious of each breath she drew, and hearing his as well. His breaths quickened.

"It's good to be home," he said.

She studied him. "Yes?"

His fingers twittered on the railing. "It's harder than I remembered," he said. "Being normal. My brother teasing me. Acting if she were my sister when she hugs me and praises me." He wouldn't look straight at Anaea, his voice strained as if he were apologizing for the words. "Hypermentals get a sense of each other, sort of a taste of strong thoughts. I will never know how easy I am to read."

"You could leave again," she said. "I'd go with you." That excited her, an unexpected lifting of wings.

Gwydion faced her. "Anaea," he said, "if there's anything this journey taught me, it's how lucky I am to have a place like this – a refuge."

The question lingered in his voice, and she had expected it, though not so soon. Somewhere in the back of her mind, she had seen this weekend as a test, all judgement suspended until the last evening. But his expression made it difficult to demur, or to say she needed more time.

She knew what her answer had to be, and there was no point

in putting it off. She wanted to hold on, to this moment, to him and this place, but she couldn't.

She caught herself shifting to look away and instead made herself square with him. "I can't stay, Gwydion," she said. "I've lived in a bubble all my life, and I can't go back to that."

She thought again of Orithia, desperate to believe that Themiscyra was the world. She thought of his concept of hiraeth, the crushing pain of losing a homeland. There could not be two more different people, and yet both were content in sanctuary. She . . . was not.

Gwydion flinched as if she had drawn a weapon on him. His eyes lifted reluctantly, studying her face. He came to a conclusion long before he spoke; she could see him marshaling painful thoughts into the right form.

"All right," he said. "I won't ask if you're sure. But you've seen the choices available to you. Which way will you turn?"

14

IT WAS NOT AN EASY QUESTION, ALTHOUGH HEARING IT, WITH the implication he wouldn't argue, filled her with relief. "I'll let you know tomorrow," Anaea said.

His dismay, restrained under the surface, deepened. "You won't stay the weekend, at least?"

"I feel it would be under false pretenses," she said. "The idea of my staying here is to decide, and I have. I don't want to impose on Sophie."

"It's not just that," he said. "They're grateful to you. I'm grateful to you. For giving me back my life."

Only she and Gwydion knew the full truth of that. "It was an even trade," she said. "I need to leave." Was it eagerness to see what other places had to offer? Was it fear she might change her mind? She wasn't sure, but she felt invisible hands pulled her onwards. "You could come with me." She tried again, even though she knew what he would say.

He shook his head. "I can't. Everything I need is here."

Everything – or Sophie? Anaea surprised herself with

bitterness. Why did it matter to her? But more than that, she felt despair for him. It would never get better.

"Maybe here isn't the only place you can find it," she said.

"There's nowhere like home. I can't leave, not when the voyage of the White Hound almost took me away forever." He pulled away from the railing. "Promise me you'll be careful? You're not like anyone in the known universe, and things that might be safe for others could be dangerous." His tone was soft, rueful; it apologized for his words. "You could spend a lifetime traveling and not reach every place."

She knew, with that gentle segue into advice, that he wouldn't be convinced. He had been her anchor in this strange universe, but would be no more. The enormity of it left her numb. "I know," she said.

They were both subdued for the rest of the night, a silent ache suspended between them. Sophie and Adrian noticed, it was evident, but neither asked. Anaea didn't want to explain until she had chosen her destination, and that was the thing that kept her awake that night.

On the face of it, it was an obvious choice. In the Collective, where women, if not the ones she knew, made the decisions, things would be easier, more familiar, probably more pleasant. She was good at moving with the flow; they would hardly notice her, as long as she learned the trends and kept up a quota of good deeds.

That was the very thing that pulled her away. She knew that world – if not entirely, then a quiet reflection in the shelter of Themiscyra. And the white serenity, its sameness, bothered her.

She would find disorder in the Empire, even in places less fiercely independent than Eastwood. The top levels of society made few rules except when impulse demanded, and there was no sure way to avoid pitfalls.

Perhaps, she considered, the challenge of living would be what she needed.

Anaea swung out of bed and tapped the link, browsing guides. She was going to the Pinnacle Empire.

*

She told Gwydion in the morning she had decided upon Nissyen on the far side of Annwyn. His reaction was short and shocked.

"You're going over to the Pinnacle?" he said. "Why? You don't know what goes through a male mind—"

"She's a woman," Sophie said drily. "Of course she doesn't. What's going on here?"

Anaea hesitated, not sure she would have an ally.

Gwydion leapt in. "It's dangerous," he said. "The big cities are chaos. Women on their own have few protections." She was surprised to find that, even living in the Sanctum, matriarch thinking had made him sure which was the greater of two evils.

"At least she could choose a smaller city, or a station commune like Manawydan. A center for the arts," he addressed Anaea then, face taut.

Anaea shook her head violently. "I've been indoors and contained all my life," she said. "I want to be under open skies and feel earth."

Only then did she realize what she had said, and flicked a furtive look at Sophie, but if the woman was pensive, it was not to do with any hidden import in her guest's words.

"Every city, every place known to man is inherently contained," Sophie said. "Drawing boundaries is what people do. It's only a question of degree." She paused, studied Anaea. "There are few population centers outside the large cities on Annwyn. Nissyen is not as bad as some. Certainly, you would not be comfortable among the scattered farmers and isos."

Anaea recognized the terms isos, used to describe people who cut themselves off both in virtual and physical space, often hundreds of miles from the nearest population center and dozens from a neighbor who they might see twice a year. It was beyond Anaea to imagine what that would be like.

"You're all right with my leaving?" Anaea asked.

"Of course not," Sophie said with a smile, "but it is your decision, and one cannot keep a person in place by nailing down their shoes."

"By what?"

"Folk expression. People" – she gave Gwydion a gentle but pointed look – "used to hold construction together with iron spikes known as nails."

"She could pick a safer destination," Gwydion said. "She's not—" He caught himself. "She isn't familiar with cities or the warlords."

Anaea relaxed, releasing the tension of what he had almost said. His protectiveness unsettled her, but she couldn't believe there was such cause for alarm. It was the first time she had doubted him, and it shook her more than leaving.

"Hundreds of people emigrate every week," Sophie said, "if not more. Whatever makes you think you need to protect her?"

*

That settled the matter. The next shuttle to New Athens was at three o'clock in the afternoon, with off-planet transit an hour later and then a change of vessels on the other side of the Bridge. Anaea was astonished how simple it was to arrange transportation across light-years and corridors. The calculations automatically synced with galactic time.

Adrian seemed ready to question her chances of survival in the Empire, but a glance from his wife silenced him. She heard the brothers talking in the hallway; when she leaned out to ask Gwydion a question, they stopped. Was it a conspiracy amongst the gender or amongst the family?

As three o'clock approached, a light mist settled over the Sanctum. Adrian handed out weather bubbles to shield them from the rain. Anaea declined. Penelope seemed eager to frolic in the damp, and what might have been an awkward trip was occupied pulling her away from puddles.

They arrived early. Adrian snagged an arm around his wife; she rested her head on his shoulder. Gwydion talked Anaea through the checklist they had reviewed two hours ago. He was anxious, so she forgave him: for himself, he would have done it thrice more.

The shuttle descended and disgorged a few passengers, met by Sanctum relatives. The bell sounded for boarding. Anaea glanced around, realized she was the only person headed in that direction. She squared her shoulders, picked up the duffel-bag Sophie had given her, and started forward.

"Good luck," Gwydion said.

She turned. "Thank you," she said. "For your hospitality and understanding – for everything." She held his gaze longer than those of the others but she could still see them out of the corner of her eye, nestled, serene.

It was a decision she made suddenly, hoping it would help him with the pretense he struggled to maintain. She dropped the bag, hurried back to him and clasped his arms with her hands. She kissed him.

He was stunned, then responsive, his lips soft against hers, unfamiliar contrast to a trace of roughness on his skin. They pressed gently, instinctive, no thought. She didn't have to stretch up to meet him, an ease which briefly delighted her. Her brain pivoted with points of light, seeking definition and not finding it; too hazy, too light, to come back to the ground. Her body tingled, warm as an imagined summer.

She broke it off before it became too confusing, before she didn't want to stop. His eyes were too large and intent, hunting for something in her face.

"Anaea . . ." he said.

"Don't talk," she said, aware the explanation might sound like an excuse, hoping he would come to it on his own. Her heart thundered, drumming up half-formed thoughts.

"Now that's a goodbye," Adrian chortled.

That knocked Anaea out of her thoughts. She scampered to retrieve the duffel-bag, was afraid to look back. She hurried onto the shuttle, Penelope at her feet.

"Anaea, don't forget—" The singing doors swallowed his last words.

Anaea's heart descended with the shuttle's rise. The kiss had been a distraction for Sophie. The rush she had felt was the rush of the unfamiliar, of physical contact new to her, nothing more. She stayed at the window and watched the Sanctum shrink long past the point where she could make out any details.

Don't forget what? No matter what he had intended to say, she knew she wouldn't.

The leaving hurt, and she took a deep breath to steady herself. Maybe, she thought, her real calling in life was to say goodbye.

Or maybe, just maybe, this was the beginning of something new. The wildness of the Pinnacle Empire promised something completely unknown, and she was surprised to find a little tingle of excitement at the possibility of danger. Had her adventure with Gwydion opened a new side of her, something more daring?

Probably not, she thought wryly. She was still herself, a little shy, a little awkward, a girl out of place, except now, she had an expanse in which to search for somewhere she fit.

*

NEW ATHENS WAS bewildering, but Anaea remembered most details from her previous trip. There was a bad patch with Penelope and permits, but Sophie had walked her through the process, and she was able to convince the officials it was an unrecorded species without raising eyebrows.

The guestlink was removed at the spaceport. Interminable lines, pleasant, smiling faces and too many personal details later, Anaea boarded the Io. It was a live-in spaceship, meant to accommodate thirty people as seamlessly as if they had never left home. The onboard clocks recorded artificial ship time, which was easier on the brain; they could worry about time dilation at the other end.

The primary decorating colors were sage green and drab pink. Anaea found it medicinal, which was not unpleasant for her, but a few passengers complained. She watched them, trying to study without being noticed.

A stick-thin elderly gentleman traveling with two stammering secretaries was a businessman bound for Independence. The matronly woman and her son; seven years old, with a penchant for climbing fixtures were bound for Centurion Station to see her husband, a soldier stationed there. It was obvious from the tightness around her eyes she didn't approve of his occupation. The child was more interested in the adventure than seeing his father.

A portly redhead was also bound for the DN-48 system, but not for Annwyn. He was a biologist tasked to study lifeforms on the planet, Avalon. He didn't speak unless his head was ducked and his eyes down, but he cooed to Penelope as if she were a child and tossed her candies from his pocket.

Anaea studied the kearl critically that evening. Was she getting fatter?

"We may have to put you on a diet," she said.

Penelope hissed.

Shipboard food came from an automated dispenser, charged to your account. The central system was designed to answer hundreds of questions, from directions, though it was impossible to get lost, to how long the Io had taken to construct. In short, the crew had done everything possible to ensure contact was unnecessary, and consequently were ghosts.

The trip across the Bridge seemed to take longer than Anaea remembered. Gwydion had said her shuttle was more advanced, but then again, travel time through hyperspace was nebulous. She savored the light feeling in her body, but not everyone did. The male of a young married couple threw up hourly.

They emerged with a thunk of dead weight. Anaea was glad there were no viewing portals: she didn't want to see Centurion Station looming over them.

"All passengers please assemble in the main corridor."

Anaea scampered out and stood behind the mother and son. The docking door opened.

Bright lights blinded Anaea; an acrid scent hit her nose: old grease and something less pleasant. As her eyes adjusted, the corridor swarmed with mountainous forms. Fear hit her, low and visceral.

"No one move!" The voice was loud enough she swore the hairs on the back of her neck went white. "This is Centurion Port Authority, and this ship and everyone on it are under investigation. If you give us trouble, I guarantee it will be the last thing you do."

Those mountains were soldiers in grey uniform. Flat faces stared at the travelers, summed them up and found them wanting. Some glowered; most maintained a predator's gaze.

Their leader's uniform was trimmed in gold. He did a rapid head-count, his lips crinkling in distaste. "All right," he said, "march out."

The landing bay was dim but spotless. Cleaning fumes wafted with the shadows. Another group of soldiers had rounded up the crew, who looked miserable. Only the engineer seemed calm, sneering.

"In my father's time," the leader commented, moving to a position where both groups could see him, "you lot would have been tossed back across the Bridge, with or without your ship. None of you are worth my energy," he continued. "Take their bags and frisk them."

It was a methodical process with the threat of violence below the surface. Catching the tension, Penelope growled and arched her back. Anaea wished she could do the same, or better, shrink into a corner to hide.

When two soldiers approached Anaea, she offered her duffel-bag. The kearl snapped her teeth.

The soldiers stopped and stared. "What in starfire is that?" one demanded.

"Little beast wants to bite us," the other said, reaching down. Penelope danced back, wrapping the leash around Anaea's leg. "Come here, you little—"

"Penelope, easy, he's not going to hurt you," Anaea tried, but there was no hope of the kearl minding her. She spun to keep herself from being tangled in the leash.

Faint, throttled snickers rose from the passengers. The leader strode over in search of the source of the commotion.

"What is the meaning of this?" he demanded.

Anaea flinched, and a trickle of anger rose within her. She remembered what Gwydion had said about being direct, and then her body was ahead of her thoughts. She intercepted the leader's pointing finger with a firm hand, a doctor's hand.

"Your man is scaring my pet," she said. "Ask him to stop."

A rasping sound backed up in his throat. Before he could speak, warm brandy laughter washed over them.

The leader whirled to face the origin: a wiry figure in an elaborate uniform. "I'll take care of this one," the arrival said, reaching out to take Anaea's arm, and because his grip was firm but not harsh, and because Penelope did not shy away, Anaea let him.

She realized that might have been a bad idea as the clumps of people in the landing bay shrunk and they walked under the bulk of another ship. This one was thick, broody, with evil-looking protrusions.

She cleared her throat. "Sir—"

"You have no need for concern, and nor do your fellow passengers," he said. "It's a routine search. Have to let the boys blow off steam somehow. Unless that is a ship of rogues and villains?"

Still feeling uneasy, Anaea chuckled at the amusement in his voice. "No, sir."

He waved a hand in front of a sensor panel. It opened to allow them into a dim corridor. "Who are you, then?" They exchanged introductions; he was the division captain. "I'll drop you off at processing," he said. "You can stay in the civilian barracks until your ship arrives."

"I'm booked on the Barricuda," she said. "Is it delayed?" Then she wondered how a captain would know about the movement of a random ship.

"Not so much delayed as discouraged," he answered. "Warlord's orders. The two ruffians who fly the Barricuda ducked some tax." He shrugged, unconcerned. "You should get your travel permits transferred to the Bleak. Reliable sorts; no one's broken them yet."

"Thank you for the advice," Anaea said, pleasantly surprised.

"Think of it as repayment for the shock of arrival." He opened another door to a dingy chamber. "Through here."

Anaea turned to ask a question, but the door had closed, and on this side it looked armored. She joined the line of people waiting to be processed.

The questions were fewer, but more penetrating, and often repeated, as if the wary guards expected falsehoods that could be revealed by asking the question more loudly. They were openly contemptuous of her Collective credentials, her money vouchers, and her very presence. Twice, she was bounced back in the line while they moved someone else forward.

She requested the ship transfer timidly and received a martyred look. "It'll be done." He slapped a wristband on her like those from Eastwood. "Next!"

Cut loose from the bureaucracy, she spun aimlessly until her steps took her towards an exit. She found the civilian barracks by dint of looking for the only open door.

It turned out to be a room almost as large as the landing dock, divided into countless alcoves with beds. Holographic light rose up from some entryways, sheltering the occupants. Newly accustomed to the wide spaces of the Sanctum, Anaea felt her shoulder blades itch with the urge to pull in and be smaller.

Some alcoves had digital placards with names; others were blank. Anaea wandered, hearing mothers shushing children, two teenagers laughing boisterously. Finally, it occurred to her there was no allocation of spaces, and she could choose as she would.

She wound to a corner, three spaces from the nearest occupied bunk. She pressed her palm on the panel and it lit with her name, translucent walls materializing for an illusion of privacy.

She stood for a moment, watching the bunk. She had chosen to come here, yet even the penitent quarters in Themiscyra were more comfortable.

Anaea tossed the duffel-bag on the bed and chivvied Penelope inside, looping the leash around the bedrail. She rummaged and learned the plastine toy she had purchased for the kearl had gained a Sanctum-born sister in transit, a bright pink rabbit. "Thank you, Sophie," she said, shaking her head.

She hunted up the visitor mess hall, which served bland gloop. The man on duty at currency exchange treated her to narrow looks and subtle jibes. Out of the corner of her eye, she noticed two men haggling over vials filled with a viscous grey liquid.

It was Lisle extract, a controlled substance with psychoactive properties. The biologist from the Io had gone on about it at length; how the Lisle was a beautiful creature, bushy like a fox and coiled like a snake, and it was shame to milk it for human misuse.

As if thinking about him had summoned him, he turned the bend. Stunned, she stared at his face, mashed and bloodied, and his escort – neither for show nor blowing off steam now. He could hardly walk; the soldiers dragged him when he faltered. She stumbled backwards.

"Smuggler," the exchange officer observed in a bored voice. "Too many people think they can drop down to Avalon in the guise of studying the wildlife and they won't be caught."

"He doesn't look like that kind of person," she said.

The officer snorted. "How would you know?"

She had no answer for that. "What will happen to him?"

"If he's lucky? He'll stand trial on Annwyn. If he's not . . ." The officer shrugged, dismissive. "Doubt he'll make it there."

He dismissed Anaea, beckoning the person behind her. She stood motionless, seized with the urge to run after the biologist, as if she could do something to help.

Consequences in imperial space were dire, whether the offense was real or imagined . . . and how would she even know which was which?

*

There was no simulation of day and night on Centurion Station: the lights never brightened, never dimmed. Anaea simply chose to collapse and call it morning when the alarm roused her.

She was still on edge as she ventured out to board the Bleak. She approached the ship with four other passengers. They looked like she felt, rumpled and red-eyed.

The loading dock dropped, and a heavyset woman in garish clothes and fluorescent make-up ushered them aboard. She had a stunner at one hip and a broad-barreled blaster at the other. The first mate who greeted them was dressed and armed just as fully.

He smirked, looking the group up and down. "Aren't we a sorry collection. Settle in and strap down. The first one to complain is on the menu if we get stranded in space. Rita! Ramp up, full throttle and tell the monkeys on control if they don't make way for us, we'll make our way through whichever ship's ahead on the roster."

Anaea turned and was surprised to find the dock had retracted. The first mate's tone was jovial, but the heavy arms made her nervous. Had the advice from the division captain been double-edged, some kind of trap? What had she walked into?

Even if she could turn back, she had no way of knowing if there would be a better berth. She had to keep moving forward.

15

The Bleak was a cargo ship, not a passenger liner. The smallest of its four bays had been set up with prefabricated room-units, walls not thick enough to block out the sounds of the crew shoving, jostling, rejoicing in their work. The low, restive sounds of animal cargo thrummed like engines, and Anaea wondered if the Bleak was carrying the contraband animals for which the biologist had been arrested.

The departure from Centurion Station jarred bones and rattled the walls. The room-unit had a rudimentary webbing system; Anaea clung frantically and winced as she heard Penelope shriek. Just as she could feel her stomach consider the benefits of divesting its contents, the bouncing slowed.

"Oh, because you—" the woman's voice crackled overhead, then paused as she seemed to realize she was on the loudspeaker. "Y'all can unstrap and go about your business. Mess is across the hall, and it lives up to its name. No wandering."

Anaea released herself from the restraints and oozed to the floor. Penelope clambered into her lap, tail twitching, and groomed her clothing. Anaea stroked the kearl and let her do as she pleased until something ripped under agitated paws.

"Easy, you," she said, scooping a hand under Penelope's belly and lifting her away. "We're fine, see?" She placed the creature on the bed and stepped outside, still wobbling.

A slim young man with an improbable mop of teal, cherry and chestnut hair knelt by the access panel for his unit and prodded at the circuits. He started and looked up, flashing her a grin. He had his hands in the guts of the panel, but showed no self-consciousness at being caught.

"Hey," he said. "Just trying to short the overrides. Wouldn't want to be locked in here."

"Is that legal?" Anaea winced when it came out of her mouth.

He took no offense, grin broadening. "As long as I don't get caught, it's in the rules of the game. Wits to wits. Anyone who uses shoddy old prefabs like this without some heavy mods deserves to be caught with passengers roaming wild. Sec!" This seemed to be a request to wait, for his head whipped around and the panel had his attention. It emitted a series of sickly beeps, then a crackle and finally silence.

"Done," he said. She saw the gadget in his hand then: a bewildering series of protrusions, only some of which she could identify. It obviously wasn't a single device, but three or four discrete objects fused together into an improbable but workable whole.

He thrust it in her direction. "Tobias Risingsun Mortimer, but most people call me Flick."

She regarded the gadget at a loss. "Ah . . ."

"Oh! Sorry." He tucked it into his belt and offered his hand instead. "Good to meet."

"Anaea Carlisle," she said. "It's good to meet you, Tobias."

His nose twitched. "Flick."

"Flick?"

"Like the flick of an old switch," he said. "I'm a Tweaker. The universe is in binary and it's always turned to the wrong digit, hmm? Do you want me to fix your door?"

"No, I think I—"

"Don't mind getting locked in?" He planted his hands on his hips; she noticed the length of his fingers. "Well, suit yourself, I suppose."

"It's not that," Anaea said. "I don't want to get in trouble."

Tobias – Flick – stared, eyes widening in exaggerated surprise. "Sorry, I'm not sure you're making any sense."

She had to laugh. "Are you always like this?"

"Being me, I'm not sure I would notice the difference." Flick tipped his head. "I'd offer to buy you a meal, but seeing as it's served free, that would be tricky."

She had skipped breakfast. "I am feeling somewhat peckish."

"Peckish? I haven't heard that word since the last time I saw my grandmum. Well, peckish it is; you want to come?" His gesture undulated his whole body. He was oddly made, with too much nose and too short a torso.

Anaea followed him into the mess. The food service was automated and dispensed anonymous squares of synthetics. Flick loaded up on imitation pastries; Anaea chose oatmeal.

"No wonder you're so skinny," he said.

"This is all I wanted." Anaea wondered why she sounded apologetic.

"I have a fast metabolism," he continued. "I pack food away like no one's business. My grandmum used to say she would have sold me into slavery except the question always came up: 'Is he cheap to feed?'"

Anaea felt her cheeks cool. "Slavery?"

Flick blinked owlishly, then burst out laughing. "What do you Collective people think of us? We're still the same people under the skin. Less difference between you and me than between different countries back on Earth."

Anaea thought this was disputable, but even had she tried, he was still talking.

"There's no slavery like that. Of course there's long-term binding agreements and that sort of thing, but you have laws for that, too." Flick grinned wryly. "I came this close to crossing the Bridge to look for my fortune, but then the dice came up for Defiance."

It took her a moment to realize that was the name of a place, not a description of his course of action. "Did you find what you were looking for?" she asked.

He made a face. "Not so much. Took more than I'd expected to carve out a niche. Local Tweakers didn't like a young hotshot horning in, and the hypermentals keep a lock on all of Independence's big cities. I don't need someone looking over my shoulder from fifty feet away, it's creepy.

"Anyhow, I finally stumbled into some payoffs and stashed up a sum, but with all the work, the cost of being away from home, the trip back . . ." He shrugged, peering almost quizzically at the remnants of his pastry. Anaea couldn't figure out when he'd had time to eat it. "I'm not much better off than I would have been if I'd stayed."

"I'm sorry," she said.

"At least I have something to show for it," he said. "And grandmum—" His face pulled in, the first sign of reticence she had seen. "It will be good to get home."

"Where is home?"

"Nissyen, near the Silver district; locals call it the Cauldron," he said. "Born there. Probably die there." This bit of fatalism was delivered with a glint in his eyes.

She took the opportunity to press. "Is there anywhere in that district you recommend for a new arrival?"

"Nowhere," he said. Her face must have been startled, for he continued, "You might not understand. I know your matriarchs keep the luckless from falling too low because helping them gets some kind of payoff, but the Cauldron is a poor area. Filled with people who know survival is an art-form. I love my home—" his expression flushed, set with pride "—but I don't expect anyone else to share that sentiment. You would probably be more comfortable uptown."

But she wouldn't, and he was so friendly it was on the tip of her tongue to say something. She swallowed it. He was still right: she had no sense of his world. How did she begin if she was always turned away for ignorance?

"Why are you traveling to Nissyen?" he asked.

"I'm looking for a home," she said.

"What was wrong with the one you left behind?"

She smiled. "It was too isolated. They didn't want to admit the rest of the universe existed."

Flick barked laughter. "There are times I don't want to admit the rest of the universe exists. Does that mean you're going to shun me? But it's been my experience," he continued, sobering, "that you don't find a home. It finds you."

"Let's hope it does," she said. The thought seemed impossibly far away.

*

THEY ATE A second meal together later on. Flick talked about his experiences in Defiance, his inventions, and his grandmother, who seemed to be the only family he had. Anaea pieced together what a Tweaker was: a salvage expert who could give anything that might otherwise have been thrown away a new form and purpose, and an inventor without government sanction or funding. A unique product of the Pinnacle Empire.

She found that by phrasing her questions in an open-ended manner, she could keep Flick talking while sharing little in return. His cheerful spates of information sputtered out occasionally into jokes or questions, but he seemed more interested in what she thought of the crew or hypermentals or philosophy than personal details.

"I mean, supposing they give every child an aptitude test," he said. "Whatever they turn out to be good at, that's what they do in life. It'd be efficient, right?"

"How could you possibly design a test that would cover all variables?" Anaea asked.

He crinkled his nose. "Neural mapping on a particular field of tests could manage that, but you're avoiding the point. Would it be good for people?"

"I don't know," she answered. "I'm not an expert—"

"You don't have to be an expert!" he burst out, gesturing wildly with his fork. "You just have to be human. You just have to have a heart in things."

She wondered what he would think of her home. "I suppose just as a thought exercise—"

The ship shuddered. Anaea's plate slid out of her grasp and clattered on the floor. An animal bellowed.

An unfamiliar voice thundered through the overhead. "Captain of the Bleak, you have twenty seconds to surrender. Passengers of the Bleak, the warning shot you have experienced represents only a fraction of our firepower, and your only chance is to prevail upon your ship's commander not to test it."

The voice faded out, and was replaced by the tail end of creative cursing from the Bleak's captain. ". . . frighten the passengers into mutiny, of all the—"

"You're on broadcast," someone else said. The overhead hissed silent.

Anaea rose in a flurry, blood humming in her ears. Pragmatism pulled her panic into stillness. She looked to Flick for reaction, hoping to see him serene, even bored or amused, but he sat shaking his head like a furry dog. The two other passengers in the mess clung to each other even though they were strangers, faces white.

"Everyone remain calm," the captain's voice continued. "They don't know who they're dealing with. The Bleak has outgunned and outrun every decent pirate in the sector."

"What about the indecent ones?" Flick said *sotto voce*, though his voice cracked on the words.

The deck pitched. The furniture was secure; nothing else was. Anaea tumbled, landing elbow-first in a corner with the remnants of two or three lunches. Voices yowled; animal or human, it was impossible to tell. Her arm throbbed.

Flick grabbed her wrist before she could stand. "Should've known a berth like this wouldn't have high-grade inertial dampeners," he said. "Stay down. Crawl along the fixtures. Though really, where are you going? It's raining food, what more could you ask for?"

She recognized his manic cheer as panic and swallowed. The sound exploded in her ears. She focused on something she could control. "My pet," she said.

"She's safer in the pod," he said. "The padding will—"

The world flipped over again. Anaea managed to hold on until it righted, eyes squeezed shut. Someone shouted from the corridor.

A crackling explosion popped over her head. She thought she might have shrieked; Flick's fingers dug into her arm.

"That was inside the ship," he said.

She managed to collect herself enough to ask, "How do you know?"

"Because if it came from outside, at that volume, we would be venting atmosphere . . . and people." Flick's free hand conducted an emergency search of his belt. "Nothing's gone loose."

Their flight path steadied, and it seemed to Anaea the ship had slowed. She remained in a crouch, trying to find where her heart had landed.

"I think we're okay." Flick spoke softly, as if afraid louder words would contradict him.

"Does this happen often?" Anaea whispered.

He shook his head. "Not in my experience."

The beasts on board squealed like torquing metal . . . or damaged internals sounded like a pack of hyenas. Anaea shivered. The people on the other side of the mess picked themselves up, the homely young man clinging to the severe older woman.

Two crewmen burst into the mess, weapons drawn, flanking

the first mate. Rivulets of sweat pasted his hair to his brow. "You!" he said, pointing at Flick. "Did you mess with your lockpad?"

Flick smiled uneasily, backing off and using Anaea's shoulder as a shield. "Well, you know, sometimes those things just malfunction."

"We don't have time for you to be cagey," the first mate said. "Are you a Tweaker, boy?"

Flick drew himself up. "Man."

The female crewman fixed her aim on him. "Stop being cute."

"Yes, yes!" Flick's hands flitted up in surrender. "I'm a Tweaker. I swear I didn't do any harm——"

"You're on repair," the first mate said. "We evaded the pirates and entered an asteroid belt, but the weapons system is shorted. If we poke our nose back into open space, it's going to get shot off."

"What about your engineer?" Flick asked.

"He's busy with the life support, which they also hit. More important, don't you think? Besides, the weapons are a foreign installation." The first mate scowled. "Do you want to get to our destination, *boy*?" The word conveyed contempt and menace in the same heartbeat.

The tension in the air buzzed. Flick seemed to be as anxious about attempting the repairs as denying the crewmen. Anaea understood why. What would happen if he tried and failed . . . or worse, if the repairs didn't hold through encounter with the pirates?

The young man dithered. "I'm going to need a hand——"

"I'll help," Anaea said.

All four looked at her as if she had suggested growing extra limbs. "You have any experience?" the first mate asked.

"I know enough to follow instructions," she said with more confidence than she felt. She had interned in engineering, studied her mother's specs with interest, but she had decades of divergent technology to contend with.

Flick offered her a weak smile of gratitude. "Yeah, I suppose

Anaea can help me," he said. "But I can't promise anything, understand?"

The first mate turned on his heel. "This way."

"You shouldn't have gotten yourself into this," Flick whispered as they followed. "I don't know what they'll do to me if I can't fix it."

"Then better you have help," she said.

He ignored this to insist: "They could dump me out in space. They could dump both of us."

Her disbelief reached her lips before the chill of nerves did. "Surely they wouldn't go so far—"

"They can always claim the pirates got us. No one would know otherwise." He jammed his hands in his pockets. "We can't help, we're dead weight."

Anaea fell silent. Flick had someone who would look for him. She did not.

"There are eight empanelments," the first mate said as they entered the engineering area. "In groundman's terms, one for each cardinal direction, plus two up, two down. Bridge controls are operational, but the central conduit is another story."

The weapons control conduit had once been three featureless plastine pillars, their secrets sealed beyond touch. Now coils and block protrusions boiled out from broken seams, heaped together into an asymmetrical beast.

Flick hissed. "Now that's a jabberwocky job."

"Impressed?" the first mate asked, missing his tone. "It's not bad for a high-tech system rolled into an antique."

Anaea suppressed the urge to laugh as she saw the strained look on the Tweaker's face. He seemed about to make a sarcastic remark; then his eyes went to the first mate's holster, and his expression blanked.

"It will do," he said. "You can leave now."

"And have you pocket spare parts? I don't think so," the first mate said. "You two – watch him. I want a preliminary report in ten." With that, he disappeared, leaving the two armed figures to loom over the impromptu repair crew.

Flick removed a tool from his belt. "Come on, Anaea, help me with middle panel."

The panel groaned as they opened it and emitted a puff of acrid smoke. Flick shoved his head inside, starting a patter of analysis under his breath. He hooked a reading device from his belt, but consulted it rarely.

"Hosed," he said. "Someone thought they were building in redundancies, but they ended up with fishtails. It's useless for our purposes."

"Can you alter the chain protocol?" Anaea asked. "They can't all fire at once."

He scrunched up his face. "Difficult, but – yeah. Look for a bright yellow switch . . ." He yelped, jerking backwards as sparks sprayed. "What a jabberwock! If something growls, back off. It could blow."

They spent several moments sorting through the wreckage, Flick calling out parts, Anaea locating them. The machine hummed and crackled, spitting energy and the occasional curl of smoke. Every time, she fought the impulse to leap back. Finally, the Tweaker thunked on his heels.

"Put through to your boss," he told the crewmen. "I've got a sitrep." He panted, hands twitching on his knees.

The first mate's voice came on the overhead. "What is it?"

"I can get you one, two, five and eight," he said. "Those are the empanelments that will still work. The others need to be replaced."

"Unacceptable." At those words, the crewmen toyed with their weapons. Anaea backed up and tripped over a coil. She steadied herself on the pillar, feeling panicked and silly at the same time. Her heart quivered.

Flick swallowed, hiccuping over nerves. "Unavoidable."

Silence, a locking of wills without faces to match. Anaea heard her heartbeats counting the time, loud as thunder. Finally, the first mate snorted. "Do what you can."

Flick made a little sound and whirled back. "Can you calibrate laser output, Anaea?"

She shook her head. "I've never seen a weapon system before."

"You've never seen . . ." His hand came down on the panel to steady himself. "Where did you come from again?"

Anaea realized her slip and took a verbal step back. "Of course I've seen them, but not this close."

He didn't seem to believe her, but after an anxious glance at their minders, he let it go. "I can talk you through the process."

It was sweaty, fiddly, tedious, made worse by its urgency. She scrubbed at her face and was surprised when her hand came away black.

Flick halted, sudden stillness. He shook his head, once, twice, as if it would dislodge his thoughts.

"Flick?" she asked.

He jumped, banging his hand on a coil. His lips tightened, not quite smiling. "What if I told you it's not going to work?"

She read his expression, a new kind of fear, weighing the odds. "Is that what you're telling me?"

"I don't want them to put you in the middle," he said softly. "You don't know anything, huh? Just tell him—"

"Tell me what?" the first mate inquired.

Flick's smile appeased, but without hope. "My first estimate was optimistic. Can't be done."

He narrowed his eyes. "Coming out of this alive should be sufficient fee."

"It's not about that. There is such a thing as impossibility, you know."

Anaea stayed silent, still confused by what he had been trying to tell her. She longed for the easy and private exchange she could have had with Gwydion: confirmation, coordination and trust. Yet she knew more about Flick now than she had known about Gwydion when she had agreed to help the hypermental leave Themiscyra.

"Look, Anaea is seeing the same things I am," Flick said, rolling his eyes at her in mute appeal.

"I'm not an expert," she said, "but I think—"

"You think." The first mate gestured, and both weapons trained on her. She longed to close her eyes, but couldn't look away. "That's the thing about thinking. It changes so easily."

"Hey, keep her out of this," Flick said.

"Then give me the solution," the first mate replied. "A half hour ago, you were confident you could restore half the system. What's changed?"

He stared, jaw slack. "There's a power-knot in the fifth empanelment," he said slowly. "It's a physical problem in the firing mechanism. Outside, on the hull of the ship. To be fixed, someone has to go out there, and it that has to be done on the ground, under atmosphere, with twenty less variables," he added, color returning to his cheeks.

"We have the emergency suits and appropriate gear." The first mate lifted an eyebrow. "We could always put you out there without it."

And this was the ship, Anaea thought, dizzy, the captain at Centurion Station had recommended as better and safer than its peers.

"We face pirates without weapons," the first mate continued, "better than even chance we're all ashes. You may want to tempt the odds, but I don't – and I've got the guns."

"The calibration is highly technical," Flick said. "I have to be on this side."

"Easy." The first mate shrugged. "We'll send your girl out there."

"She's not my—"

There was no other choice. She made herself speak before the courage left her. "I'll do it," she said. "Just tell me what you need."

16

F LICK PROTESTED, BUT WHEN PRESSED FOR ANOTHER solution he twined his fingers together and muttered. The first mate guided her to the airlock with every courtesy except holstering his weapon.

The atmosphere suit flowed against the lines of her body, releasing a thin coating of gel to fix itself in place. She grimaced as it bonded to skin. She was used to similar technology, but had liked it no better under practice conditions. Hopefully, it worked as well as the suit she remembered. The uncertainty jarred her, wedging a shard of panic in her mind.

The first mate rapped through the protocols, speaking so fast she missed pieces. He did not look inclined to answer questions, and she couldn't make her mouth move to ask them. But the protocols were familiar, and she began to relax. She could feel her heartbeat against the suit, and it was slow and steady.

She found the communications relay and turned it on. "Flick?"

"Top o' the morning to you." He sighed and tried to joke. "I expect a discount on my ticket."

Anaea drew a deep breath and released anxiety with it. "I'm ready to go out."

"Break a leg."

A short tether, meant only for the transition to the hull. Grip-gloves for her hands. They were misnamed, for they applied magnetic energies rather than physical force. The first mate did a distracted double-check of the equipment and pushed her into the airlock before she could wonder what he might have missed. It closed, sealing her away.

Her breath blurred against the face-plate of the suit. The airlock depressurized, and the weight of her body trickled out; it was like dissolving. She let herself flow with it. Then the exterior door slid away, and clear, sharp blackness beckoned.

She curled her fingers in the gloves and inched along the wall. Her right hand grasped nothing. She brought it around to the side of the ship and shimmied, a graceless manuever. She breathed a command to the inside of the suit and the pressure holding the boots decreased.

"Don't let it all the way up," Flick said. "It will keep you steady."

Anaea knew this, but wasn't sure she would have remembered. She turned to her left and found the floating lead of the long tether. Feet braced. Grip-gloves relaxed. Movements slow, not that the suit allowed anything else. Breathing just as slow, a meditative pitch against the increasing thump of her heart.

She caught the hook at the end of the tether. She tried to latch it on the bar on the hull and missed. A nervous giggle popped up on her lips.

"What's so funny?" Flick asked.

"You had to be there," she said.

"No, thank you."

She secured the hook on the third try and popped the bar into place. It was some of the most important emergency equipment a ship had. It would hold, had to hold. It was the only thing to keep her from tumbling out into the emptiness.

An image of the hodge-podge weapons relay flashed through her mind. She suppressed the ill taste in her mouth, turning away from the hull.

Eternity held out its hands before her. From them tumbled gem-like asteroids, hanging as if caught in mid-fall. Flashes of light leapt out at her, then disappeared as she sought the source. She tried to guess the distance between some of the asteroids and failed. She stared in wonder, could have watched forever. Fear became a distant whisper.

"Anaea, we have to do this." His voice and its quaver brought the fear back along with her mission.

"Sorry. I'm here." She turned and slid the grip-glove along the hull, inching like a spider. She kept running through the interior of the ship in her head, wondering when it had grown. She fought to stay calm.

Finally, she reached a curve. "Flick, I'm at the corner," she reported. "Where do I go from here?"

"Footwards," he said. "Just keep going until you can't see where you've been."

Anaea blinked at his description, but released her left foot to comply. The other came with it, and she spun, dropping with the torque of her body. Her grip-glove slid along the metal, doing nothing to slow her momentum.

She gasped out the commands. The grip-glove activated. The rest of her continued to tumble and jerked hard against the tether. The impact echoed in her teeth.

"Anaea?"

She secured her feet before replying. "I'm okay. Just a slip. Heading down now."

"Footwards," he corrected.

She smiled shakily and said nothing, working her way along the hull. Moving down – footwards – meant almost no line of sight; she had to go by feel when she could feel nothing through the suit, slipping by inches and using the suit's protocols cautiously. Sweat ran along the hollows of her neck, and the gel oozed out to meet it. Space might be cold, but she would never know it.

Flick's directions were accurate: as the curve of the hull disguised the asteroids she had first seen, she spotted the blackened bulk of the weapons empanelment to her left. She tried to suppress the nauseating sensation the pirates would appear as soon as her eyes were not on that portion of space and shoot off the small target.

The grip-gloves squeaked in protest: she was clenching her fingers. She made her hands ease and worked her way over.

"I'm here," she reported.

"You made good time," Flick said. His voice was nervous, covered by a breezy tone. "There should be four panels around the firing barrel. You'll know the correct one because it will be blackened."

"Err," she said, "there's only one that isn't."

"Buckets of bolts!" He said it as a curse. "The only thing to do is to start at the top. There should be a latch bar on the left and right sides of the panels."

She struggled to get the grip-gloves around the small latch on the top left panel. As soon as she pulled, it popped free, revealing dull silver circuitry.

"What do you see?" When she described it, he responded with a chittering sound.

"That's not it?" she asked.

"Nope. Keep moving."

What if she had to open all four? She thought her shoulders would give way first. Gritting her teeth, she crab-crawled to the next panel and found the bar was partway fused to the panel.

"Break it," he said. "They're going to have to put in for proper repairs when they landed anywise – don't you dare look at me like that. Ah, not you, Anaea, the dame with the gun."

Anaea turned the grip-glove to its highest setting and pulled. The metal snapped; the plate came away and drifted over her shoulder. She reached for it, was still anchored, and winced as resistance ripped through her arms. She freed herself in time to grab the plate and shifted it to her right hand so her dominant hand was free, not that handedness mattered much with the clumsiness of the gloves.

"I think I see it," she said. Of the five coils, three were dark and opaque. She described it hastily and was met with silence. Had the relay died? She shifted anxiously. "Flick?"

"Anaea, I think you had better come back," he said. "The sensors are picking up anomalous motion. Could be the pirates."

She looked down at the open panel and was unnerved to realize her primary feeling was frustration, not fear. The words rushed out of her, against sense and reason. "I'm here," she said. "I don't want to back out now. Can it be done quickly? Did I find the right panel?" Frenetic energy washed over her. She wanted to move, faster than the suit could possibly let her, and hanging in stasis was torture.

Flick made a noise of astonishment. "You—" He paused, obviously considering the time eaten up by arguing. "Squeeze each coil, then remove it. I should be able to tell from the readings."

Involuntarily, she glanced up the hull of the ship and fingered the tether. She could – she should – retreat. But if the pirates had found them and the ship didn't have weapons, this would all be for nothing.

It took her two tries to get a grip on the first coil. She pinched it.

"Got it. Pull it out."

Sweat inched down her brow, pulling a curl with it. The gel oozed around her temples, but the faceplate was the only part of the suit designed not to adhere.

"Recording readings – check," he said. "Replace it."

"That's not the one we need?" she asked.

"Can't know until we've tried all of them," Flick said. "I need to compare the readings. Anaea—" his voice dropped "—first mate says if it's pirates, they're firing the engines."

And she would be pulled along in its wake, a loose toy to be smashed against the hull. Anaea had trouble breathing, felt as if her heart stuck to her tongue. She knew she likely wouldn't see the pirate ship until it was too late, but all the sense in the universe couldn't keep her from craning back to look. With her right hand occupied with the loose plate and only her feet anchored, her senses swam as if she were tumbling.

If she turned back now . . .

She had no guarantee she would make it, that they would even risk opening the airlock. Her first attempt at words went nowhere. She forced air into her throat.

"I'm going to the other side," she said.

"Go."

She repeated the process. The coil stuck fast until she heaved; she suspected it was partly fused to the board.

She shot another frantic glance into the asteroid field. She tried to be soothed by the stillness, but instead, the shimmering of stars turned optical illusion, mimicking movement. She shivered, turned to the central coil. Though her fingers twitched in the gloves, she managed to keep them still enough to return the coil to its place. "That's the last one."

The silence stretched on, or maybe it was the combination of eternity and sweat. "Flick?" she asked.

His sigh gusted in her ear. "No pirates – we're clear," he said. "The anomaly was just that. False alarm. You can take it easy."

Anaea realized how fast her heart had been beating only as it slowed. "If it's all the same to you," she said, "I'd like to get finished as soon as I can."

"I hear you. Let me tabulate. Like I said, a jabberwocky through and through." He made another clicking sound. "Remove the central coil again – just let it float off. Squeeze the top coil and press down it bends. Then replace the plate. That should do it."

Anaea pulled the coil out and opened her hand. It hovered until she batted it away with the back of the glove. She watched the trajectory out into space, then reached for the other coil.

She flinched as she pressed down, expecting it to break, but with a whine, it torqued around the middle. She replaced the plate, frowning. "Flick, this isn't going to hold."

"Doesn't have to, not in the long run," he said. "Tamp it down as best you can and come back up. We're done."

"We're done," Anaea echoed. Inside the suit, accessible by touch, were the controls for the tether reel. She nudged the slow retract with her elbow.

The world whipped into sudden black-on-black motion, the reality of flying against a sensation of stillness caused by the unchanging landscape. Her stomach bent over itself in protest. The tether yanked her back and up – headwards – until her shoulder slammed into the hull, and she twisted about. She lifted her arms instinctively to shelter her head and regretted it when she collided with the ship again. The faceplate shut down, and she spun.

"Anaea! Are you all right?"

"Gwydion?" she wondered.

"Did you hit your head?"

She found herself clutching the bar to which the tether was affixed, unsure if she had blacked out and sore all over. She stared muzzily at the airlock door and mustered words.

"No. I'm bruised, but fine."

"What possessed you to punch the emergency retract? I know I'd want to get out of the great black as soon as possible, but that had to hurt."

"I didn't . . ." She paused, trying to replay the first mate's explanations in her mind. He had skipped over that detail, and she had assumed the suit operated the same way as the versions she knew. She bit down a protest of how that didn't make sense and amended, "It was an accident."

Two minutes later, she was inside the ship, peeling off interminable layers. The faceplate came off first, and she gulped in air, not caring there was no difference between the suit's breathing apparatus and the cycling system on board. Bits of gel stuck to her hair; others adhered to her skin and came off with a rip. By the time she stood in only her clothes, she felt like one mass of ache and itch.

The first mate thanked her in a handful of words and disappeared. Flick was more effusive: he pounced her in a full-body hug that made pain flare up, something that distracted her from the awkwardness of a near stranger embracing her.

"I owe you one," he said. "You're welcome to come stay with me on Nissyen. I know I told you how rotten it was, but it's what I have, so – it's yours."

"All I did was follow directions," she said. "Someone had to."

Flick snorted. "Speak for yourself, I'm terrible at following directions." He looked down at himself, wrinkling his nose at what had rubbed off her shirt. "Eww."

"I'm going to take a three hour soak and then apply some patches," she said. First, however, she needed to check on Penelope. She stumbled, her limbs moving of their own accord.

The chamber was a mess, pillow shredded, blankets strewn everywhere, the chair toppled. At first, she assumed it was the result of the Bleak's jostling; then, she realized two of the blankets were draped over the chair in the deliberate fashion of a nest.

Dark eyes peered out from the shadows. Penelope chittered.

"Bad kearl," Anaea said with no conviction. She bent down. Penelope scrambled out of the nest and leapt into her arms. Somehow, soothing the kearl was exactly what she needed.

*

WHILE ANAEA WAS ensconsed in the ship's facilities, eyes closed and thoughts floating, the Bleak left the shelter of the asteroid belt. Anti-climax to the past few hours, the pirates were nowhere to be found. Who knew whether they had given up or found better prey.

She was surprised to discover the lightness of hyperspace did not improve the dragging ache in her bones; if anything, it made her more aware of their stiffness. The patches helped, but she still felt wrung out and thin, a weaker version of herself. She missed being able to chatter with Orithia and the other girls; they would cluster in the corner of a mess hall after a rough day and grouse about the elaborate plans their instructors had clearly made to torture them.

She wobbled back to her room and found Flick there, kneeling on the floor and trying to coax Penelope out with a piece of cheese.

She put one hand on her hip, trying to feel indignant. "I locked it."

"Oh, well." He flashed her a sheepish smile. "I thought I'd wait for you. See how you were doing."

She was too tired to point out he could have waited outside. "Thank you, I guess. There's no need to fuss, though."

Flick popped up and leaned against the wall. "What kind of animal is that?"

She told the lie on autopilot, dropping onto the bed. He nodded and went back to brandishing the cheese.

"She doesn't like me," he said mournfully.

Anaea thought it was odd, for the kearl had warmed quickly to Gwydion. She shut off that line of thought with a sharpness that ached.

"Was the first mate satisfied with the repairs?" she asked.

"Does it matter if he was?" Flick said, looking sour. "Yeah, he said it was a good job. All's well that ends, I guess."

Penelope scampered out from under the chair and hopped onto her lap. Anaea winced, shunting her to one side.

"Hey," he wondered, "how's the pain?"

"Better," she said. "I coaxed one of the crew mates into letting me use the ship's medical pack, which had some stronger patches."

Shaggy brows flew up. "Those are for doctors."

"I have some basic training," she admitted.

He whistled. "A little bit engineer, a little bit doctor, what's it you actually do with yourself?" But the question was either rhetorical, or he decided to make it so out of politeness, for he continued, "I'd like you to come by my grandmum's home, when you can, if you don't mind doing another favor for me."

"What sort of favor?" she asked. Penelope bumped against her hand. She scratched the kearl behind the ears.

"My grandmum's last message came through complaining about some aches," he said. "Got me worried, but she would never waste money on a doctor. So—"

"I'm not a doctor," Anaea said. "I'm not anything." That was truth, spoken without thought, but stinging as soon as she said it.

Flick pursed his lips as if he would dive head-first into an argument on that point, but then he shook his head. "Just a look. If you don't detect anything, you don't, but at least it's something, and she's not going to mind a visitor."

Guilt warred with the desire to have a friendly place to stay and a growing curiosity about this shady side of society he seemed so convinced she could not handle. Finally, she said, "I can't promise anything. But you offered me your hospitality, and I would like that."

Flick's glinting eyes ducked out of sight with his nod. "That's a deal, but you're going to cause some comment. You seem like an uptowner."

"Tell people I'm evading a warlord who was overly interested in me," she said, remembering the story Gwydion had given in Eastwood.

"Oh, I'm not sure they'll believe that," Flick said, but his grin proved him to be teasing. "Then again, I suppose warlords do have incomprehensible tastes."

Penelope chittered as if understanding the tongue-in-cheek insult.

"Sorry, little one," he said. He offered a hand to Anaea. "Deal?"

She clasped it in hers. "Deal."

*

By the time they dropped out of the corridor in the DN-48 system, Anaea felt more human. She and Flick, occasionally joined by another passenger, talked of casual things, never touching upon personal subjects.

There was a viewscreen available to the passengers, and once they neared the third planet, Anaea went to watch. Both planet and moon were marbled spheres of blue and green, but easily distinguishable: Avalon was far larger than its inhabited satellite. The approach showed, through cloud cover, landmasses in winding, peninsular fingers.

Nissyen was on the far side of Annwyn, the side of the moon that faced perpetually outwards. She had a disconcerting double-view of planet and moon during the approach, which vanished as proximity to the smaller mass eclipsed the larger. A technician cleared them for descent; the captain bellowed at everyone to strap to the webs. Anaea fumbled herself in with Penelope clutched to her chest. Her tail beat a fervent tempo against Anaea's stomach.

The landing seemed to take forever. Even after the jarring stopped, there was no announcement on the overhead. Instead, a knock came on her door.

"Come in," she said, expecting it to be Flick. She was surprised when the first mate entered, and struggled to free herself from the web. "Is something wrong?"

"Nothing is wrong," he said, waiting for her to extricate herself. When she had, he handed her a pouch. "This is yours."

She pushed it open with one finger and found three small gemstones inside. Her eyes widened.

"A job well done is worth paying for," he said briskly. "We honor our debts." There was a touch of defensiveness in his voice.

"Thank you." She was heartened, more than he would know. The money didn't matter: she had enough, she judged, unless her search went on longer than she cared to think about. But there was gratitude here, a reckoning even for things that could be taken by force. It was something.

He nodded curtly and departed. A minute later, the captain instructed everyone to join him in the main corridor. Flick jostled her in greeting.

The ramp descended. Flick paused at the edge for a dramatic hauled breath. Then he pelted forward, pulling her along. Penelope hissed as the leash tugged in Anaea's hand.

"Home," he said, looking around the unprepossessing interior of the bay. "I'm finally home."

Anaea wondered if it might turn out to be home for her, as well.

17

THEY WOUND THROUGH A SERIES OF UTILITARIAN CORRI-
dors, the only decoration an infestation of scrolling text:
directions to customs and other locations, advertisements
and warnings. These last were accompanied by short bursts of
static that hit the base of Anaea's neck. Even after three or four,
she continued to crane back; it was impossible to ignore.

But Flick did ignore it, bounding ahead, chattering, something about a local sports team, an old friend, the lousy rainstorms
and the fact the whole spaceport needed a circuitry overhaul. "It's
going to go up in sparks one day," he predicted.

Anaea knew it was unreasonable, but jumped even so.
"Err . . ."

"Oh, not now," he dismissed it with an airy wave.

Customs proved to be much busier than on Eastwood or
Elysium. A press of people separated her from Flick. Penelope
clung to her ankles, bristling.

Now that Anaea had official credentials, the spindly agent was
less interested in her. "Purpose in Nissyen?" he asked.

"Vacation."

"Length of stay?"

"Two weeks." She hoped that would be enough to decide whether to stay or go.

For the first time, the agent fixed her with a square look. "Long way to come for a pleasure jaunt," he challenged.

She met his eyes. "Yes." Her heart quickened, but she said nothing more. Could a minor functionary cause trouble for her?

The agent shrugged. "Hold out your wrist." When she did, he slapped the back with a thin stick that flexed and adhered to the skin. "Two weeks, this will start emitting counter-pulses. None of the standard services will work for you. If you want to stay longer, file before that. You take your chances getting back into the complex otherwise. Any questions?"

Anaea shook her head, though she wondered what happened to people who missed the deadline. When they met up outside the customs area, Flick waved away her concerns. "Those sticks aren't hard to remove," he said. "Not if you're connected. And I know people who won't have forgotten they owe me favors." He wet his lips nervously. "Same goes for the reverse."

Anaea started to ask what he meant, but then they emerged into cold autumn air and harsh buffets of the wind and passing crowds. The acceleration sidewalks were sparsely populated; the strip between swarmed with upright vehicles; little more than platforms with hand grips. A few were designed with baskets for passengers, but they were the minority.

Anaea yelped in surprise as one passed overhead. Penelope's claws dug into her ankle.

Flick seemed to think nothing of it, weaving across the street with no announcement of their destination. His face glowed. "Home!" he said. "Nothing like it in the universe."

Nissyen was a city of scarlet and squares. Its thrusting angles and blood buildings, some bright, others dappled roan or brick, were interrupted by a thicket of smaller construction, more varied and shoved in wherever room might be made. Anaea vaguely sensed it was clean, the streets antiseptic in their tidiness, but the whirl of people, commotion and architecture made it all seem dusty and chaotic.

"Where are we going?" she asked.

"Cab-port." He hooked his arm through hers and steered her along. "Not going to call ahead, just drop in and surprise her."

The cab-port was a shelter bracketed by public terminals like those on Eastwood. A billboard loomed over it. The billboard shifted to show a miniature model of the city under flickering platitudes: "your victory awaits," then, "a new beginning starts here," and Anaea stopped reading. A dark face in profile accompanied the text.

Anaea noticed as the image moved that there was a crude moustache scrawled on the board's screen, with obscenities curling around it.

Flick studied this, making a face. "Not terribly clever. It's sort of a game," he explained. "Cleaning sensors will kick in soon. It's a victimless crime."

"Is that the warlord?" she wondered.

"Sure thing. I'm a little surprised he's still gracing billboards, honestly." Flick grinned.

Anaea summed up that statement and the graffiti. "He's unpopular?"

"No more than any warlord and less than some." He leaned forward, craning his neck down the street. "Don't think I see a cab. But he had a record tenure when I left. I would've thought someone had dug him out by now. Makes you wonder – ah!"

The cab was identical to the other vehicles swarming the streets, and its driver plunged them into the melee with unreasonable glee. Anaea clenched her fingers in her lap and banished the question of why the cabs weren't automated. If she were navigating this traffic, she would want to be in control. Though if it was all routed through systems, there wouldn't be such chaos; somewhere in the past was a vicious circle that had ended up here.

Penelope burrowed into her lap. Soothing the kearl before she ripped through her trousers calmed and distracted her in turn.

Her brain settled on a different concern.

She wished she hadn't told Flick she would observe his grandmother. With genetic diseases, she was on firm ground. She had covered poisons and atmospheric risks as an intern, but new ones could have developed. Only a handful of bacteria could thrive in a closed system like Themiscyra, and viruses she was clueless about. Only the common cold was familiar, bursting out in patches and vanishing before anyone could deal with it.

"You get used to it," Flick assured her, mistaking the reason for her pensive expression.

"Hmm? Oh." The buildings lost height and luster deeper into the city, shrinking in on themselves like squat beasts. Glass and steel rubbed elbows in disharmonious clusters, but there were no empty spaces, just places where the buildings were shoved less tightly together. The boisterous patter of haggling scratched the air. Cooking scents wafted over the faint blood-taste of electronics.

As they went east, the gaps showed themselves. At first, it was a work in progress here, an extra alley there. Further on, buildings stood blank and vacant, and structures torn down were piled in careless ruin. The appearance of dustiness gave way to the reality. Once beautiful facades now crumbled.

To Anaea's eye, the change wasn't all negative: the sky bled downwards, filling spaces with the purple blush of twilight, and vacant lots housed swaths of teal foliage. Vehicle traffic thinned, but the crowds below were more driven, aggressive: heads down, eyes forward, shoulders leading.

The cab put down at a port near an old stone bridge. The brass plate on its surface dated it to 2338, twenty years after planetfall. Once, it had gone somewhere, now it was only a barrier. Ocean dampness rose from under the arch.

Flick paid the cab driver and hopped out. He insisted on taking her bag and scampered ahead. He halted in the archway.

"Into the fairy-mound we go, under the arch where mortals fear to follow," he quipped. Then he was gone under the bridge.

*

DESPITE FLICK'S THEATRICS, Nissyen on the other side of the bridge seemed little different. It was slightly darker and the colors more subdued, but that was due to the scarceness of artificial light. A handful of lights flickered on now; they whined in pain.

The streets were almost deserted. The only people who moved across them darted, disappearing within buildings as if hurtled by gravity. As quickly as automatic lights came on, they disappeared, a firefly flash across her line of sight.

A low growl, more felt than heard: machinery, punctuated by the snap of voices, the rumble of violence. Flick halted her with a raised hand.

"Hug the walls," he said. "Stay in the shadows. Come quietly."

Her breathing rang in her ears as she followed him; the click of Penelope's claws seemed equally loud. She tasted questions on her tongue, but waited. Her heart pounded, though she couldn't identify a source for the anxiety. At the next intersection, he quick-stepped into the shade of a public terminal, body pressed against the frame. He swore softly.

Anaea hurried to join him. Four blocks down, two scarlet vehicles idled on either of the street. Unlike the cab, these were hulking, armored brutes with opaque windows. A group of people in uniforms moved from residence to residence, pounding on doors, swooping down on the few people on the streets.

Three men cornered a middle-aged woman; she repeated the refrain: "It's not mine, I don't know where it came from." Her voice faded with the realization they did not believe her. One of the uniformed figures manhandled her into the vehicle.

The figure that held Anaea's eye was the only one not moving in this determined sweep. The woman stood atop one of the vehicles, a thin, angular form. Her lips moved, issuing orders, presumably into the earpieces of those below. Her black hair was worn in a close shear that resisted curl.

"Who's that?" Anaea murmured.

Flick frowned. "Don't know, though she looks familiar somehow. Don't need to know her name to know she's bad news."

"What's going on?" she asked.

He wrenched her arm, pulling her around the side of the terminal. The leash pulled taut, drgging the kearl with her. What she couldn't seescared Anaea as much as the sudden motion. She imagined those uniformed men materializing before them.

The approaching evening spat the crackle of machinery, the creak of metal, but it brought nothing more. Flick inched about the terminal and took a scouting glance. "Cross the street," he said. "Now."

With that, he was gone, and she had to throw herself after him. Either sensing the urgency or just eager to run, Penelope bounded along beside her. Anaea risked a glance in the direction of the armored vehicles. A fight had broken out, the aggressors – or were they the defenders? – two burly men, one armed with a chair.

"Anaea!"

She hop-jumped and found herself in the shadow of the next street. Flick took her arm and pushed on.

"Could be more than one group," he said. "Stay sharp."

"Who are they? What are they doing?" she pressed.

Flick's eyes surveyed their surroundings before he spoke. "Law officers. It's routine," he said, but the forced lightness implied otherwise. "They come down here occasionally to see what kind of questionable activities they can dig up. Scour the neighborhood until they've met their quota. I should have realized why folks are lying low."

"I don't understand," she said, trying to stay calm. "If they haven't done anything—"

He cast her a look that stopped just shy of being disgusted. "Of course they've done something. It's practically tradition around here. All's fair if you don't hurt anyone and you don't get caught, right? It's within warlord's rules."

"Oh," she said, feeling herself on the edge of a mental precipice. She couldn't wrap her mind around this distinction: the difference between what was allowed, what was against the law, and what was only legal if you could get away with it.

"We're almost there," he said.

She shortened the leash, shushing Penelope when the kearl growled protest. The sound echoed. Anaea winced, peering up from between braced shoulders to see if they had drawn attention. Flick tugged her along at a faster pace. The sounds of the patrol diminished.

The buildings down the next street were dilapidated and almost off-kilter: they seemed to tilt at angles, as if time and gravity had drawn them into a slope. Flick led them to an apartment complex. The main door blared red and reminded him of a no-pets policy.

Flick rolled his eyes. "Tell that to the rats," he said. Anaea hoped he was joking. He spouted off an override code, and it slid open.

Anaea breathed easier when the door closed behind her. Flick laid his hand on the palmpad and told it to put on the law-lock. She assumed that was meant to keep the authorities out.

No elevation tube or lift platform, just a series of rickety steps down three floors into a hallway. Penelope sniffed judiciously and then pressed against Anaea's leg. Flick knocked on one of the doors.

"Who is it?" a crackly alto voice asked. "Put your hand on the plate so I can be sure it's you."

"It's me, Tobias," he said. "I brought a friend."

"In that case, don't bother to put your hand on the plate. You could easily fake being someone else."

Flick glanced back at Anaea and grinned sheepishly. The door slid open.

The apartment was small, spartan and crooked, though every effort had been made to spread its tidiness out so it appeared more prosperous. The lights were rose-tinted.

The occupant crushed in Flick in a hug accompanied by a cloud of floral scents. "I missed you, Tobias," she said. "You can't imagine how long I pictured you hacked to bits or strung up somewhere like a living machine."

Flick coughed, and Anaea wondered how far that second statement was from the truth. The woman pulled back to examine him. She was slender, short, with strains of silver in short hair that otherwise matched her grandson's in color. Her back was straight and her movements easy, but wear set into the lines of her face and the thin weight on her bones. Anaea couldn't tell what combination of age and preventative treatments that implied.

"You are never to leave so long again, do you understand?" She chuckled. "Of course, if you hadn't made a muddle of it, I might be saying the opposite."

Flick colored, the red trickling down his neck. "That's not fair!"

"Oh, it is," she replied. "Now introduce me to your friend."

"Grandmum, this is my friend and most recent savior of my tail-bone, Anaea Carlisle," he said. "Anaea, this is my grandmother, Marianna Risingsun."

Penelope chirred.

"And her companion, Penelope Carlisle," Flick added.

"It's a pleasure to meet you, Mrs. Risingsun," Anaea said.

"Marianna, if you please." She took the younger woman's hands in hers. She gave a reflexive shudder, as if the motion pained her. "You're welcome in my home."

"Actually, we were hoping she could stay for a while," Flick said, trotting out a boyish smile. "I promise I'll foot the bill—"

"Scrubbing the sink would do, but that's usually too much to ask," Marianna said drily. She reclaimed her hands; Anaea noticed they were red, darkening angrily closer to the wrist.

"I would never impose," she said. "If it's a problem—"

"Don't be ridiculous." Marianna clicked her tongue. "My home is open to anyone who enters in the spirit of friendship. Flick, you're on the couch, but I suggest you poke your head into your room to make sure I haven't left anything out that might embarrass you."

The sound he made was more eloquent than any speech. He ducked through one of the apartment's three inner doors.

"Perhaps you'd like some tea—" Marianna paused, her face working as if an unpleasant taste had touched her lips. "Just one moment, Anaea, I'm sorry." She disappeared behind another of the doors.

Anaea was left standing alone. She felt a curious sense of intrusion, as if merely to look would be rude. Her eyes flitted, not settling on anything. She heard Marianna choking and winced, resisting the urge to barge in.

Penelope crawled onto a chair and inspected its fringe. Anaea hurried over to extract her before the dangling threads could become impromptu toys.

"Stay put and behave," she said, chivvying Penelope into a perch on her shoulder. The kearl mouthed her ear, but didn't bite.

Flick bounded back, cheeks flushed. He ducked his head to avoid her gaze, then popped up again, apparently recovered from whatever childhood relics he had removed. "Sit down," he said. "Grandmum got rid of the carnivorous chair before I left." He lowered his voice, continuing, "You know, not too late to change your mind and go uptown. I'm not proud; I know there are better places."

Anaea tried not to make it obvious she was studying her surroundings. The room had more personal touches than her quarters at home had. It had been easier to leave it blank and bare than to figure out what she wanted.

"You're too hard on yourself," she said. "And I like your grandmother. I'm staying." Sensitive to his mood, she added nothing about whether it would be imposing, even though part of her squirmed.

Marianna returned with a determined smile on her lips. "Now! Tea." She moved into the kitchen alcove and started the brew. Anaea noticed the woman scooped herself three times the amount of sugar. Symptom, a decreased sense of taste, or habit, a sweet tooth? "Now, tell me how you met and what brings you to Nissyen with my grandson."

Though Marianna had mostly addressed Anaea, Flick took charge of the story, and she was content to let him do so, jumping in when his embellishments of her role became too much for modesty to bear. She was surprised how honestly he related the adventure, from his misdeeds to the violence the Bleak's crew had threatened. He seemed to have no concerns that Marianna would be upset by the risks her grandson had tumbled through.

That belief seemed well-founded, for she listened and tsked occasionally with approval, arched an eyebrow at this remark or that, but remained serene. She tidied off two cups of tea and started on a third. It was good tea, sweet and minty. Anaea felt relaxation seep into her bones.

"I didn't do badly on Independence," Flick defended himself, "helped a few OGIs with deep pockets—"

"Ogees?" Anaea wondered.

Flick stepped on her foot. "You're one," he muttered.

Marianna cocked her head to one side, noting the exchange. She said nothing, sipping.

"Actually, that's why Anaea is here," Flick continued. She realized with a start that he was weaving her chosen alibi into the story. "Wanted to avoid the mitts of a grabby warlord. Seeing as how Avidan doesn't let anyone poach on his territory she figured here would be doubly safe."

"Mmm," Marianna said with the façade of a smile. "Avidan has plans for the region. Things are changing."

Flick cocked his head to one side. "Like what? What's going on?"

"That's not a matter for your friend's worries or the eve of a homecoming," Marianna said firmly. She rose, collecting the cups and sweeping to the alcove to wash up. She rolled up her sleeves, and Anaea got a good look at the rash. She stared in surprise. Of the possibilities she had chased around the inadequate training in her mind, that had not been one of them.

Penelope chirred in her ear, inquiring. Anaea stroked her fur absently and stood. "Flick, could you point out where I should put my things?"

His brow crinkled, and he opened his mouth, obviously to say something about how it was self-evident. Then he caught her expression and popped up, waving for her to follow.

He closed the bedroom door behind him and put his hands on his hips. "What?"

"I'm pretty sure I know what's wrong with your grandmother," she replied.

18

Flick smiled weakly, as if he wanted to make a joke and laugh off her words, but was too nervous to do so. "Already?" he said. "Is it something serious?"

"It's just a theory," Anaea said. She began to doubt her first thought. How could something common to Themiscyra be found here? The Cauldron seemed its polar opposite, gritty and messy where the station was pristine and ordered. "Is there an artificial growing environment here?"

Flick frowned. "How do you mean?"

"Hydroponics," she said. "For plants."

His expression snapped into focus. "Oh! Come with me," he said.

"Where are we—" she started to say, but he was ahead of her and out the front door.

He guided them up the stairs to the fourth floor. "This way," he said. "Grandmum sent me updates about the progress with her messages – the owner is probably breaking zoning laws, but it's worth it."

Thick herbal scents drifted down; Anaea inhaled, feeling the tickle in her nose. Penelope chirred inquisitively. "What's worth it, exactly?" she asked.

Flick pushed open a trapdoor. "This is."

Perhaps it had once been a penthouse suite – now greenery enveloped it, the floor mounded with bushes and flowers, the walls host not only to climbing vines, but to rows upon rows of plants that swayed in rootless suspension. Nesting pots rested on beams criss-crossing the room. Only the ceiling was clear, made of glass.

"One of the residents here retired a decade ago," Flick said. "Industrial accident. He got lucky – paid enough to live until he breaks the hundred mark. Pretty close to that now, I think." He shrugged. "Anyhow, this has been his occupation since."

"Couldn't he have afforded—" Anaea bit her tongue.

"Some place uptown?" Flick grinned. "He could have, but then he wouldn't have had the resources for this. Better to have something to flaunt."

"It's beautiful," she said, tightening her hold on the kearl's leash. "It may be the problem, though. Does your grandmum help?"

"Now and again," he said. "Why?"

"Search the underside of the pots," she said. She could be wrong, or it could be something else, a species native to this vast planet. "Look for a purplish moss."

Flick scampered off under an archway of vines. The air was warm and humid, caressing the skin. Anaea found it soothing, even as she worried about other plants, most of which she had no name for, all of which could be toxic or provoke allergic reaction. Penelope sneezed in her ear.

"Anaea!" Flick called.

She ducked through the maze of greenery. He held out a pot for examination.

"This is it," she said. "If your grandmother handled any of these – the moss carries a bacteria. It causes a rash like the one I saw on her wrist."

Flick looked impressed. "Hydroponics, huh."

"I worked with them back home," she said.

On those words, the expression grew more profound. "What didn't you do?"

She couldn't explain to him it was a condition of where she had been raised, that hydroponics were the norm and this type of infection common. His praise, and the fact she couldn't correct him, made her more aware of the gap between them.

"The medicine for it isn't uncommon," she said. "A doctor—"

"Don't worry," he said, "I can find it." The corner of his lips pulled up into a grin and he crushed her in a hug. "Thank you. Again. I have to admit, I'm worried about getting used to having you pull my tail out of fires."

"It wasn't much of a fire," she said. "It's not life-threatening by any means."

He wrinkled his nose. "You just can't take a compliment, can you? Come on. There are a few delivery companies down here that have arrangements with the police, so we can order in a proper feast even during a raid. A homecoming, a cure – it's worth celebrating."

*

It was a pleasant evening. Flick described his escapades on Independence, and Marianna responded with local news. She seemed concerned about the presence of surveyor teams in the Cauldron, but Flick waved it off.

"They like to use their fancy widgets and measure and scowl when the area shifts about impossibly," he said, "but they never do anything."

Anaea was more surprised by his stories and the fact that he told them in front of his grandmother with no hesitation. Business in imperial space was dominated by corporations as ruthless as the warlords, and they did not take kindly to competition from Tweakers. That, to Flick, was most of the fun.

"You slip right under their noses and steal their best customers," he said. "Anyhow, I'm not dealing in the real dangerous stuff, weapons development and that. Those businessmen never travel without a pistol and a saber, and I don't think the latter's always for show, either." He pondered. "Or maybe it's an epée."

"I hope you stayed within Defiance," Marianna said mildly. "The law is stricter outside the capital."

"Oh, yeah, I know if they dumped me into a raptorhound run, I'd be puppy chow," Flick said blithely. "I wouldn't even be particularly entertaining."

Anaea knew what a raptorhound was, but had never seen one: the male of the last pair in the Preserve had shredded his mate and pups ten years before she was born. They were native to Independence, most closely resembling saber-toothed canids with scales armoring their throats. Vicious, hearty, capable of surviving on any fodder: the stuff of a nightmare.

Which meant his casual statement left her as much sickened as confused. "Why would they dump you in with raptorhounds?"

His brows drew down as if he couldn't figure out if she might be joking. "Some warlords'll use that instead of a criminal sentence. Entertains the locals and gives you a sporting chance . . . sort of."

She half-closed her eyes, trying not to picture it. "Oh."

Flick bounced on to the next topic. "Oh, grandmum, I've got to tell you about this chick I met on the south side."

Anaea awoke the next morning without the comforting lump of Penelope by her side. What had roused her was a buzz that moved through the walls and made the bed frame twitch. She dressed before she ventured into the hall.

Marianna sat on the couch, stroking the kearl and watching a blurry holographic broadcast. The blonde siren reciting the news flickered as if rain were falling through her.

Marianna halted the broadcast with a wave of her hand as Anaea entered. "How are you this morning?" she asked.

Anaea resisted the impulse to rub her ears. "What is that?"

"Scrambler service," Marianna said. "I don't understand the technical side, but it helps to prevent scans from tracing back to this apartment."

"Is that necessary?" she asked.

Penelope rolled over, displaying her belly. Marianna chuckled. "The landlord requires it with the rent," she said, "but there are things to be said for privacy, whether or not one intends to abuse it."

Anaea blushed. "I didn't mean—"

"I didn't take it that way," Marianna assured her. "Tobias left to see to some errands, greet some old friends, and possibly make trouble amongst all that. Feel free to grab some breakfast in the kitchen. I put in extra sausage for Tobias."

By the time Anaea returned with a plate, the buzz had stopped, though it echoed in her ears.

Marianna regarded her with piercing dark eyes. "You said last night you were hiding from a warlord. Is this a temporary flight, or a permanent one?" Before Anaea could answer, she continued, "I see by your look there's no easy answer to that question." She offered a slight smile. "I will insist Tobias take you on a proper tour of the city. We have few tourist attractions and even fewer a native remembers, but you should see our best face."

"What are they?" Anaea asked.

"There's Branwen's Tower, an annex to the warlord's fortress, technically. Built by the first man to grab power here, for his wife," Marianna said. "The exterior is twisted like a Gordian knot; the interior is works of art within a work of art. I find it over-stimulating, but it's popular with the young and dreamy-eyed."

She continued, naming a few more places, but Anaea snapped to attention when she said, "The Wainwright Library. Supposed to be the largest on the planet, and I imagine if that weren't true, Avidan would fix it."

"An archaic library? With books?" Anaea was surprised at the excitement in her voice. She flushed.

Marianna did not react as if it was foolish. "That kind of

thing interests you, does it? Yes, the Wainwright is a model of historic preservation and such nonsense. I hear they have a lending collection, as if this were three hundred years ago." Her tone was clipped, disapproving of such frivolity, but then became thoughtful.

"If you want to see the old art at its best, there is a local man you should meet," she said. "The rest of the city may not agree, may not even know, but the Cauldron brews the best of Nissyen."

Penelope, apparently tired of the cosseting, squirmed out of Marianna's lap. "I would love to meet him," Anaea said.

"Well, then." Marianna clapped her hands and made to rise. She wobbled as she did. "Shall we?"

"It can wait until you're feeling better," she said.

Marianna paused. "So Flick told you I was sick, did he?" There seemed no harm, so Anaea explained. The old woman chuckled. "He might not have worried you. It's inconvenient, but I hardly have the luxury of lounging about indulging it. The matter will clear itself up."

"It won't," Anaea said, "and it leaves you vulnerable to other infections. It's a persistent fungus, and it spreads deeper into the lungs if you let it."

"Does it, now." Marianna seemed unconcerned, though she smiled. "In your professional opinion, is it hazardous for me to walk a few blocks?"

Backed into an answer, Anaea admitted, "No. But—"

"Then put your companion in your room and we shall go," Marianna said.

That was that. They climbed the wavering steps and left the apartment. Marianna leaned on her occasionally, but otherwise moved well. Out in the sunlight, there was no sign of the chaos of the previous night. The streets gleamed; light danced off the buildings in teasing whorls, creating the illusion that the top floors were translucent.

A few vehicles criss-crossed the streets, duller and bulkier versions of the uptown models. Their drivers kept one twitchy hand on the controls as if expecting they would have to race away at any moment. The foot traffic was equally edgy, dart-eyed, hunch-shouldered, though most paused to greet Marianna. As Anaea watched with bemusement, a brunette maybe a decade the old woman's junior, or a few thousand credits more vain, chattered about sweet cream.

"Aren't you worried about being stopped? After last night?" Anaea asked.

Marianna shrugged. "What will be, will be. Why should we halt our lives for maybes? In any case, they're unlikely to come through. The woman who ran last night's raid is one of Blake Avidan's battle trainers, and she used to be one of us. She knows better."

"Do you know her?"

Marianna paused. "No one knows her now."

Anaea knew better than to indulge her curiosity. She continued walking, her attention caught by a shifting billboard across the street, broken and drizzling letters.

Marianna indicated they should cross and headed for what Anaea assumed was a demolition gap. Then she realized there was a building, or at least three and a half walls with shelter and privacy. She hesitated, casting her guide a quizzical look. She remembered the hermetic book room in the Sanctum. How could works be preserved in a place like this?

Marianna never slowed, ducking under burlap to knock on the faded plank door. "Justin? Are you in?"

Anaea noted with surprise the door had no evidence of electronic locks or surveillance. She knew some people lived like that on Annwyn, isos in particular, but she had assumed it was restricted to far-flung barrens and marshes, not cityscapes.

"Marianna, is that you?" The voice was rich, tawny. The door opened; the speaker was a middle-aged man with too-green eyes. He was poorly dressed, barefoot, wearing leather gloves. One cheek bore a series of black smudges.

"Justin, this is Anaea," Marianna said. "She would like to see the workshop."

"Ah?" The word carried a wealth of meaning, as did the faint smile that accompanied it. "This way. Mind your step."

Anaea followed into a place of twining shadows. It opened up with a burst of light into a tiled chamber, lined on two sides with glassed-in bookshelves. In the center, commanding the attention, was—

She stared. The black iron machine was as mesmerizing as it was archaic, a labyrinth of gears whose purpose lay open to the eye even as it eluded her. Even through the complexity, she could tell there was no electronic component to process commands; it was a thing without mind, streamlined to simple cause and effect. It sat still now, but looked somehow poised for action.

"What is that?" she asked.

"A printing press," Justin said. "Built by a pre-colonization historian and come here as . . . call it spoils of war. All of these" – he gestured around him – "were printed with this apparatus, except for the top shelf, which are found volumes.

"Presses and books became flimsier as they evolved," he added. "Go back further and you find the book as it should be."

"So you say, Justin." Marianna sounded amused, indulgent.

Did that explain the open environment, that the room was not double-sealed and void of outside influence? It astonished her to think of this ancient beast turning out the array of treasures on the shelves. Forgotten history, and yet it lived, cried out for attention.

With a brief glance to confirm it was all right, Anaea went to study the shelves. The books were thick and hardbound, each one distinct, whether bound with leather, cloth or spun-glass. The titles on the spines seemed to be hand-lettered.

"Take one out and look at it," Justin said, more direction than invitation.

She did, careful as surgery, opening it to the title page: *Bound In Ice*. A delicious scent rose up to greet her, pungent and acidic and not entirely pleasant, but that was part of the charm. The typeface was smooth, distinct, setting the scene of a female mercenary in the lowest polar regions of Independence, her hover-sled a useless relic in the unrelenting white.

Pages turned and words marched away, defined, immutable. Their physical presence curved into her brain and drew Anaea in, descriptions caressing her with imagined cold. She read without thinking, head bent, as if the building had melted away and the sky-slashing mountains on the page surrounded her. The story stretched out—

"Ahem," Marianna said.

"Oh, let her be," Justin said, laughing.

"I'm sorry," Anaea said, blushing. With an effort, she lowered the book. "How do you decide what to print? There are so many classics and other works to choose from."

"Why limit yourself to that?" The bookmaker waved to the top shelf. "Look for yourself."

There seemed nothing different. Anaea picked the fifth book, a botanical treatise, and turned it over, looking for a clue.

"Inside," Justin urged. He clearly wanted his visitor to discover for herself.

Anaea scanned the first pages. "I don't see anything."

"The date." His voice overflowed with pride. "The copyright date."

It was recent, just last year. She frowned slightly.

"Not everyone knows what it means, Justin," Marianna said.

Justin ducked his head like a child. "That's the date when a work becomes protected by law. It can't be replicated without its author's permission. There used to be—"

"It means it was published on that date," Marianna interrupted.

"Oh." Then it settled around her like a hug, and she repeated, "Oh." A new world from the old; the scent and progression of unchanging type did not end. For the first time, she felt at home, not in a place but in a knowledge.

What sense did it make? She knew nothing about the process;

it was a myth to her. She had no creative spark and no mechanical talent. Flick might be able to make the printing press dance, but she had no idea where to start.

She had only experienced this feeling once before, when watching an unconscious Gwydion and drawn in by his presence: she wanted to know. It gnawed at her that she didn't.

"Do other people do this?" she asked.

Justin laughed, and Anaea liked him more for the sound. It was delighted, ready to share a secret. "Fringe groups here and there," he said. "Artists on Manawydan Station make a good living. I don't know if the matriarchs have much traffic, but there must be girly romance novels to be preserved, and new ones to be written, for that matter."

Could that be home? Yet the thought scuttled away from her. She couldn't stop moving yet.

She turned her attention to the printing press. "How does it work?"

*

Anaea's head buzzed when they returned to the apartment. Justin had invited her to return in a few days' time for a bookbinding; he was waiting for a shipment of cloth. Part of her felt guilty for chasing a whim when it seemed the universe waited for her to make a decision.

Flick appeared an hour later, covered in soot and toting misshapen packages. He spilled them out over the couch, presenting his grandmother with a case of medicinal patches.

"They're, err—" He might have rehearsed a lie, but he lost it and gestured like a frustrated haggler.

Marianna chuckled. "It's all right, Tobias, your young friend told me about the unofficial exam. Is this the medicine?"

He dropped his arms, deflated. "I thought you would refuse to take it if you knew."

"Where would be the sense in that?" She tsked.

Flick grumbled under his breath as she applied a patch near the rash.

The rest of his packets contained widgets, circuit-cubes and a bright pink bow for Penelope that the kearl deigned to wear. When Marianna suggested a tour uptown, he beamed.

"I love the Tower, just for trying to retro-engineer it in my head," he said. "Now's the best time to see it, too. Angle of the autumn sun."

They walked out of the Cauldron and caught a cab through Nissyen's winding thoroughfares. The city seemed to double and triple back on itself, revealing curves where there should have been none and unexpected, impossible skyscrapers that vanished when one looked back.

As the layers of Nissyen peeled away, they proved to be a web around an iron and stone core. The central building was made for ground siege, the city cringing back from its perimeter.

"Warlord's fortress," Flick said, his voice hushed; a superstitious quaver. "Used to be a refuge bunker."

"From?" she asked without thinking.

His face tensed before he decided she wasn't joking. "Y-Poisoning."

She studied the walls. She felt the disease looming over her as it had not since Themiscyra. Society had cascaded out from its impact: warlords reigned because Y-Poisoning had cleared the way.

The exterior of Branwen's Tower gleamed like a pillar of pure gold, though up close, elaborate filigree greeted the eye. The seams holding the tower together were invisible even on the tenth look. It was made to impress and demand attention.

Within, each room overflowed with its own distinct style, from archaic impressionism and surrealism to scentwaves and angular realism. The tower boasted bedrooms, gathering rooms and bathrooms the size of the Risingsun apartment. The pool on the lower level adjoined the gaming room, consoles, cages, and a rack of blades.

A holo placard informed visitors that the lady had kept her

own raptorhounds for amusement, and that she had participated in the pinnacle of female sport: fencing, as elegant and delicate as the lady herself.

Branwen had been an ornament, Anaea realized, as was the entirety of the Tower. It had not been a residence for decades, instead preserved as a spectacle and display of power. The warlord owned this, could afford to consign it to people on the street.

She shifted her focus to those people. Young couples, wildly diverse in size and complexion and mode of dress, but all with one thing in common: cupped elbows, clutched shoulders, the man guiding their steps and tightening his hold when another crossed his path; the women sweet and soft with lowered eyes. An older couple leaned on each other. Families strung out along halls, mothers chasing children while the fathers lounged together.

Gossiping, Anaea thought, bemused, like new interns on Themiscyra, without a care for their free-range offspring.

A cluster of teens sketched on virtual pads. Occasionally, their leader would point out another feature, and they flocked to observe it.

"Students," Flick said, sounding disgusted. "Uptown twits whose parents are too dumb to realize they're wasting money on high school. Any of them tried to go walkabout, they'd be hairsprayed to a detention cell before you could blink."

"Did you not go, then?" Anaea asked.

His expression suggested she was an alien. "Of course I went, not that I couldn't dance rings around youth curfew. It strapped my parents something fierce, but I made something of it. I mean, the government's either going to force you to pay or lock you in the house until you're eighteen, so what else are you going to do?"

Anaea let that question float into silence, disquieted. They continued their tour until Flick lured her out with promises of a good meal.

They took a cab to a busy commercial district and then walked, dodging vehicles, to a blue-lacquered restaurant specializing in curries made with native and cross-bred spices. Some of the flavors were new to Anaea and made her taste buds dance.

She felt safe, and she knew what it was: anonymity. She wandered through Nissyen cloaked in it, her oddness hidden and no one curious enough to seek it out. Chance skipped by her without touching. The visitor band on her wrist was hidden under her sleeve.

Flick chattered in the cab back to the Cauldron, gesticulating rapidly. He jumped from nuances of the Tower to his school experiences: a target of bullies, he too had learned the value of crawl-spaces. Then he moved on to pointing out aspects of the city, contorting his body and stabbing alarmingly at the horizon. The driver told him to settle down.

Anaea paid the fare, and they crossed under the liminal bridge into pools of shadow. She blinked, surprised. It was as if sunset had happened only on this side. Surely not that much time had passed? Of course, Annwyn's day was three hours shorter than galactic standard.

Lights pulsed into bloom and voices built as if the day had barely begun. Their wariness was tempered by the power of darkness. Flick seemed to absorb it, swaggering as they moved down the street.

He stopped at the corner as someone waved. "Hey, can you get the rest of the way back on your own?" he asked. "I made some headway this morning, but I still have catching up to do."

Anaea glanced down the streets. It wasn't that far. "Of course," she said. "You be careful."

Flick grinned. "Yeah, I'll do that," he said, and hurried away.

Anaea continued towards the apartment complex. The early evening chill was refreshing. Her thoughts roamed far ahead, planning without planning, dreaming of Branwen's Tower and an endless stream of printed words.

Then her anonymity failed her.

19

THE TRIO COULD HAVE BEEN FOLLOWING HER FOR BLOCKS. She noticed them only as they closed, two buildings away, then ten paces, locking onto her with purposeful movements. She quickened her stride and looked for a place to detour, hoping they would walk past. Her skin prickled.

An alley beckoned – no. She hadn't been raised to be wary of shadow, but she knew that was a bad idea. She told herself she was too keyed up. There was no reason to accost her: she showed no sign of wealth, and hadn't she just proved she fit in?

"Where are you going in such a hurry?"

She pretended she hadn't heard, that the words hadn't been aimed at her like gunfire. How fast could she move without breaking into a run? She told herself she wasn't frightened. The quiver in her body wouldn't listen.

Two of the men cut into the street, moving to flank her. Both were a half-head taller than she, strong, athletic. "Gone mute, have you?" The speaker had a thick, blustery accent.

Anaea doubted a civil response would neutralize them. "I can't linger," she said. "I'll be late for an appointment."

"I think you'll be missing that." The voice came from behind her, cool poison.

She jumped, spinning to face the bristle-bearded figure. He was shorter but broader, a powerhouse of a man. Her eyes swept past him, scanning the sidewalks. She was not alone, but she might have been invisible; no one even looked her way. It left her stiff-kneed and bewildered.

"I can't—" She strained for something sensible to say. "Who are you?"

The one with the accent spoke again. "The welcoming committee." All three wore ochre with hard paneling: crude armor. How had they come up on her so fast? She backed up to the corner and still found herself surrounded by the grinning trio.

"Your new best friends." This drew snickers from the other two. It was an ugly humor, and she knew she was to be the punchline.

Anaea hesitated. In each direction, she was putting her back to someone. Panic built; it heated her skin. "In that case, I feel welcome. Excuse—"

The bearded figure grabbed her arm and snapped her backwards. Her feet left the ground. She stumbled in a circle of fishy breath, laughter, and eyes filled with incomprehensible hunger. Blankness hit her where understanding should have been. What did they want?

"No hurries, little tourist," the one with the accent said. "We're holding a party, and you're invited."

The third – did he speak? – stroked her arm, and the pieces tumbled into place in her brain. Panic squeezed her and hardened thought into determination. She twisted to face him, quivering like a leaf. She waited for him to move, her decision surprising her.

His hand tightened, pulled her in; he brought his mouth down, smirking, wordless. Awkwardly, somehow with enough speed, she jammed her knee into his stomach. He stumbled back with a snort of pain. She pushed into his right shoulder, taking advantage of the momentum to clear her path.

Her feet threw her forward. Harsh arms caught her midsection, hauled her back. She had a dim flash of memory from an old holo-movie. Twisting, she went for his eyes with her hands, no intention, no hope of burrowing into them, just blind panic. He jerked away to protect himself and she fell the other direction. She slammed her back foot against the pavement before she could topple.

She was free.

Running was the easy part. They swarmed after her. They were faster than she was, she had nowhere to go—

A clang of impact from a thrown object, and one of her pursuers dropped. Startled, she turned her head. That slowed her too much; the others reached her.

A dark blur slammed into the bearded man, resolved into a slender human form. It – she – blocked his attempt to swing at Anaea and caught him by the elbow. A sickening crack, a pivot, and he was down on the pavement, clutching his arm and too winded to howl. His companion reeled, clutching his head.

The woman turned to face the third figure. She was armed, ostentatiously so, with a blaster on either hip, but her hands went nowhere near them. "I'd keep running," she said.

Anaea stared. It was the woman from the raid. The trainer.

Maybe the three men recognized her; maybe they only knew they were outclassed. Whatever the case, they fled with frenetic scrambling that would have been comical, had their previous intentions not been ice in Anaea's mind.

The woman hissed through her teeth. Up close, she was striking, the broad, flat face making her dark eyes stand out. A series of small scars feathered down one side of her chin. "Idiots," she said.

"Thank you for saving me," Anaea said.

"If you hadn't fought back, I would have left you," she said curtly. "This is no place for a woman who won't defend herself."

The statement stung, but at least she had acted. She would not have to find out whether that was true. "I was sure I wouldn't "escape." It was almost a peace offering, to excuse the cowardice Anaea knew had not been far from her thoughts. It would have been so easy to curl up and cover her head, even knowing it wouldn't have protected her.

"Odds weren't in your favor," the trainer said. "Lucky they were stupid." She shook her head, then performed a regimental snap to face Anaea and offered a hand. "Dezba Moon, combat trainer for warlord Avidan." Her voice carried a touch of pride.

"Anaea Carlisle," she said. "Pleased to meet you." She blushed and added, "Even under the circumstances."

Dezba's snort sounded like laughter. "Likewise. Are you new here?"

"How can you tell?" She had lost her faith in her anonymity, but she had not been gawping or uncertain on unfamiliar streets. The Cauldron was huge; surely not everyone knew their neighbors by sight.

Dezba's face shifted, one brow tilting upwards. "You have a manner about you," she said. "Too soft, too tentative, like you're trespassing." A beat, and she added, "You've also got a visitor band. My com is picking it up."

"Oh." Anaea wanted to ask how she could fix that, how she could walk as if she knew what she was doing, when she didn't, when it would take years to reach that level of comfort with things even a matriarch would take for granted, but this was not a person to confide in. She smiled, polite façade. "I appreciate the warning."

To her puzzlement, Dezba burst out laughing. "You appreciate – how far from home are you? No one talks like that."

"Apparently, someone does," Anaea said before she could stop herself.

The laughter trailed off; Dezba nodded. "Point. You shouldn't be out here unprepared."

The woman was right, and shame trickled up from Anaea's core. Was she helpless? Did every step have to be made in company? "Then what should I do?" she asked, realizing she was challenging Dezba and wanting to shy away, but the words were spoken. She recalled what Marianna had said earlier. "I can't hold my life for maybes."

"I said you shouldn't be unprepared, not that you should hide." The voice was crisp, clipped. "Get yourself a stunner. You look as if you can afford it. Or come to me, if you decide to stay. I can teach you how to defend yourself."

The offer surprised Anaea, but it seemed genuine. "Thank you," she said. "I will."

Dezba nodded. "This way?" she inquired, starting up the street.

Anaea hesitated, unsure how wise it was to lead the person responsible for last night's raids to her hostess' doorstep, but there seemed no way to dissuade her. She hurried ahead. There was no reason to believe that Dezba would have any special interest in where she stopped.

The trainer said nothing, and something about the silence, though it was not unfriendly, encouraged Anaea not to break it. When they reached the apartment complex, she climbed the steps and realized Dezba had not followed, had in fact turned to stride in the other direction.

"Thank you," she called after. The woman did not look back.

*

"Anaea? What happened to you?" Marianna reached up to brush a lock of hair away from Anaea's face. "You're as white as a blank wall."

The words flowed downhill out of her. "I was attacked," she said. "A group of men. The – someone came to my rescue." She didn't want to divulge the identity of her rescuer. Dezba might be the enemy.

Marianna's eyes darkened as she guided her visitor into the apartment. One arm slipped about Anaea, rubbing her shoulder.

"Where was Tobias? No, don't answer that yet," she said. "Let's get you comfortable and get a hot drink in you. Then tell me everything."

The older woman cajoled her into taking a shower. Anaea lost herself to the luxury of hot water, letting it unkink her thoughts along with her muscles. When she ventured into the main room, Marianna pressed stewed chocolate and cookies on her, along with a heated blanket. Penelope scampered up from under the couch and hopped onto her lap.

"You don't need to fuss over me," Anaea said.

"Of course I do," Marianna said briskly. "It's a mother's right." Something in Anaea's expression must have caught her attention, for she added, "Goodness, child, did your mother never coddle you?"

"Well . . ." Hard to imagine her solo parent having such impulses.

Marianna shook her head. "Scandalous," she said.

By the time Anaea started her story, holding her cookie out of the kearl's reach, the anxiety had faded to faint nausea.

"Those craven thugs . . ." Marianna's ire rang in her voice, yet there was no lecture, no recitation of the precautions Anaea should have taken.

Flick returned, humming to himself as he palmed in. "How are you ladies?"

Marianna descended on him like a storm. "What were you thinking? She could have been seriously hurt."

He blinked in confusion. "What happened?"

Anaea stirred on the couch, wondering if she should intervene as Marianna blasted her grandson. Penelope squirmed deeper into her lap, deciding the matter.

Flick turned wide eyes on her. "Anaea? Are you all right?"

"I'm fine," she said.

"Only by luck," Marianna interjected. "I don't even like you going about unarmed, and you're not a young woman with no clue of the back ways and no business ties to protect you."

"But it's never been that dangerous," Flick protested. "No one would make trouble with the Black Gang—"

"It's changed, Tobias," she cut him off. "The streets are rougher. The Gang isn't as pervasive as it used to be. The strong and the stupid ignore the rules they put down. I know you're so used to wandering the fringes that you take for granted no one will notice you, but that doesn't apply to her. Or any woman."

That last statement puzzled Anaea until she turned it over. The default assumption in Nissyen, as irrational as it was, was that women were less capable; easier targets. How one could look at Marianna or Dezba and think so was beyond her understanding, but it meant she would be in more danger than Flick even if she looked as if she belonged.

"You'll get her a stunner," Marianna concluded. "One of those watered-up versions your friend peddles."

"Juiced up, grandmum," Flick said.

She waved it off. "You know what I meant."

Flick sidled over and perched on the edge of the couch. "Are you sure you weren't hurt?" he asked. "I'm sorry I hared off on you. I didn't think." He swallowed, the contrition tightening in his throat. "I'm glad nothing happened."

Marianna sniffed and drew breath to make a comment. Anaea shook her head.

"It's past," she said. "Let it go."

"If you leave now," the older woman could no longer contain herself, "I can hold dinner and you can get it sorted out tonight."

The last thing Anaea wanted to do was to go back out into those shadows, even accompanied, but she could see arguing with Marianna would be futile. "All right."

*

"At least let me split the cost with you," Flick argued as they took a lift to the third floor of the building. The hover chamber glowed an eerie blue, coating their skin. Anaea looked up, saw striations in the projector mechanism and realized the color was damage, not an affectation.

"It's not your fault," she said. "I can manage it." How to tell him she had sold off a shuttle with no technological equal? She had no money concerns as long as she reserved the resources needed to leave this world, and right now, that desire burned inside her. Stubbornness made her push it aside; she hadn't learned enough . . . and then there was the book maker.

Flick sighed. "All right, all right. Just don't tell my grandmum."

The third floor landing was a confused melee of holographic signs, the prosaic scratches of a moneylender swirling into plastic representations of food and then blank space. Apparently, if you wanted to visit the final business, you knew what it was.

Flick headed to that door. It opened as he approached, and, inexplicably, he ducked. He peered up and blinked. "Oh. Well. I suppose he turned off the prank channel—"

"You came early," said a bass voice, "I'm reprogramming it in honor of your homecoming."

"How sweet," Flick replied. "Come on, Anaea."

They entered a cluttered chamber with dim, pulsing lights. At first, Anaea thought it was rotated at a sixty-degree angle. Then she realized that furniture, workbench and fixtures were all oriented in different directions, placed so improbably the only clue to up was the fact that four of five chairs had their seats angled in that direction.

"Didn't expect to see you so soon," the voice continued. "I thought you'd have more social rounds first."

The speaker stood beneath a holographic screen, tweaking a three-dimensional diagram. He sidestepped out from under it; it vanished in a swirl of light. He was a stout young man, broader than any woman she had ever seen, but not especially tall, a few inches shorter than she was, in fact.

"Hello, miss," he said, cutting a bow.

Flick snickered. "When did you turn into a matriarch?"

He made a face in response. "There's nothing wrong with the occasional courtesy."

"This is my friend Anaea," Flick said, "she's looking for a stunner, one with a lot of pings and bleeps. Anaea, this is my friend – and I use the word loosely – Richard, but call him Rip. He's also a Tweaker, but he specializes in weapons. We used to study together under White Thomas, before he retired."

"Pleased to meet you, Rip," Anaea said. He shook her hand, his grip crushing. Something else occurred to her as she reclaimed it. "You never told me what you specialized in, Flick."

"Blends and programming," he responded. "Fusing two things together so they work in unison."

"Why you can't just use each thing separately is something you never explain," Rip said.

Flick stuck his tongue out. "Jealous."

"We all do repairs," Rip explained to Anaea. "Try to stay within our areas of expertise. Professional courtesy." He clapped his hands together and moved to a cabinet affixed to the wall at a thirty-degree angle. "Stunners. Light grade, heavy? How much power do you want?"

"Something legal, Rip," Flick said. "Or at least only a little on the shady side."

"You've gotten boring in your old age."

"Go stick your head in a power conduit."

"Thought that's how you got that hairstyle."

Anaea listened to the banter, bemused. The words were sharp, but spoken with confederate grins. "It doesn't need to be anything high-powered," she said. "It's for self-defense."

"Then you'll want a bodylock on it," Rip responded. "I'll need a palm print and DNA sample to work one up. No good having a weapon for self-defense if someone can snatch it and use it against you. Here, what do you think of this?"

He tossed something at her. She started to duck, then managed to catch it. It was a sleek, white cylinder with hollowed handgrips, much smaller than she had anticipated from seeing Dezba's showy weapons.

She turned it over dubiously. "Is this—"

"Too cumbersome for you? Need more of a handle?" Rip inquired. "That's a popular style because it fits into a neckline holster. Visible, because it has to be, legally, but not obtrusive. Melds well with the bodylock, too. Some people consider them a fashion accessory."

"Since when do you know anything about fashion?" Flick asked.

"It's a narrow burst, easy to hit with but no precision," Rip continued, ignoring his friend. "If you want a targeted weapon or a crowd-sweeper—"

"I thought you weren't selling those any more." Flick sounded uneasy, gnawing his lip.

The shrug was flippant – too flippant. "Times change. You adapt. I don't bruit it about, but it pays." He cleared his throat forcefully. "Well enough I can offer a good deal on whatever you're looking for."

"I don't know," she admitted. "I just want it to work and hope I never have to use it."

Rip extended a hand. "I'll put on a paint attachment and you can do some target practice. Flick, you want to be the target?"

Flick made a gesture Anaea presumed was rude. "I thought playing target was part of your marketing scheme."

Rip shook his head, not rising to the bait. He called out a command. A board dropped down along the far wall. Holographic outlines of people materialized in front of it. He reached back into the cabinet, snapped something on the end of the cylinder, and tossed it back to her.

"You want to try with sims later, that's fine," he said, "but I find people tend to freeze up when they have to look at faces."

Those words sent a chill through Anaea, causing her fingers to stiffen as she adjusted to the grip. She knew it, of course: the presence of the stunner alone might not send any foe running.

Was this thing her future?

She could get out of the Cauldron, but there were risks uptown, too; there was a reason the natives had so readily accepted the story she was hiding from a too-friendly warlord. Even if she returned to Collective space, there were criminals and dangerous places, softly spoken, but still there.

Perhaps this universe was the ruin Asteria had claimed.

No. Images flicked through her mind: Branwen's Tower, the Mallories arm in arm, the hotel in Eastwood and the books, the old and new. There might be ruins, but not everything had collapsed, and new growth had sprouted up in the gaps, like the greenhouse on Marianna's roof

She focused on the outline and pressed her fingers into the grip. A spray of bright blue paint haloed one holograph's right arm.

"That's just going to make him angry," Rip said, moving up behind her. "Square your stance like this and squint. Now aim."

*

By the end of the practice session, Anaea thought she could hit a motionless target. She had never learned to shoot on Themiscyra: she had no interest in working security. The closest she had come was team sports and a few old-school arcade games. Rip was patient and encouraging. Flick heckled, but his barbs were directed at his friend, who bantered back comfortably.

That night, Flick dragged two crates into the living room and spread out plastic sheeting. "Grandmum gave me permission to work out here until I have a new office scoped," he said. "Do you want to lend a hand?"

Anaea sensed he was trying to keep her busy and was grateful. Besides, this Tweaker's art might be a handy tool. She listened, complied, snapped and prised apart the various pieces and circuit-buttons.

Anaea had thought she wouldn't sleep, feared dark dreams,

but she had only a few seconds to reflect before exhaustion drew her under.

She and Flick resumed their task next morning. The bulk of the completed devices, including dinner plates with secret compartments, went into the crates. The others, he said, had to be delivered.

At first, she was too keyed up to notice much about their surroundings as they wove through the Cauldron. She noticed first the precautions he took: surveying each cross-street with a reading device on his belt, sometimes stopping to rouse some burly gatekeeper out of a nearby building and obtain permission to advance. These individuals were all male; she saw no women out and about.

Then the tumbledown nature of the buildings imprinted itself on her. Some had broken walls, holes punched into them by unknown impact. Others sunk in their foundations. Most were sound, but betrayed peeling paint, cracked plastic, smeared dust and dirt left to accumulate until there was vague artistry in the patterns. Businesses had become homes and vice versa.

Flick didn't haggle; smiling faces accepted the trade before disappearing behind their barricades. After an older mother closed her door, he turned to Anaea and said, "Most of their furniture is Tweaker-made. The place used to be a bank. They even found a use for the vintage vaults."

"How do you have so much work, so quickly?" she asked.

"Pulled a few strings, got some overflow from the man who works the north side of the Cauldron, and there were people who knew I was coming back. I'm the best at my specialty." Those words, said off-handedly, rang true.

The last thing Anaea noticed as they made their rounds was the patchwork of social routine, taut wariness contrasted with bellowed greetings and friendly insults. Vehicle traffic was sparse; the acceleration sidewalks shorted out unexpectedly. The tempo of the world had been forced to slow down.

After the last delivery, Flick pulled her through the door to

Rip's building.

The other Tweaker pressed the stunner on her. "Make sure it recognizes you," he said. "Fire at the wall."

She adjusted it in her hand and squeezed the grip. The air pulsed, shimmering with discharged energy.

"Going to have to ask for payment, miss." Rip's tone was apologetic.

Anaea took the pouch she had received on the Bleak from within her sleeve and dropped two of the gemstones into his hand. She had intended to use them all, but Rip's stunned expression told her to stop. She had new respect for the captain's gratitude.

"Could you use another practice round?" he asked, recovering. "It might serve you in good stead."

She agreed, and he called up the target board. Flick suggested they make it a contest. Anaea noted the fierce expressions and snarled comments with a hint of bemusement. It grew ever more heated until she pulled ahead of Flick in points, sheer luck, and the boys banded together.

She was still laughing when they left, feeling safe despite the tumbledown chaos, or perhaps because of it. She turned her face up to the cloudy sky and soaked in its dizzying expanse.

*

The next morning found an overtired Anaea – she had forgotten local time and lost two hours of sleep – with Justin and his cloth binding. She watched as he applied it to three books: copies of the novel *Falling Stars*, the twenty-first century work from which the planet Perica had been named. Reality imitated fiction.

"These books, respected, but not locked away or cosseted, will last a long time," Justin said. "Their permanence is more certain than that of any database, and they remember a legacy of centuries." He looked up, his smile tentative. "Perhaps you think I overstate."

Anaea shook her head. "No. What will you do with them?"

"Most, I keep for myself," he admitted. "There could be profit in them, but they are too much like my children. I couldn't sell them. I do give some away, though, to the worthy."

"How do you decide who is worthy?"

He leveled a finger on her. "That look," he said. "The one you're wearing right now."

She started to reply, but the door burst open. Flick slid across the tiles. "Anaea!" he said. "You've got to pack. You need to leave the Cauldron. Now."

20

A NAEA BLINKED, TAKING IN HIS STANCE AND PANTED breaths. "What's going on?" she asked.

Flick flapped his hands at her. "What's going on is you're packing. Grandmum will help you."

Justin put down his work, ensuring each tool was properly aligned before he looked up. "If there is a problem in the Cauldron, I would like to know," he said.

Flick expelled air out of his lungs in a rush. "I guess you had better know now, seeing as you have the most to pack. They're planning another raid of the neighborhood, a deep raid, this time. Someone gave them names." His face pinched up in anger. "When people told me that things had changed around here, I didn't think."

"We've all survived raids before," Justin said.

"They're going to press anyone they find without legal identity into hard labor," Flick said. "Bring the Cauldron down around our ears. Destroy whatever buildings don't match their code. Clear us out for whatever project the warlord's people have in mind. Probably want to put in matriarch boutiques." He said that as if it were the crowning crime.

"I have identification," Anaea pointed out. She stifled the qualm it was manufactured. She had to trust in Phailin's work. "I'm not in danger. I can help," she said.

"I need to do an inventory," Justin said, "determine how much I can move. Then I'll know if I need help." He sounded resigned, or perhaps it merely seemed that way with how much calmer he was than Flick, who looked fit to vibrate out of his skin.

Flick surveyed the room with darting eyes. "Of course you'll need help," he said. "But come on, Anaea. This isn't your fight."

Then what was? she wondered. "Can you use my assistance?"

Flick wavered. "Well, yeah. You're not profiled as a Cauldron resident, so you might be able to help us get some things under the radar. But—" arguments bubbled in his face, then popped in rapid succession. "Just make sure you always have your stunner close."

She touched its resting place with one hand. "Done."

"She has the will to be one of us," Justin said. A smile played across his lips, then disappeared as he turned his attention to the shelves. He scanned them with intense focus, as if burning them into his brain, but his words remained calm. "No use hoping this building isn't on the condemned list. Have to save the books."

"Save yourself, too," Flick advised. He ushered her out. "Some of us are meeting for a tactics session. Normally, the invitations would go out street-side so they can't be intercepted in virtual, but I'm here, so the messages went over the net." He grinned, taut. "Which I suppose means it's my fault if anything goes wrong."

They entered winding back streets and another access tunnel which led into the phantom corridors between buildings. Anaea was reminded of the quickways through Themiscyra and felt oddly at home, for all the twists and turns couldn't have been more different. The place where Flick halted should have been on the condemned list: four stories of skeletal construction with only the highest floor in any way complete, four half-walls and a jostling floor.

The perch made Anaea ill, but it had an obvious purpose: it was easy to see the expanse of neighboring structures, without being seen in turn, and impossible to sneak up on. She found herself a shipping crate for a seat and tucked her feet under her.

A small knot of young people, Rip included, had made it there ahead of Flick. The rest arrived within moments. Greeting banter made the floor vibrate, but it was short and perfunctory.

"Why are you in charge, Tweaker?" asked a man with a salt-and-pepper beard. "As I heard it, you just got back into town."

"He knows what the scheme is," Rip said.

"And he's related to Marianna," someone else said.

Anaea wasn't sure why that should matter, but it silenced the man. To her eye, Flick's challenging look around the room was more comical than anything else, but it roused no objections. He dropped a metal button to the ground. Light flared out, forming a three-dimensional viewscreen and a map of the area.

"Anything in red is a building we know for sure they're going to destroy," Flick said. "Orange is best guesses—"

"Shift the Etson Complex to red," said a blonde woman. "We've had someone nosing about."

"Put the bank on the orange list," Rip said.

Two or three other suggestions went up on the map. The combined intensity weighed uncomfortably on Anaea's skin. Somehow, it reminded her of players in a game: focused, deliberate, as if the right moves were all they needed.

"We can shunt some folks uptown," Flick said, "but I'm hearing this is going to be a long haul, and that doesn't solve the problem of coming back to an empty hole or a donut stand."

"Who's in charge?" the bearded man asked.

"Dezba Moon," Rip said. "At least, on the face. It could come from Avidan himself."

Anaea buried her fingers in her palms to control her dismayed reaction. She couldn't be surprised – what did she know of her rescuer? – but she wished it were otherwise. She hated to think of the woman as an enemy.

"Tell me about Moon's tactics," Flick said.

"She's a skirmisher and familiar with the patterns of the neighborhood," a girl said. "My dad says she hits the slow side on purpose."

"To lower our guard," the beard retorted.

"Or earn our gratitude." Rip sounded thoughtful.

The conversation continued as Anaea tried to match her meeting with the woman to the debate circling the room, and the upheaval to come. She had the terrible feeling Dezba might be more than equal to the task.

"Has anyone tried negotiating with her?" she asked.

Silence descended. Most of the room stared, expressions ranging from stunned to hostile. A few people snickered with restrained tension.

Rip coughed. "I'm sorry?"

Anaea resisted the urge to shrink into the shadows. She had started; she could only finish. "What does the other side really want here?" she asked. "I find it hard to believe they – she, whoever – want to pick a fight just for the sake of it. Or to hold workers against their will if there's another way. You say she came from the Cauldron. Maybe she never left it."

"What an empty-headed, childish idea—"

"If they want anything from us, they can come take it!"

"Who are you to stand up and—"

Voices blended in an incoherent roar. Anaea jerked backwards, trying to formulate a response, but even her loudest shout would have been lost.

Flick shoved his hand into the center of the map. A high-pitched wail pulsed through the chamber. People subsided, wincing and rubbing their ears.

"Now that we've let the whole city know where we are," he said, "back to the point at hand."

"It's worth a try, isn't it?" Rip said. "If we have to give up something, it's better than giving up everything. It's rough down here, and there's only so much looking over your shoulder you can do until you pull something."

"Maybe until you pull something," Flick said under his breath.

The other Tweaker grinned, acknowledging the poke but not rising to it. "So what do we have to bargain with?"

*

It was a little after noon when Anaea left the Cauldron for the warlord's fortress. Flick had given her a communication button that fit inside her ear; Marianna had given her the confidence to approach that dismal place.

The cab-ride left her vaguely nauseous and trying not to wobble as she walked. The main entrance was three stories high and half as wide. People passed back and forth with purpose, never slowing, but when she stepped under the arch, her body shuddered with pitched vibrations like those that warned of approaching vehicles on Eastwood. That memory was so strong she almost hurled herself to the ground.

Feeling ridiculous and anxious in equal parts, she passed under the arch into a narrowing tunnel. Gates meant to withstand massive force flanked her; probably less effective than the electronic field and perhaps not closed for years, but they still made her shiver.

At the end of the tunnel, a manned guard post. The liveried figures raked her with their gazes, instantly identifying her as an interloper even though her sleeve was over the visitor band.

"Name and business?"

"Anaea Carlisle," she said, "I'm here on the invitation of Dezba Moon." That was, she thought with her heart pressing against her throat, even accurate.

The men straightened, avoiding her eyes. "Go on through," the speaker continued. He queried the computer at his station, and added, "End of the corridor, lift to the ninth floor, immediate right and the fourth door down. Don't get misplaced."

Anaea nodded and walked through. She remembered the guiding lights in the hotel walls in New Athens, but there was no such coddling here. She fervently hoped she wouldn't make a wrong turn that would get her arrested. Even her presence here was risky: she represented black market traders and unregistered residents.

The corridor was steel grey, lit from below. At the end, it opened into an octagonal shaft. She shivered as she stepped into space and floated upwards. A hive of activity buzzed through the corridors she passed, people in uniform snapping along as if programmed. She expected to be stopped at every point.

The ninth floor was the highest, which surprised her: the fortress seemed much larger from outside. She hopped onto the corridor ledge and took the first turn. Solitude surrounded her, unnerving enough that she counted doors twice before she palmed open the fourth.

It opened onto a courtyard with old-fashioned cobblestones and thick foliage clinging to the walls, disguising their artificial nature. Anaea realized why she had assumed greater height for the fortress: the walls rose three stories and ended in a force dome.

Dezba Moon stood in one quadrant of the courtyard, holding an archaic fencing blade and following a holographic light in an intricate pattern. Anaea took a step forward; the cobbles clicked under her feet. Dezba whirled, the blade flipping around in her hand as if she would throw it. Then she recognized her visitor and her lips twitched, not to be mistaken for a smile, but it was something. Amusement? Surprise?

"Miss Carlisle," she said. "Tired of ducking and dodging?"

Reflexively, Anaea's hand came up to the stunner sheath. "No," she said, "but I did take your advice. Thank you." She tried to make it obvious in her voice that she was sincere, even grateful. Her consciousness of it felt false.

If it was forced, Dezba didn't seem to notice. "Physical discipline hones the mind – but good." She loosened her grip on the weapon. She turned the blade over idly in her hand as she continued, "If you're not here for that, then what?"

Anaea had the strange feeling she suspected. "I'm here on behalf of some people from the Cauldron," she said. "They want to talk about compromise."

"Compromise?" Dezba snorted. "Was that your idea? Cauldron residents don't simper about compromise." In a single flow, she sheathed the sword on her belt and crossed the distance between them, catching Anaea's elbow with one hand. "Walk with me. Explain yourself."

Anaea ignored the personal implications of that question and the twitching in her stomach. "Raids on the Cauldron will cost you time, injuries – if not lives – and hassle," she said, then hastily tacked on: "and money. Some of those demolitions you've planned will mean constant harassment from the previous tenants, people who haven't done anything wrong."

"You mean they haven't been caught," Dezba said. The words were sharp, but dark eyes hinted at humor.

As they moved into the shade of a willow, Anaea risked a smile and the response, "That's the refrain I seem to hear a lot."

Dezba laughed, a short bark. "Because it's the truth."

"The Cauldron folk want to offer a way to spare you the grief and embarrassment," Anaea said, hoping she sounded confident. "First, a voluntary work-force for any improvement done within the neighborhood. Second, there's a few architects who could identify which buildings—"

Dezba's hand came down like a knife. "Stop," she said.

Confused, she turned to face the woman. "What?"

"It's impossible," Dezba said. "They're in no position to set terms. That they even dare to offer is throwing down a gauntlet. I'll choose to ignore that because it comes from you, but if the Cauldron wants to trade with withered spoils, they had better earn the right."

This sounded like a foreign language. "You haven't even heard the full terms," Anaea said. "They're—"

"Doesn't matter."

Was that irritation in Dezba's look? A trickle of fear ran through her for the Cauldron folk. "What do you have against them that is so powerful?" she asked. "Do they really not have a chance?" For a second, she was speaking that language, gibberish on the tongue.

"Of course they have a chance. A good chance." Dezba's look softened, a trace of reminisce. "I used to be Cauldron-folk. Ran with a crowd under the Tweaker White Thomas."

The name traced recognition on the inside of Anaea's thoughts. White Thomas. Hadn't Flick said – yes. Both he and Rip had trained with the man. The coil was tighter than she had imagined, and yet Flick didn't seem to know Dezba personally. What, then?

Anaea shook her head, trying to understand the more pressing point. "So why fight people who used to be your allies?"

"Because I didn't come to this point by giving ground. Neither did Blake, and my actions represent him." Dezba's lips thinned. "You don't belong here, Anaea Carlisle," she said. "This is not your turf, and no matter how much you train yourself, you're never going to feel comfortable."

Anaea wondered if she meant in the Cauldron, Nissyen, or perhaps even the Pinnacle Empire, but it didn't matter, for the woman only echoed thoughts drifting just out of reach for the past several days. She admired the people, enjoyed the city and its secrets, could even accept that life here was a series of challenges, but she had no instinct for it. She had been at home on Themiscyra, where at least she understood the life, even if she wasn't sure of her place in it.

"Suited or not," she said. "I'm not going to walk out on them." She held the other's eyes.

Dezba's gaze raked hers; then, unexpectedly, her chin dipped. "You make friends so fast and lightly, then?" she asked, but the barb was absent from her voice. She turned, posture straightening. "Tell your friends that two mornings from now, the plan is to send a stealth team by dawn to plant smoke missiles in three buildings: the bank and the two towers nearest."

Anaea blinked, trying to figure out the implications of this information. "Thank you," she said.

"That's all I can do for you," Dezba said. "Go."

She wasn't done, questions buzzing on her lips. She studied that sharp face and saw she would have no answers, saw also the woman was on edge. If pressed, would Dezba change the plan and negate the warning?

"Once you've passed that on," Dezba said, "get out. We expect criminals to behave a certain way. An ordinary citizen in the same waters will be bloodied and broken to discourage anyone else to follow her—" the pronoun might not have been chosen deliberately, but her eyes flicked back "—path."

The urge to question died, dissolving in the pit of Anaea's stomach. "Thank you," she repeated, stepping backwards. Dezba didn't respond, pacing away. Anaea watched the woman for a few seconds more; then she ducked out from the shadow of the willow.

The journey through the fortress gave her plenty of time for fruitless thought. She had failed – but what more could she do? She had no power to bargain. Her resources, the seeds of an ordinary life in a new universe, seemed like nothing now.

As she approached the guard post, a chill thought occurred to her. Would Dezba change her mind, hold her as a member of the resistance? She stiffened her spine and tried to look assured as she approached the booth.

The four guards watched her with level gazes, vigilant. One tipped his head to his companion, murmuring. She fought the urge to scramble backwards, and then the other man laughed, their secret conversation resolving into leers. She felt undressed before their eyes.

Embarrassed, flushing, she focused on the fact she was almost out, was not under arrest. She passed under the gate arch. She tensed anew as the senior guard, who had not joined in, touched the com panel in front of him.

"We're overdue for relief," he said.

Anaea stepped past the guard post. Autumn sunlight swept her face. It was all she could do not to break into a run. She waited until she was well out of sight of the fortress before hailing a cab.

The jostling, swerving chaos of the cab was a relief. She tapped the earpiece and called Flick.

"What happened?" he asked, his voice nasal with anxiety.

She explained, and his exclamations told her the result had been half-expected. He was grateful for the news about the dawn raid. "We can use that," he said. "Turn it back on them."

"Do you trust what she told me?" Anaea asked.

Flick remained silent for a moment. "I do," he said. "She's an honorable opponent. If she gave an advantage, she meant it."

Then something had been accomplished, though Anaea felt no pleasure. As much as the Cauldron residents treated this like a game, it wasn't. "Good. What's next?"

"You should move uptown," Flick said. "Nothing more you can do."

"But—" the protests swirled at the roof of her mouth. He was right, or almost. This was not her world. On Themiscyra, crime was almost unheard of, contained, controlled, as her entire life had been. Literally: no open skies and broken buildings, no pathways that couldn't be found on the schematics.

But there was something she could do. "I'm going to help Justin get out of the line of fire," she said. "Thank you for everything."

"Good luck," he said. "Can you call Rip with this? I'm going to have my hands full."

"Will," she promised, tapping the call off. It wasn't their last conversation, she told herself.

Rip was more vocal in reaction. "Should have sent you with a better stunner," he said, "except I suppose they wouldn't have let you through the guard post."

Anaea restrained the urge to point out she would never have shot Dezba to solve their problems. "Can I ask you a question?" she said.

"I think you just did, but I got plenty of sleep last night. I can handle two. What's on your mind?"

The cab stopped, and she asked him to hold as she paid and dismounted. She started towards the Cauldron arch. "White Thomas," she said. "Flick said you both trained under him. Dezba said she ran with him, and I was wondering . . ."

"Never met her," Rip said. "Might have been before my time. White Thomas was on the streets for decades. Really sharp fellow. He was always more interested in Flick than me, though. Sort of treated him like a son. Spent a lot of time with the family. Why do you ask?"

She hesitated, not quite sure. "Just puzzled by a few things."

Rip left it at that. "I'm going to lay out some plans. Call me if you need anything."

She hurried down the Cauldron streets, conscious of eyes glossing over her form, but most moved on, and the few that lingered seemed aware of the stunner's subtle bulge. She tried not to wince, not to stare, but her nerves sang.

She reached Justin's workshop and knocked.

"Come in," he said when she announced herself. She pushed the door open and crossed the gloom.

She was surprised to find the workshop untouched; no boxes, everything still assembled. "Why haven't you started moving things?" she asked.

Justin smiled wryly from where he calibrated letters. "I'm not leaving."

21

WHAT? WHY NOT?" ANAEA ASKED.

"I did the math," he said, "and I can't move everything in time, even with help. The press won't fit through the door in one piece, and I'm afraid to disassemble it."

"You could break the wall. Move at least some things," she said.

He shook his head. "The thought of losing even little pieces, of being uprooted . . . I just don't have the strength." That weariness reflected in his voice, soft and colorless.

"Being uprooted isn't the worst thing in the world," she said. "It means opportunity, a chance to start anew." Her words took on an intensity she hadn't expected. She braced herself in front of him, tongue drying out against the roof of her mouth.

"Maybe you'll even find some place – something – better," she finished.

Justin did not move, barely ventured another smile. "Do you speak from personal experience, Anaea?"

That silenced her, sent her whirling into uncertainty. She

didn't know. Had the women of Themiscyra painted this universe accurately, in spirit if not in fact?

"I'm taking the chance," she said quietly. "You should do the same."

"I've taken more than my fair share of chances. I'm done." Justin sighed. "I do have something for you, however."

Anaea glanced about, her mind skipping ahead to plan. If she didn't argue, if she simply took armloads and left . . . but there was too much.

Justin returned with a packet of books wrapped in plast-seal. On the top was one of the copies of *Falling Stars* he had been working on: grey cloth woven with faux-silver thread, the title embroidered in black. "These are yours," he said. "Take them, cherish them – read them."

She drew her hands to her body, wanting to reject the present and the surrender it represented. Somehow, she ended up fumbling with the package. "You'll come with me, at least?"

He shook his head. "I'm not in danger."

She started to form her argument. Dezba had spoken of destroying buildings. Anaea had no confidence the authorities would evacuate them first.

The soft purr of an engine and the rumble of voices made them both stop. Justin started to open his mouth; Anaea was ahead of him, hurrying to the door with what she hoped was silent step. The cold of the marble seeped up into her feet.

She reached the door and pressed her face to the old-fashioned peep hole. An official vehicle rumbled up the street, uniformed policemen alert inside. She tensed, but it drove by the workshop and turned the next corner.

Anaea's nerves took another turn. It was the direction of Marianna's home. Maybe a coincidence, but what if it wasn't? "I'm going to see where they're headed," she called back, setting the books down.

"I don't think that's a good idea," Justin said. "Let them go."

She turned back to him, shook her head. He might have given up, but she could not.

She slipped out onto the street and dashed across, not looking for traffic. It was quiet and still, more than it had been the night she arrived. Anxiety tasted icy in her mouth.

She wasn't quite running as she rounded the bend, saw the officials turn again, heard them arguing, a mechanical grunt of temper. She quickened her pace, skidding, sliding, and tapped the link.

"Anaea?"

"Flick," she said, "where are you?"

After a puzzled pause, he asked, "Are you okay? You sound out of breath."

"Where are you?" she repeated.

"At home," he said. "Grandmum rang me for some help. There are also supplies here. What about you? I thought you were on your way uptown."

Anaea bit her lip as the vehicle parked in front of the steps. "Flick," she said, "they're at the complex door. Get out now."

But get out where? she wondered. Could there be a basement exit? They needed time.

Flick swore. "But we – how did they – okay. Go home, Anaea, and don't worry about me."

If only either of those were possible.

Arguing with him, telling him what she intended, would only waste time he needed. "All right," she said. "Be careful."

He snorted. "Little late for that."

As the call ended, Anaea waved her arms frantically to get the officers' attention. Two turned and spoke to their comrades; the squad paused on the steps of the apartment building.

"Officers . . ." She didn't have to pretend to be out of breath. She hunched over, seeing she had their attention, counting the seconds and wondering how long she could draw them out. She straightened when she saw annoyance in their gazes and blurted out, "You need to come quickly. Please."

The brawny man who seemed in charge frowned. "What seems to be the problem?"

Breath, then another. Try not to think too hard of Flick and his grandmother, as if they could somehow sense it. "I've found a body, a man, a young man, I mean, younger than I am—" babble had never come easily to her; she tripped over it "—in an alley back a ways, and I think he might be dead."

The officer's expression tensed, then relaxed into the patina of routine. "You and you," he said, indicating two of his people, a man and a wiry woman, "go with her." He turned back to the complex, dismissing the matter.

That wasn't good enough. Anaea's thoughts scattered in search of some other way to draw attention.

"Where is this body, then?" the woman said brusquely.

They were too close. She retreated, gesturing. Her other hand settled at her neckline. She rehearsed the actions, the shot, the turn, the repeat. Smooth and easy. Pretend they were targets. Never mind she had first fired a weapon only days ago.

"Just back here," she said. "Well, not just – it's a few blocks down . . . shouldn't you call a medic? He might be alive."

"I've got a kit," the man said. "If he can be helped, that will stabilize him for a doctor's care. Around here, though, he probably got what was coming to him."

The other officers had the complex door open. No more time. Anaea stepped back until her hip bumped against the side of a public terminal. The impact scattered her nerves. "That's a cold philosophy," she said.

A smirk pulled at the woman's lips. "That's the way—"

Anaea jerked the stunner out. Her hand shook so hard she could barely see. Half-blind, she squeezed the grip.

The blast clipped the woman in the thigh. Her legs shuddered as a surprised flush darkened her face. Anaea fired in the direction of the man and dove behind the terminal. The sickly taste of her heart's blood rose into her throat.

Shouts echoed from the apartment complex. Anaea snatched a

breath that made the spinning in her head worse. She desperately wanted to look back – no. She forced herself to scan the street, guessing where she might be able to run without presenting a clear target.

She saw the route: around a parked float-cart, behind stone front steps, and no more than three paces from there to the street corner. She plunged forward, seeing only that safety. A hissing of sparks exploded behind her. The shot hit something between her and them. The officers howled for her to stop, sounding more like a mob bent on revenge than authorities demanding their due.

She rounded the bend. There was no cover, when she had been sure of comforting shadows. Absurdly, she thought of Penelope and hoped Flick had taken the kearl.

The cross-street leapt out at her. She strained towards it, lungs throbbing.

A halo of bright light surrounded her. It soothed for a heart-beat, before her body tingled and her limbs went numb. The world dipped to one side, swayed to the other, and upended itself in pieces.

Anaea's forward momentum carried her and then crashed her into the pavement. Pain sliced holes in the disorientation. Someone must have winged her with a stunner – a passing hit? Maybe she had distracted them for long enough that Flick had slipped away. Maybe there was a chance she could explain it as a misunderstanding.

She pushed to her hands and knees. Her body remembered the motions even if she couldn't feel herself making them. The stunner had rolled out of her hand and wedged in a gutter. She rocked forward, but knew she couldn't reach it even before she felt herself overbalance.

She skidded on all fours, then clambered upright. The blood shot to her feet, making her dizzy. The next business had a decorative porch. She somehow made it there and oozed behind its shelter, her back against the faux-wood pillar. She knew the authorities were right behind her.

Real wood, she realized as her finger picked up a splinter. Of course. Wouldn't it be cheaper here, on a wild planet? Time seemed to ooze.

"Don't move," the female officer called. "Step away from the building and keep your hands up, and we won't have to shoot."

It occurred to Anaea to point out they didn't have to shoot, it was a conscious choice, but her tongue wouldn't wrap around the witticism. There was nowhere to go. She followed their direction. They were dim, bobbing shapes in the back of her eyes.

One dark slash jumped out from her left. It grabbed her, tossing her about like a child's doll, and forced her wrists behind her. She hung limp, unresisting. "You're under arrest for assault on police officers, resisting arrest and false report," a male voice said. "You have the right . . ."

His voice faded into the background. Anaea's world shrunk.

*

THE POLICE PRODDED, dug, searched every inch of her, as if they might scour some hidden threat off her skin. One officer yanked the earpiece out. After a cursory inspection, he smashed it underfoot. As thehe stunner blast wore off , she started to feel the rough handling. The officer shoved her into their vehicle; her shoulder struck the wall, jarring her hard enough it ached in her teeth. Anaea curled up, the vehicle's lurch rattling in her bones.

She heard the driver communicate with a superior, his surprise when he was directed to the central holding facility. She remained as tense as her sore, watery muscles would let her, waiting for word about their original quarry. She couldn't be afraid for herself, not until she heard how Flick had fared.

"Can't believe we had to abort our search for this," the driver grumbled.

"What's Moon going to do about it?" another wondered.

"You don't have to worry. You were just following orders." The lead officer scowled.

Anaea sucked in a breath. Of course Dezba had given the order. Anything else would have been too much coincidence. Yet how? Pieces jostled around in her thoughts, refusing to settle.

The central holding facility was inside the warlord's fortress. The vehicle stopped past the gate as an aperture slid away, and down into darkness they plunged, so swift Anaea had a dizzy vision of a facility powered by the planet's core.

At the bottom, they hauled her out of the vehicle and down corridors into a blazing white chamber of undetermined size. Niches dotted the length at random.

"Stand back."

Anaea tried to ask questions, but they ignored her. They hauled and shoved her like a loose crate, finally depositing her in an alcove. A wall of light flared around her, blunt and blinding.

She realized the setup of this jail: force walls encompassing a tiny square of space, enough to sit or stand, to curl up but not lie straight. Contact with the walls was uncomfortable: they vibrated at a touch. She tried to guess how many alcoves there could be, and gave up.

Though sick with nerves, she dozed. When she awakened, she tried to pull herself upright and found the walls slick and unhelpful. Their buzz made her bruises ache. She noticed a panel and laid her palm on it.

"Prisoner is allowed three calls," an overhead announced.

She thought about contacting Rip or Justin, then discarded the idea. She had already brought trouble on Flick; she didn't want to draw attention to anyone else. She wondered: were communications private? These people seemed to guard their privacy with teeth, but she wasn't sure that extended to prisoners. Particularly not from the Cauldron.

"List of lawyers, please," she said.

The data overwhelmed her. How could she begin to make an informed choice? It seemed this was one thing the Empire and the Collective had in common: they both valued the legal profession, whether it was to defend the law or bend it. At last, she selected a man whose details seemed promising and put through a call. He promised to meet her within the hour.

She remained standing, collecting her thoughts. Was she destined to break the laws everywhere she went? She managed a wry smile despite the sick panic at her core. Maybe for the best she had left Gwydion behind. She wouldn't drag him down with her.

The wall of light phased out. "Your lawyer is here," a guard said. He led her to a nondescript room. The dimness was a relief to her eyes.

The lawyer was a portly man in his forties with a crooked set to his lips. After they exchanged introductions, he said, "Are you aware of the gravity of the charges against you?"

She shook her head. "I'm from – they do things differently at home."

"The assault, the flight, that's almost expected, though the fact you're not a native and shouldn't be used to the game is a point against you," he said. "Conspiracy and aiding and abetting, on the other hand, those are more serious charges."

Anaea blinked. "What?"

"They didn't inform you?" The lawyer gave her a sharp look. "You've been charged with assisting widespread criminal activity in the Cauldron, as well as aiding the escape of two known instigators."

"Oh." Anaea wanted to smile, found her lips cold. If the police hunted Flick, interpreting her actions as a diversion would have been an easy conclusion. "But they can't prove my intentions."

"What else would you be trying to accomplish?" He cocked his head to one side.

Anaea shook her head, half to clear it, half hoping some idea would fall into it. What had she gotten herself into? "What's my situation?" she asked.

"If I were in your place," he said, "I would plead guilty and invoke the kindness of anyone you know. It's hard to argue with the facts, and defending the rest is chancy at best. You're far away from home with no allies."

She couldn't call on the Cauldron folk to defend her from the charge of being associated with them. Plead guilty – and then what? The sick sensation in her core expanded until she could feel it pressing her lungs. "How long do I have to decide?"

"Unless the warlord moves it to his personal court, the backlog is running eight days. Almost a week," he said. "And you don't want his personal attention."

"Thank you." Anaea swallowed, fighting to breathe. "Will you take my case, however I decide?"

The lawyer frowned. "If you value life and limb, I would highly advise you to take immediate steps toward a deal, but yes. I'm yours to command."

The words were so odd she laughed, a brittle sound. She stopped when he stared. "I'm just not sure I can command anything," she said.

He frowned. "I'll return this time tomorrow with some preliminary information." He saw himself out.

Anaea expected to be dragged back to the cell, and was relieved when no one came. She sat there for several minutes, enjoying the semi-dark and the illusion that she didn't have to move. Everywhere her thoughts turned, she ran into claustrophobia.

The door opened again, and Dezba Moon entered.

Anaea scrambled to her feet, though once she had the chair between herself and the woman, she had no idea what good it did. "Why did you come after him?" she asked. "I never meant to do anything illegal—"

"Save your breath. That's not a defense." Dezba's lips quirked, betraying humor. Then the face returned to flat affect. "Do you feel betrayed?"

Anaea hesitated. Was this an attempt to get a confession? Yet Dezba knew enough already. "Yes," she said. "To give with one hand and take with the other . . ."

"Enough." Her voice was sharp, warning. Anaea blinked, confused. Were they being monitored? Did that mean the information Dezba had given earlier was still accurate? How did that make sense? Dezba showed no inclination to explain. "I would have left you alone. But I wanted to know my enemy, so I checked the ships' logs to see who you had traveled with. When I saw the name, I knew I needed to act."

Anaea worried her lip. "Tobias—" she used his real name with the hope of sounding distant "—is surely not that dangerous."

Dezba barked laughter. "Not the younger Risingsun. The elder."

"Marianna?" she asked, confused.

"White Thomas was her second husband. They accomplished a lot together." The expression that flickered across her face was not a smile, not a frown. "I saw some of it. Heard about the rest." Her voice hardened. "But now she is the enemy, and has to be dealt with as that deserves."

The history made sense now, the tangle that linked them. It was a bond almost like family, a matter not for outsiders, even though it affected the warlord's followers and the Cauldron alike.

"You wanted me to leave Annwyn," Anaea said. "Can you help me?"

Dezba fixed her with a sharp look. "You got what you wanted: their little family is gone like smoke. It's only fair you face the consequences."

Anaea had broken the law and could not run away from it again, as much as a voice screamed and clawed inside her. She vowed if she somehow made it out there would be no more. She would be a model citizen, even if she never found somewhere to call home. She could not see a way to freedom, much less to sanctuary.

She flashed to the scene in Valasca's office and remembered her terror then. Now the chief doctor seemed mild, Thalestris even supportive in her way. Was loss of memory worse than loss of freedom? She twisted back and forth over the question.

"Take care of yourself, if you can," Dezba said, and saw herself out. The guard arrived moments later to take Anaea back to the blazing cell.

∗

MEALS APPEARED AT intervals, marking time. She had no contact with the outside world, nothing to look at but the faceless light. The cell made it impossible to stretch out or lie down comfortably; her muscles seemed permanently stiff. If she forgot the quiver of the wall and tried to lean, it jarred every little ache. Her mind looped around and around her time in Nissyen, choking like a noose.

"What happens if I plead guilty to the lesser charges and contest the others?" she asked the lawyer. "What am I looking at?"

"Two years – local, not galactic – with the possibility of parole in one," he said. "I would highly recommend you take anything you're offered. I will repeat that I believe you should consider pleading to all charges."

"How long?" she asked.

"Seven to ten. Out in five if you have good character references."

He was so matter of fact that at first, she thought she had misheard. Five years? Character references? Acid swam up from her stomach. "What if I fight and lose?"

"Much longer," he said. "This is a sensitive subject. The warlord is looking to make a point. Worst case scenario, they decide not only are you guilty, but you know more about the organization. There's a sentencing provision for extreme measures . . ."

She bit her lip. "Such as?" The lawyer hesitated long enough to make her shiver. "No, don't," she said.

Five years. No risk of more, no risk of – torture? She should take it, but every instinct beat against the certainty of that cage. How could they prove it, even if it was the truth? Even here, hypermentals couldn't collect evidence without permission. It seemed a strange civility, but the lawyer had assured her of it.

"If you're innocent . . ." he trailed off.

She looked up, met his eyes. "I have to fight," she said.

"Most people do," he said with a trace of resignation. "I

suppose we wouldn't be people if we didn't. Well, if that's what you want, I'll make it happen."

22

THREE MORE DAYS PASSED. A DATE WAS SET FOR THE TRIAL. Her body throbbed with the contortion needed to sleep or sit. It was too hard to stand for long. The cramps of sleeping curled up left her numb. The other facilities of the cell were adequate, but no less unpleasant.

When her lawyer arrived, his lips trembled. "Miss Carlisle," he said.

"Is there something wrong?" she asked.

"Your friends," he said. "Well, the people you allegedly sought to aid?"

Until those words, she had thought she was too exhausted for the burst of anxiety. "What happened?"

"I'm not clear on the details, but they've won a coup," he said. "Drove off a group of builders, and instead of destroying the site, they finished the construction, made themselves look good and made fools of the officers who tried to arrest them. Half the city wants to know why these upstanding citizens are being persecuted. The warlord is backing off the restructure plan before opinion blows up in his face."

Anaea resisted the urge to laugh, delight washing over her. "Isn't that a good thing?"

"Not for you," he said. "Any case connected to this goes to trial and the media will pounce on it. Right now you've been postponed indefinitely."

She blinked, confusion toppling around her. "They can do that? But—"

"They can do that," he confirmed.

"Oh." She sucked in a breath, collecting her composure. "I'm still glad. Those people were—"

He held up a hand. "Don't say anything more."

"What happens next?" she asked.

"What happens?" he echoed, puzzled. "Nothing. You wait."

"Until . . ."

"I can't say. No one can."

Numbed into silence, she didn't stop his departure. The entrance of the guards awakened her voice. "I demand an appeal," she said, trying to force the quaver out of her voice. Setting a firm line was the only way she had any hope. "You can't just—"

She didn't see the guard move. His arm struck her across the chest. She staggered, her right leg twisting under her. Pain flared up her ankle as if the muscles had been set on fire.

"Women like you stay quiet," he said.

Anaea wobbled for balance. As soon as she managed it, she regretted it: she couldn't put weight on the ankle.

"That's enough," the other guard said. "Back to her cell."

She had to limp, almost hop, and the effort of keeping up filled her attention. It wasn't until the force-cell flared around her again that her reaction caught up with her. She curled up and sobbed, her hands braced against the floor. She fought the urge to dig. It was stone, nowhere to go. At least a criminal sentence had an end, but now she couldn't see one.

She stopped counting meals. She had no idea how long it would take for the political dust to settle. The thought of Dezba crossed her mind occasionally, but the woman had made it clear

Anaea was on her own.

Any summons from the outside was a welcome break in the routine. She sat at the table again, head in hands. It might be good news, might be bad again, and she didn't know which way to jump.

She heard the door open. The shadow hesitated on the threshold.

"Anaea?" a familiar warm tenor voice said.

She jerked her head up, staring. Ignoring the flash of pain from her ankle, she crossed the distance and crushed him in a fierce hug. "Gwydion," she said, and that moment of warmth eclipsed the past several days. She pulled her head back to study him and felt the strange, sudden urge to lean closer and—

"I missed you," he said, his voice genuine and intense. His expression devoured her.

Anaea tightened her hold on him in answer. His presence made her warm and dizzy. She felt safe, sheltered; the pain and confusion blurred into the background. She made herself release him and stepped back. "You didn't come all the way here for company," she said.

"I've been tracking the feeds from Nissyen since you left," he said. "Because I know Sanctum police, I have access to data before it becomes news. That's how I heard about your arrest. I told Dr. Anders I was leaving with or without her approval." His eyes dropped; his expression would have been sheepish if it weren't so grave. "She sent me with her seal as her representative." He reached for her hands and lifted his eyes to hers. When he spoke again, it was the well-remembered starlight in her mind.

Anaea, how do we get you out of here?

She stared. It took her a moment to remember how to frame her thoughts. *What do you mean?*

Jail-break, if we have to, he responded. *You did it for me, remember? I'd still be locked away from everything I knew.*

Which was the situation she was in now. *They must know*

how to deal with hypermentals here. Never mind risky, it could be impossible.

That would be a last resort, he said.

She asked him some inane question out loud about his trip, which he answered. If only the arraignment were soon; it would easier to escape en route to the courtroom than from these depths. Her brain buzzed around that.

Hypermentals have some political pull here, don't they? she asked. *Just on basis of what they are?*

Memories of overloaded hypermentals and the impact they had, Gwydion said. *Yes. I have Dr. Anders' voice, as well, for what it's worth.*

Anaea bit her lip. *The people I acted to defend just scored a major victory. I've been told the warlord has delayed my trial until things quiet down. Maybe—*

I see where you're going, he said. *I can do that. Is there anyone I need to talk to?*

She filled his head with thoughts of Flick and Marianna. *They'll help, I think.*

He hugged her again. "I'm going to help you get out of here," he said. The words seemed loud and hollow after the internal conversation.

"I'm . . . not sure you can," she said.

"I can," he said, a promise. He lingered uncertainly, some speech or decision flicking across his face, then he hastened out.

Anaea dropped against the table, heaving out a breath giddy with pent-up joy and relief. There was light, and he had brought it with him.

*

In the middle of the night, according to the meals she started counting again, a pair of guards dragged her out of the cell. She got her wits about her enough to ask where they were going, but got no answer. They entered a room furnished like an old-fashioned study.

The rich wood shelves concealed who knew what behind false leather bookbindings. Anaea knew the real thing enough to tell the difference, but there were several genuine volumes as well. The room smelled of cedar and smoke, filled with a rich red light.

The guards tightened their grip on her arms, though she hadn't been struggling. The figure behind the desk – tall, athletic, dark – rose at her entrance.

"You're Anaea Carlisle," he said. His voice cut like a whip, as did his eyes, a startling pale blue. She would have thought he was blind, save for their intense focus.

"Yes." She wasn't sure what else to say.

"You have five minutes to explain yourself," he said, "or I have you and your adorable little sycophant executed. Better to deal with a single shock than so many bleeding-heart whimpers. Public attention may be on you now, but it will fade."

Anaea's eyes widened. Alarm and realization slammed into her. She was bleary from captivity, but there was no mistaking the face from the billboard: Blake Avidan, warlord of Nissyen.

She swallowed. "What am I explaining?" she asked. Hope scampered through her. Gwydion had succeeded with their plan, spread word of her plight – none of which mattered if the warlord could not be swayed.

"Why you flouted the law and the imposed order of Nissyen, and got caught." There was a flicker of amusement in his expression, but like Dezba's, it vanished under cold assurance. "Why you think you deserve freedom now."

She could answer honestly, but would he accept it? Gwydion – he had mentioned Gwydion. She pushed through the fear and tried to think loudly, seeking him.

"If you're hoping for guidance from your companion," Avidan said, "don't. I have him under control."

There was no menace in his voice, only certainty. Anaea's

stomach knotted. What if – no. Focus. The truth had served her before in warlord territory. She had to trust that.

"I never meant to flout anything," she said. "I was helping a friend. Two friends. People who made me feel welcome even though I was unprepared for everything in their world." Her eyes strayed to the shelves. She could smell the leather, almost feel pages under her fingers.

"There was no planning or malice. I did the only thing I could think of to keep them from being arrested, and I expected the consequences." She tried to swallow, but her throat was dry. Avidan's brows shifted, a twitch to the eyes that couldn't be read. "I got caught because I had no time to plan, but even if I had, I don't think I would have managed much better. I'm not meant to be here."

"Meant?" he rumbled.

The words knocked her off on a tangent. "I don't mean in a cosmic sense," she said, "I don't believe there's a God directing the path we take, though I recognize a universal consciousness." Or maybe it was that simple: this part of the universe would always reject her, in the same way an allergic reaction caused a rash.

"I mean I don't fit in here. I could learn it intellectually, but I wouldn't grasp it emotionally," she continued. "I know I bear some guilt. But if people only fought charges when they were innocent, would there be any need for courts?"

Avidan barked laughter. "Most people fight to avoid their guilt, yes. However, you . . ." he trailed off, the silence interrupted only by the crackling of the fireplace. She stood tense, trying not to waver.

"Are you willing to make a statement to that effect? That you are a foreigner acting out of personal interests and not otherwise concerned with how Nissyen runs?" he asked.

"Yes," she said.

"Then I release you," he said. "On the condition your departure is permanent. I have no time to wrestle with this, and I have no intention of doing it twice. If you return, even for a day-trip, I will make an example of you. Do you understand me?"

She swallowed hard, nerves thrumming in her ears. But how hard could it be to avoid a single city? "Yes," she said.

He nodded. "Good. I'll call the media."

Anaea blinked. "But it's late," she said. Relief flowed up through her, filling the spaces of her mind and awakening thoughts that had been dead for days.

"Early," he said, "but why should that matter? Wait here."

*

In less time than she had anticipated, Avidan had a crew of six reporters in his office. She repeated her explanation in a daze as they lapped up her words.

"What is your opinion of politics on Nissyen?" one woman asked.

Avidan narrowed his eyes, then dropped back in his chair. Even that slight movement caused the reporters to freeze as if they might stampede out of the office, but they relaxed when he did. That display of power startled Anaea: this one man was stronger than Asteria, the founder of her home, and he had done nothing more than take control.

"I don't have an opinion," she said. "I would need to know much more to form one, and I don't mean to stay and do so."

"What are your plans?"

"Are you being thrown off the planet?" another bulled in.

Anaea winced. "Of course not," she said, and wondered if in fact that was a good description. "But I don't know where I'm going next. My friend—"

"Are you satisfied?" Avidan interrupted. "Or is this to be a puff piece?"

His question cleared them out. Without moving from behind the desk, he continued, "Get your friend and make your departure. Half my enemies are not this much trouble." Somehow, that didn't seem to be entirely a complaint. He added, "But if I see you again, you'll be one of them, and I'll let the raptorhounds have you."

The words were so mild, tinged with a hint of humor, that Anaea didn't know what to make of them. Compared to the brute force of the guards, the blank assault of imprisonment, Avidan seemed too reserved for such a threat . . . not that she intended to return to find out.

The guards returned the items Anaea had been arrested with, but not the stunner. Under the circumstances, she could not protest. They led her to a chamber where two men and an empanelment of force generators held Gwydion under surveillance. When he saw her, he stumbled to his feet, getting tangled in the chair. That and the flush on his cheeks told her he had been drugged.

"Let's get out of here," she said.

He was coherent enough to direct her to his hotel, but neither of them could walk without the other's help. As much as he tried to let her do the leaning, his weight bore down on her sore frame. She helped him sit on the bed.

"Sorry," he croaked, "they dragged me to the fortress. Told me this was the only way to be sure I wasn't influencing you."

Tentatively, she kissed his brow. "You saved me."

"I think you saved you," he said, then groaned and slid back on the bed. "Make it stop spinning."

He was asleep two seconds later.

Anaea sat with the light on, finding time for thoughts crushed by the situation. Where would she go next? Why had Gwydion come so far for her? Could she ever feel safe again, when it was so easy to be thrown in a cage and forgotten? What about Penelope? What about her things? The after-images of imprisonment flashed on the inside of her eyelids. She shuddered and forced her eyes open.

The door light flashed. The screen under the palm panel read Tobias Mortimer.

Flick! She leapt to her feet and pressed her hand on the panel. "How did you find—"

Her intention to hug him in greeting was forestalled when Penelope leapt to her shoulder from the duffel-bag Flick carried. She reeled backwards with an awkward hop tokeep from falling over.

"Sheesh, you'd think I had tortured her," Flick said. "I guess I just give off the wrong pheremones or something."

Anaea buried the side of her face in the kearl's fur. "Are you all right?" she asked. "The things I heard – or didn't hear . . ."

"I'm fine," he said. "There were some hairy moments and some losses—" he bit his lip "—but we're doing better than I could have expected. I owe you for getting me out that night. When your friend from the matriarchs asked us to kick up a fuss, it was the least I could do – here, take your stuff before my arms fall off."

She did so, noticing the packet of books peeking out from the duffel-bag. "Justin's gift," she said. "How is he?"

Flick closed his eyes. "He's dead."

She sucked in a sharp breath. "How?"

"It wasn't a patrol, if that's what you're thinking," he said. "The workers tried to do some preliminary work on the building and it just . . . came down. Everything more than three feet from the door got buried. That—" he nodded to the packet.

"Was still waiting by the door," she finished his sentence, vividly remembering setting it down. He had left it for her return.

"Yeah." Flick smiled wearily. "Figured something like that when I opened it, saw the dedication on the first book. He signed it to you."

Sensing her mood, Penelope pressed against her face. Anaea gently peeled the kearl into her arms, her heart running faster. Justin dead. She had hardly known him, but he had showed her something that changed her perception of the world. She almost felt it had died with him.

"I'm sorry," she said, remembering he had been a friend of

Flick's family, his acquaintance, his loss. She wasn't even sure she had the right to grieve.

"So am I," he answered. He dropped the duffel-bag to give her a one-armed hug. "Mind if I come in?"

They sat at the table as he filled her in on events in the Cauldron, and she related her experiences in prison. She shied away from her fears and the pain; it was easier to pretend neither existed, and she didn't want him to feel responsible. He shook his head in astonishment at her description of Avidan's behavior. "I guess only the crazy ones become warlords," he said. "Either that, or the job drives you nuts. Look, wherever you go, you can always call on me and Grandmum. You know that, right?"

"I know," she said.

He stood. "Travel safe. Or travel wild, I guess . . . but stay in touch."

"I will," she promised.

She had expected to collapse after his departure, with relief or grief or certainly exhaustion, but her brain continued to spin. Penelope fell asleep on her lap.

"Anaea?" It was Gwydion, clear-eyed. The nap must have flushed the drugs from his system.

"Flick stopped in to say goodbye and thanks," she said.

He nodded, studying her face. "Is everything all right?"

She decided against explaining. Right now, it was too close and painful to share, even with him. "Let's just get out of here," she said.

23

Anaea and Gwydion left the next morning on a passenger shuttle. Afraid that she would be stopped if she took the time to see a doctor, she had relied on a medkit to bandage her ankle, grabbed some patches for the pain. She had to wait it out. She didn't want to think about it; the physical ache brought the rest tumbling back, but she couldn't tune it out: the process of standing in line, waiting, made the ankle swell and throb.

Once aboard, she found a place by the viewscreen and watched Nissyen diminish to a speck on the winding peninsula, then vanish, along with the lingering pain. She had only seen one city, and that seemed impossibly vast. It was hard to imagine an entire planet reduced to dust in the distance.

The copy of *Falling Stars* rested in her lap. "We are all creatures of our past, real and imagined," Justin had written on the inside cover.

"How are you feeling?" Gwydion settled next to her.

"Like I need another three showers," she said, "but good. Relieved." The word wasn't strong enough for what she wanted to express, and she shook her head.

"Did you find what you were looking for?" he asked. "Would you have stayed?"

"Some of it." She glanced down at the book. "No. I was leaving when everything happened. I liked the freedom, and there were good people, but I don't have their instincts." Yet she had replaced the stunner with a conventional model. It remained in her bag, sealed and probably never to be used, but it was there. It was a thing she would never have been allowed on Themiscyra, much less felt she needed. The uncertainty clenched her throat. She was still no marksman. Surely she wouldn't need it in matriarch space . . .

"Your friend Flick is a character," Gwydion said. "Sometimes I felt as if I needed a translation guide."

She laughed. "I suppose you might. He has a heart as big as the sea, though."

"You're one to talk about seas," he said lightly, smiling.

She ducked her head. "I've only seen them from above."

"We'll have to fix that." He watched out the viewscreen. "Anaea, does Dr. Anders know where you're from?"

"She suspects, at the very least. Why did she send you after me?" Anaea rubbed the silver cover of the book in counterpoint to her thoughts.

"I'm one of only four hypermentals in the Sanctum," Gwydion said, "and Adrian is another. She tends to bend a little for us. And it comes with a request. Matriarchs on the planet Solomon are locked in debate about privacy zones; areas, like the Sanctum, where the planet-wide nets don't function. Dr. Anders asked if you and I could listen to what's happening on the ground." He swallowed; it was obvious the idea intimidated him. "I'm ideal because a lot of those same issues come up with hypermentals, so I can ask questions. You're an outsider, so you might see other things."

And Phailin suspected just how much of an outsider. Anaea bit her lip. The idea of some political mission depending on her observations made her slightly nauseous, but if she could help the Sanctum, she owed them. Compared to where she had been, it surely couldn't be dangerous. And they wouldn't be spies, exactly . . . just observers.

While she looked, just as intently, for signs that she might be finding her way home.

"I think we should do it," she said.

"I was hoping you'd say that," he said. "We won't be there in any official capacity, but Dr. Anders wanted to . . . edit your background ties. There's an older couple who retired in the Sanctum who are blood relations of a local comitissa. If they had a daughter, she would be of interest. Enough to get us in the door."

Anaea bit her lip, uncomfortable with the deception, but she could see no harm in it. "All right. Where are we going?"

"The name of the city is Serendipity."

She laughed, surprised. Maybe that was the first sign. Could the universal consciousness be sending her where she needed to be? "We'll see about that."

*

MUCH LATER, SHE sat in their shared cabin with Penelope on her lap, reading the first chapter of *Falling Stars*. She stopped at the description of a binary star sunrise, wondering why the flowery prose had her dabbing at her eyes.

Because in any other media, that description would have been updated to match the current style. It was the stamp of time Justin had loved.

"Anaea? Are you all right?" Gwydion had been surfing history records.

"I'm fine," she said, but gestured for him to join her on the couch. "I met a book maker in Nissyen." At his encouraging look, she told him the rest of the story: how Marianna had introduced them, the printing press and his personal library, and finally Justin's refusal to leave that had led to his death.

"I'm sorry," Gwydion said, "that's horrible." He rested a hand on her arm, tentatively. "At least he didn't see his life's work destroyed."

"I hadn't thought of that," Anaea admitted, remembering the last time she had seen him: his weary refusal, the final gift. She leaned against Gwydion. His presence made her feel warm, safe – but also something else that intruded into what she had meant to be a moment of grief.

He let the silence linger before he spoke. "Books," he said. "It's an archaic art, but it suits you."

"Are you calling me archaic?" she asked gently.

He colored. "I didn't mean . . ."

She meant to laugh and tell him it was a joke. A tickling sensation interrupted her, the urge that had passed her by when he showed up in her cell. This time it was not a mysterious thing, but a specific and deliberate suggestion.

She leaned up and, for the second time, kissed him.

He made a surprised sound against her lips, then pressed closer. It was gentle, inviting, wrapping around her thoughts and making her head tingle. She felt his breath through hers, as complete as the touch of minds.

His hand cupped her cheek. Each finger left a warm imprint on her skin. She turned her head into the touch and deepened the kiss. She tasted fire and savored the feeling. It felt like a homecoming to some place she had only imagined.

He broke off for air, his eyes widened and intense on hers. "Anaea? I thought you were putting on a show for my family."

"They're not here now," she said softly.

He smiled weakly, lowering his hand. "I noticed."

She could laugh it off and things would be almost the same. She hesitated on that brink, but her heart still hummed with the kiss, and she could not lie.

"Gwydion," she said, "I've realized how much I missed you, and that you mean more to me than an ally." The words buzzed in her throat. "I think I'm attracted to you. I don't know how it goes with men—"

His eyes lightened with recognition. The glow went deep under her skin. "Something like this, I think," he said. "I chased you across star systems, remember?"

The part of her on tenterhooks dropped with relief. She drew in a swooping breath, but then a thought made her hold it. "I know I'm not Sophie—"

"You don't have to be," he said hastily, but there was no strain in his voice. "Just be you. That's enough."

He meant it. She breathed out and leaned into him, surprised how comfortable a frame so different from hers could be. The angles she had thought would be inconvenient instead provided a solid resting place.

She tilted her head up to kiss him again. She had expected to be more sure of herself, but the sensations startled her anew. She rediscovered what a kiss was like, even as his presence made it familiar. Could Hiraeth, she wondered, be longing for a person?

The meal call interrupted them. Anaea dithered between this newfound comfort and food, and because of the bland diet from prison, the latter won out.

She gave him a tentative peck on his cheek, and felt absurdly like she was putting a mark on him. "I hate to leave, but – can we go?"

"Name the destination." He threaded his arm through hers and pulled her up, letting her lean on him to steady her ankle. She sensed, joke or not, that he meant it.

*

THE SHIP ENCOUNTERED no pirates or other trouble until it reached the Bridge. There was no need for a change of ship, so the plan was to bypass Centurion Station. Anaea was relieved: she didn't want to spend another day in bleak imperial housing If she thought about it, her little room on Themiscyra hadn't been much more elaborate, but it had been more cozy because it had been safe, and it had been hers.

She and Gwydion spoke to all hours about her discovery of books and his departure from policework; about her beliefs and his religion; about family and community and not belonging to either. Sometimes they clung close to each other; other times, the nearness seemed awkward, charged. She shied away from more. This was a new, fragile thing, and it needed care.

Their transport had a viewscreen in the main lounge. Part of Anaea didn't want to see the Bridge again, as if simply watching it could summon trouble. The urge for vigilance won out. She curled in a chair nearest the screen, taut. Penelope groomed herself in her lap, restless and often turning about, trying to knead Anaea into stillness with her paws. Gwydion rested his hand over hers.

The sight of space's expanse reminded her of star-dancing, the virtual simulation the women of Themiscyra loved as a past-time, where the music and the flickering starfield responded to the dance. Orithia had invited her the day she had found Gwydion on salvage. She remembered begging off until the weekend, caught up in her confusion and assuming there would be time. Now she wished desperately she had gone that night.

The fingers on hers tightened, a gentle squeeze. Guilt flashed through her. She shouldn't be pining for the past, not with possibility, and a mission, at hand. She reassured him with a smile.

As if the universe had decided to mock her attempts at equilibrium, the red-slashed ships of the Bridge authority filled the viewscreen.

Anaea jumped, swallowing her breath in a hiccup. The move dumped Penelope off her lap. The kearl chittered indignantly and scuttled off to sulk. "What's going on?" she asked, first of Gwydion, and then the other passengers in the lounge. No one had answers.

The captain's voice filled the lounge. "We've been halted by Centurion Station. There is no need for concern. They are searching for a fugitive and have no business with us."

"Could Avidan have changed his mind?" Gwydion murmured. She shot him a sharp, startled look, and he paled. He obviously hadn't meant to say the words out loud. He shook his head. "Surely not."

But she had to do the math, even through panic. "Could a courier ship have beaten us here?"

"Communications in-system are limited only by the speed of light," he said. "Send a message to a courier stationed near the hyperspace corridor and it would be possible."

"Please remain where you are," the captain continued. "Let's make this as painless as possible."

If they were looking for her, staying mute here would not be painless. She twined her hands in her lap, leaning in to Gwydion. "Can you hide us?"

"I could," he answered, "if we conceal ourselves somewhere, I can dissuade them from looking. But if we do that . . ."

"We're admitting we have something to hide," she finished his sentence. "And we don't. Avidan set us free."

"He wants you out of sight," he said. "Surely bringing you back would be counterproductive."

Before she could stop herself, she pounced on the uncertainty in his voice. "Who says they'd bring me – us – back?"

That decided Gwydion. He rose in a rush, attracting curious eyes from others in the lounge. He managed a casual smile even as his fingers clutched hers. They inched towards the door under the flat stare of a grey-haired woman.

"Wait – Penelope," Anaea said. She lowered into a crouch, crooning to the kearl. Penelope pretended a fit of deafness, nuzzling up to a young man for a portion of his cake. Anaea suppressed the frantic urge to laughter. It might come to nothing, but she wanted to get out of the lounge while they could, and nothing more than the kearl's stubbornness stood in the way. She wished she had left the leash on, but Penelope still hated it: she had never needed one at home.

In this area of space, it wasn't the pets who needed leashes.

The lounge door opened and four imperial officers entered. Anaea straightened, fingers still laced with Gwydion's, and trying to make her face look as natural as possible. It wouldn't matter if she was the one they were looking for.

The grey-haired woman slanted her narrow gaze in their direction and sniffed in a manner that might be taken for triumphant. They had tried to escape and been caught at it.

The men spread out, speaking briefly to each of the passengers. They passed Anaea and Gwydion without a glance back, focusing first on the ones who were seated. One checked a holographic imprint on his palm. They were looking for a specific face.

Their search brought them back around to the pair. The black-clad officer towered over her. His regard sharpened.

"In a hurry to go somewhere, were you?"

She was: anywhere but here. Numb, she shook her head.

"We were on our way to our quarters when the announcement came through," Gwydion said. He shifted with the obvious intent of standing in front of her.

The officer reached out to stop him. "Don't move." He focused on her, hardly giving her companion a second glance.

They were looking for a female, then. Her stomach swirled, her thoughts flashing back to imprisonment, the vibrating walls, the fear of being lost forever. He gestured to the man with the holographic imprint. They bent over the image. Anaea tried to stretch onto her toes without being too obvious, but her right foot wouldn't let her.

Her heart nearly flew out of her chest when small claws pulled at her pants, scrambling up her leg and hip. Penelope swung onto her shoulder. "Now you come over," Anaea said, wishing she could find the humor in it. The kearl nipped her ear.

The officer looked up, studied her. Gwydion tensed to readiness, though there was little he could do.

"Not her," he said to the others. "Let's go."

They swept out of the lounge. Anaea stumbled to one side, leaning on Gwydion. The other passengers exchanged looks ranging from puzzled to indignant and relieved, but none, she was sure, felt the same chest pounding she did.

"We're fine," Gwydion said, steering her back to a chair by her elbow.

"We're fine," she echoed, but she didn't really believe it until the ship flashed into hyperspace. Part of her hoped the imperials never found who they were looking for.

*

Days later, they arrived in the Tau Ceti system. Solomon, second earth, first colony, was the innermost planet of six, a brilliant pearl of blue. Less than a fifth of its surface was landmass, but it had housed the nerve-center of the colonized universe, until Y-Poisoning. In the back of her mind, Anaea realized she had considered Solomon almost mythical.

Two hours of security protocols before the ship was permitted to land, and another two to process their identification and luggage, took only a little shine off her awe. Penelope was cranky and restless by the time they left the antiseptic spaceport. A new guestlink itched against Anaea's collarbone.

Serendipity was green: not just the predominant tone of buildings, sidewalks and street signs, but the jeweled tones of flowerbeds, crawling vines and immense trees. Even public uniforms matched. The sky was a tantalizing patchwork of blue, the air thick with pollen and perfume. Penelope sneezed, shaking out her fur.

Anaea marveled as they walked, forgetting the low throb of her ankle. "How do they maintain this?"

"Carbon dioxide rations," Gwydion said. "If you produce too much, there's a fine. The plants off-set that, of course."

"Oh." It still seemed beautiful.

Two minutes down the acceleration sidewalk, they reached a hotel and checked in.

The room was palatial with green-tinted windows. Warm sunlight poured in, an afternoon that matched the master clock:

Solomon's twenty-five hour day was the basis for galactic standard. "Can we afford this?"

"For a few days, yes," Gwydion said. "And why not? It's nice to indulge every now and again."

Anaea scooped Penelope off one of the beds, extricating a tassel from her mouth. "That would be why not," she said.

He chuckled. "Hopefully, we'll get a reply from Dr. Anders soon. I sent a message from customs, but it won't travel at any great speed. In the meantime, you should write to the regina, see if you can get an invitation."

"Why would she be interested in me?" Anaea asked.

"Even if you aren't here in any official capacity, the Sanctum is your residence of record," he said. "So you'd be a curiosity to her."

More, Anaea thought wryly, than the regina would ever know. "What do I say?" she asked.

After some time dithering over tone, humility and flowery language, Anaea found herself reciting the message and hoping it sounded natural.

"Regina Linscott, I hope this message finds you well," she said. "My name is Anaea Carlisle. Phailin Anders spoke of you highly, and since I have business in the area, I thought I would send my greetings. I hope we can meet as friends."

A little compliment, a little lie. A hint she might have political leanings. It wasn't perfect, but with no tongue-tripping, she saved the message and sent it.

"If she tries to find out what business I have, she's going to be very puzzled," Anaea said.

Gwydion chuckled. "She might assume it's something deep and mysterious."

She shuddered. "I hope not."

He leaned over and rubbed her shoulders. "Between the two of us, we can do anything," he said.

She resisted the urge to melt into his touch. "It's sweet of you to say," she said.

"By which you mean that's nonsense." His voice was soft with amusement.

"Yes." She tipped her head to give him a quick kiss, he leaned in, and the next several minutes were blissfully free of any thought.

Heads bent over the viewscreen, they planned for a day as tourists. Their itinerary included investigating the city's book-craftand its most famed sights, the foremost of which was the Flying Sphere, a tower atop which a zero-gravity force dome allowed a view of the entire city.

"I'm not sure I could relax at that height," Anaea admitted. "Do you want to check in with the Hypermental Charter?"

He shook his head. "I'd rather not. Groups of us tend to forget about personal space and inner thoughts. It gets disconcerting."

There was little information to be found on either the local matriarchs or the legislation Phailin feared. On the ship, they had read about Linscott and studied the few news articles that discussed the changing tide. It was not a topic much in popular debate. Did no one care?

They ordered dinner: a mishmash of local specialties, some of which should have clashed and yet still smelled heavenly. Anaea had a forkful to her mouth when her link buzzed.

It was a recorded message, audio only.

"Miss Carlisle," said a silken voice, "your presence in my city is a mystery and a delight. You are invited to my estate for an evening meal at the time of seven and thirty. Your bodyguard is, of course, welcome to accompany you. Identity yourself to my secretary, Karen, when you arrive."

Anaea blinked. "Bodyguard?"

"I suppose she just assumed." Gwydion looked abashed.

"But you're not . . ."

"I could be if I needed to." His voice was serious.

She found herself warmed by the protective note in the words. "I know," she said, "but that's not what I meant. You're not my underling."

"I am, as far as they're concerned," he said. "If you are a businesswoman, or anyone of import, I must be an assistant, bodyguard or . . ." He flushed.

She decided not to ask. "That was fast," she said, after replaying the message. "I wonder what the quickness of it means?"

Gwydion cast a rueful look to their untouched feast. "Means we ordered all this for nothing."

He changed into a black suit a size too large in the elbows. She dressed hastily, pinning the outermost strands of her hair so they held the rest back. No more than a dusting of make-up; she had no familiarity with applying it, and felt it best not to seem other than she was. She regarded herself in the mirror and sighed. None of Themiscyra's prized outward tranquility.

She stepped out of the bathroom and jerked at Gwydion's sharp breath. "What is it?"

"You look beautiful," he said.

She wore the dress she had purchased in the Sanctum, peacock blue and draped off one shoulder. She had no jewelry, leaving an expanse of cream skin at the neckline. She loved the dress, yet was conscious of the fact she didn't live up to it. The ankle bandage felt huge and conspicuous.

She shook her head. "I'll be fine," she said.

"I wasn't flattering you for reassurance," he said.

She flicked him a startled look and lifted a hand to her cheek. She was sure compared to Linscott's companions, she was plain, but she smiled and said nothing.

They had decided Penelope was well-behaved enough to come, and that a little curiosity about the kearl wasn't a bad thing. Better, Anaea thought, the matriarch focus on her pet than herself.

When they entered a public car, the front panel lit. "Reading clearance from Regina Linscott," the automated voice said. "Conveying."

They soared high, passing businesses and then entering a residential area. The homes were widely spaced and heavily landscaped, to the point where some were nothing more than suggestions under the shroud of green.

As the homes increased in luxury, a trend appeared: many were constructed within the branches of an artificial tree, two or three stories off the ground. The realism of the faux branches grew in proportion to the size and opulence of the dwelling, but every tree echoed the last, a pleasing pattern of harmony.

Finally, the public car swiveled to a halt in front of a cherry wood fence. A gravel avenue wound between flowerbeds towards a manor suspended in the cradle of three massive old-growth trees. Anaea stared hard, but couldn't shake the conviction they were real.

A hover platform stood under the canopy. There was no security visible: no guards, no checkpoints, no force field posts. A little nonplussed, Anaea followed Gwydion onto the platform.

As they ascended, she stroked Penelope's fur. The kearl perched on the padded shoulder of the dress, a watchful sentinel.

The underside of the manor mimicked the treeline, so the predominance of white marble and angular columns in the antechamber startled Anaea. Offices split off in all directions.

A short, stout man emerged. He had dark brown hair and a neatly trimmed beard with a hint of fuzz over the lip. She blinked at the facial hair. She had seen it on several men by now, but it struck her at odds with his polished manner.

His mild green eyes sharpened before he dipped in a bow. "May I help you?" he said in a gravelly voice.

"We're looking for the regina's secretary," Anaea said.

"You've found him."

Anaea blinked in surprise. "But she said Karen—" Gwydion's fingers squeezed her arm in warning, but not quickly enough.

The man seemed to think nothing of it. "My parents thought it would be an advantageous name," he rumbled.

It's not uncommon over here, Gwydion said. *Give male children a neutral or feminine name to improve their chances.*

She felt her cheeks heat. The color intensified when she realized the secretary was witness to this reaction. *Oh.*

"You are Carlisle?" he asked. On her nod, he smiled and bowed his head, with no trace of irony. "Welcome to Serendipity. I hope you enjoy your stay."

"Thank you," she said. "I'm sure I will."

"This way." The lift rose as they entered. "Interesting pet." He extended a palm towards Penelope. The kearl's nostrils flared, but she allowed the approach until he was close enough she could sniff, then nibble his fingers. He never jumped, turning his hand to stroke her neck with one thumb.

The platform halted. The marble floors were striated with gold. Baroque curlicues gave the ceiling an illusion of vaulted roundness.

"You're good with animals," Anaea said.

A shrug. "I work here."

She smothered laughter behind a hand. Gwydion grinned at her sideways.

Karen headed briskly down the corridor. "I've arranged for everything to be brought from your hotel," he said.

Anaea blinked. "We didn't expect—"

Karen turned and held out a portable pad. "I need your confirmation."

Anaea hesitated. She wanted to meet her hostess before being lodged under her roof.

Gwydion touched her thoughts. *This helps our purpose, even though I'm surprised by her level of interest.*

I at least expected to carry my own belongings, she said.

I'm pretty sure that's not allowed. Rueful humor in his thoughts.

Biting her lip, she pressed her palm on the pad. It beeped in affirmation.

"Thanks," Karen said. The pad disappeared within his vest. He moved to a pair of double doors at the end of the hall. They opened with a grand, artificial groaning of hinges.

For a second, Anaea was blinded by golden light; then, she was conscious only of the hundreds of faces that reflected back on her.

24

Disoriented, Anaea pulled back. As her eyes adjusted, she realized the multitude of people was only a handful: an illusion created by mirrored walls. The obsidian floors were highly polished, picking up ghost images of the occupants.

A tall, voluptuous woman with a labyrinth of sculptured jet hair crossed the room to meet them. Though her face was severe: high cheekbones, a patrician nose and ice-white skin: the smile welcomed. "I am Traviata Linscott, regina of Serendipity," she said, bowing her head. "Welcome to my city and my home."

"Anaea Carlisle," Anaea said, inclining deeply, until Gwydion's hand on her back stopped her. "This is my dear friend, Gwydion Mallory."

One of Traviata's fine brows lifted a fraction, but her face did not change. "Mr. Mallory," she said without a nod.

He responded with a bow. "Regina."

Traviata paused to address Karen. He moved like a shadow, retrieving another chair for the dining room beyond. If Gwydion's "upgrade" from bodyguard to friend was unexpected, the regina made no point of it.

"Come." Traviata guided Anaea and Gwydion into the room. Her file said she was in her forties, but she looked younger and moved with the poise of centuries. "May I present Upala Manuel, marchionissa of the Meira region—"

Upala, a pale, petite young woman with bountiful red hair and freckles, dimpled and dipped her head. "Charmed." She wore a frilly, multi-layered gown of seashell pink.

"—the Mrs. and Mr. Ellen Petrarch. She's a comitissa from Verity, the next country over," Traviata continued.

Ellen was an older, sour-faced woman, her husband a rangy shadow next to her. She performed the half-bow that seemed most common on the streets; he dropped lower.

Anaea's understanding of the various ranks was sketchy, but she knew a comitissa was the second step up from the base tier of the ruling classes, a baronissa, who would have direct hand over a community of a few thousand people. It was certainly above the many relatives who were treated as matriarchs, which was a heriditary honor but had no post or power.

"And finally," Traviata said, "visiting from Elysium, baronissa Morgan Dennison."

Gwydion had paled before she spoke, but until then, Anaea had been too overwhelmed by their surroundings to notice the familiar face. She caught her breath, then forced it out.

Morgan flashed a cool, shallow smile. "I'm already acquainted with Mr. Mallory," she said, "and I've met Miss Carlisle."

"Miss Dennison," she said with a small nod. "It's good to see you again." Could the woman somehow harm them? Poke holes in her story? She glanced to Gwydion, but he stood very still, not looking anywhere but straight ahead.

"On a first-name basis, please," Traviata said. It wasn't relaxed informality: itwas a command, her lips hinting at a frown.

"We shall be eager to hear stories of your Sanctum, Anaea,"

Ellen said, turning towards Morgan as if anticipating her agreement. "Its mysteries intrigue us."

"I find your city even more intriguing," Anaea said, hoping that might head off questions.

It seemed to be the right thing to say, for significant looks flitted between the three female guests. Mr. Petrarch looked sour.

"What is that remarkable creature with you?" Upala asked in a flute-pitched soprano.

"This is Penelope; she's native to my home colony," Anaea said. "She's very attached and doesn't like to be apart from me. I hope that's all right."

Traviata waved it off. "If you judge the creature is trained enough to be in public, I'm certain it is fine. Now that we are all arrived, shall we?" She stepped to the dining table, a gilt-silver piece with a holographic tabletop. It came to life as she neared, gold snowflake flourishes dancing around the edges and ebbing inward in autumnal colors. Anaea tried not to stare.

Nothing marked the seating, but everyone seemed to know where they were supposed to be. Anaea ended up on Traviata's left, across from Upala, with Gwydion beside her in the added chair. Ellen dominated the far end. Morgan sat across from Gwydion, her smile fixed.

Traviata tapped the table. Rather than the flock of servants Anaea had expected, this summoned mechanical platters shaped like butterflies and beetles. They descended, sprouted limbs, and set the table in a flurry. One stopped before her and offered a choice of drinks; bewildered, she tapped the appropriate antenna.

The robots disappeared, leaving a soup course with crescent bread. The table waited on Traviata to take the first bite, and then the meal started.

"It has been a lovely day," Upala said after a few bites, "quite cool for summer, but I find it refreshing."

"There is something to be said for a bracing breeze," Ellen agreed. "You had an ideal day for your arrival, Anaea."

Anaea started. "I thought the weather was always like this," she said.

Upala laughed far more than the joke needed. "Oh, if only!"

"So we tell the tourists," Mr. Petrarch said, his second remark of the night.

"It's less humid here than it is at home," Morgan observed. The small talk continued, and Anaea recognized it as a ritual, a required part of dinner. She tried to relax, though her spine prickled as she wondered what the consequence for fouling up might be.

The soup was delicious, with a subtle spice that struck the back of the palette and trickled down. Penelope perched on her feet, tail twitching. Gwydion kept his head bent, looking up only when necessary.

When the salad course arrived in another flurry of bejeweled insects, Traviata took the conversational reins. "What diversions will you seek in our fair city, Anaea?"

"I hardly know where to start," she said, hoping to keep the others talking. Every time she had to speak, she felt as if she was being tested.

"Oh, I have many suggestions," Upala burst in eagerly. "The tourist spots are well-known for a reason, of course—"

"Advertising," Ellen observed in a crackly voice.

Upala colored. "Not just that," she said, and they went several good-natured rounds on that point before the elder conceded. "Of course, there's the Serendipity Countryhall, where we gather for planet-wide announcements, and we may be doing that very soon." Her voice was proud.

"No politics at the table."

Traviata's tone was mild, but Anaea heard the cut underneath, and Upala wasn't the only one to flinch. Meekly, she subsided, and Ellen took up the thread until Morgan asked nonchalantly about local hotels.

Gwydion's thoughts touched hers as the third course was

served, local seafood. *Are you all right? You have an odd expression on your face.*

She was surprised he had noticed with his eyes turned down. *I was only wondering if it would be polite to ask how many courses there are.*

He didn't laugh; an impression of warmth brushed her thoughts. *If you could phrase it as a compliment . . .*

Upala cooed at Penelope under the table. The kearl remained aloof, playing with the leash. "She's not very friendly, is she?" the marchionissa commented.

"They bond with specific people," Anaea said.

The fourth course was lamb; sheep had thrived on Solomon, according to Upala. A heavy scent of mint and rosemary filled the air.

As Anaea lifted the first bite to her mouth, before the insects had retreated into their aerial alcove, Morgan wondered, "Why didn't your daughter join us tonight, Traviata? I would have enjoyed her company."

"Eve had soccer practice tonight," Traviata said, with a touch of disapproval. "Some important game this weekend."

"Team spirit is very well and good, but it does provoke a frightful amount of violence," Upala said.

Traviata bestowed a benevolent smile upon the young woman. "Best she excise such masculine impulses from her system in her youth."

"Soccer is a game of the mind as well as the body," Mr. Petrarch observed mildly. "I'm sure she'll learn from it."

Ellen patted her husband's hand. "We enjoy watching the games," she said.

There were three more courses: beef steeped in wine sauce, a palate-cleansing lemon ice, and chocolate pastry. Anaea had been certain she was stuffed, but this last was so perfect it demanded a clean plate.

Though she strained for political undertones or hints in personality that might indicate where one woman or another stood, the conversation remained firmly fixed on the pleasant and trivial. Eyes rarely shifted overtly to Traviata, nor did she often make a gesture more pronounced than a smile, but they all played to her, and she directed them with her attention.

Anaea discovered one more thing: Mr. Petrarch was feeding Penelope under the table. She kept her face straight and said nothing.

The insects cleared the final courses and Traviata spoke a blessing, humble thanks to her God for the meal. Shortly after, Ellen made her excuses and departed with her husband in tow. A subtle jostle ensued between Upala and Morgan as to who would leave next, the women pointing out each other's busy schedules.

Morgan lost. "I should be on my way," she said airily. "Alas, this isn't entirely a pleasure trip, as much as I might wish . . ." Her eyes strayed to Gwydion, but when she continued, she spoke to Anaea. "We must sit down together sometime and discuss our mutual territory."

What did that mean? Anaea wondered, disoriented. "I would be pleased to," she said.

"Thank you so much for the invitation, Traviata." Morgan sailed out.

"I did want to speak with you in private," Upala said. "I'm having some difficulty with social credit distribution in my district—"

"Once my guests are comfortable, I will be pleased to advise," Traviata said, "but it's hardly courteous to rush anyone on a full stomach."

"Oh, of course," Upala said lightly. Her eyes were warm with devotion. Anaea recognized it with a start: she had seen it on the face of interns with a crush on their superior. She wondered if the feeling was returned or even noticed. "I didn't mean to rush you off," the redhead continued, expression apologetic.

"That's all right," Anaea said. "I'd like to get settled in." Not to mention the food left her feeling half-asleep.

Gwydion looked relieved. "As would I."

"Upala, wait in my office, would you?" Traviata led the way into the hall. "I arranged for you to have adjoining chambers," she said. "I trust that is satisfactory?" Without waiting for an answer, she continued, "I hope you will feel free to stay as long as the spirit moves you."

Anaea smiled, but did not reply. She wanted to like Traviata, but remembered the woman's subtle hand over dinner. Did she tolerate people who didn't obey her?

They returned to the lift and ascended three floors into a cherry wood hall. The doors were native snow wood, each with a different pattern of greenish whorls. Near the end of the hall, Traviata stopped and palmed open a door.

It opened into a rotunda sitting room, with three adjoining doors and a glassed patio entrance at the back. The furniture was carved from snow wood, the accents deep veridian.

"I will be occupied until the noon hour, so you will want to order breakfast into the room," Traviata said briskly. "If you need anything, don't hesitate to call. The lifts will take you to any part of the manor. Again, welcome to Serendipity."

The door on the right entered Gwydion's smaller room; to the left was the bedroom and the bathroom. The latter, to Anaea's puzzlement, had a glass window in the door, discreetly curtained. She had seen panels in the hotel rooms, but this was different.

"Gwydion?" she asked.

"Matriarch fashions," he said. "What can you say? I'm going to check to make sure everything made it."

Her heart leapt. The stunner! She hurried into her bedroom and found everything unpacked. That alone was enough to make her shudder: the thought of someone pawing through her clothes to set them out was unnerving. Penelope bounded in after and leapt onto the bed.

The books were set up on the dresser. She let her fingers linger over the spines before she continued hunting. She found the duffel-bag in the bottom of the bureau, with the weapon in the folds.

She let out a sigh, told herself she was being silly. It was hers, and she had permits to prove it. She was thinking too much like an imperial. But who should she be thinking like? Was she a woman of Themiscyra, a matriarch, someone else entirely? She clutched at her identity and tried to put words to it. None came.

"Anaea?"

His voice broke her stasis. She returned the stunner to its place and hurried into the sitting room. The kearl chittered, but remained ensconced in the pillows. "Are you all right?" she asked Gwydion. "Seeing Morgan must have been a shock."

"I'm fine," he said, "and I'm sure there's nothing to worry about. She might be a little irritated and try to needle us, but I doubt she has more plans than that." His voice was slightly high, as if trying to convince himself.

"You don't think she might pursue you?" Anaea asked.

"Why? I'm not that interesting."

"You're interesting to me," she said, pecking his lips with a kiss.

He caught her hand and pulled her in. His lips were warm and gentle and still tasted of chocolate. She had thought she couldn't handle another taste of it; she was wrong.

He broke off. "Anaea . . ."

"What is it?"

He glanced about anxiously. "I've heard that matriarchs monitor their visitors. I don't think we should . . ."

"Oh," she said. "Of course." She didn't want their affections to become someone else's entertainment. "I suppose that means we shouldn't talk about our plans for taking over the planet."

Gwydion laughed. "I was thinking we would raze Serendipity and put a book factory in its place."

"That's not a bad idea," she said, smiling.

He brushed his lips to hers again, more tentatively. "What's the plan now?"

"Right now? I just want to relax. Do you think we could pull up a game?"

The manor had access to a vast number of modules. The

head-to-head mode had few entries, reflecting how gauche it was to compete; Anaea went for a puzzle sequence instead. Soon immersed in the game, she forgot the mission Phailin had sent them on and everything the evening had brought. It would keep until tomorrow.

*

Anaea awoke with saffron sunlight streaming across her face. Bemused, she realized it was genuine: she had left the curtains open.

She padded out to the balcony. As long as she didn't lean on it, her ankle no longer throbbed. The balcony overlooked the trees, a graceful downward spiral of intertwined branches and translucent leaves. Squinting, she saw a hint of reflection. Below lay the glass floor of a courtyard.

She went back inside and changed. She found herself trying to shield her body without being obvious about it and blushed.

She returned to the sitting room to find a sleepy Gwydion on the couch, stroking Penelope. The kearl chittered in greeting.

"Breakfast?" he suggested.

The menu was vast. They made their requests, delivered by the ubiquitous metallic insects. Without a dining table to protect her, Penelope seemed more wary of the creatures, but after a few whacks with one paw to which the machines did not respond, she settled down.

As they were finishing, the wall flashed. "Karen Partridge," the overhead announced.

"Come in," Anaea said.

The regina's secretary entered, betraying a faint smile with his greeting bow. "Good morn to both of you. I've come to see if everything is to your satisfaction. Do you require anything else?"

"Everything is fine, thank you," Anaea said.

"Is any of our time spoken for today?" Gwydion asked.

"Not as yet," Karen said. "The regina wishes to dine with you again tonight."

Anaea almost asked if there would be as much food, then stopped herself.

"If that is all?" Karen tipped his head in inquiry.

"Please. I appreciate the courtesy," Anaea said.

"May I also suggest the better grounds for new books would be in Mount Pharos," he said. The door closed behind him.

Anaea blinked. "Did he—"

Gwydion put a hand over hers. *Talk to me.*

He just told us we were being recorded, she thought, *without being overt. Just referencing my interest in the printed page.*

Yes.

Anaea chewed on a cold piece of toast. *I like him.*

Gwydion squeezed her hand, then stood. "I'm going to look," he said. "Maybe poke into security, as I'm supposed to be a bodyguard."

Anaea pushed down laughter. "Make sure I'm safe," she teased.

He grinned and slipped out.

Anaea went out to the balcony, Penelope scampering at her feet. She leaned on the rail, looking down at the courtyard. From this vantage-point, the flower-beds seemed to grow out of crossed branches, an appealing optical illusion. She also noticed the rail had a gate with a half-moon arc of metal. A hover platform, well-disguised.

"Want to go down, Penelope?" she asked. The kearl purred and bumped her good ankle. "I'll take that as a yes." She scooped Penelope into her arms.

She stepped off the balcony into air. The system lowered her gently. She realized there were several identical balconies, and hastily memorized the position of hers. She landed in scattered leaf-cover.

In the courtyard, trees within the trees and flowering bushes formed a maze. Anaea wandered, smiling as the kearl broke from the leash to chase an insect – a real one. The trees rustled above.

The sound intensified into a crackle. She frowned, turning her head. Something dropped out of the branches and slammed into her.

25

SHE SKIDDED FORWARD AND HIT THE GROUND. SOMEONE landed on top of her; the impact knocked her breath out. Her instincts screamed, her shoulders tensing. Penelope dashed up, hissing, her tail rampant.

"I'm sorry! Are you all right?" The shape scrambled up, resolving itself into a white-clad adolescent boy. "I guess I leaned over too far."

Anaea's chest hurt too much to speak. She blinked until the spots cleared from her eyes, but the embarassment from overreacting remained. She was safe here, physically, at least, with no threat of warlord police swooping in.

The boy looked young – ten or eleven? – and had a mane of auburn hair. He seemed affected not at all by his tumble from the tree, anxiously poised for her recovery.

She pushed into a seated position, resting a hand on the scruff of the kearl's neck. "Penelope, no," she said. "It's fine." She rubbed at her collarbone, the ache subsiding as she caught her breath. "No harm done."

His intensity did not lessen. If anything, brown eyes widened further. He shunted from one foot to the other, indecisive, then reached a conclusion and thrust down a hand. "Let me help you up."

She accepted the hand and pulled herself upright, right foot swinging awkwardly. Penelope burrowed against her leg. "Thank you."

He released her hand and bowed low, almost to the point of overbalancing. "Gilford Linscott, at your service," he said.

Now that her heart had calmed, Anaea had to bite her lip to keep from laughing. Gilford, that would be Traviata's younger child, which put him at thirteen. He must be small for his age, or she had no idea what a boy-child should look like, which was more likely. "It's good to meet you, Gilford," she said. "I'm Anaea Carlisle."

"Oh, you're the off-worlder from the radical cult," he said enthusiastically, then blushed, ducking his head. "I mean, it's a pleasure to make your acquaintance."

Radical cult? Was that how people on Solomon viewed the Sanctum? She wondered what they would think of Themiscyra. "Hardly a cult," she said gently, "but I see news travels fast."

He flushed, head dipping lower, though he snuck a sideways look up at her through one curl. "I heard you let men keep their names."

It took Anaea a second to figure out what he meant; then she laughed. "Names aren't so important," she said, "and everyone should have the one they prefer."

Gilford straightened, meeting her eyes. "In that case, I'm Gil. It's less stuffy. You don't strike me as stuffy." He cocked his head, but it was not quite a question.

"I like to think I'm not stuffy," she said.

"Gil!" a voice echoed from elsewhere in the courtyard. "Stop scampering around like a monkey and come help me with this sim."

Gilford made a face. "My sister," he said. "I should go."

Anaea stepped forward. "I'd like to meet—"

"No, not now," he said. "She's not very – I mean . . . I wouldn't want you to . . . bye." On that note of finality, he darted away.

Puzzled, Anaea shook her head. She had no idea what to make of the young man. She wandered the courtyard, admiring the flushed color of the trees, but did not go far, not wanting to disturb the siblings. The grove felt cozy, sheltering her from the sky while still providing glimpses. Finally, she returned to the lift, luckily remembering which one it was.

She had only been sitting on the couch a moment when the wall panel flashed. "Upala Manuel."

"Enter," Anaea said.

The redhead flounced in wearing a lacy white shirt and neon-green mini-skirt, her smile piercing. Penelope dove under the couch.

"Good morning, Anaea," Upala trilled. "I hope you slept well? It's a beautiful morning, simply marvelous – the best day since, well, yesterday, I suppose, but the superlative shouldn't suffer for that little fact. I hope you have no plans for the day? If so, you should cancel them: I have something better."

All this was spoken at rapid fire pace. Anaea watched in bemusement, then belatedly realized she had been left space to respond. "Well, I hadn't planned—"

"Excellent!" Upala beamed. "Let me steal you away. I know some sights you simply must see, and I need your advice on an important matter."

Anaea blinked. "My advice?"

"But of course! Come, come, the morning is slipping through our fingers." She darted to the door, beckoning. "Come as you are, even though your color scheme is rather drab for daylight. But we can fix that!"

"What's the important matter?" Anaea wondered.

"Oh, in good time," Upala chirped, leading them through the manor. "One shouldn't hurry these things. Or perhaps I'm just prone to waiting until the last minute. It gives one a rush, don't you think?"

Anaea smiled without commenting and tapped her link to send Gwydion a message. Her mind whirled, colliding with anxieties. Why did Upala want her counsel? Had she said something, done something last night which had deeper implications? Was it Phailin's reputation?

They descended to the street. "I follow my predecessor in not having a personal car; it avoids ostentation," Upala said airily, touching her collarbone, "so we will have to wait a moment – ah! There we go."

A public car took the bend at a roar and stopped in front of them. How much of a sacrifice was it, Anaea wondered, not to have a private car when the city's transport leapt to response?

Upala ascended with a hop. "Come on!" Once Anaea was seated, she plopped down opposite, hands clasped, gaze intent. "That boy of yours is a tasty morsel."

Anaea blushed. "It's not . . ." She shook her head, realizing how it looked. No wonder so many people had thought twice about their situation before. Was it social nicety to claim innocence whether or not it was true?

Upala seemed oblivious, gesturing as the car rose. "The Rosewater District," she said, "finest in the city, residence by invitation only. Such women who have had the poor taste to ask will never grace these fine streets." She paused for effect, then added, "I myself have a small cottage here, though mostly my duties keep me in the Meira neighborhood, on the west side, along the shore. Many would say the prettiest property within city limits. It would be unfair of me to agree, but . . ." She flipped her hand nonchalantly.

"Each manor here matches a color palette designed to create a harmony of tones. Perfection." She twisted to point at a larger house, peach with massive windows. "Every home here is a gift. I made the primary contributions to that one."

"Oh." Anaea tried to imagine that system of mutual largesse and failed. "So you're expected—"

"Expected!" Upala sounded horrified. "Nothing of the sort.

Generosity of spirit isn't the same if it's forced. Every matriarch I know is overflowing with it."

Upala continued to narrate as the public car wove into Serendipity proper, but her remarks became less informative and more exclamatory: "Oh, look at that sculpture, what does it look like?" "Isn't that couple sweet?" "Oh, feel the breeze, Anaea!"

Anaea tipped her head back as they passed under an arch of flowers, inhaling deeply. As the car continued, a scent touched her nose, so subtle it was almost lost beneath the flowers: clean, crisp, a touch of lightning on the tongue. At the same time, the sheer span of space dizzied her. She had never realized how comforting a cocoon the passages of Themiscyra were. She wanted to reach out for walls that weren't there.

"We're almost to our first stop," Upala said. "It's a bit of a journey, but worth it. My little secret."

"Did you grow up here?" Anaea asked.

Upala tipped a shoulder. "About a hundred miles south, next country down. I left when I realized that being no one wasn't going to net me anything." She laughed. "Little girl, big city, it seemed to add up nicely."

Anaea opened her mouth to ask a question, but Upala had bounced out of her seat. "Oh, here we are!"

Anaea hurried after. The building was a government complex, a towering tree of metallic emerald, easily one of the tallest in Serendipity. Glass doors parted as Upala entered; workers spun about to welcome her as she headed for the hover-lift. She accepted their greetings with a merry smile and not a word, sailing onwards.

"Brace yourself," she said, "it's a sudden start."

Anaea was used to the long vertical distances of Themiscyra, but the surge of the lift surprised her. She found herself clutching her companion's arm.

Upala giggled and patted her hand, a gesture of confederacy. "I did warn you," she mock-chided.

Veiled windows rushed past. Above, gold split the green light as the dome irised open. They rose onto a rooftop platform.

"Never mind the Flying Sphere," Upala said. "That's all very well if one likes the novelty of bouncing about, but this is the best view in Serendipity."

Anaea stepped off the lift onto the roof and faced east. Here she could see the patchwork, the planning, the city growing in its divided beds like the largest garden imaginable. Tall spires broke the landscape; business districts thrust in rolling hills next to residential areas. Serendipity tapered off into mushroom clumps of attached towns, nestled in a landscape she could almost smell and touch.

Then she turned in the other direction, and she forgot everything else.

Past Serendipity lay the ocean, an expanse that seemed larger than space, dotted with the stars of swells, boats and sandbars, and further out, distant lands and things the eye could only imagine. Anaea leaned forward, recognizing the scent as if by some primitive instinct. The vastness made her feel as if she could reach out and touch it.

"You've never seen the sea before, have you?" Upala's voice was thoughtful.

Anaea pulled back, feeling the hairs on her arm tingle. She should explain herself, have some story ready, but it wouldn't come. She stood in silence, watching the black specks of birds that skipped across the endless grey.

"Of course I have," she said, "just not like this."

Upala leaned against the rail. "No one's ever seen it like this."

Anaea could have stared forever, but she felt the curiosity of the redhead's regard. She pulled herself away. "Thank you," she said. "I think you might be right."

Upala inclined her head modestly and led the way. As the car rose, she was quiet, almost meditative. Then she chattered, pointing here, peering there as if Serendipity had been structured for her personal amusement. Though overwhelmed, Anaea almost found it admirable. There was something lovely about treating the world as a series of delights.

"We have the largest on-site shopping center in the known universe," Upala said grandly. "Paradise given form, with a breath of perfume. Do you want to go?"

Anaea shook her head. "I don't have anything I need."

"Need?" Upala laughed. "It's not about need, it's about joy and whim. But I suppose going in without a target in mind could be overwhelming. One could wander for days . . ." Her expression was wistful. Then, she clapped her hands. "Onwards!"

Even though she had seen the city from above, Anaea gave up hope of keeping track of their direction and where they were in relation to the Rosewater District. She leaned back as they drifted under a canopy of exotic blooms.

"Now," Upala said, her lips acquiring a pensive quirk, "there is the matter which I wanted to discuss with you. I hope I can trust you to give me your honest opinion?"

Where was this leading? Anaea wasn't sure whether to hope or worry. "I'll do my best," she said.

Upala nodded. "Well, you see, I've had this invitation from a young male reporter, and I'm undecided how to approach it," she said, tone serious. "The potential scandal . . ."

Anaea wondered how she could have any insight on the subject; wondered, too, if this might have something to do with her purpose in coming to Serendipity. Could she hope she had stumbled into information? "What does he want to interview you about?" she asked.

Upala blinked, her eyes round with confusion. "Interview? No. He had the audacity to ask me on a date. A young man of no connection to the matriarchs, with prospects but no power. And he approached me."

It was Anaea's turn to be puzzled. "What do you need from me, then?" With relief, thoughts of politics and dangerous decisions started to fade from her mind.

"I told you." If the redhead looked irritated, it disappeared into brightness. "Counsel! He is more bold than he has a right to be, but he is handsome and well-spoken." She pursed her lips. "I don't wish to be seen as desperate, reaching down for one of the masses. I want to know what you think."

Anaea wanted to laugh, but it seemed a serious request, and she was afraid of insulting this volatile woman. That it seemed so obvious made her stop and consider, as much to look for nuance as to appear she was thinking about it.

"Take away everything else, and he sounds like a person you're interested in," Anaea said. "Isn't the rest just a matter of interpretation?"

"Interpretation is important," Upala demurred.

"Then give it your interpretation," Anaea said. "Can't you do that?"

"Hmm." The redhead scrunched up her brow, thinking. "He did ask me. Kindness to our inferiors and such. Do you know, your answer was very similar to the one Ellen gave? So much for my theory that generations think differently."

Anaea blinked. "What?"

"Oh, I've asked several people about this," Upala said blithely. "One must have a thorough background before making such a decision."

Could she not make the decision for herself? There was no polite way to ask, so Anaea let the conversation lapse. She had started to think she might understand the matriarchs; now she could feel the sense escaping her.

"Here we are," Upala said.

The public car broke through a ring of ancient oak trees, which must have been planted soon after Serendipity was founded, and approached a building comprised of mushroom-like clusters. The central dome floated above the rest.

"The countryhall," Upala explained as the car passed through ivory gates. "It also used to be the home of the regina, until the Rosewater District became so fashionable, that is. The private quarters are impressive, in a way, but so . . . quaint."

They dismounted and walked through riotous gardens to

the main entrance. Everything was carved of native wood, often blending together so the whorls and grains of one tree disappeared into the fibers of another.

A long hall led through clumps of attached offices and agencies of state. It opened in the central dome, an aerial expanse of snow wood. The window at its peak coruscated with fractal color patterns, changing the light in a slow, mesmerizing pulse. Rows of benches ringed the chamber; they looked like stone, but when Anaea put her hand down, it sank into soft plush.

"This is it," Upala announced, "the place where we come for dialogue that involves the entire planet. When someone speaks, their countryhall appears as a hologram in the center."

Anaea tried to picture the room full. "How many—"

"Everyone but the baronissas," Upala said. "Of course, there are always those who don't have the decency to show up." She exhaled a sigh, resting her hand on a bench arm with an ostentatious splay of fingers.

Amused, Anaea took the hint. "Where are you?"

"Oh! Right here, in the second row," she said. "I've only spoken a few times, but my contributions—" she colored. "One doesn't like to boast."

"It must be something to see," Anaea answered.

"You might well see it, if you approach Traviata properly." Upala shifted a look sideways. "I could even help, if you have a purpose beyond curiosity."

Anaea hoped Phailin didn't intend for her to conceal why she was here. With the circumstances of the Sanctum and the minds of these women, it was not hard to figure out. Still, until she heard otherwise, she wasn't willing to disclose what Upala hunted for.

"Isn't curiosity enough?" she asked.

"Always!" Upala laughed. She didn't seem perturbed by her failure. "Otherwise, what excuse would there be for gossip?"

Anaea spread her hands. There seemed no answer to that.

Upala sat on the arm of her bench, swinging one foot. "If

there is something I can do for you, please ask. I can promise I'm a sympathetic ear."

"I'll let you know," Anaea said.

Upala circled the countryhall, recounting a story from the last session. Anaea strained, but she heard nothing connected to privacy in the monologue, except that Upala took a dim view of anyone else having any when there were entertaining tidbits to be had.

As they left, the marchionissa said, "Do you want to take the shore tour on our way back?"

"Isn't that in the opposite direction?" Anaea asked.

"Yes, it's sort of a long circle about, but it doesn't take that much longer, and the scenery is lovely," Upala said, then dangled the word, "Seashore?"

Anaea had always thought the sparkling white sand in holograms was an exaggeration: now she saw that projections did not live up to the real thing. The water called to her, endless. It took her a while to force her attention back to the shore.

Serendipity's beaches were pristine and teeming with sunbathers and swimmers. People in uniform scoured the beaches, collecting trash and ocean detritus.

When asked, Upala beamed. "Work program," she said. "Gives the unemployed some way of earning a living. Even a little cheaper than the machines."

The public car progressed leisurely down the beach. By the time it detoured towards the city interior, Anaea had grown accustomed to the ocean . . . almost.

They returned to the manor, Upala still chattering. As Anaea eased down, she settled into her seat.

"Duty calls," she said, "but it was a lovely morning. Do call on me, hmm? I'm certain I can be a friend and ally."

Anaea found Gwydion, and they compared notes. He hadn't learned much. The staff working the manor regarded their mistress with a mixture of affection and awe. Everyone seemed to have a personal story about the assistance she had given them.

Where does she find the time? Anaea wondered.

Maybe she's discovered a sleep substitute, Gwydion said.

Anaea chuckled. *Maybe.*

It's no less improbable than anti-aging.

Anaea fell silent. Themiscyra had perfected that: Thalestris had been a young woman at the time of the founding, and Asteria had seen the Y-Plague infestation as a grown woman and still functioned as middle-aged. She wondered how much of the schism the woman had experienced.

Her link buzzed, and she tapped it. It announced a package had arrived at a depot just outside the Rosewater District.

She met Gwydion's eyes. *Phailin,* he said. *Knows you might be here, and might be watched.*

Anaea rose in a rush, fast enough to be unsteady. "I'll be back."

At the depot, the machine dropped two items in her booth: a message tube and a sealed box. Her hand hovered. What would Phailin have sent her?

She broke the message tube open.

26

Phailin's face appeared in miniature. "Thanks for taking this on, Anaea," her voice said, "I appreciate it. I'm sorry for the cumbersome method of contact, but matriarchs are insufferably nosy. I expect your hostess will try to eavesdrop. I'd almost be disappointed if she didn't, to be honest."

Despite herself, Anaea smiled.

"People will want to know why you're on Solomon. Be honest. They will piece it together, and if you don't evade, they'll waste their energies looking for more complex motives. The truth is the best offense. Under no circumstances play favorites. It's way too easy to make an enemy by association or perceived slight."

Anaea grimaced. She knew what that meant: talking to Morgan.

"One more thing," Phailin said. "If Traviata takes an interest in you, that's good. She knows minute details about the lives of everyone around her. For that same reason, you need to keep her at arm's length. Don't let her put you under her microscope."

Anaea bit her lip. It was too late for that.

"As for the other package you're receiving, don't use it unless you have to. Light and faith to you, Anaea Carlisle. Keep our boy safe, too."

"I will," Anaea promised as the face disappeared.

She pulled the other box onto her lap and opened it. It contained a pair of gold bracelets, and after a moment, Anaea realized the first had a series of buttons and wiring, the second designed to fit within and conceal these. She had to squint at the writing on the interior rim to guess at its purpose: it was an electronics jammer.

Its presence chilled her. It would have felt more appropriate in the wild imperial territory she had just left. Phailin anticipated trouble. If they were spies, it was a public sort. But she realized she knew very little about what hid behind the smiles and coordinated sympathy of the matriarchs. It might be no less dangerous.

In the public car, she tapped her link. "Morgan Dennison."

The call buzzed five times in the bones beneath her ear, and she thought it would go unanswered. "Morgan here. Why are you calling?" The tone was cool and neutral.

"I was hoping we could sit down over a late lunch and talk. I don't want to draw lines between us."

"Well." Her voice warmed subtly; the tone shifted. "Come to my quarters in an hour. I'll have something ordered in."

Anaea winced, thinking of the surveillance and Phailin's warnings. Did Morgan not know she was being recorded? Should she warn her? "It's a lovely day to be outside."

Morgan sniffed. "Then we'll picnic in the garden. Until then, good day." The call clicked silent.

Anaea sighed. There was no going back now.

Once she reached the manor, she explained Phailin's message to Gwydion: a silent transfer covered by dialogue about the homes she had seen. He winced in the same places she had. Penelope dozed under the couch.

We can't leave now, he said. *That would offend Traviata, and we'd never get anything done with the regina annoyed with us.*

I know. I wish . . . She sighed, glancing at the crystal

mantelpiece clock. "I should go," she said, "I have a meeting with Morgan."

"Morgan?" Gwydion's voice went up several pitches. He jerked to his feet. Penelope hissed and retreated further under the couch.

"Relax," she said. "I want to see if we can mend some ties. I thought it would be a good idea."

Gwydion shook his head, looking dubious. He seemed about to say something, changed his mind; she expected telepathic contact to follow, but there was nothing. "Good luck," he said. "Lots of it."

She squeezed his arm. "Won't need it."

She didn't believe it, but left him on that note and descended to the garden. She told her heart to stop jumping around. There was nothing Morgan could do to them, surely? Whip up bad feelings, at the most . . . but that meant a lot to these women.

She found Morgan leaning against a gazebo wall, wearing a gold tunic and flare-legged pants. An assortment of sandwiches were set out on the bench.

Morgan rose, a soft smile curling her over-reddened lips. "Anaea," she said, "come, sit. I'm sure you want to get this over with."

Anaea approached, puzzled. "Over with?"

Morgan quirked an eyebrow. "I assumed you were turning over your man. Isn't that purpose of following up on my invitation?"

Anaea felt as if she had been punched. She fought with what to address first; confusion won out. "Why would you think that?"

"You echoed my words, especially those of lines and territory," Morgan said. "I know that concession is difficult for the pride . . ."

"It's impossible," Anaea said. "He's not mine to give up."

Morgan laughed, high and mocking. "Oh, really? He doesn't strike me as the wandering type, to avoid commitment to a woman."

The assumptions made her stomach clench. She tried to find a grip on her anger. On Themiscyra, men had been enigmas, monsters, whispers, but she had never seen them like this.

"I don't own him," she said. "I wouldn't own him even if we were partnered." She knew there were differences between marriage and life-ties, but she was sure neither made the spouse into a possession.

"Oh, don't give me that." Morgan looked disgusted. "Men belong to us. They're our pieces to put through the game as we see fit."

Anaea shook her head. "I don't agree with that. I—"

"Has that Sanctum of yours rotted your brain?" Morgan sniffed. "You know that's how our world works."

Anaea swallowed, resisting the urge to bolt from the gazebo. "Why do you still want him? Why would you pursue a man who wants nothing to do with you?"

"No man denies a woman of my stature," Morgan said in a low voice. "If I let him walk away, I admit I am not that woman."

Anaea's mouth tasted like blood, but she pitied Morgan. It was a terrible expectation. Was it self-imposed, or did the matriarch society force it on her?

"I can't help you," she said. No hope of not making enemies now. "I won't stop you from talking to Gwydion, but I will stop you from badgering him or hurting him. I don't want us to be on opposing terms."

"No, you don't – do you?" Morgan's voice softened, but revealed layers of chill. "You're worried about your precious Sanctum, and what will happen when I return home. You should be. Your sweet, innocent displays reek. You don't belong here."

Anaea stood numb. She couldn't help the thought that here, again, she was told there was no place for her. Maybe there was no escaping the environment that raised her.

Morgan turned on her heel. "Go away. I weary of you."

Anaea recognized the superior sting in that dismissal. She tried to say something, but words froze somewhere between concept and speech. She backed out of the gazebo and hurried through the garden, still locked in ice.

At the bend near her balcony, she encountered Karen. He bowed formally.

"Miss Carlisle," he said. "I hope you are well."

She was surprised to find she had a smile to offer. "I'll be fine."

Karen glanced behind her. There was something significant in the look, but it did not linger. "The regina wishes you to dine with her tonight at six-thirty. It will be the two of you."

It was the last thing Anaea wanted to do. She struggled to keep her face neutral. "I will be there."

He started to turn, then paused. "Miss Carlisle?"

"Karen?"

"I suggest the sage and white outfit." Without waiting for a response, he resumed walking.

Anaea blinked after, bemused. Then she went to arm herself for dinner.

*

Traviata's private dining room was carpeted in plush crimson with a snowflake-lace table. It was meant to be cosy, intimate: instead, it pressed familiarity into such a small space that Anaea had trouble breathing. She had taken Karen's advice and worn the scallop-necked, sleeveless blouse with the ankle-length skirt, and it turned out to be the right choice, as formal as Traviata's cerulean dress.

"Anaea," the hostess said. "I hope the day treated you well."

"It did, thank you," Anaea said. "You have a lovely home, and I spent an enjoyable morning with Upala." She was surprised when the words didn't sound as stilted as they felt.

"Ah?" Traviata arched an eyebrow. Her tone was neutral: it could be interpreted as probing or dubious. "Please sit."

Anaea settled into her chair, fingers knotting in the skirt. "She seemed to think I might have an opportunity to see a countryhall session."

Traviata paused with one long hand on the back of her chair.

"You haven't – no, of course. Are our ways of governance that interesting to you?" She tapped the table. The insect servitors flurried down, the whirring of their wings preventing an immediate answer. "What to drink?"

"Water, please," Anaea said, a little fervently.

The robots deposited a blue-and-green salad and scurried away. Traviata cut a bite, waiting for a few expectant seconds before she began to eat.

Sensing it had been left to her whether to pursue the subject, Anaea said, "I'm sure Serendipity is different enough from New Athens I could learn something."

"Truly?" Traviata sounded surprised. "Your curiosity does you credit."

Anaea felt like a young intern being praised on her second week of rotation. She ventured, "Then—"

"I will consider it, on the understanding you would only be an observer," Traviata said. "Your voice has no place in our debates."

Anaea's head jerked, startled by the directness. "Of course not," she said. "I don't imagine any of the small things I occupy myself with are significant enough for your countryhall."

"That's a swift dismissal." By her tone, the regina had taken those words for an opposite meaning. These verbal nuances! Couldn't one just mean what was said?

"I met your son today," Anaea said, attempting to shift the subject.

"Did he intrude?" Traviata asked. "I'm sorry. You know how long boys take to grow up, if they ever do."

"No, he didn't," Anaea said. "We ran into each other in the garden. He was sweet, a young gentleman."

"Was he." The regina added, "My husband and I wanted another girl, of course, but Gilford has acquitted himself well. He has a sensitive side that will make him an excellent nurse some day."

Anaea tried to imagine the exuberant young man as a doctor's assistant and had trouble. Then again, perhapsere all boys of his age were like that.

"That's a good ambition," she said. "I have some medical training, myself, and I admire the people who devote their lives to it."

Something seemed to amuse Traviata, but she did not voice it. "He will adjust."

The insects descended, clearing away the salad. To Anaea's relief, their next burden was dinner casserole, obviously intended as the main course.

"I've heard you spent several years in an asteroid colony," Traviata said. "Tell me about that?"

"Not much to tell," Anaea said. "It was very quiet, very isolated, but everyone had to be self-sufficient. We knew help was too far away for a shout."

"Then you returned to populous space to live with relatives. To see the universe?" the regina surmised.

Anaea smiled slightly. This much wasn't a lie. After a few general questions, Traviata veered into the more recent events of her history, and she had to scramble, while keeping her face straight, sometimes using the food as a pretext, and always feeling it was obvious.

It was conversation, not interrogation. Surely only the subject matter made it feel otherwise. "Is Eve your heir, then?" she asked.

"Keep in mind we are not a monarchy," Traviata said. "Although I was my mother's only child, I earned what I have, as will Eve. In no other way can we respect the position." She interrupted this lofty speech with a smile.

"I hope I'll have an opportunity to meet her," Anaea said.

"Tomorrow," Traviata said. "A birthday celebration for a marchionissa, and of course, you are invited. No gift is required."

More social events? "Thank you."

"This asteroid of yours," the regina said, "did it cleave to Collective philosophy, or Imperial?"

Anaea blinked. She had located it in space as near Perica. "Collective, of course . . ."

"Very good," Traviata said.

She diverted the conversation into lighter topics, but Anaea could not shake the feeling that something significant had passed with that answer. But what misstep could she have made?

*

Anaea gave a pleasant description of dinner to Gwydion, kissed him gently, and then, when he touched her mind, said, *Get me out of here.*

They caught a public car and swept across the city. Sunset was only a hint in the length of the shadows. They reached the shore and found a drinks stand. Scurrying along the sand, they found a place on the far side of a dune and dropped down to watch the water. Anaea felt the prickle of sand in her ankle brace and didn't mind in the slightest.

She told him everything about dinner with Traviata, but kept her encounter with Morgan to herself, other than to say it had not gone well. She was relieved when he didn't press. The single moon, Sheba, was almost full, turning the landscape blue.

He put his arm around her and tipped his head against hers. "I think you acquitted yourself well," he said. "It might not even be a test."

She laughed. "Might not?"

He joined in. She could feel it vibrating in his chest. "Well."

Anaea set down her drink and edged closer, folding his hand in hers. The warmth washed over her like a second sea breeze.

"I don't understand," she said softly, "how you can feel for a person and treat them like a possession. Or how someone could let them."

"You really don't understand that?" His voice was soft in her ear, enough to be distracting.

"No, I don't," she said. "Maybe that was what was wrong with Orithia and I. I can't imagine feeling that way about someone."

"I guess you have to be there," he said. "Maybe there's a point where you care for someone so much that being theirs is a part of being yourself."

Tired and nettled, Anaea pushed herself upright. "Are you speaking from experience?"

As soon as the words were out, she regretted them. He could say that was how he felt about Sophie, and she neither wanted to hear it, nor to remind him. He could simply say no, and that was a slap, even if she expected it with their relationship so new. Or there was a slight chance he could say something else, and she didn't want that, either, not here, not now.

She reached up and kissed him fiercely. Maybe he didn't want to answer, for his response was swift, his mouth, sweet with the taste of the drink, hot on hers. His hands played down her back, drawing her closer. She ended up in his lap, surrounded by his strangeness, moving into it.

Her position meant the skirt rode up. One of his hands slid down her hip and caressed skin, working up her thigh. She pulled at his shirt and was fascinated anew by the lines of his body. She expected softness, found ribs instead, almost overbalanced them both. The sound that escaped him vibrated her spine. It shot fire to her nerves. His hand roamed . . .

Then paused as he stiffened. He jerked back, head twisting. His hands fumbled, grabbed her shoulders.

"Anaea," he said, "please. Just – enough."

She stared, head spinning. They had been moving in a direction she wasn't even sure how to follow, even as she ached for it. "Gwydion," she started, "I didn't mean . . ." She paused, bewildered how to finish that sentence.

He shook his head. "This goes any further, I won't be able to hold back. And you're sheltered in ways no other woman is. I don't—" He blushed.

"You don't have to worry about me," she said, a sick feeling in her core.

"I'm also devout," he said, "and we just don't. Not outside of marriage."

"We don't even have marriage," Anaea said.

His eyes widened. "No marriage?"

How had that not come up in their discussions? Not important, perhaps, not until this moment. She found herself flush against the wall of a concept and a distinction she didn't understand, and worse, flush against a barrier between them. Her instinct was to question, to figure it out, but asking him those questions now, it would seem as if the debate was about something entirely different.

Carefully, she rocked back on her heels and wobbled upright. Sand clung to the front of her legs. The distance between them loomed like space itself.

"We have life-ties," she said, her voice sounding thin and flat to her own ears, "but they're not a requirement for anything life has to offer, except contributing to a child's genetics, and that's more complicated for us."

Gwydion flinched, looking down. "I . . ."

"I'm not trying to guilt you," Anaea said softly. "I'm only . . ." Embarrassed, disappointed, confused, or maybe none of that. This whole conversation implied futures she had never considered, and couldn't, not when they were in the middle of a mission, when she didn't know where the universe would take her. She had been raised to believe every person would find their place in a greater whole, and now she felt out of touch with that, if it had ever been true.

"Let's go," she said. "Things are going to take off tomorrow."

"Anaea, please don't—" Gwydion closed his eyes. His features spoke volumes, made apologies, made excuses, and she stood motionless through it, pretending she didn't see. Her throat closed tight.

He sighed and rose. "All right. Maybe we can make some headway."

Even when they spoke on the car-ride back to Traviata's manor, about strategy for the next day and who might attend, Anaea heard no more meaning than she had in the hiss of the waves.

27

ANAEA AWOKE EARLY THE NEXT MORNING TO GREY SKIES and a smattering of rain. Having seen the outfits at the private dinner, she knew her wardrobe wasn't prepared for a party, and she was fairly sure she wasn't, either. Ruefully, she wished shopping were not such a foreign endeavour. This was not a trip for Gwydion, and she didn't want to deal with sugary Upala. She wondered what Orithia would have made of it; her friend's idea of dressing up was making sure she had no grease stains.

"I wish I could talk to you, Penelope," she said. "I'm sure you have good fashion sense."

The kearl chittered smugly. Anaea left, gnawing a breakfast pastry brought by one of the spiders. She met Karen in the hall.

"Good morning," she said.

He bowed. "Good morning, Miss Carlisle. If you are interested, I will send to your link a list of popular boutiques in the area."

She stared. "Are you a mindreader?"

"Merely observant." He smiled slightly, but humor warmed his eyes.

"In that case, please." Anaea drew a breath. "Karen?"

The smile widened a fraction. "Yes?"

She hesitated, heat coming to her cheeks. She had almost asked why he was so nice to her, but to ask the question was not fair to him. Being in the Collective had her looking for ulterior motives everywhere.

"Never mind," she said.

He dipped his head. "Miss," he said, and vanished.

She headed out into the city, guided by Karen's list. The boutiques were small, intimate, staffed by gushing clerks. They insisted she try everything on: "You can use a virtual double, but it isn't the same as feeling the fabric on your skin."

Not the same, indeed, for she wouldn't have known the person inside the whirl of dresses was her without the tingle of silk and the gentle weight on her body. Even through her worries, she started to feel giddy.

She bought three dresses and left two boutiques empty-handed, feeling vaguely guilty, which seemed to be their strategy. On an impulse, she found a public car and searched the directory.

It took some finding. Like most cities, Serendipity did not advertise its less prosperous zones. She finally found an area marked Oakwood and instructed the car to pass through.

When the vehicle turned the bend, the expanse of green surprised Anaea. Then she realized it was paint: sometimes sun-faded, sometimes yellowed, but glossing over the plasteel veneer of identical buildings. Each was shaped like a tree, mimicking high class homes. Regulation flower boxes perched on every windowsill.

There were few people on the streets, but each wore the same cream tunic and trousers. Heads whipped about in the direction of the public car; people stood at attention, even children. They relaxed after Anaea passed.

Low, squat buildings rested in between the trees. It took her a moment to identify their functions: a public kitchen, an entertainment node and a dispenser for clothing. It was then, as she realized how much had been made communal, that she noticed the size of the windows and the lack of blinds. Every home stood bared to view.

It was quiet, tranquil, safe, but she found herself averting her eyes from the windows. It felt like she was prying, even though people must be used to it. Was this better, the occasional lost secret or embarrassing moment aired, than being dumped in a place falling apart, hiding off-grid, outside the system?

She didn't know.

Anaea reached over to the controls. "Book printing, please."

She spent the rest of the day touring a print factory. The books were personalized to order. She purchased a slim volume; it smelled of green leaves and new growth, not the heavier scent she had grown accustomed to. She inhaled deeply, found it refreshing. It was heady, too, to touch pages made with new wood, trees grown in a place she had thought long fallen into ruin. She wished she could show the women back home.

Then she thought of the lies, the tales, the conspiracy, and the wish faded, first in a flash of anger, and then with sadness. Did Thalestris, Valasca and the others understand what they had left behind?

She returned to her chambers and lost herself in preparations. The luxury of a hot shower with real water was something she would never tire of.

She shimmied into the dress, a floor-length sheath of pale lilac with orchid lace at the shoulders. The shoes were flats. She was tall in comparison to most of these women. No need to emphasize it, and she still didn't trust her ankle

Gwydion knocked; she called him in. His face lit in a smile; then it faltered slightly. "You look like an old-fashioned portrait," he said.

There was no reason to feel awkward around him, she assured herself. It was easy enough to forget last night. She wasn't convinced, and ached even as she tried to hide it. "Is that a compliment?"

He chuckled. "Well, yes." Still hesitant, he offered his arm. "Shall we?"

She threaded her arm through his and pecked his cheek. "Onwards."

The party was in the courtyard, a sea of shimmering gold lights. Sunburst sparkles floated in the air, scattering when they collided. Subtle artificial breezes kept the temperature cool.

Anaea and Gwydion emerged into the garden at the fringe of a crowd of vibrantly dressed people, chattering, mingling, striking poses. White rose petals carpeted the ground; when Anaea's foot disturbed a patch, a ripple in the floor readjusted them. She jumped, staring down, and quickly caught herself. She pulled her gaze up, but couldn't resist peeking now and then.

"Are you Anaea Carlisle?" The speaker was a leggy girl with curly black hair. She wore a maroon sheath dress, and kept shifting from one foot to the other.

"I am, yes," she said, "and this is—"

The girl grabbed for Anaea's hand, shaking it enthusiastically. "I'm Eve Linscott," she said. "My mother said I should watch for you. And my brother thinks you hung the stars in the sky, but don't tell him I let you know. This is your bodyguard?"

Again, Anaea let it go. "Gwydion," she said.

While Eve transferred her attention to Gwydion, Anaea studied the girl. Eve was sixteen, only three years younger than she was, but obviously still growing. Her eyes were dark pools, something pensive flickering beneath their surface.

"Come on," Eve said, "I'll introduce you to the birthday – err, woman. Follow me?" She clopped awkwardly in high-heeled shoes.

They threaded through the crowd, passing bubbly concoctions and bite-sized tidbits proffered by mechanical butterflies. Near a raised platform stood a portly older woman with a cluster of family in her shadow. The marchionissa acknowledged them with a lofty smile and introduced her family. Her daughter beamed and blushed, eyes averted.

"I hope you are finding Serendipity to your liking," the marchionissa said, her tone a borderline command.

"There is much beauty to admire," Anaea said with perfect honesty. She felt more than saw the wisp of Gwydion's smile.

"Happy birthday again, marchionissa." Eve gave a tug to Anaea's arm. Once they were away from the platform, she said, "I always feel as if she's staring into my thoughts somehow. So I'm supposed to entertain you until dinner begins," she continued. "How would you like to be entertained?"

Her tone was serious, but her eyes were bright. Anaea laughed. "Actually," she said, "your mother said something about a soccer match. Tell me about that?"

Eve ducked her head. "You really want to know?" she asked. "My mother's sort of embarrassed and doesn't like me talking about it in public."

"I'm your guest," Anaea said, "and I would like to hear about it." Feeling she needed some sort of cover, she added, "We didn't have much time for sports where I grew up, and the years since I came to the Sanctum have been far too busy."

You're getting better at spinning tales, Gwydion said.

She restrained a wince. *I wish I weren't.*

His thoughts pulled back with a pulse of surprise. He had been close as a heartbeat; now he was withdrawn. *It was a compliment.*

She wanted to apologize and somehow couldn't, and then Eve was answering her question.

"I'm part of the Eastside junior league," Eve said. "There's a Rosewater division, but they're not very good. Too concerned with their nails and makeup. I almost tried out under an assumed name." She smiled ruefully.

"Your mother?" Anaea asked.

"After a fashion," Eve said. "She didn't want me playing at all and would have preferred I stayed in Rosewater if I had to, but it was more that I was concerned Eastside would accept me just to curry favor with her." She brushed a curl out of her eye. "Had a heart-to-heart with the coach. Made it clear if I couldn't keep up, I didn't want to play. As it turned out, I'm one of their best strikers."

"This will sound silly," Anaea said, "but how is the game played?"

It was the right question to ask. Eve lit up, rattling on merrily about the rules, strategy, and her fellow players until she was interrupted by rude snickering.

"You and that silly game," Gilford said. "Put the ball in the net. Anyone can put a ball in a – oh." He straightened, tugging at his tie. "Hi, Anaea. I didn't see you were my sister's victim. Good to see you." He flashed a nervous smile. "May I say that you're looking lovely tonight?"

"Would you want to say something that corny?" Eve asked.

Gil flushed. Gwydion stepped forward, interposing, "I don't think we've been introduced."

The boy clutched the offered hand with evident relief. "Gil Linscott, sir."

"Gwydion Mallory."

At the name, Gil underwent a transformation. He stiffened, dropping the hand. His examination became a guarded stare.

He was jealous, Anaea realized with bemusement. Which meant—

The lights above exploded in a shower of gold. Streamers rushed past, drawing her attention towards the dais, where Traviata stood.

"Dinner is served," the regina announced.

The crowd parted them, whisking Gwydion away to another table, Anaea next to Eve, and Gilford at the foot of the main table. Mr. Petrarch sat behind Anaea at the adjoining table, and he smiled faintly as he nodded to her.

"We have a particular delicacy tonight," Traviata said. "I hope everyone enjoys."

The jeweled insects swirled down with four covered platters per table. One landed in front of Anaea. When the lid rolled open, she jerked in her chair.

The platters were filled with pale, iridescent larvae, twitching spasmodically. A few attempted to climb the rim, but it was too high.

Anaea stared. She knew the color had drained out of her cheeks. Was this an elaborate joke, and on whom? She flicked a glance at the guest of honor to gauge her reaction.

The marchionissa looked delighted. "Wherever did you find these?" she asked.

"Mindfire worms," Eve said. "Hallucinogenic. It's fun for a party. I'm surprised my mother is letting me try them." She flicked an uncertain look up the table. "Considering . . ."

Anaea stopped with her hand a reluctant inch from the serving tongs. "Considering?"

"You're supposed to kill them right before you eat them, that's the best time," Eve said softly. "Except if you haven't made sure they're dead, they can burrow up through the back of your mouth into your brain."

Anaea jerked her hand away from the tongs. A swift look down the table showed a few others who made no move to fill their plates, including Gil, who wrinkled his nose emphatically as he folded his hands in his lap. Anxiously, she followed suit, minus the nose.

She flinched when Upala, at the upper end of the table, blithely bit into one of the creatures. The redhead lolled back in her chair and released an, "Ohh . . ." of satisfaction.

"Anaea," Morgan said, "aren't you going to have some?"

She had spoken loudly enough to arrest the attention of the table. Eve squeaked under her breath.

The marchionissa arched a fine brow. "You're not fond of mindfire, miss Carlisle?"

Anaea tried to keep her panic in check. "More for everyone else," she said.

"Oh, but you must try it," Upala urged.

"Indeed," Morgan said softly, "it seems a discourtesy . . ."

Courtesy was not enough to change Anaea's mind. It was all

she could do to keep her breathing steady. "I mean none."

"You're as thin-blooded as that boy of yours," Morgan said.

Anaea flushed, but was puzzled. Did Morgan expect to goad her into trying the delicacy? The last two worms on the platter before her writhed, seeming to leap for the rim; she flinched.

"Anaea," Traviata said, her voice carrying without any impropriety of shouting, "tell me what you think of the seasoning."

She could scoop some of the broth, surely. Her hand shook on the ladle as she reached for it. The whole table fixed on her. One diner had his mindfire worm pinned down with a fork as its gyrations grew increasingly more frantic.

"My daughter can instruct you where to stab," the regina continued.

Anaea froze. To insult Eve's skill and mother, daughter or both? To annoy the subject of the party and convince the table she was a coward? None of that was of great importance, but somehow, she found herself taking a firm grip on the tongs.

Done properly, there was no danger. Certainly the rest of the party showed no concern, or if they did, it was swept beneath smiles.

Anaea scooped up the worm in the tongs. It pressed against the plastic as if trying to ooze through. She dropped it on her plate and jumped as its coils arched towards her hand.

Snickers echoed down the table. In truth, they didn't bother her; if anything, she would rather know it was a laughing matter.

Eve leaned in, nudging her elbow. "You need to strike it below the second vertebrae, there," she said. "One good, hard blow."

Anaea fought the impulse to close her eyes as she drove the fork down. Something squished, a quivering that went up into her hand. The worm went still.

"What are you waiting for?" Morgan asked.

"Oh, do let up," Upala said. "She's savoring the moment."

The worm hadn't moved, or was that camouflage? Anaea turned her fork, collecting it through the center of the body. The squelch as the fork went back in turned her stomach. She scooped it into her mouth and swallowed as quickly as she could.

It tickled up her throat. Was it moving? Before she could panic, a pleasant warmth spread up into her palette and a halo of color formed behind her eyes. The table danced with iridescence. She tasted the sauce, faintly, almondy, enough to disguise the rubbery texture.

"The sauce is very good," she said faintly. The words vibrated like lightning in her throat, setting off symphonic bursts of bell-ringing in her ears.

"My compliments to the chef," the marchionissa said. With those words, the spotlight turned from Anaea. She leaned back in her chair, watching the colors dance and whirl every time she blinked. The world changed, flitted, soared by her eyes.

The subsequent courses were not nearly so dangerous, and a merry clatter of conversation filled the courtyard. To her surprise, the marchionissa brought up the topic of trade tariffs, and no one objected or deflected into more frivolous subjects. The words swelled in her brain like a symphony until the mindfire faded.

She listened with interest, but there was nothing helpful to her situation. She cleared her throat. "Have privacy zones made it more difficult to enforce these tariffs?"

"Precisely," the marchionissa said, "which is one of many reasons to remove them. It's outdated legislature from a time of suspicion and fear. People clinging to an old paradigm."

"It was necessary then," another woman agreed. "However—"

A third frowned. "I disagree that everything of the old should be regarded with disdain. The ways of Terra—"

"Why do you bring this up, Carlisle?" Morgan interjected. "You have special interest in the topic. What are you trying to get us to do?"

Blood rose in Anaea's ears; the lingering mindfire made it sound like singing crickets. No denials, Phailin had said. "I'm not trying to get you to do anything," she said. "The Sanctum has certain beliefs, but I lived most of my life in a region where isolation was not a privilege, it was forced. Is it wrong to want the rest of the picture?"

She was going to be called out as an imposter, or the table would go silent . . . but neither of those things happened as Upala chirped, "If you want my opinion, you're making it far too complicated. Of course we don't need privacy zones. Imagine never being alone, always having someone else to support you, if only by agreeable silence."

Ellen Petrarch snorted. "Imagine feeling as if your actions were hemmed in by public censure. There are always things that people don't need to know about each other."

A few more people weighed in. Their opinions were forceful and direct, no looking for permission here. Anaea slid a glance to Traviata, but the regina was expressionless, engaged in dialogue with the birthday marchionissa.

Eve misinterpreted the glance. "Oh, me?" she said. "I don't think I really know enough about it to make a decision, and it's so complex, how could I figure it out?"

Anaea started, hearing herself only a month ago. How, indeed? She realized she had been making similar decisions ever since leaving home, without thought. The idea unnerved her.

The topic drifted, but Anaea had heard enough for now. She concentrated on the meal and her neighbor, quizzing her about the game she loved. Eve seemed grateful to have a comfortable topic of conversation and bloomed with words.

An enormous cake, seven feet tall, marked the end of the meal. The green and gold layers spun slowly. The marchionissa cut the first piece, and then the insects descended in a swarm to finish the job.

Anaea was too stuffed to eat more than a few bites of decadent chocolate. She rose from the table with relief, watching as people split off to dancing, drinking and other entertainments. Holographic displays burst to life.

"She's not going to open the presents?" Anaea wondered.

She only realized she had been speaking out loud when Eve

gave her a furrowed-brow look. "Of course not," she said. "That just encourages people to compare and judge; who spent more money, who better understands her, and so on."

"Oh," Anaea said. There had been no real purpose to birthday presents on Themiscyra, but the girls still exchanged them, eager to display not extravagance but personality.

Eve flipped her a smile. "Of course, she still gets to make those judgements in private. I'm going to drag Gil off for a game. Catch you up later?"

The girl scampered away, leaving Anaea amidst the buzz of conversation and the scintillating decorations. She turned her face up, watching the starbursts as they shifted through constellations.

She hunted for Gwydion, wondering if he had learned anything at his table. The crowds shifted to reveal him standing by a willow. The marchionissa's daughter stood next to him, laughing buoyantly, and leaning in with a glow in her eyes that made Anaea's breath catch. Angrily, she drew herself up, her mind bubbling with demands. She remembered the touch of his firm, square fingers and now it made her flush with embarrassment.

She let it go with a shake of her head. She had no right to be jealous, to turn possessive. They had made no promises. Maybe she was not so far from understanding these women. The thought made her bite her lip.

Fingers latched into her arm. "Anaea?" It was Ellen Petrarch, eyes sharp and measured. "A moment in private, if you please."

28

THEY STEPPED INTO A ROOM OFF THE COURTYARD. IT housed a labyrinth of garden maintenance controls. "You want to see privacy zones maintained," Ellen said without preamble.

"I believe Dr. Anders does, yes," Anaea said. *And I feel much the same,* she added silently.

Ellen cracked a dry smile and moved away from the door. "There's a powerful consortium bribing matriarchs to abolish the zone laws in several major cities: New Megiddo here, New Troy and Little Sparta on Elysium, and both Perica's primary population centers. Money being the root of power, I suspect those places are lost causes."

Anaea sucked in a breath, stunned Ellen would share the information with her. "How do you know?"

The older woman shrugged. "My husband and I are very good listeners, and we like things the way they are."

"So do I." Anaea rushed the words out.

Ellen's lips twitched. "So I assumed."

"What about other cities?" She glanced out the window

overlooking the courtyard, but saw only shadows thrown against trees.

"Some locations, I have no information about," Ellen said. "Some locations, the consortium is leaving alone because the matter is decided one way or the other, and nothing is going to change the minds of the locals. New Athens is one such place. Dr. Anders' old stomping grounds, yes?"

Anaea nodded. "What about Serendipity? The debate seems to be lively."

Ellen grimaced. "You might say that."

Could she push for more information? "So are there—" she paused, rephrased the question. "Is the consortium concerned about Serendipity? I mean, as much as you can make out?"

"No, they're not," Ellen said shortly.

How invested was the comitissa? Anaea shook her head to clear it. "Is that a good thing?" she asked.

"Hard to say. Traviata," Ellen said. "When she decides, whatever she decides, that's the way the city will jump."

"She can't make decisions for the others, can she?"

Ellen smiled wryly. "Not directly, but she makes herself heard. I've always been grateful not to be too close to her."

"You were at dinner the night I arrived."

"A social necessity. I have no problem with her on a personal level." Ellen shrugged. "We should go. One of us may be missed." Before Anaea could reply, she stepped out. "Wait a few moments before leaving."

"But what about—" Anaea found herself speaking to empty air. She slumped against the console. Serendipity came down to Traviata Linscott. In that respect, she was in the right place, but what did she do with that knowledge? She had only been asked to gather information, and she had done that.

When she headed back into the courtyard, the bursts of color dizzied her anew. She found Gwydion standing near one of the entertainment displays, sipping a glass of cider.

He was alone, no sign of the marchionissa's daughter, and

Anaea was embarrassed by tingles of relief. "How are you holding up?" she said.

"Feeling like part of the scenery," he said. "I don't really mind it, though."

In the guise of kissing his cheek, she murmured, "As soon as we can make our excuses, we need to talk."

*

Gwydion had no answers for her, only more questions, but they agreed on one thing: Phailin had to be informed. The next morning, Anaea told Karen she was shopping for gifts for friends back at the Sanctum and hurried out into the city. To cover, she made a stop at a glass shop and found a striking blue-and-silver vase that would fit perfectly in Sophie's house.

She almost collided with Upala Manuel.

"Anaea, what a pleasant surprise!" the redhead cooed. "What brings you out on this fine day?"

Surprise? Could it be coincidence? Startled, she clutched the shopping bag. "Hunting for presents to bring home," she said.

"Oh, truly?" Upala smiled warmly. "Then you have excellent taste. This is one of the best places for glasswork in the city."

Then it was chance? Unsure, Anaea moved towards the street. "I admit I don't know much about craftsmanship," she said. "I just know what looks pretty."

Upala edged along with her. "Would you like some company? I can help you find the best boutiques."

"No, I have other stops I need to make," Anaea said. "I wouldn't want to hold you up."

"Oh, I don't mind," Upala assured her.

What was the worst outcome if the matriarch joined her on the way to the depot? Anaea wasn't used to being so paranoid. "If you're sure . . ." she made herself hesitate. "In that case, I'll meet you outside the shopping center in an hour?"

Upala's brow furrowed in a delicate frown, quick to dissipate.

"Oh, certainly. Don't be late. Until then!" she carolled, flouncing away.

Anaea let out a shaky breath. Probably nothing more than a chance encounter, and she was jumping at shadows.

She stopped the public car a few blocks short of her destination and walked. She recorded a message to Phailin, wishing they had established some codes, and sent it with the vase.

Then she steeled her nerves and went to meet Upala.

The next several hours disappeared in a blur of vibrant tedium. On her way back, she received a dinner invitation from another matriarch, and it seemed polite to accept. While confining her conversation mostly to the delights of the city, the baronissa diffidently expressed she felt more comfortable with the privacy zones in place.

Though at first, she tripped over her tongue, Anaea felt herself begin to pick up the rhythm of matriarch speech. She could be polite, phrase things just so; maybe not with native experience, but she could pass.

Anaea stumbled back to Traviata's manor, drained. The first day in an intern rotation was less taxing. She flopped on the bed, drifted and woke up to the chime of the computer. "At balcony door, Gilford Linscott," it announced.

She blinked hazily and rubbed her eyes. "Come in," she said.

He entered, hands behind his back and a furtive expression on his face. Penelope twined through her arm, watching the boy with a twitch of her tail.

"Good evening, Gil," she said. "Did you enjoy the party yesterday?"

He wrinkled his nose. "Not really," he said. "Bunch of old women who think they're amusing and only manage to make themselves laugh. They sound like cackling crows." He remembered his manners in a rush, "What about you?"

"I enjoyed myself, I think," she said.

"What about the mindfire? My mother won't let me eat it." Gil hesitated, frowning. "Not that it's her objection that's stopping me. I wouldn't, anyhow."

Anaea fought a smile. "It was like having a lightshow in your head."

"Huh. Guess that could be cool." Gil seemed to come to a decision. He hop-advanced forward and swung a bouquet of flowers out from behind his back, brandishing them like a weapon. "These are for you."

The flowers were lilies and daffodils, vivid turquoise and golden yellow. Tentatively, she reached out to accept them. What else was there to do? It seemed hurtful to refuse a gift, and they were lovely: an explosion of disorganized color.

"Thank you," she said, "but you really didn't have to."

Gil hovered, looking as if he wanted to say more. He pulled back, tucking his hands behind his back again. "I thought you'd like those better than a traditional arrangement. Less fussy."

"You thought right." Anaea hunted for more to say. While waiting for inspiration, she sniffed at the flowers and almost sneezed as the potent aroma snaked into her senses. Once the rush cleared, the tangy sweetness tickled her nose. "They smell amazing."

"All natural, too," he said proudly. "I don't care for the engineered strands. That's like giving a person a piece of plastic: not romantic at all." He pinked and wobbled, on the brink of a question. Anaea wanted to interrupt him, but her scampering mind couldn't find anything to say. Romantic? She remembered his jealousy from the previous night.

He let out his breath in a rush. "How long will you be staying?" he asked.

"Not long, I'm afraid," she said. "I have business duties to perform." Though the duty was to herself. No question of staying here, but another city like it? Could she begin anew with the matriarchs and find equilibrium?

"Oh." Gil's shoulders dropped. "I guess I have to decide whether I want you to run into aggravating delays or not." He hurried on before she could reply, "I guess I should go. Good night, Anaea. If there's anything I can do . . . I mean . . ." He fled the balcony.

Anaea watched after him, biting her lip. What could she do? She didn't want to hurt him, but she had no idea how to respond to the overtures. He was too young, and as an aristocratic male, too unfamiliar in his impulses and beliefs, for her to fall back on the strategies she had used a few times on Themiscyra. Certainly she couldn't claim it would be awkward because they worked together.

Gently, she batted Penelope off the flowers. "Not for you," she said, but the kearl's dark eyes were so wide that she chuckled, removed a flower from the bouquet, and offered it. Penelope snatched it and scuttled under the bed.

Anaea sighed and went to find a vase.

*

THE NEXT THREE days progressed in a whirl. Some invitations included Gwydion; few needed him to speak. Most of the women supported maintaining privacy zones, but some seemed to have invited her for the sole purpose of a furious lecture, and others never admitted business topics at their table.

Anaea never noticed Morgan's influence until Karen pointed out that two prominent matriarchs had avoided her completely. A third woman invited her to dine, then canceled the invite not once but twice, citing important emergencies.

"I suppose that's a snub," she said to Gwydion, "but mostly, I'm relieved."

He smiled wryly. "If only she knew, hmm?"

On the third day, Anaea spent the afternoon with a matriarch a few years older than herself who had been assigned to monitor one of the poor districts. "You have to ask: where do hypermentals fall into this?" the woman said. They sat on a veranda overlooking the ocean.

"Under the laws that already exist, surely?" Anaea answered.

"That's why there's so much energy devoted to registration and training."

The young blonde shook her head. "Nothing stops a hypermental if they truly wish to do something, and there are more unregistered individuals than most people know. I work frequently with the police. Those people are their worst nightmares, and there isn't much to be done." She sighed. "It doesn't help that certain matriarchs put them to use—" Her hand flew to her lips. "You don't want to hear this."

Anaea, tense, wanted – needed – to hear, but she recognized the blonde back-pedaling to protect herself. "I wasn't aware things were so unsettled," she said.

The woman smiled wryly. "No. You wouldn't be. I've often wished for ignorance. Which, I suppose," she continued, her tone lightening, "is why I support privacy zones. Not for the sake of the people inside, but for the sake of the people who would otherwise have to know about it."

It was meant as a joke: cued, Anaea forced a laugh. "Well, that decides me," she said.

"I hear you're interested in bookcraft," the blonde said in a quelling tone.

Though Anaea tried, she couldn't push the conversation back to hypermentals. It lingered in her mind as she returned to Traviata's estate.

This isn't news, Gwydion admitted when she explained, pretending to be absorbed in a news report. *In law enforcement, you always know they exist. But it was a minor issue in New Athens, and reined in enough that no matriarch would dare . . .* he trailed off. *Traviata?*

That's what she implied. I don't know. Anaea couldn't keep frustration from spilling into that thought.

I can find out more from the Hypermental Charter, he said.

She looked up from the couch, startled. *Are you sure? You said you weren't comfortable around them.*

A little sacrifice. His smile was weary. *Let them read me. There isn't much to see.*

Don't put yourself down like that, she protested.

He rose, crossed the room, and kissed her brow. "Do you mind if I leave you tonight?"

"I'm sure I can find something to do," she said, and she did, drawn to the sea for a sunset stroll with Penelope. All the holographic oceans in Themiscyra were a drop to this one and its endless variety. It was hot even after dark; she came back sticky and sand-coated, and minding neither. After a shower, she settled in with one of Justin's books and lost herself in it.

It was late when Gwydion returned. He beckoned her onto the balcony in the guise of watching the stars, tucked an arm around her shoulders.

She pressed close. "Talk to me," she said.

Both thought there was no surveillance on the balcony; not sure enough to speak openly, but convinced enough it felt private. His cheek pressed against her hair.

Yes, he said. *Traviata Linscott hires a hypermental under the table. He's been out of the city, though.*

Oh. So they were safe, at least on that front.

I would have known if someone had come close, he said. *As long as we were together.* She needed no thought to realize he was considering the times that hadn't been the case.

Anything else? she asked.

Nothing solid. She might be in contact with others off-planet. He paused, then echoed their thought. *Phailin. I know. But there's nothing to suggest she's especially interested in the Sanctum.*

And what about me? Anaea wondered. She tipped her head to study him. *We still need to tell her.*

Yes. Tomorrow. He stroked her cheek with a finger, worrying at his lip as he did. *There's something I would like to do, Anaea. To protect you in case a hypermental comes calling.*

He took a deep breath. *I would like to form a telepathic tie between us. If someone tries to brush your mind, I will know about it, wherever you are. It's not intrusive,* he rushed on, the words seeming to pile up in the space in her head, *I might feel a strong emotion from you, or vice versa. But I understand if you aren't comfortable.*

She watched his eyes, tentative, worried. She wasn't sure whether this was necessary, whether it was jumping at shadows, but she trusted him. "Please," she said.

Gwydion nodded, placing the fingers of both hands against the pulse of her neck. A tide of wordless thought washed into the front of her mind, then licked deeper, stirring up eddies of memory. She saw Orithia when they had first met; the New Athens skyline; the city within the city of the Cauldron . . . her heartbeat quickened.

Done, he said, and she felt an alien flicker of relief; reflection, not her own feeling. Startled, her eyes widened on his.

"Oh," she said.

"How do you feel?" he asked.

Anaea considered, then for answer, drew him in for a grateful kiss, knowing – hoping – he would feel what she meant. Underneath the kiss, she sensed hints like tender words on the tip of the tongue.

He broke away, hand sliding to the back of her neck. *I guess we know it works.*

She was about to suggest testing it further when a crack came from the foliage. She tensed, jumping upright. He instinctively placed his body between her and the balcony. Part of her found the gesture absurd.

Further snaps, branches breaking, leaves distressed. The figure causing them stumbled into view and stared up at balcony, cheeks flaming.

"Gil," Anaea said, relieved. "Gwydion, it's Gil. Relax."

She hadn't said "only," but it was obviously how the boy took it, his body stiff as a machine. 'Yeah, it's not important," he bit off. "Forget it." He turned and fled into the courtyard, a crashing giant now he was no longer trying to go unseen.

Anaea rushed to the balcony lift, then paused. If she followed him, found him, what would she say?

"He'll be fine," Gwydion said. "I do know something about it, remember."

She nodded, watching over the courtyard. "Sorry," she murmured into the night.

"Things will be better in the morning," Gwydion said. "Always are."

He was wrong.

∗

ANAEA ROSE BLEARILY and started to order breakfast with twice as much coffee. This was one area where the warlords reigned supreme, but matriarch coffee was still noticeably better than Themiscyra's. Perhaps it was due to the use of real coffee beans, including hybrid strains.

The console beeped. "Traviata requests the honor of your presence at breakfast."

She whimpered and indulged in a childish moment by curling up under the covers until Penelope pawed at them to reach her. She would have to dispatch the message to Phailin after breakfast.

She wandered through a shower and changed into the first thing that came to hand. She dealt with her hair by the simple expedient of pinning it up.

The private dining room door was ajar when she reached it. She poked her head in.

Traviata, luminous in ice-blue, smiled with a pallor to match her gown. "Come in. Close the door."

Anaea did so. "How are you this morning, Traviata?" she asked.

"It looks to be a glorious day." Traviata waved a hand. "Please, sit. And yourself?"

She perched on the edge of a chair. Conversations with the regina still felt like an arcane test, and her head was too muddled to be sure of focusing. "I'm well, thank you."

"Are you sure about that?" The matriarch arched an eyebrow.

Anaea frowned. "Should I not be?" A linguistics nuance? Or was there bad news from the Sanctum?

"That depends." Traviata's tone was brisk as emerald butterflies dropped down, laying out scones and jelly. "Can any person who lives a life not her own be well? I'd think it would strain the psyche."

Anaea managed not to freeze, reached for a scone and pulled it apart with automatic motions. "I don't follow you."

"Then allow me to be blunt," Traviata said. "My sources have told me all your carefully composed records rest over a history where no one has ever met you. So someone has to ask the question: who are you, Anaea Carlisle?"

29

THE WORDS ECHOED INSIDE ANAEA'S HEAD, BOUNCING off six different answers that each depended on what Traviata knew. Her body vibrated like a drum, pounding in panic.

"I am Anaea Carlisle," she said. "That is – has always been – my name."

"You don't exist," the matriarch said, her voice a steady tide. "Someone has done an excellent job constructing you a identity, but they cannot fake years of the invisible footprints made in social circles. You pretend to an identity you do not have."

The scone crumbled in Anaea's fingers. "I'm not—" she stopped herself. To say anything more would be to admit Phailin had created this version of her, performed whatever fraud had been necessary. How had Traviata found out so quickly?

"You might claim Phailin permitted you this charade," Traviata said, "but it will do you no good." Her smile was a thin, condescending thing, encased in iron. "For one, without investigation, we have only your word. For another, that does not change the fact you have made fools of us and lived as an imposter in my home."

Anaea planted her hands on the table. "Then I'll leave your home," she said, "with the deepest—"

"No." Finality in that soft word. "You won't."

She blinked in confusion. "But I—"

"You are a secret bundled six times around to protect yourself," Traviata said. "Whatever you're trying to hide is either highly unsavory or dangerous, or both. Would I be correct if I said that you would do almost anything to protect it?"

Would she? Anaea's thoughts whirled as she sank back. It would be easy to confess to Traviata. The women of Themiscyra would face the universe again, and no one would blame her.

No. To reveal Themiscyra to protect herself was wrong, and she was equally certain Traviata shouldn't be the first person to hear those words. Would she try to orchestrate the station the way she did her parties?

"Almost anything," she said.

Traviata's lip quirked, humorless. "I see. Then you will do exactly as I direct for the duration of your stay. Are we clear?"

Anaea wet her lip. "Or . . . ?"

"The evidence I have is quite sufficient for me to short-circuit due process and have your head ripped open," Traviata said. "Your friend goes to prison for collusion. Hypermentals, you should understand, have to be sedated."

Anaea swallowed; the sour feeling in her stomach pressed downwards, made her legs shake. The burning buzz of the imperial cell crowded into her ears and bones, never mind telling herself this was a different place. Even if she thought an explanation would set her free, and she didn't believe that, she couldn't offer Themiscyra into those hands. Traviata would make a tool of it, she had no doubt.

"I understand," she said in a small voice. "How did you learn this so quickly?"

"Don't you think your deception skills assisted me?" Traviata spiked a brow. "I did have some assistance from Morgan, in exchange for a few concessions."

Anaea jolted forward. "You can't give him to her," she said, "it's not—"

The matriarch held up a hand. "You're not in a position to make requests," she said, "but I shall not be depositing your friend in her care. While hypermentals are not the exalted gods the imperials sometimes make them, the Charter takes a dim view of enslaving its own."

"It also takes a dim view of using rogues to gather information," Anaea said, rushing the words out. But what did she have to lose?

"I shall pretend, for your sake, that you did not say that." The matriarch dismissed it with an airy gesture. "No, Morgan had other interests, none of which are your concern."

The room shrank around Anaea. She took a deep breath, trying to contain the claustrophobia.

Anaea? Gwydion's voice curled around her thoughts. *Are you all right?*

He must have felt the shift in her emotions through the link. *No,* she responded. *Neither are you, nor Phailin.* She paused, trying to sort out the jumble and figure out where to start. *Traviata knows I'm not—*

Stop. His thought was sharp and alarmed. Her eyes widened as she tried to blank her mind, project nothing, consider nothing.

"I have him monitored," Traviata observed. "Do you take me for a fool?"

Realization fell into place. She pushed down the urge to call out, reminding herself the link went two ways: she would know if he had been hurt. Anger flared. If the other hypermental attacked him . . .

"What now?" she asked.

"I think my first assignment will cause you no distress: befriend my daughter." Traviata smiled faintly, but it vanished as she continued. "As you do this, you will encourage her to abandon her forays into sports. They are embarrassing."

Anaea stared, relief reaching her first – this was all the woman wanted? – and then being buried under an avalanche. Confusion why Traviata would go to such lengths for a small matter, worry about what might be next, contempt the woman would be so anxious to dissuade her daughter, and regret. She didn't want to urge Eve away from something that made her happy.

The regina exhaled a sigh. "However, if you have a problem with that . . ."

The words chilled her. "I'll do my best," Anaea said. "But I can't guarantee she'll listen."

"Of course. I understand." The matriarch's tone, even when guised with a softening of manner, emphasized her high expectations. "Are there any other questions?"

Dozens, none of which Anaea could force herself to ask. "Nothing."

"Then finish your breakfast." Traviata bit into a scone as if nothing had happened.

No chance of that, with the knotting in her stomach and the tightness in her throat. "I think I'm done."

A long sigh, and then a languid wave of one white hand. "Go on with you."

Her composure in ruins, Anaea fled.

*

Gwydion met her in the doorway, his face pale. "Are you . . ."

"Are you all right?" she spoke over him.

He pulled her into an embrace. She wrapped her arms around him and held tight. For one brilliant instant, everything was fine, just by virtue of being close.

It shattered. "Does she have a hypermental watching you?" she asked.

Gwydion nodded against her hair. "What happened?"

There was no point in trying to hide from surveillance. As they retreated into her suite, she spilled the story. "I don't know which way to jump," she said. "Is it ridiculous to be worried, because she means to ask casual things of me, and the only reason she used so much force is because she could? Or . . ."

"Or," he echoed as they sat on the couch.

She touched his hand to initiate mental contact. *We won't get our message to Phailin now.*

Maybe, he replied. *An opportunity might arise.*

She had trouble finding room for optimism, but nodded. He tipped her chin up to kiss her. She responded fiercely, not caring what ended up on record. His hands tightened on her back as if he wanted to fuse the two of them together.

Anaea broke the kiss, sighing. "I need air," she said. "I thought I would head to the shore. Coming?" It was one way to see how much leash they had. Would the hypermental follow? Surely not close enough to hear and see everything; that would attract too much attention. Could Traviata track their links without going through formal channels? Her heart rose. Too tedious to monitor them twenty-five hours a day.

Gwydion rose, pulling her with him. "Sure," he said. "I could use it."

They headed for the hover platform with forced chatter and hollow smiles. She kept hold of his hand. The platform ascended from below.

A flurry of gold fabric and red curls popped between them and the platform, resolving itself into a beaming Upala Manuel. "Oh, Anaea, what fortune! I was looking for you. How are you?"

"I'm fine," Anaea said, her voice weak. "And yourself?"

"Delightful. You remember that young man?" Her smile tried to be mysterious and failed. "What are you about?"

Upala's buoyant manner jarred against the backdrop in Anaea's head. "Gwydion and I are on our way out," she said. "Could we meet later? I would like to ask you about something." Though what could she really ask the woman? She could hardly open a discussion about Traviata.

"Oh, why wait?" Upala reached out to claim her arm. "I'll

come with you. You don't mind, do you?" Her trill left room for no other answer.

"We're just headed to the beach," Gwydion said, uncomfortable. "I imagine you've memorized every grain of sand by now."

Upala laughed as if it had been a statement of great wit. "Oh, impossible. Might I? I simply must get out of here."

Anaea touched Gwydion lightly on the arm. Their eyes met. There was no need for telepathy to communicate the thought: Upala was their chaperone, Traviata's idea of a guard; probably not aware of her role, but reliable for chattering every detail.

"Very well," she said, "but you know the beach better than we do. Show us where to go?"

*

THEY RETURNED TWO hours later. A few moments alone to whisper, always with Upala within line of sight. The prison was subtle, even if the redhead herself was not. She left them on Traviata's doorstep, swooping off to consult on either dress design or regional administration; Anaea couldn't tell which from context.

Gwydion touched her hand as they headed inside. *The hyper-mental trailed us,* he said. *Never more than five hundred feet out, never closer than a hundred.*

Is that significant? she wondered.

It means he's stronger than I am, but not by much. Gwydion sighed. *I think. Hope.*

She kissed his cheek. *I'm sure you're right.*

She wandered out to her balcony, Penelope bouncing at her heels. She picked the kearl up. "What got you so cheerful?" she asked, tapping the creature's nose. Penelope bumped into her hand.

In the courtyard, a startled yelp, then laughter. Anaea leaned forward and saw a lean shape whirling in one of the open spaces, responding to a holographic program. She thought it was Eve.

Impulse nudged her, but she was reluctant to follow. Was it already time to play out Traviata's command, like a ship on schedule for repairs?

She told herself not to think about it. Just go down and see what was happening.

The route turned out to be less than straightforward, but she found it after a few turns. Eve sat on a bench, adjusting her sneakers. She grinned. "Hi, Anaea. Do you want to play on my team?"

Anaea blinked. "What?"

Eve gestured to the frozen holographic players. "I finished warm-ups and was going to run through a program."

Anaea hesitated. On the one hand, this did not seem the best way to strike up a conversation to dissuade her, and on the same hand, she had never been much good at athletics. She had only taken the ankle brace off that morning.

"Well, I don't—"

"You could be the goalie," Eve said. "You mostly get to stand there. You contribute by being in the way. I mean—" She pinked, but her eyes were wide and hopeful. "Please?"

Anaea gave in. "All right, but you have to remember I don't know anything."

A little over an hour later, she discovered that "just standing there" was one of the hardest things she had ever done. The holographic ball hit her chest, legs and – once – her face, the impacts bruising, even though the pain was transient. She was relieved when Eve canceled the program.

Anaea lay down where she had stood, staring up at the sky. Eve bounced over and sat by her head, hands clasped over one knee.

"So we need to talk," she said, "about my brother."

Anaea thought about sitting up and decided against it. "What did he tell you?"

"That he thinks you hung the moon in the sky, that he brought you flowers . . ." Eve let out a breath. "That he saw you with your friend Gwydion last night, and he thinks the punk deserves a drubbing." This last had a lilt in her voice, obviously a quote.

Anaea appreciated the fact Eve didn't call him a bodyguard, knew his name. "I never meant to upset Gil," she said.

Eve shook her head. "When Gil gets caught up in something, it happens in his head without much input from the rest of the world." She bit her lip. "But I know what it's like to be stuck on someone and not want to realize they don't even see you."

There was history in her voice, recent history. Anaea hesitated, wanting to ask, afraid to intrude. "I hope I haven't been that stupid," she said. "I like Gil, and I think he's a good young man. But—"

"I know. I told him he was too young, that someone your age wants a man, not a boy." Her eyes were serious as she imparted this wisdom. Anaea tried to look as if this were some knowledge of sisterhood. "I'm not accusing you. I'm just asking you to let him down gently. Talk to him, you know? If he goes after Gwydion, he's going to get his pride smashed."

The idea of having that conversation with a mysterious male creature made her nervous, but how could she refuse? "Of course," she said.

Eve smiled, lopsided. "Thanks. Got to protect my little brother, you know? I'm the only one who will." Her eyes turned upwards. "Do you want to come to practice tonight?"

"I won't be participating, will I?"

Eve laughed. "No, I promise. I thought, since you seemed so interested in the game . . ."

Interested, Anaea thought ruefully, in its flaws: what made it worth giving up. "I'd like that," she said.

"I leave at sixteen hours," Eve said. "See you then." She flitted to her feet and scampered off. Anaea returned to her room, unhappily contemplating strategies that might turn Eve away from her hobby.

The soccer stadium Eve's team used to practice was an older building, verging on ill-kempt; something Anaea had become familiar with in the Cauldron, but was surprised to see here.

The coach, an emotionless woman in her fifties, watched with narrow eyes.

Eve was in her element, commanding attention when off the field and setting the pace on it. She slowed only to call encouragement to a teammate. She was never hesitant or unsure; she went head to head with the coach over a few plays. Anaea wondered if her mother had ever seen this side of her.

During lulls in the practice, Anaea read, savoring the feel of the book as much as the storyline. This drew a few frowns and whispers from the soccer players. She paid it no mind. She expected to be viewed as strange and archaic.

It was sunset by the time the coach called a halt. Eve flopped next to her, chattering about the players, asking if she had noticed this strategy or that move: an unstoppable stream of words.

"I hardly know the game," Anaea admitted, "but it looked impressive."

That turned Eve into a teacher as they walked out to catch a public car. The spate of words slowed when they entered the Rosewater district.

"You really seem to love it," Anaea said.

"Yeah. There are days when it's the thing I wake up for." Eve squirmed into the seat, eyes half-closed.

"Is that what you want to do with your life?" she asked.

A slow rise of one shoulder. "I don't know. How can I? My mother has expectations, but it's not as if we're in a monarchy." She sighed. "It would be nice. A life where your mind and body get to be the same instrument."

Her stomach tightening, Anaea sought the things that had frightened her at Themiscyra, the well-meant advice that had paralyzed her in choosing a career. "You have to be careful with a decision like that," she said. "Do you think the positive aspects will always outweigh the negatives? Five years down the road, ten? Or might turning it into a career take the mystery out of it?"

Eve sighed again, the sound whispering into silence. "I don't know," she admitted softly.

Anaea watched the Rosewater district flash by, regulated opulence, no residence outshining the next. She clutched the book on her lap and took comfort in how out of place it was.

"Maybe that's why I like the game," Eve said. "You don't have to think about the future. The moment is the important thing. Look too far ahead, and you'll lose everything else."

Wasn't that how Anaea had approached this impossibly large universe? Taking it moment by moment had gotten her this far. "Maybe you're right," she said.

*

After a banal morning, Anaea received a call from Traviata.

"We need to speak," she said. "Now."

"What—" Anaea started, but the connection had been severed. Biting her lip, she followed her link to a garden room adjoining the courtyard.

Traviata moved data-points around a three-dimensional grid. She looked up when Anaea entered.

"If you've called for an update on your daughter," Anaea said, "I've learned something that may surprise you. She gains more than physical skill from—"

Traviata held up a hand. "I did not ask you to comment on how I raise my daughter. I am sure there are many suitable ways to mold her in the proper image; I desire it to be done my way. Are we clear?"

Anaea stared. The words buzzed on the inside of her lips: how Eve was learning leadership and strategy through the game as effectively as any course that could be drummed into her head, how it might burn out like any other phase when she had taken what she needed from it. It was an impassioned argument, and somehow, she could not speak.

"I see we are," Traviata continued. "Your next task: I want you to meet with the Petrarchs. They seem to like you and may be more forthcoming. I want to know how strongly Ellen is set against the privacy zone legislation, and anything else of interest she might impart."

Anaea was surprised, perhaps a little relieved, that the regina didn't seem to suspect how fully Ellen Petrarch investigated. The Petrarchs were allies, of a sort. Time alone with them would be welcome. Time to say things that would not get back to Traviata.

Would it be a good idea to seem reluctant? She tried it on for size. "I don't like the idea of betraying their confidence," she said.

"That's what politics is. Get used to it." Traviata's tone thinly disguised the order. "If it salves your conscience, remind yourself you're under duress. Is there anything else?"

Anaea shook her head. "Nothing."

"Then be about it." Traviata turned her attention to the display.

Anaea slipped out, taking deep breaths to unknot her stomach. Once calm and able to muster a smile, she tapped her link and sent a call to Ellen Petrarch.

"Anaea," the woman greeted her, then continued, "I was just about to contact you. We need to talk."

30

WHAT'S GOING ON?" ANAEA ASKED, SURPRISED.

"We should speak in person. Can you come?" Ellen's holographic image arched a brow.

"I was calling to ask if we could sit down for dinner." Coincidence or not, the timing made Anaea nervous.

"What I have to say is best done in private. Perhaps an early meal," Ellen said. "Fifteen hours works for you?"

That much time to worry? "That would be perfect."

"Until then."

Anaea spent the day in reading and research, or tried to. She found her focus wandering, dropping into pits of worry. She spent too much time fussing with her hair and the novelty of make-up before she caught a public car. Even in front of a mirror, she couldn't find confidence. It didn't help that she wasn't sure what to aim for, the standards she had grown up with or the glossy elegance of the matriarchs.

The Petrarch residence was austere: a cream-white building with grey trim. The scalloped molding and ancient sheltering tree were its only adornments.

Mr. Petrarch met her at the roots. "Anaea," he said. "Good to see you. How is your small creature?"

"Fat and lazy from life here," Anaea said.

"As are my cats." He gestured. "After you."

As she stepped into the lift, an old-fashioned mechanical elevator with glass walls, she felt a prickle along on her spine. "What—?"

"We have our own privacy field," he said with a slight smile. "I prefer that people not even know the kind of tea I drink."

"I don't blame you," Anaea said.

His eyes crinkled. "Most would impugn my drink preference as putting on airs," he said.

She laughed, feeling more at ease. The lift doors opened onto an unvarnished patio. "You've already said almost as much as you did the entire party," she said.

He shrugged. "To be expected." He guided them to a dining room paneled in cherry wood. Ellen met them.

"You look well today, Anaea," she said, her brisk tone not inviting response. "Please, be seated. Seltzer?"

"Please."

Ellen scooped up a pitcher and poured; there were no robot servitors here. "I wanted to speak with you about—"

"Really, Ellen, doesn't the child even get time for pleasantries?"

She fixed her husband with a stern look, then smiled. "If we get business out of the way, we can relax," she said. "You can draw her into one of those arcane board games you're so fond of. My husband has the flaw of a competitive urge," she explained to Anaea. "I have a data stick you can review at your leisure. Still, you should hear this first.

"We've been receiving more information about the consortium's movements and interests," Ellen continued. "They've fixed eyes upon the Sanctum. No surprise to you, I'm sure. They have people inside: two psychologists compiling reports, attempting to show how unhealthy life in such an isolated enclave is, and a spy."

Was that how Traviata had learned about her so quickly?

Anaea wondered. "Do you have names?" she asked. "Phailin should know about this."

"No names, unfortunately," Mr. Petrarch said. "There's a limit to how deeply we can pry without being discovered."

"In tracing these movements, we noticed some individuals seemed interested in aspects of the Sanctum that have no relevance to privacy zones," Ellen said. "They've studied recruitment practices. They've studied the agents the Sanctum has posted off-planet, particularly with exploratory crews."

It was so unexpected that Anaea blinked. She felt a cold squeeze in the pit of her stomach before she understood why. Exploratory crews – Gwydion – Themiscyra . . .

Mr. Petrarch held up a hand. "Hold on, Ellen. Miss Carlisle, are you all right?"

"I'm fine," Anaea said. "Please go on."

Ellen shrugged. "I understand they recently pulled information on resident hypermentals, but that doesn't seem anomalous to me," she said. "However—"

The ceiling lights flashed red. Everything powered off. The silence vanished under Anaea's heartbeat.

Ellen rose in a rush. "What—"

"Ellen and Patrick Petrarch," an authoritative voice rang through the overhead, "this is the Serendipity Restraint Service. Please remain where you are."

Patrick, Anaea thought. She hadn't even known his first name.

Ellen cursed under her breath. "I have the data-stick on me."

"This is my fault," Anaea said in a rush, "I—"

"No," Mr. Petrarch – Patrick – said. "The regina suspects our leanings. Yours are evident. All that was needed was a team prepared to move at the right time."

She opened her mouth to insist that it had been her doing, but he held a finger to his lips. The doors opened, and six uniformed policewomen entered. Their stunners were lowered to a polite half-tilt, but they were obviously ready. Dread rippled through Anaea. She had brought them here, following Traviata's command.

"Mind the furniture," Ellen said crisply. "It's antique."

"Matriarch, I regret to inform you that you and your husband are under arrest on suspicion of espionage," the lead officer said. "We've been authorized to search your persons and the premises."

Ellen spread her hands. "As you will."

"Stand to one side, please, miss." The officer's command to Anaea was calm as rain, nothing like the imperial barks she had faced, but its softness was not up for debate.

The police impersonally patted down the pair and came up with the data-stick. There was no surprise, no inquiry. The lead office fixed her with a bland look. "You're free to go," she said, then started reciting the couple's rights.

Anaea whirled, afraid she would see accusation in the Petrarchs' eyes and knowing herself as guilty as they could imagine. Her mind flailed for some explanation to give them, but found nothing, and blinded by those thoughts, she found herself on the street, knees shaking and hating herself for it.

She should have been able to do something, but what? In old holo movies, this was the part where someone made a brave stand and shouted for everyone to run, but those hadn't been the faces of people who would run.

It was tempting to start walking and go wherever her feet took her: coastline, continental shuttle, spaceport. It was clear now she wasn't being assigned harmless errands. Was Traviata trying to see how far she could push? Anaea feared she didn't have the spine to push back.

Anaea? Gwydion's thoughts, frantic, crackling with anxiety, slowed her forward plunge as if she had dived into cold water. His presence decided her: she couldn't abandon him.

I'll explain when I get back. She didn't have the energy for more.

She walked the Rosewater district and eventually slouched into the manor. She laid her head against a column in the foyer.

"Headache?"

Anaea whirled. The dripping-sweet voice belonged to Morgan, decked out in an emerald gown. Luggage fought for the privilege of a secure spot on the overloaded hovercart behind her.

"I'm fine," she said. Her voice sounded hoarse to her own ears.

"Are you sure?" Morgan smiled. "I got what I wanted. Did you?"

Anaea's throat tightened. "Are you still—"

"No, not your boy, though if you're weary of him, I'll take him off your hands. It might be a kindness." The woman shrugged. "No, what I wanted was new surroundings and a better position, which I now have. Exploration oversight here on Solomon. There's said to be a big mission afoot, so it may turn out to be more of a boon than my benefactor knows."

That second touch on a raw nerve made Anaea flinch. "Good luck to you," she said.

Morgan snorted. "You're the one who's going to need it," she said, and strode into the lift.

Anaea turned away and noticed Karen standing in his doorway. He advanced, laying a light hand on her shoulder. "My sympathies, miss Carlisle," he said.

The warmth in his voice made her smile. "Thank you."

She managed to regain her poise and make it to her door. When Gwydion opened it, she fell into his arms, her head buried against his shoulder. She was surprised to realize the main emotions coursing through her were frustration and anger; they vibrated into his skin.

"What happened?" he asked.

She started to speak, got through a few fitful sentences before she realized she might say too much, and tried to switch to thoughts. Instead of a coherent through-line, she ended up dropping it on him as waves of images.

"Easy," he said softly. *I hear you. I think the Petrarchs will surprise Traviata.*

She pulled back to study him, thinking. *If only we could—*

He stiffened; she felt a frisson of fear and violation trickle down the link between them, and then, for an instant, felt as if she had been shoved against a wall. It passed before she could open her mouth.

Our guardian is getting nosier, he said.

He has no right to our thoughts. Her mind was chaos, emotions and thoughts bouncing off each other in random collisions . . . and one made cool, logical sense. *Can he sense when you're studying an object with your powers?* She remembered he could pick up impressions by touching things.

No. Not unless he were closer to my mind. He pulled them onto the couch. Penelope twined around his ankles. That startled a laugh out of him, brittle, high, and echoing.

Start looking, when you can. She framed the thoughts slowly, carefully. *Traviata's things – and Upala's, too. I don't want to ask you to do this . . .*

He picked up on the nuances under the words: she was probably shouting them in her mind. His face tensed, the color fading; even Penelope bumping under his chin didn't change his expression. Finally, he nodded.

You're right. We should think offensively. Fight back their way. He squeezed her hand.

She thought of the stunner still hidden under her luggage. If Karen hadn't betrayed it by now, he didn't intend to. She could use it, if she had to. *Maybe not just their way.*

*

THE NEXT MORNING, after a breakfast of bland coffee and cold pastries, Anaea queried her link for Gil. It was Saturday, so she was surprised to find him up and about, location logged as his room.

After a moment of hesitation, she took the lift and placed her palm on the recognition panel. She heard a thump, a yelp, and then scrambling as if there were three times the number of people inside. The door finally opened to reveal Gil with hands thrust in pockets, chin up, eyes combative.

"What do you want?" he demanded.

"I want to talk," she said. "Can I come in?"

The querulous expression remained a second longer, then evaporated as he ducked his head. "Sure. Come on, sit down."

Anaea lingered on the threshold, feeling as if she were stepping into a foreign world. It looked as if the contents of five rooms had been stuck into a mixer and spat out. Gil seemed to have a fascination for snakes and vintage spaceships. She blinked when she saw something that looked like the launchpod from the Themiscyra colonization, which was enshrined on the station. Somehow, it made her feel more at home.

"My mother was a starship engineer," she said. "This reminds me of her."

"Really?" he asked. "What kind of ships did she work on?" His eyes skimmed across the holographic representations, lingering, almost greedy.

"Small shuttles, mostly." Belatedly, Anaea realized this was not a detail incorporated into her cover story. Well, there was no harm now. "But those little hoppers helped a lot of people."

"Hoppers." Gil grinned. "I've never heard them called that. So what did you want to talk about?" The defensiveness returned with those words.

Anaea had thought through six ways to start, and somehow not settled on anything. "If I gave you the wrong impression, I'm sorry," she said, stumbling into it. "I think you're a gentleman, and I've been told those are hard skills to learn." Her heart thumped in her chest. She wondered if he could hear it. "And if you were five years older, maybe." Who could tell what five years would do to him? "I am glad to have met you."

Gil turned this over, his cheeks ruddy. "What about him? My competition?"

"Gwydion and I have been through fire together," she said. "We've saved each other's lives. We've been in situations I hope you never have to face. I trust him with everything I am." She paused. How did she explain what their shared adventures had forged?

"Do you love him?" Gil asked, as much curious as challenging.

"I—" It was eerie, finding no words on her tongue. "—don't know," she finished. How was a person sure? She cared for him deeply, no question, and the sensations she felt when she was near him seemed impossible. She knew things about him she couldn't put words to. Was it as easy as saying it?

"Huh." Gil huffed out a breath. "I guess that's an honest answer."

She stood in uncertain silence, hands twisting. Her eyes turned to the launch pod, following lines she had almost memorized.

"Interesting old clunker, isn't it?" His voice was proud. "Had it forever. Near as I can tell, shipbuilders stopped designing for improvement a long time ago and just focused on style. This one doesn't have much of that, but it doesn't need it."

"Gets on just fine without," Anaea agreed in a murmur.

"You want to see what I have?" He cocked his head.

She took it for a peace offering and smiled. "I would love to."

She left feeling lighter of heart, though that unanswered question gnawed at her. She shoved it down: it was too soon to think about love, too much complication. She also worried a hint of the thought might slip through to Gwydion.

She wondered how hypermental couples kept from driving each other crazy.

She returned to her quarters to find a package waiting. She held her breath when she saw Phailin had sent it. If it had been brought here, then she was not the first to see it. She opened the lid and found a message tube. She felt along the seal. Broken. Someone had opened it, and made no attempt to disguise the fact.

Anaea cracked the tube. Phailin's face appeared, strained and tired, but wearing a genuine smile.

"Hi, Anaea," she said. "Thank you for your last message. Gives me something to work with. We're going to make this go away. We have to." She shook her head. "Removing privacy zones would kill the Sanctum. Makes me wonder if that isn't the motivation of some.

"I want you to come back after the debate this upcoming Cloday," she said. "It's going to get hotter from here out."

"It's going to get hotter?" Anaea asked the image as it faded. She sighed, staring at the pieces of tube in her hands. Phailin needed to know about the new developments, but there was no way to reach her. Was there?

She knew from Gwydion that once a message tube was on a shipment, it would take a court order to intercept it. Would Traviata go to those lengths? Worth risking that she wouldn't.

But not now. This would be the moment Traviata expected a move. She dumped the pieces, feeling at last she had some kind of plan.

*

Sunday afternoon, thirty minutes before the last shipment of the week. Upala was supposed to be out with her paramour; Gwydion was on a call with a member of the Hypermental Charter, which would hopefully keep their guardians on edge.

She left the manor at a leisurely stroll, then hurried to a public car. The fresh evening air swirled around her, tickling her cheek. She enjoyed the solitude, not even minding the sensation of the link against her collarbone. After some debate, she had left the bracelets in her quarters. She could use them to ensure her invisibility, but once discovered, they couldn't be used again.

She directed the public car to a business four blocks south of her intended destination. She hurried through the crowds, receiving shocked looks when she pushed and jostled to quicken her pace. She saw the shipping station ahead.

"Anaea!" a familiar voice caroled.

Astonished, Anaea lost a step . . . then dropped her head and barreled forward before her hesitation could be seen. Just act as if she hadn't heard the woman, but wasn't Upala supposed to be cozied up on a date? Why would she drop that to come here?

Anaea ducked around a pair of gossiping teenagers and

sprinted for the door, adrenaline overcoming logic. If she could just disappear from view—

The door seemed to take forever to respond. She darted inside, looking for someone to hide behind, but because it was a weekend, the station was almost deserted.

"Anaea, good heavens!" Upala's laughter preceded her. "Whatever is the matter with you? You look as if you were on some dire mission."

Did Upala know she was a designated guard? Anaea wished she were sure. "I am," she said.

"Why, so am I," Upala said. "And quite put out about it, I must say. Traviata told me there was an urgent inbound I simply must pick up. Can you imagine? To be relegated to mere courier, to the detriment of my social life." She exhaled a gusty sigh. "We can go together?"

"No." Anaea managed to sound firm, not sharp, though her nerves crackled. "I have to leave a message for a dear friend, and I need to be alone."

"Oh, sweetheart," Upala said, squeezing her arm. "That's very brave of you, but that's the last thing you need. Let me come. I won't say a word, I promise. Silent support, hmm?"

Anaea fought back the urge to scream. She extricated her arm. A thought in the back of her mind stopped her before she could be too blunt. If Upala had no idea she was an appointed guard, but realized Traviata wanted Anaea under surveillance, she might redouble her efforts for the regina she clearly adored.

"Upala," she asked, "how involved are you in Traviata's politics?"

The pretty brow furrowed. "Well, my district is under her control," she said, "so anything she passes down comes to me?"

"Has she ever asked you to do anything more personal?" Anaea pressed. "Help her with a pet project?"

"Of course, and I am always at her service." Upala turned wide eyes upon her companion. "But do you mean to ask if you are such a project? Anaea, don't be silly. I only want to make you feel at home, and the more you do such strange things, the more I worry."

Her gaze was deep and earnest, and looking at her, Anaea couldn't tell if it was the truth or a perfectly orchestrated lie.

31

THERE ARE TIMES," ANAEA SAID, "WHEN YOU AREN'T READY to talk about a difficult situation."

Upala looked thoughtful, eyes downcast. "I suppose that makes sense."

Anaea's heart leapt. She was ready to take that as victory, but then she saw the furtive flick of the girl's gaze. Whether because she was a spy, or because she thought she knew what Anaea's own good was, she suspected Upala would prevail upon the staff to allow her to listen.

She couldn't take the chance of further condemning the Petrarchs, not even to warn Phailin. She bit her lip. "Thank you."

Upala made a little shooing gesture. "Then go on."

Anaea felt false and obvious as she made herself hesitate. "Maybe – I'm not quite sure what I want to say yet," she admitted. "Maybe I'll come back later."

Upala clapped her shoulder. "You can do it," she said.

It was all Anaea could to keep from shouting and shaking free. "No, truly. I think it's best to wait."

"Well, let me know if you need me, hmm?" The redhead sailed

on without waiting for an answer, a sudden shift in mood. "I should see what silly thing Traviata has dispatched me to retrieve. What a bother! But I suppose my loss is your gain."

She sailed to the counter and had a discussion with the cleric. She came back with a theatric scowl.

"Nothing," she said. "Apparently, it was delayed in transit. I will be doing this all over again in another hour." She heaved a sigh. "I need a drink. Would you join me?"

Anaea scrambled to shift gears. She might be able to start an offensive move. "Certainly," she said. "Where do you recommend?"

A few moments later, they settled into a bar suspended in spot gravity. Their table hovered fifteen feet up. Anaea, who was used to zero-gravity environments from Themiscyra, was not as impressed with the novelty as some of the patrons seemed to be.

Upala tugged her sleeve. "Oh, do be a little more jovial," she said. "I'm sure whatever problem you have with your friend, you can work it out, or you can work out your feelings with your bodyguard."

Anaea caught her breath as if she had been punched in the stomach. "I—"

Upala wrinkled her nose. "Oh, please don't tell me you're a good religious girl," she said. "None of us have time for that."

She had no intention of explaining whose spirituality was the issue. "So are you joining your date after this is cleared up?"

Upala shook her head. "No, the mood was ruined. I really will have to have words with Traviata. Still, I suppose I could use the time to finish the research compiled for me for the debate. I don't see why it has to be so complicated. Why should you want privacy unless you have something to hide?"

Apparently unaware she had maligned Anaea's motives, she pressed onwards, alternately complaining and expounding with waves of her hand. Anaea fought to follow the words, looking for something useful in the morass, but she found her attention wandering, and the potent fizz of the beverage made it difficult to focus.

"Honestly," Upala concluded, "the primary pleasure I derive from these kind of affairs is seeing what everyone has decided to wear."

Belatedly, Anaea realized that was her cue. "Speaking of fashion," she said, "I've noticed you have a few hats that . . ." she trailed off, reaching frantically for the term.

"The retro bonnets? Darling, aren't they? Even if they do hide one's luxurious locks." Upala tossed her head in demonstration.

Hoping she wasn't committing an obscure social misstep, Anaea ventured, "Do you mind if I borrow one? I have a lunch date it would be perfect for, but I would feel silly buying something I'm only going to wear once."

Upala stared as if this were some foreign language, but the urge to generosity won out. "Well, of course I would be happy to lend you something. I'll swing by with my favorites tomorrow and you can choose, hmm?"

Anaea nodded, relieved. Should she request social credits for something like this, she wondered, or would it be insulting?

The conversation bounced to other topics. ". . . seems so eager to discover we're not alone in the universe," Upala said at length. "The last time we had alien neighbors, it was the Derithe and . . . well."

"Is this the project Morgan is joining?" Anaea asked cautiously.

"Is it?" Upala made a face. "You're probably right. She would want to be on the front line."

Anaea stirred her drink and tried not to feel as if someone were drizzling the ice along her spine. "There's a front line?"

"More like front dots," Upala said. "It's a silly thing—" she gestured with the umbrella from her drink. "There are cases where an exploration ship didn't return. Sometimes, they send out a crew to retrieve it. Rarely, there's nothing to find. Some heavy thinkers are convinced there's a pattern of disappearances in one area."

Could it be somewhere else? Could she be so lucky? Anaea sipped, rehearsed the casualness in her mind before speaking.

"Which area, and why would they think that? Hyperspace is so unpredictable."

"Oh, I don't know." The redhead waved her hand again. "Something about debris trails and other dull technicalities."

"So you don't really think there's anything out there?" Anaea's head buzzed. The thought intruded that if this was Themiscyra, the factor which had given them away was not her retreat with Gwydion, but decades of salvaging ships. She felt guilty for being relieved. Did that absolve her of trying to prevent it, if the threat of discovery existed? Did she want to?

"No, but I wish Morgan joy of hunting." Upala shook her head. "Such a beastly little bully."

Anaea wanted – needed – more detail, but she could tell her companion knew almost nothing, and trying to pry it out of her would show more interest than she dared. Instead, they plunged headlong into the depths of polite conversation. By the time Upala headed back to the station for her package, if indeed there was a package, Anaea was exhausted.

She returned to Traviata's manor and met Gwydion's eyes. Neither word nor thought was exchanged; he sighed. As for her worries of home, she kept them to herself.

*

The next morning, Upala arrived with eleven retro bonnets, from yellow plaid with sunshine ties to a translucent version that shifted colors in the light. Anaea studied them, looking for which might be oldest.

It turned out to be the most technological of the bonnets, she discovered when her hand lingered and the redhead grimaced. "Why would you want that one? It's been out of style forever."

"These things go in cycles, don't they?" Anaea reasoned. "It could be the next thing soon."

Upala formed her lips into an "o," as if this were great wisdom. "I knew there was a reason I never threw anything away," she said. "Well, if you like it, you're welcome. Try it on!"

She did, fighting with the plastine ties as they darted through her fingers. The bonnet shimmered, making streaks of blue seem to appear in her hair.

"Gwydion?" she called, throat tightening. "Come over?"

He entered, smiling nervously at Upala. She dimpled and twiddled her fingers. "What did you need?" he asked.

Anaea tilted her head, showing off the bonnet. "What do you think?"

He stepped forward, touched her cheek. The warmth of his fingers wandered through her. His hand lingered on the bonnet, ostensibly catching a curl beneath it. She saw his eyes widen slightly.

"I can hardly see your face," he said.

Upala giggled. "Oh, if that isn't a line."

Anaea quirked an eyebrow. "What do you think?" she asked.

"He's a man. He doesn't know anything about the really important things in life." Like fashion, apparently.

"I think it's perfect," Gwydion said, holding her gaze.

Her heart leapt a little in triumph. "I think I'll borrow this one," she said. "It will only be for a day. If you truly don't mind?"

"Would I have brought them if I minded? No, and you can keep it as long as you need." Upala tsked and swept out, as merry as she had come.

Her thoughts running round and about each other, Anaea tried to carry on a casual conversation with Gwydion about their visitor's foibles to cover the private discussion. Her skin prickled, waiting for that telepathic touch.

There's not much, he said. *Clothing keeps impressions, but not like a record. It's flashes, hints. Another hand that touched the fabric, stroked it . . .* the thoughts carried undertones more clearly than his blush. *An older woman with eyes like the sea.*

Anaea could see hints of her, as if reflected through a broken mirror. She thought she would recognize the woman if she saw her face. Would she tip their hand if she studied Upala's records?

Traviata would expect her to look into her watch-dog.

Anything else?

Gwydion's eyelids fluttered. *Words . . . pieces . . .* "I've made it go away, dearheart."

She blinked. *Made what go away?*

He started to shake his head, then caught himself. "Well, she's still very much a mystery to me."

That was it, their piece of trivia. Would it do any good? Determination hardened within her. "Maybe not to me," she said, and she said it as a promise.

*

MONDAY MORNING MEANT the younger Linscotts were in school. Anaea browsed records, taking care to mix her time between Traviata, the Petrarchs, and even Morgan as she searched for the mysterious woman. The latter gave her a pretext to touch the periphery of the Solomon exploration mission, but unfortunately, public records had less information than Upala.

In the meantime, Gwydion took pretexts to wander, laying hands where he could. He came back perturbed and frustrated.

Everything in the house pulses Traviata, so much that it disguises anything else, he observed. *She's such a strong soul, I think she would obscure wars fought on this ground.*

She smiled wryly. *Such as ours?*

And too many others, I imagine.

She almost missed the face when it flickered by on the records. She jerked back to it, staring. Gwydion leaned in and called up the next image, squeezing her shoulder.

The previous marchionissa, he said. *The woman who gave Upala the job made something go away. Something serious.*

She refrained from biting her lip. *Does that help us?*

Maybe. He leaned his head against hers. *Something else is bothering you.*

She jerked, feeling stung, hemmed in, and she hadn't expected it to come from the one person here she trusted. *Don't read my mind.*

He stiffened, withdrawing from her side. "I wasn't." His speaking out loud was pointed, though the words were gentle.

She closed her eyes. "I'm sorry."

"Don't be. We're difficult to live with." His smile was tenuous. "Or maybe that's just me."

"It's not you." Her mind drifted to Sophie Mallory. What was living with a hypermental like? Never sure if their attention was concern or intrusion?

Talk to me. Please.

She flipped to a puzzle game before answering. *It may be nothing* – her emotions overwhelmed that thought – *but I think the exploration mission may be looking for Themiscyra.* She outlined what she had heard. Maybe it was just the focus required for Gwydion to read her surface thoughts, but the more she explained, the less it seemed like a leap, and the more it seemed like inevitability.

His silence made it worse. After several moves in the game, she squeezed his hand.

It makes sense, he said. *Do you suppose your presence or mine—*

She shook her head violently, converted it into staring at the three-dimensional board. *I can't think like that.*

We have to be careful. If Traviata begins to suspect the connection . . .

Anaea went cold. She hadn't considered that aspect.

He laughed at one of her moves, kissed her ear. It was strange, that little affections could make the world right; she would never have thought it possible before. *But as long as we're here, we have the freedom to investigate. On site.*

Gratitude pulsed through her. *Thank you.*

They spoke no more, devoted to finishing the game. It was such an activity of nothing that she wanted to cry out, but it had its place: camouflage.

Dinner was a formal affair, a house-party to which the younger

Linscotts had been invited. Gil grinned and waved as she and Gwydion entered. He opened his palm to reveal a holographic model of a Derithe stealth ship, then tucked it away before anyone could reprimand him.

"It's just a guess, of course," he said. "We don't really know how they were built inside."

Traviata orchestrated dinner conversation, steering it onto the topic of the debate the next day. Anaea sat on pins and needles and spoke only when called upon, but was relieved there were no tasks, no private commands from the regina.

Upala sat on her left and spoke in bright bubbles, oblivious to any somber words ventured at the table. She diverted the conversation into her favored subjects several times, even to the point of asking the assembled what they would be wearing, and Traviata let her with an air of maternal indulgence.

Eve, seated opposite Anaea, stayed quiet, eyes downcast. She pushed her food about with the fork, eating little. As soon as the meal ended and social mingling began in the lounge, she disappeared.

"I hope she's all right," Anaea murmured to Gwydion.

"Anaea?" Traviata beckoned from beside a holographic display. "Could I borrow you?"

She and Gwydion exchanged looks; she felt a pulse of reassurance through the link. She crossed the room, setting down her drink on the way and trusting one of the countless insects would collect it. "Is there a problem, regina?" she asked.

Traviata arched an eyebrow. "There's no need to be so formal," she said. "I simply wanted to invite you to try a new word-sequence game. It evolved from the gambling over on Twin Fires, but it is stimulating."

Anaea smiled nervously. "Maybe one round?"

Traviata summoned the game. An opalescent pearl field shimmered around them, letters in pairs dropping like diamonds. She frowned, waved, and the letters became puzzle pieces. The pieces looked three-dimensional if Anaea looked at them directly, but if she tipped her head, she could see past them to the party. Sounds reached her as a muted lapping like waves.

"I'm not familiar with this game," Anaea admitted. As she said it, rules text swirled past her left eye. Simple enough: a matter of combining letter pairs in a holding pen. It was a cooperative game, three players versus a dealer.

"Should we ask—" Anaea began.

"No, we'll use virtuals." Traviata snapped her fingers. A holographic figure appeared to her left; a fourth hovered over them.

Anaea paled. They were Mr. and Mrs. Petrarch.

She felt her fingers clench and forced them to relax. "What is this about?"

Traviata inclined her head. "Play."

Anaea reached out, hand cupping to catch a falling set of letters. They tickled her palm. She placed two in rapid succession, hoping to create a difficult sequence for Traviata, but the illusory Patrick interjected, finishing the first word.

Traviata arched a brow and plucked another pair of letters out of the air. They continued like this for a few minutes, and Anaea's heart settled.

"You will be attending the debate tomorrow," the regina said.

She started, reminded herself it was an opportunity to learn more, even though she was backed into a corner. "Thank you," she said, bowing her head.

"Don't thank me. You have a job to do. I've already put you on the docket." Traviata paused, frowning as the holographic Ellen disrupted the pattern she had been building. "Harder than it looks, isn't it?"

"I don't like being volunteered." Anea's voice was quieter than she would have liked. Her heart sped up, drying out her mouth.

"Everyone likes to be known as a selfless contributor," Traviata said. "You will stand up, introduce yourself, pronounce your affiliation with the Sanctum, and support the removal of privacy zones. Talking points will be provided."

"You think if it comes from the Sanctum, the place which

has the most reason to want its privacy preserved, it will quiet other objections," Anaea said.

"It's certain."

Anaea looked away, watching the phantoms of the dinner guests as they mixed and laughed. Incredible, to have this conversation in plain view, but it was also the perfect cover. She tried to calm her racing thoughts. She had to make a stand somewhere. "Maybe this is worth more than my reputation to me."

"Is it?" Traviata inquired idly. "If you force me to call you out, Anaea, I still achieve my objective. Do you see what the Sanctum is capable of doing behind its privacy zones? Terrible, abusive practices. We must put a stop to them." Her voice turned syrupy, almost a purr.

Anaea's decision rose as a cold thought, anger first, but then affirming itself as logic. She looked at Traviata steadily, weighing, hearing Ellen's calm tones, Eve's wistfulness, seeing Gwydion flinch as the rogue hypermental touched his mind.

It was not enough to escape. She had to do more. Glimmers of a plan formed, plucked from possibilities and whispers and 'perhaps,' but it was what she had.

"So you want me to betray the Sanctum." Her voice stayed quiet.

"Don't blame yourself," Traviata said airily. "You've been maneuvered into this, and the fault is not your own. I was going to award you social credits for the assistance, but if it salves your conscience, I will refrain."

Anaea caught a falling vowel pair and turned it over. "I won't accept anything."

"By the way," the regina continued, "I am aware you and your bodyguard have private conversations. The system analyzes pauses, hesitations and unexplained movements. I have not intervened because I do not want to start a hypermental clash, but don't abuse the privilege."

Those words relieved Anaea rather than alarmed her. It was obvious Traviata thought she and Gwydion could say whatever they wanted, because it couldn't affect the outcome. She had been underestimated, and it would help them. There was hope. Unexpectedly, Anaea found heart: she was beginning to realize this maze of words could work for her.

"I understand," she said, then nodded to the board. "Let's finish this game."

32

AFTER THE GAME ENDED, ANAEA MINGLED, HER BRAIN roiling, but her chaotic thoughts had a direction. By the time she could gracefully excuse herself, she had a plan.

She returned to her room and put on the show: she burrowed on the bed with her face in the pillow and managed tears with the theatrics. She convinced Penelope, at least, for the kearl squirmed down the bedpost and nuzzled her neck until she looked up.

She ruffled Penelope's fur. "I'm sorry I brought you here."

The kearl snorted and flicked her tail as if she understood.

As Anaea removed the bracelet, she turned it over and slid the inner casing out so she could glance at the workings. There were several settings, as she had suspected; she had to hope the highest one was enough.

Gwydion appeared in the doorway. "Anaea? Are you all right? I was sandwiched between two chatty matriarch daughters."

He looked so genuinely distressed that she laughed. "You're too good a listener."

"It was hard to get a word in edgewise."

His eyes were quizzical, worried. Had he felt her distress

through the link? Was her outburst keeping him silent? She bit her lip. Why was it he slipped away when she tried to get closer?

"Well, you must try," she said, and hoped her meaning was evident from her eyes.

What did Traviata really want?

She told him, letting the emotion spill into her thoughts. He pulled her into his arms, tentative, then visibly relieved when she wrapped in close. She could feel his heartbeat, and it made her own quicken. *If you have to do this,* he framed the thought, *Phailin would understand.*

She shook her head. *I won't do it. Not to Phailin or the Sanctum. If we run, we lose our chance to track the exploration mission.*

He had focused, unerringly, on the thing that bothered her most about her plan. Her limbs tightened as she fought tears anew.

She took a deep breath. *I can't do anything, even if it is Themiscyra, even if I know.*

Still. That one word offered everything: forgiveness, support, rescue.

She savored it before she made herself reply. *I left them. That has to be the way it is.* She wished she were as convinced as she tried to be. She added, *I have a plan.*

He watched her intently as she explained, not interrupting. When she finished, he said only, *I'm going to need a boost.*

I'll do my best to get you that. She squeezed his hand. *Are you willing to do this?*

His eyes never left hers. *I trust you.*

I – she lost the train of thought and blushed. *Thank you.*

The leaders of Themiscyra had been wrong, she thought with sudden clarity. If there were people like Gwydion in the universe, then it was worth embracing.

*

Anaea slipped out an hour later in search of Karen. She found him in his office, working with data stacks.

"Can we speak privately?" she asked.

He regarded her thoughtfully, then nodded for her to shut the door. Once she had, he tapped a command on the desk. "We can talk," he said. "No one will overhear."

"I'm in a bind," she said. "Gwydion needs a stimulant, but I think Traviata would take it the wrong way." She watched him, eyes level. If he asked, she wouldn't lie.

Karen frowned. "Traviata is a cautious woman, not given to paranoia."

Anaea nodded, reading between the lines. She tried to stop her heart from sinking. There would be another way, but it would be hard. "I won't ask—"

"I'll aid you," he said.

She felt her jaw loosen. "But—"

"Officially, I don't know of any problem between my employer and yourself," Karen said. "One of my roles here is to see to the comfort of guests."

Anaea blinked once, twice, then more frantically. Why was she tearing up? "Thank you," she said. "You don't owe an outsider—"

He held up a hand. "Do you know how I started in this job? It was rhetorical, for he continued, "My girlfriend and I were seventeen. Full of ourselves. I dropped out of school to make money for us. Didn't value a free education. The system caught up with me, and I was arrested, because education is more important than independence." Irony lined his voice. "Someone got a lot of social credits for turning in the young truant.

"My sentence was community service. Desiree left me." The inflection in his voice indicated cause and effect. "Part of my service involved working as an assistant for a volunteer organization. Any credits I earned went to them, of course, but I discovered I liked the work. I also developed an idea how much a good secretary could influence his surroundings. I worked my way up from there."

Anaea squinted, trying to work out how old he was.

"Thirty-four," he supplied.

She blinked. "Are you sure you're not a hypermental?"

"Don't need to be." He smiled wryly. "My point is I came into this world from the outside, from beneath, a position where I was underestimated. And there's nothing wrong with any of that."

"I hear you," she said, "but I don't think I'm going to be in this world for long."

Karen arched a brow, his expression quizzical. "Where else would you go?"

Anaea lifted her shoulders in a shrug. She tried to disguise how much the question bothered her: where else was there to turn? "I don't know."

"Well, best of luck to you." He shook his head. "I assume you need this right away?"

How much had he guessed? "Yes."

"It will be handled by morning. The last guest will be headed home soon, and the regina has some late business to handle. You should go." He added, "You'll be under record again as soon as you open the door."

"Good evening, Karen," she said, and stepped back into Traviata's constant surveillance.

*

The package arrived with breakfast. Anaea met Gwydion's eyes across the table, and her heart snapped against her ribcage.

We're ready?

She felt more than heard the questioning note and suppressed nervous laughter. She reached out and gripped his hand.

Maybe this wouldn't do any good. Maybe Traviata had too much control over the situation. But there was a chance the right speech during the debate would raise questions – about the Petrarchs, about other things. It was better than running.

They had an hour before departure as part of the regina's

entourage. It was too much time even if Anaea remembered every trick she had been shown with make-up, and she had neither the focus nor the inclination.

They rose from the remnants of breakfast. She leaned in, kissed Gwydion, and found courage in the touch of his lips, the breath that joined hers. It was a long, slow kiss, an exploration of where she ended and he began, and synchronized their heartbeats.

He pulled her closer, a crushing hold, a note of desperation she felt in her bones. If this went bad . . . the matriarchs hid their violence under regulations and euphemisms, but it was there. Real danger, whichever way they turned. Whichever way they were forced to turn.

Her mind ran ahead of her as she basked in a heat that grew more potent. If this might be the last moment, what did watchers and vows matter? The world could stand on their doorstep, the divine could judge, but they were the only ones in this moment. The physical differences between could hardly intimidate her now.

Gwydion broke off the kiss and made an incoherent sound. She lifted a finger to his lips.

"Don't—"

The overhead chimed. "Upala Manuel to see you."

They groaned in chorus, then locked eyes. Anaea burst out laughing a second before he did, and the humor, however welcome, a rush of sea breeze over her soul, made the heat evaporate.

"I suppose you ought to answer it," Gwydion said, even as he tightened his hold. She was surprised how strong it was.

"If you want me to, you need to let go," Anaea said.

"Well . . ." He chuckled.

She heard herself laugh again, shaky. She kissed him and pulled free. "Come in."

The door opened, and Upala flurried in, filling the room with her presence. "I just wanted to see if you were ready," she said, "or if you needed any help with – you're not planning on wearing that old-fashioned bonnet for the debate, I hope?"

Anaea was tempted to say she had planned her outfit around it. Feeling a trifle guilty for thinking it, she said, "No. Don't worry, I'll be ready on time."

Upala wrinkled her nose, looking dubious. "Are you sure?"

Behind Anaea, Gwydion stifled laughter.

"I'm sure," she said. "I won't embarrass you." Except that was a lie, and she felt it even as she met the woman's eyes.

"Oh, of course not." Upala dimpled. "I have a few calls to make before we depart – until then?"

"Wait." The word came out ahead of Anaea's thoughts. "Will there be anything on the exploration mission at the debate?"

Upala looked puzzled. "That's not a matter for the Collective, not yet," she said. "Though I'm sure it will gossip its way out long before a formal report is made. Why do you ask?"

Morgan. Gwydion's thought was a light tap in her mind.

"Miss Dennison," Anaea said. "I wanted to know if she would be present. We didn't part on good terms."

"No, Morgan shan't be attending," Upala said. "She hasn't the rank. Oh, Anaea, you must simply relax and enjoy yourself," she continued. "It's a great honor to attend."

"Oh, I'm looking forward to it." She forced eagerness into her voice.

The redhead smiled vaguely and flounced out.

Anaea dropped and groaned into her hands. "Did I just make a fool of myself?"

Gwydion rubbed her shoulders. "No."

What if Upala noticed special significance in what she said? Anaea told herself there was no point in worrying: after today, her origins would be a moot point.

She let out a breath and stood, going for the blue dress and remembering Sophie, remembering the security the Sanctum represented. She knelt for the matching flats and slid the stunner out from its hiding place. The cool surface pressed against her outer thigh, hidden beneath the flutters of the dress.

The bracelets went on, and there was no more time.

Her stomach roiled as she and Gwydion approached the lift. His nerves reflected off hers, echoing in the link. Penelope curled up on his shoulder, face buried in the crook of his ear.

A gangly figure in a scarlet sheath dress darted out and almost collided with them. She bounced backwards onto her heels.

"Sorry, Anaea," Eve said. "I was looking for you, though. Mother wants Gil and I to come along, thinks it's important for us to be seen." She curled a strand of her hair around her finger. "Well, for me to be seen, not so much Gil."

The uncertainty struck a chord in Anaea. She smiled, feeling the expression crack. "You'll be fine."

"I would be impressed, if I saw you for the first time," Gwydion said.

Eve tipped her head up, not quite strutting. "Thanks," she said. Her expression turned pensive. "Do you remember our conversation about my long-term plans, Anaea?"

The lump in Anaea's stomach congealed. The last thing she wanted to hear was she had succeeded. "Yes, I do."

"You asked me if having it as a career would take the mystery out of it." Eve puffed out a sigh. "I thought about that for a long time. I asked myself all those questions. What I came out of it realizing was there isn't anything in the world that could live up to that scrutiny. For me, I mean." She flushed. "I'm sorry if you feel differently, but that's how it looks to me."

"No," Anaea said, "that's exactly right." Those questions had kept her paralyzed for years longer than Eve. Somehow, she had said the right thing to help the girl avoid the same fate, even though that hadn't been the message she intended.

Eve grinned. "Come on, we don't want to be late."

Traviata greeted them with a chill nod as they entered the foyer. She stared at Gwydion and the kearl, then offered an elegant shrug. She wore a high-collared gold tunic with crystal buttons flowing down the neckline. No pretense of humility here: the outfit was expensive and reveled in it.

When they descended, three public cars waited at the street.

It turned out to be a sizable group, with Karen and two other assistants.

Gwydion stiffened, glancing towards the last car. A nondescript middle-aged man with wispy black hair sat in the corner, hands folded, apparently ignoring the illustrious procession.

Anaea breathed out, slowly. *Is that him?*

Yes.

The hypermental had shown himself; things were coming to a head. Anaea dug her fingers into her palms as she seated herself. The trip passed in a blur, masked by meaningless conversation.

The car halted. The rogue hypermental dismounted. No one commented, but Anaea watched him disappear out of the corner of her eye. She had expected this: Gwydion had informed her a pair of hired hypermentals monitored the debates to be sure no one eavesdropped.

Does that mean they might hinder us? she had asked.

I doubt it. They know me now, and most of us, when it comes to a choice between normals and another hypermental, support each other. He sounded sure, but there was no telling what would happen.

She climbed down in front of the cumulus cloud domes, swallowed by the vibrant explosion of flowers, and a burst of people, as cloying and as colorful. Some seemed to be spectators, eager for the first rumors of the debate, but others moved with purpose. Penelope chittered, pressing closer against Gwydion's neck.

The crowd drew back from Traviata as she advanced, leaving her a path as wide as a queen's. She smiled and acknowledged the occasional face with the air of one granting a favor, yet if it seemed condescending to Anaea, no one else appeared to notice.

The power of this woman took Anaea aback once more, but if she was unquestioned mistress of this place, then they were about to enter the eyes of dozens more women who were equally powerful.

Upala giggled and blew a kiss to someone in the crowd.

Just shy of the entrance to the central chamber, Traviata

paused. She kissed her daughter's cheek and said formally, "I will see you after, dear."

Eve bobbed her head. "I'll be here." As she turned, Anaea caught a hint of green fabric under the red. The girl had her uniform on under the dress; perhaps there was a practice scheduled during the debate.

Anaea bit down her laughter. Standing behind his sister, Gil caught her look and grinned.

Gwydion hugged her with one arm. "Good luck," he said, his voice soft.

"Same to you," she said.

A wave of Traviata's hand was enough to sweep them into the chamber. Rainbow light descended over the assembly, blending them into patchwork sameness. A holographic sphere dominated the space in the center like a diamond, each facet depicting another room; people moved in flicks and flurries of multiplied motion. Anaea looked away, dizzied.

Traviata's place was nearest the sphere, Anaea's four rows back. Upala flounced off with one of the assistants in tow, and with Karen behind the regina, Anaea was finally alone. She glanced behind her, seeking the nearest exit. Then she slipped down in the plush faux-stone seat and focused on the debate.

The regina of New Megiddo served as chairwoman and moderator; her image expanded and remained off-set to the sphere, watching the speakers as they raised their voices. Supporting data swirled onto the consoles in front of each seat. The same ritual, Anaea knew, occurred on the other two planets in the Collective, and perhaps a session on the Twin Fires station.

An older woman spoke of tradition as if no other consideration should matter. A younger girl of high rank spoke dreamily of a united world, one with no secrets. Anaea snuck a glance over at Upala: the redhead leaned forward, hanging onto the words.

A third woman, a creature of hard angles, claimed the abolishment of privacy zones was necessary to decrease their dangerous reliance on hypermentals. "Should we trust them or the evidence of our own senses?" she concluded.

The moderator's image rotated in Traviata's direction. "I understand Serendipity has a piece to say."

"Not from my lips," Traviata said, "but from a person I believe better understands the implications than most of us; indeed, she lives them." She turned, her eyes finding Anaea's, and the smile pierced. "Anaea Carlisle of the Sanctum."

Murmurs rippled through the chamber, buzzing in Anaea's ears. Across the sphere, other figures turned to each other, the sum of their motion causing the sphere to flicker and shudder.

Anaea rose and advanced to the projection dais. Her ankles wobbled; she thought she would pitch forward.

"Regina Linscott has graciously allowed me to speak in support of the abolishment of privacy zones," she said, fidgeting with the bracelet. The clasp loosened under her fingers. Some matriarchs bumped heads, consulting; the others seemed intent.

"However," Anaea continued, taking a deep breath, "that's not what I came here to talk about."

33

TRAVIATA HAD BEEN STILL BEFORE; NOW SHE COILED TO spring. Her eyes narrowed.

"Soon after I arrived, I realized the debate wasn't over ethics and security, but over influence and credit." Anaea heard smothered chuckles in the countryhall, echoing faintly in other parts of the planet. She flushed, but remained steady. Better they think she was a bumpkin than a conspirator.

"This astonished me. How can such an important matter be traded and sold?" She turned, meeting the nearest eyes. Though rapt, they told her nothing. "That was how I met the Petrarchs. They had concerns about how the decision was being made." Even though she knew revealing that confidence was the right call, her stomach knotted. Easy, she told herself. If this soured, the couple were no worse off. If it went the way she hoped, the victory would be theirs.

"Pardon," Traviata said, her voice dry, "but I do not believe this is relevant. If you have nothing to say on the point, step down."

"On the contrary," the moderator said, "I find this quite

appropriate, assuming there is more to the story. Continue, Miss Carlisle."

Traviata's hands clenched, and Anaea thought she would leap up and interfere bodily, but then the anger vanished beneath her beautiful surface.

"The Petrarchs had performed an extensive investigation into a group interested in the abolishment of privacy zones," Anaea continued. How extensive? She had never found out. "They warned me someone in Serendipity was trying to swing the city, regardless of the desires of individual matriarchs."

"Enough!" the regina rose in a rush. "This person who stands before you—"

Now or never. Nausea pressed up against Anaea's throat. "Yes. You're going to tell them my history is fabricated. Which is true."

Gasps, murmurs, averted eyes. The moderator frowned. "You had better explain yourself, miss Carlisle."

"Of course." This poise belonged to a person outside of her skin. Panic bordering on vertigo whirled through her. "Only a small part of it is false," she continued. "I did come from an isolated colony. Once I left, I remained off-grid because I didn't want to draw attention to myself. That's dangerous, in warlord space. I was forced out of hiding when I tried to help a Nissyen group earn rights we take for granted. Afterwards, it was made obvious I wasn't welcome to stay.

"Phailin allowed me to change my identity not to make me more acceptable to all of you—" that was the only lie, and Anaea hoped her voice didn't quaver "—but to give me refuge from the past. That's exactly what the Sanctum is about: shelter, a chance to start anew." And could have been for her, if she had wanted to stay. "Don't we have the right to choose which parts of ourselves to show the world?"

Anaea looked around her, saw some faces blank of understanding, but more curiosity than condemnation. Heartened, a little giddy, she focused on Traviata, made herself meet the woman's furious gaze. "So you see, there are no dark motives here."

How are you doing? Gwydion asked.

Managing, she answered. *Only a few minutes.*

I'm ready.

She sent a burst of warmth down the link. "The regina was convinced my history was something criminal, something that needed to be brought to your attention." Her heart thudded in her chest. "Which meant, to her, that it was something which could be used."

"You will stand down," Traviata said harshly. "I have no patience for wild accusations."

"You gave me the floor," Anaea said, surprising herself with the steadiness of the words. "Unless the moderator says otherwise, I'm going to keep it." Her eyes flitted in the direction of that image, but the woman remained intent, waiting. "The regina threatened me, blackmailed me . . ."

She unfolded the story, leaving out Upala's possible involvement. She glanced towards the young matriarch, but her face was a mask of shock that could simply have been for the public nature of the announcement, not its contents. Anaea talked about the unlicensed hypermental, but not the Petrarchs' arrest. Let them find that for themselves.

"I want nothing more than to stay here and answer your questions," Anaea said, swallowing with effort. Her dry throat resisted. "But everyone here knows the kind of power a regina, any regina, has. I'm not safe."

She wanted to explain herself, excuse her behavior, make them understand, but she had already said too much, and she could see Traviata's fingers run across her link. No more time. She had to hope her newfound practice with diplomacy was enough. Dizzy, feeling the room start to melt around her, she put her thumb in the bracelet.

"So I'm taking my leave of you," she continued. "I'm sorry."

She jerked the bracelet cover off and pushed the dampener to maximum. Darkness rushed in; the sphere disappeared with a crack. People screamed, stumbled upright, demanded explanations.

Anaea spun and bolted up the aisle, not risking a look back. Voices shouted for backup power. She didn't dare think: fear would shut her down.

The shadowy contours of the doors jumped out at her, silent and dark. There would be a manual switch on the base, but she didn't look for it.

Gwydion, she thought, his name punching out so hard her head hurt.

Got you.

As she reached it, the doors creaked open. She pressed her body against them, wriggling through—

"Anaea!" Traviata's voice snapped across the stillness. "Don't move. Security!"

Despite the momentum pounding against her, Anaea froze, feeling sweat stick against the surface of the door. She had sickening visions of a man with weapon drawn behind her, taking aim.

The lights flickered. Someone had figured out how to overcome the dampener, or – she heard it whine on her wrist – it was almost spent. She shoved her body through the gap and heard the doors slam behind her. The frame twisted, forcing them shut.

Anaea rubbed her wrist, torquing the level down to a low buzz, enough to hide her link and hopefully keep systems from targeting her. She stumbled, twisting to scan the corridor. An alarming twinge from her just-healed ankle trapped her attention, but it subsided. Her heart throbbed in her throat.

Gwydion rushed over, catching her arm. Penelope bounded on the leash behind him. Anaea took the loop. "The back gardens are clear," he said as they hurried along. "As long as our luck holds."

He wedged open the doors to the thick, cloying air outside. They sprinted, putting distance between themselves and the chaos of the countryhall. It felt like they were moving too fast for fear to catch up: it was always an instant behind.

They approached the back gates. Once off countryhall property and into the city, with no way to track their links, they would be invisible. Relief rose within her like the heat from an engine, but it was tinged with frustration. She had fled Themiscyra, been ushered out of Nissyen and warlord territory, and now had no hope of returning to Solomon.

"Find the manual release," Gwydion said as they reached the gates. "I could push these, but—"

But that was the last push he had, his tone told her. She crouched, searching the base of the gate. The kearl nudged her hand.

The gates opened from the other side. She jumped back, startled. The arch framed the unassuming figure of the rogue hypermental, a blaster dangling in one hand. Fear caught up to her, taking her breath with it.

"Some of us aren't so easily duped," he said.

"I guess you couldn't get close enough to the countryhall to overhear," Gwydion said, "but it's done."

"Is that so?" The rogue arched a brow. "In that case, my only choice is to kill you both. I can't have you standing as witnesses."

Those words burned away everything else. "You can't," she said. "It will fall on Traviata." Her hand slid down the ruffled layers of her skirt, feeling for the weapon. She tried to keep her leg turned to hide the motion, even as her knee shook.

He snorted. "I'm better than that. I can make it look like whatever I want. Even that the police shot you." He pointed the weapon at Gwydion. The scream in her throat stopped short as his hand went still, held in rictus tension. The faces of both locked in concentration. She wrenched her stunner free.

Gwydion staggered backwards with a cry of pain. Anaea squeezed the stunner. Invisible pressure wrenched her arm skywards. The blast dissipated above. She tried to resist the momentum, but it knocked her back. She landed hard on her tail bone and saw a dark flash as Penelope streaked past into the underbrush.

"Please." The rogue sounded almost bored. "I can deal with your clumsy attempts at combat. I'll be taking that now."

Anaea clenched her fingers around the stunner even as a

force stronger than gravity ripped at it. Holding on took all her strength.

Invisible hands slammed the rogue backwards; his head snapped against the courtyard wall. The phantom pull released so abruptly the weapon thumped into her chest. Gwydion panted; he had already spent a lot of energy forcing the doors.

The rogue shoved away from the gate, expression dazed. Anaea flipped the stunner in her hand, fingers shaking. This time, the shot fired true—

It rebounded, the energies warping over her. The world went white, her senses recoiling on themselves, her limbs disconnected from her body. She thought she cried out, but she couldn't feel the vibration in her throat.

Anaea. Gwydion's thought cut through the haze like a knife. *Are you all right?*

Black spots in her vision suggested motion – too much motion, as if the men spun and gyrated around her. *Gwydion, watch out!*

She fell forward, landing on her hands. Her muscles were weak as a baby's. She fought to balance herself. A hand burrowed in her hair and yanked her up, nails scratching at her scalp. Penelope hissed, a yowl of pain from the rogue . . . she sensed more than saw him kick the kearl.

Her hand swung and found the stunner. It seemed to weigh a hundred pounds. Her heart hammered. The sensation, painful or not, was welcome in the stunner haze. All she had to do was turn the weapon a few inches, do something to slow the rogue.

Gwydion charged in, no finesse, a body to body clash. The rogue's hand ripped through her hair; it dragged her forward. She fell hard. She saw flashes of images, out of sync: the rogue smirking, obviously expecting to knock his opposite flat without effort, Gwydion blocking a blow.

Anaea pushed onto her haunches, weak and almost sick with her helplessness. She found the stunner in the grass and wobbled it between her fingers, but the two men were locked together, and the rogue pressed Gwydion, preventing him from backing off.

Forget technology. Anaea cast around her, wincing as the world bobbed, swum and danced. More by chance than intention, she closed her fingers around a landscaping stone. Just hauling it to her took massive effort, but Gwydion's cringe, the way he shrunk in on himself, pain snarling down the link between them, gave her a surge of adrenaline.

She had no plan, but the weird way her surroundings distended and the heaviness in her hand forced her to steady her aim. When the rogue lunged to follow up his mental assault with a physical blow, she hurled the rock.

It struck him below the knee. He snarled, wavering. Surprised, Gwydion still reacted quickly. He aimed a punch for the rogue's jaw, missed, but caught him hard in the face.

"Anaea!"

She scrambled for the stunner and fired. The nimbus caught the rogue straight on. He jerked, muscles rigid, then dropped.

Gwydion's hands, under her shoulders, scooping her up, urging her onwards. She babbled something about Penelope; warm fur in her arms, keening in indignation more than pain. The gate, the plunging shadows of the street, garden flowers blending into city flowers, sweet upon sweet, the hiss of electronics billowing around them—

"We've made it," he said. "We've made it."

They slowed to a walk on a narrow residential street. Penelope wound from her arms to the ground, which was just as well, because Anaea could no longer handle the weight. She felt wrung out, wet and heavy, and from Gwydion's labored breathing, she knew he was not much better off.

She reached for the guestlink against her collarbone and braced herself. It burned like atmospheric entry as she pulled, and she cried out. Breathing heavily, she dropped it and crunched it under her heel.

Not safe yet. "We have to keep going," she said. "He could still catch up to us."

"Distance," Gwydion agreed. "Let's get distance."

"We can wait to go after the exploration records," she said. "Cover our tracks first." Her heart pulled in, half-knowing if they didn't go now, they would never get there, but she couldn't put them in further danger.

"No," he said. "Now is the best time, while everyone is still confused, before anyone has a chance to figure out we might go there."

"But—" She stopped as they stepped out onto a crowded street, absorbed into the anonymity of the crowd. Even the kearl's presence wasn't enough to make them stand out. She muffled a groan, clutching her stomach. The stunner's effect lapsed into nausea.

"You sure you can walk?" he asked.

"Can you?" she countered. "We have to. Can't take a public car without turning the bracelet off." Nearby lights flickered and whined. She frowned and worked one finger under the metal, reducing the strength again. She had to keep it high enough to disguise Gwydion's permanent link, but too high would make them conspicuous.

They stepped onto an accelerated sidewalk, the mechanisms deep enough the bracelet didn't hinder it. The exploration center was far enough away from the public spaceport it would be a long walk back . . . or run.

She tried not to think about it as they passed through an industrial area carpeted with vines. To stowaway on a public ship was their best plan, but this first.

The exploration center was a two-story building with a private landing zone. It was fronted with frosted glass, showing every shape and shadow within, but obscuring detail. Exchanging a glance with Gwydion, she headed for a side door.

To her relief, it slid open as soon as the sensors picked up motion. Low-security area: they didn't have to trip any alarms by turning up the bracelet. Penelope pranced beside them, tail waving like a flag, as cheerful as if she were oblivious to the tension of her humans. The kearl had already forgotten her upset of moments before.

Anaea told herself to breathe, but a sick feeling still bubbled up inside. She led the way towards a staircase, hoping her guess was correct. If their destination wasn't on the second floor in the central block, she had no idea where else to look, and no time to do so.

They passed several secure areas. Anaea hugged the far wall, concerned the sensors might pick up the blip of the bracelet. Yet if she removed it, surely Traviata had Gwydion's signal tracked.

Around the next bend, a a secretary sat behind a smoke-glass desk that blended into her surroundings. "Name and purpose," the girl said in a flat, nasal voice.

Anaea felt an embarrassing trickle of excitement. This was a chance to practice the skills the natives valued so highly. "I'm Annie, and this is Chris," she said; it was a popular name, she had found, favored in much the same way as Karen was. "And, well, you see—"

"We're late for login," he said, picking up the cue, "because—"

She poked him in the ribs. "Hush."

The girl regarded the drama with a faint smirk.

"This is fourth time this month I've been late," Anaea said, "and if I chalk up another—"

"And if she chalks it up because of me—"

Anaea mimed a hurt look. "I wouldn't blame you."

He smiled wryly, then transferred the look to the girl, who snickered. "Yeah, and what do you want me to do about it?" she asked.

"I hate to ask, but could you turn the scanners off?" Anaea assumed a sheepish expression. "I figure I can sneak in and pretend I was already there. My supervisor will assume he missed me. I hope."

"What's with the animal?" the girl wondered.

"She's part of an experiment we're running," Anaea said.

The girl frowned, staring at her console. Anaea twisted the leash around her fingers, trying not to fidget. What if the lie failed?

"We would be in your debt," she added.

The girl looked at them skeptically. "You can't spend debt."

"You could spend social credits, though," Gwydion said. "How about we say you helped my friend here when she was . . . feeling ill? We'll think of something suitable."

She sighed and flopped back. "Fine, whatever." A glint in her eyes indicated she was more interested in the credits than she let on. "Go on through. I've powered them down. Don't get me into trouble over this. Whatever you come up with better be good."

"I won't," Anaea promised, hurrying to the double doors. "And it will."

"Thank you," Gwydion called over his shoulder.

The doors whispered open. They moved down the hall at a jog. The corridor bent and entered a t-junction. Anaea hesitated. Penelope plopped on her haunches and scratched at the collar, entirely unconcerned.

"It looks the same to me," she said.

"Oh, it isn't," a chirping voice said. "There's a right way to go, and a wrong way."

Upala Manuel stepped around the bend ahead, her hands spread before her, something triumphant and hard in her smile. "I thought you might come here."

Gwydion's eyes flicked to Anaea. *You break left, I'll go right.*

She nodded and pivoted, tightening the leash in her hand. Her body insisted she couldn't run, but what choice was there?

"Oh, don't bother," the redhead interrupted. "We're already in lockdown. You're not going anywhere."

34

ANAEA WENT STILL, HER FIRST FEELING ONE OF RELIEF: no more running. She had to remind herself to be afraid.

"How did you find us?" Gwydion asked.

"Oh, please." Though answering his question, Upala addressed Anaea. "You were a little too persistent asking about Morgan and the missions here. I wasn't sure you would come, but it was the place I knew to look."

"You don't have to turn us in," Anaea said, the words sloshing in her stomach. "All we did was embarrass Traviata."

Upala wrinkled her nose. "All? As if that weren't enough offense. You're lucky we don't throw people to raptorhounds here." Her body relaxed, oozing into a position of contentment. "And I get the credit."

"You deserve the credit." Gwydion's voice was quiet. "For a lot of things. Things your predecessor protected you from." His impassive expression supported the bluff, but Anaea could feel the vibrations of his nerves. They made her skin jitter in sympathy.

Upala paled, but recovered. "It's not the credit that matters," she said piously, "it's the knowledge of having done a good deed."

"Or a bad one."

Anaea held her breath. They knew that much from his read on the bonnet, but not much else. Inspired, she placed a hand on his arm. "Do we really need to do this? Do we need to descend to their level?"

His eyes snapped to hers. They widened as they saw her purpose, understood without the need for telepathic touch. It flushed her, filled her with warmth. Any misunderstanding they had suffered was gone.

"I won't be trapped here." His voice rasped harshly. "You wouldn't understand."

She tensed. Careful, Gwydion . . .

"If you've done nothing wrong, there's no need to go rushing about as fugitives." Upala smiled, sweet and condescending. "No need to use any weapons you . . . think you might have."

"You know exactly how wrong that is," Gwydion said.

The redhead studied his face, lips slightly parted, trying to measure him, Anaea thought. She took her time weighing. Finally, she said, "What do you want?"

Anaea's lungs hurt from holding her breath, but she didn't want to let it out too fast. "We want to leave unhindered," she said.

"And the proposal file for the mission due to be flown out of here," Gwydion added.

Upala narrowed her eyes. "Or?"

Penelope chittered, baring her teeth. Gwydion spread his hands, standing firm on the strength of nothing.

Upala pivoted, emitting a huff. "Oh, very well. I will not have you broadcasting my private affairs to all the universe, as you've shown yourself painfully capable of doing. To think I even liked you." Her eyes pierced with accusation. "Follow me. I'll remove the lockdown, tell them it was a false alarm. But don't expect me to do anything else."

"That's all we need," Anaea said, hoping it was true.

*

THEY LEFT WITH a data-stick of the proposal and promises Anaea was sure wouldn't be kept. The bracelet sparked against her wrist.

They arrived at the spaceport a ragged trio: even Penelope flagged, tail drooping. Policemen lingered on the corners, watchful, bored.

"They're probably watching for blanks in the surveillance as much as our presence," Gwydion said.

She smiled bravely. "Good thing we have a plan."

Instead of heading for the commercial area, where the monitoring net would be tight, Anaea led them to the docking area for transports and mail couriers. Low-lying smoke drifted, as if all the smog the rest of the city could not abide had settled here. Workers pushed and jostled.

She had checked the mail schedules several times. With luck, it had looked like a continuation of her attempts to contact Phailin. She stretched onto her toes, scanning for the right ship.

"Over there," Gwydion said, "with the . . . blue insignia. Err, that is blue, right?"

Black pits and scorch-marks marred most of one side of the courier in question. It hunched in its corner of the docking bay.

Anaea swallowed. They had decided returning to Elysium was too obvious and chosen a transport bound for Annwyn instead, but she now fervently wished any courier were running within the next two hours.

The gangplank lowered. A lanky youngster swaggered out and set down a battered crate. It emitted a sickly hum.

Anaea and Gwydion exchanged looks as they watched from behind a cargo crate. "So they really use dampeners, right in a matriarch spaceport?" he said. "That takes guts."

"They want their privacy." Anaea slid from her crouch with a bump, landing on her knees. "Flick mentioned something to me about crews doing this, except it's commonplace in warlord space."

He squeezed her shoulder, then settled in beside her. No chance to sneak across yet: the loading zone boiled over with personnel and hover pallets.

"We managed Upala well, I think," she said quietly. "Blackmail wouldn't have been my choice . . ."

"Worse." His voice was bleak. "She'll think I read her mind." He pulled in on himself, though he didn't object when Penelope clambered into his lap and butted her face against his shoulder. Anaea sighed and leaned against the crate, blinking against weariness as she watched the jostling.

Voices lifted in a contentious snarl on the far side of the bay. Two workers dropped their load and jogged that way, either to help or simply to gawp. She glanced to Gwydion; he nodded.

She pushed herself up, skidding sideways around the crate. She scrambled for the gangplank. The leash tugged taut; the kearl's shrill protest made her teeth ache. She snapped a gaze towards the crew, but they were absorbed.

Gwydion hauled her into the ship. A cold, thick odor, mixed parts malaise and something fishy, assaulted her nose. She turned the bracelet off as they stepped into the cargo hold.

While the crew had made some effort to confine the bulkier crates with straps or energy fields, most of the packages roamed free, sliding at the slightest jostle. It was a labyrinth and a mudpit at the same time: ideal for hiding, as long as she didn't break a traveling heirloom by accident.

They found berth behind a grey case marked "Botanical Samples." Unlikely anyone would come this far back unless, Anaea thought wryly, it was contraband.

She soothed the kearl by scritching her stomach. Gwydion crouched on her other side. She hadn't meant to, hadn't even thought it was possible, but she drifted off to sleep.

*

Gwydion shook her awake, gently. "They're checking the ties," he said in her ear.

Anaea caught herself before she could jerk upright, in no small part because Penelope dozed on her foot. Carefully, she shifted, pulling the kearl into her lap.

"Where are they?" she whispered.

He continued in thoughts. *Front of the hold. When they move back, we'll slide along this crate and take shelter behind the goldfish.*

She blinked. *Goldfish?*

Amusement, not inappropriately, swam through her thoughts. *Goldfish.*

Low voices echoed through the hold, shuffling through ribald jokes with the air of those who had told them a dozen times before. Anaea waited, fingers gripping her arms. She held Penelope firmly despite the kearl's squirms. Gwydion nudged her, and she edged into the open darkness. Blinded, she felt her heart beat faster, waiting for discovery.

She reached the edge of the crate and almost toppled backwards. A group of feather-light boxes skimmed away from her feet, but made no sound as they rebounded off other crates. She ducked behind a group of poles and felt her way through the shadows with her free hand.

The fish tank materialized like a ghost, the hand lights of the crew reflecting off the glass in ripples of white. Anaea squeezed in behind the base, trying not to feel exposed.

Penelope gyrated in her grasp, attention fixed on a cluster of fish swimming about the bottom. She stretched up, pressing her nose against the glass and sniffing at the creatures.

"Penelope!" Anaea kept her voice a low hiss as she fought to get a better hold on the kearl.

"No live cargo this time," someone said. "Pity."

"There's them fish."

Anaea froze. Her fingers loosened. Penelope stopped straining.

A snort. "Fish. I'm not talking about fish, I'm talking about great eye-pecking birds, or the mating pair of Pegai from

Elysium." The winged creatures were named after an old Earth legend. "That was some journey! They ain't as sweet as they look, I can tell you that . . ."

Anaea breathed out a small sigh as the voices retreated. The rest of the strap-check went without mishap, and the crew retreated from the hold. The last thing she heard before the doors closed was, "We're strapped down, captain. Clear to leave orbit."

Gwydion sighed, stretching out from behind the tank. "They should leave us alone for a while," he said. "Unless we knock something over."

"He's talking to you," Anaea told the kearl. Penelope proceeded to groom herself, paying the fish no further attention.

"There's a water-dispenser on the wall." Gwydion frowned. "We'll be fine with that, but food . . ."

That was one wrinkle Anaea hadn't considered. "Can't we use their systems?"

He shrugged. "Depends on how it's programmed. If it needs authorization to dispense, or keeps a log of meals, we'll have to go without."

She sighed. "I wish Orithia were here. She would be able to override it in her sleep." She felt a pang of loss. How long had it been since she had thought about her friend?

"We could always eat the fish."

She laughed, even not wanting to. "Penelope would like that. But we'll be fine. What's the outside on the trip, five days?"

He nodded. "Let's go back. I feel exposed here."

They edged through the dimness to the space they had staked out. Anaea noted a pair of pillars, holding cells for data, to be transported in a burst upon entrance into local space. At least she could be fairly confident it would hold no information about them, not yet.

She pulled out the data stick. As she did, the bracelet rubbed against her pocket. She started to remove it, then changed her mind. Better not to leave detritus behind.

The pale light of a hologram flooded the area behind the

crate as she activated the stick. The proposal – approved the day before her arrival on Solomon, she noted – scrolled by in blue: an exploration mission to the provided coordinates to map the system and either make contact with the locals, establish the reasons for the extinction of a colony there, or discover alternate theories as to events cited in attached . . .

Anaea couldn't focus on the rest. The tone of the language left no doubt they assumed there was a colony and counted anything else as unlikely. She turned to the supporting documents, flipping through diagrams and reports, overlaying them where she could to get a clearer picture.

It was as Upala had said: exploration ships disappeared with uncommon frequency in that star system. There was one case where the ship had been discovered stripped of its supplies. She wondered at that. Who on Themiscyra could have been so careless?

She pushed onwards, squinting at aftermath reports concluding the debris was not consistent with a hyperspace accident or an asteroid collision. Had her people attacked exploration vessels? To protect the secret, surely . . .

We're the pirates, Anaea thought, sickened by the revelation. So much for Thalestris' calm reason, her claims of protection: the women of Themiscyra also tried to hide the fact they were thieves.

In these reports was enough data to absolve her of personal responsibility for the potential discovery, but she felt no relief. Anxiety gnawed, poisonous and certain. This was in matriarch hands now. Morgan's hands. An empire versus a small station filled with women who had no idea what the outside universe contained, had mostly never even met a man except perhaps as a zoo curiosity . . .

She had forgotten Gwydion's presence until he put an arm about her shoulder, a soft sigh registering his own read of the findings. She leaned against him, trying to put her thoughts in order.

"Can we stop them?" she asked.

"How?"

The only thing she could think of was to convince a warlord to hold the matriarch shuttle, and what would happen then? Surely they would force the story out of their captives, and that would only set the Empire on the station. She couldn't say which was more ruthless, but the warlords were less likely to respect the women of Themiscyra for the fact of their gender.

No way to remove the trail, not now. The discovery had to be made, and neither side was a good choice for first contact.

Why did it have to be one or the other? She sucked in a breath as the idea came together.

"We don't stop them," she said. "We invite the warlords to the party."

Gwydion whistled. "That's a huge decision."

"I know. And I don't want to make it." Doubts swam in front of her eyes: it was something for wiser heads, for deep consideration; even for a committee, if one thought like a matriarch. But according to the proposal, the expedition was departing in eight days. There might be time to consult Phailin, maybe, if the next courier ran fast . . .

"But if I don't," she continued, "no one else can or will."

And it was her world, she thought. She had no right to abdicate the decision to the Sanctum's leader. Anaea still thought of it as home, she realized, despite how far she had roamed . . . or because of it? She had left the Sanctum because it was too much like Themiscyra, and yet, maybe she did understand Gwydion's hiraeth, in a way she had not expected.

"You think they'd clash with each other over the existence of the station?" Gwydion asked. "If they don't, nothing changes – two overwhelming forces isn't much worse than one – but if they do . . ."

She bit her lip. "It's worth a try, isn't it?"

"It is." He frowned. "Which warlord do we approach?"

Not long ago, she would have asked if it mattered. Now she realized the anarchic pecking order meant one warlord might be too reluctant to act, while another could spark a power struggle over the information that could delay a response for weeks, even with the matriarchs en route. It was a subject she knew too little about, with one exception.

"I am familiar with the warlord of Nissyen," she said slowly, "enough to be confident he would work with the knowledge and be able to act on it, but—"

"No," Gwydion said sharply. He squeezed her shoulder protectively, but his fingers betrayed a spasm of panic. "We can't go back there."

"I wouldn't choose it, either." As much as she wanted to see Flick again, learn first hand how things had gone in the Cauldron, she didn't want to invite Blake Avidan's wrath. Neither did she want to mention the Tweaker to Gwydion. That hint of jealousy, remembered, alien, tickled the back of her brain. She didn't want to disturb the peace they had. "But we don't have any avenues for research."

"Then we start researching as soon as we touch ground," he said, voice calm. "We have a whole planet to work with. There must be a good candidate somewhere. Whatever we need to do, Anaea, I'm behind you completely."

"I know," she repeated, tipping her head up to kiss his cheek. "It's safer than being in front of me."

*

A furtive scouting trip several hours later, after the jump into hyperspace, revealed the dispenser regulated food, but not energy bars. Gwydion returned with several. Penelope turned up her nose and returned to eyeing the fish.

"I hope she doesn't figure out the latching system," Anaea said.

Gwydion looked surprised. "Is that possible?"

"Kearls are very intelligent. It's the monkey in them, I think?"

Time crawled, and there was little to do except worry over the exploration mission. In one respite, Anaea asked, "Do you regret being swept up in this?"

"No." He stroked Penelope as he spoke. The kearl's eyes remained peaceful slits. "When I joined the White Hound mission, I thought I was just running away. When I returned to the Sanctum, I thought I had returned home, that the wandering was over. Except I still felt out of place." He smiled wryly, apologetic. "I didn't jump at the chance to travel to Nissyen just because I was concerned for you. I needed different air."

"Should I be offended?" She kept her tone light, teasing. "This can't be what you envisioned."

"Maybe not," he said, "but I left the police service in Serendipity because of a wrong I couldn't right. This is one I can affect, and that's something."

But he might not be able to right this one, either. They both knew it.

"The Sanctum is home, may always be home," he said, "but honestly, I'm not ready to stay home yet. How do you feel about going back?"

"I don't know," she admitted. "But this isn't about me."

They slept in shifts. She might have trusted Penelope to alert them, but best to be safe. Just being with Gwydion, curled up close in the darkness, was a new experience, but it was hard to appreciate the wonder with their options shrinking.

The walls blocked crew conversations, except fragments from a captain with a booming voice. Finally, after an unknown amount of time, he called out an announcement as if it were made for them. "Annwyn local space, lads. We should be down in New Glastonbury in time for breakfast."

Muttered responses, some derisive. Anaea caught Gwydion's eyes, and both cast around their designated space, a last check to be sure the signs of their presence were concealed. Penelope scampered around, under foot or hand at all turns.

The cargo hold doors opened. Anaea tensed. She stretched out her hand, looping her fingers around the leash and pulling the kearl into her arms.

Why do you suppose they're coming in now? Gwydion wondered.

Anaea shook her head and pressed against the corner of the crate, listening.

"Ping the package and let's get on with it."

"Seems like a waste. Don't suppose we could open it and no one would be the wiser?"

"You know the rules. We get dump orders, we execute them."

"Stupid, if you ask me."

"No one did."

A snort, followed by a beep. A shrill, answering sound emitted from a package by Anaea's leg.

She froze, pressing against a crate as if she could melt into it. She shook her thoughts free and twisted. Another crate sat ten feet away, not as large but enough to crouch behind. She freed one arm from around Penelope and sent a few loose packages spinning to conceal the living space they had cleared.

Hand lights struck the front of their hiding place. Gwydion squirmed behind the smaller crate, climbing over the cartons drifting there. She followed, her free hand balanced on top of a box.

It broke through with a crunch.

"What was that?" the grumbler asked. Anaea tried to twist under the thin layer of packages, but they floated out of reach.

"There's someone here." Footsteps moved with purpose in their direction.

Her head snapped up. Blinded by searing light, she could only make out the halo of the crewmen's shapes.

"Stowaways," the one in charge said. "Get the captain."

35

GWYDION TENSED, BREATH DRAWING IN. ANAEA COULD almost sense his thoughts reach out to a crate, then release it. She gradually made out the figures confronting them.

The grumbling crewman gawped. When his companion glared at him, he slouched off towards the bridge.

"Who are you? What are you doing here?" the other demanded, wielding his hand light like a weapon, though a bulk on his hip indicated he was better armed. He loomed over them.

Gwydion caught her arm to help her up. Uncomfortably reminded of her own weapon, she squirmed loose long enough to shove the case inside her shirt. Then she wobbled upright.

"We had to leave Serendipity in a hurry, and this was the first ship out," she said. Her voice quavered.

The tall figure narrowed his eyes. "Criminals?"

"Of course not." The words popped out of Anaea in surprise. She glanced at Gwydion. *Am I lying?*

I'm not sure. A hint of laughter, taut with nerves.

"Really." He kept the light trained on their faces. Anaea blinked in pain, averting her eyes.

The grumbler returned with the captain in tow, a stout redhead. The captain clasped his hands in front of him and regarded them. "Well," he said with deceptive cheer, "I'm sure you could come up with all sorts of answers for my questions, some of them reasonable justifications and one perhaps true, and no way to tell if the one and the other match up. So let's skip the explanations, shall we?"

Gwydion blinked. "Sir—"

"Since we're in imperial space, I'm within my rights to eject you into space," the captain continued. His forceful voice and conversational tone clashed, a weird trinity with the threat. "But I'd rather know what's going on." He addressed his crewmen next. "Send communications to the surface with bio readings. See what matches turn up."

Anaea cleared her throat. She had to grab some control over the situation. Would it help if she showed they had common sympathies? "We embarrassed the regina of Serendipity," she said. "Badly, at that. She's been trying to—"

"Stop," the captain interrupted with amiable finality. "I said I didn't want to hear your stories, didn't I? No, we have a few hours before we have to dock, and I think they could be educational."

The crewmen escorted them out of the hold into stabbing light. The walls seemed to torque in on Anaea, cramping three rooms together: sleeping quarters, a common area, and a perfunctory bridge. An antique cuckoo clock clicked in the connecting crawl-space.

The other two crew members shot them curious looks, then affected indifference, though the occasional tip of a head or comment whisper-snorted across the silence belied that. The tall man took charge of security, herding them to the back of the sleeping quarters. Penelope bristled, hissing.

"What's that thing?" the grumbler asked.

Anaea started to answer. Their keeper swung the light in her face. "Captain said silent, you stay silent," he said.

Hands held out before him, Gwydion settled on a bed. *If I could get to the stimulants, I could probably take them.*

Anaea shook her head. They were outnumbered in uncertain circumstances. *We wait.*

Some of the cargo is contraband, Gwydion thought. *We could use that.*

She swallowed her anxiety. *Maybe.*

It was an uncomfortable few hours. The crew flicked looks towards them with mixtures of scorn, curiosity and annoyance. Only the captain appeared oblivious to their presence.

A transmission came through, too soft to hear, leaving much to her imagination as the captain hmmed and ahhed, asking for confirmation from the ground crew.

"Apparently, you've left a whole aviary of ruffled feathers behind you," he said, "and not just on the other side of the Bridge. Some kind of heroic renegade, are you?"

"There are no charges against either of us," Anaea said.

"Yet you departed in an awful hurry, didn't you?" the captain inquired.

"She said we did nothing criminal," Gwydion said.

"I think warlord Avidan's people would be very interested to welcome you back, perhaps with a reward for my trouble." Mild word choice or not, there was no humor in his gaze now.

Anaea tried to wet her throat and ended up swallowing air. "I think he might also be interested to know," she said, "about the cargo you're carrying."

The captain snapped to, sharply enough she felt a quiver of relief in her bones. "What cargo?"

Gwydion sent images of labels to her and she rattled off the identifying codes. "At least one of those," she added, "contains contraband Lisle extract. Black market coin."

The crew tensed, one man stroking his blaster. Anaea tried not to look too closely, forced herself to keep the captain in her sights.

There was nothing jovial in his eyes now. "Then this. When we put down in Nissyen, you two get out of my sight. Dodge the law yourself. What happens after is none of my affair, but I won't turn you in."

Gwydion's thoughts slid into hers. *I don't think we're going to get a better deal. He could still threaten to space us.*

"Very well," Anaea said. She swallowed hard, not sure whether the frantic pangs in her stomach were fear or relief. Their destination was still the one place on this planet she had wanted to avoid.

Gwydion squeezed her hand. "When we get down," he murmured, "do we shoot for the wilds or try to lie low with your friend?"

First instinct surfaced sharply: yes, of course that was the right decision, to trust in Flick and Marianna. She thought it through. "Dezba, one of the warlord's advisors, knows about them," she said, "and I don't know where she stands."

"We're cleared for descent," the captain announced. "Strap in, lads."

There was one spare harness. The tall figure glared she and Gwydion into its embrace, smashed together; it was a good thing they were both thin. She clung to him, feeling ridiculous. Penelope wound about their shoulders, supported by cords meant to hold a space helmet.

The mail courier set down after a jostling, shuddering descent. Anaea felt as if something in her spine had liquefied. She slid free of the restraints.

There was nowhere to go, but the tall crewman kept a beady eye on them as he ushered them down the gangplank.

Anaea took a deep breath and coughed on the stale air of the commercial zone. Penelope pressed against her ankle as a hovercar snapped by at unsafe speeds.

"Let's see what's leaving the city and when," she said, taking charge. "Then we can decide what to do from there."

Dodging workers and vehicles not particular about who they ran over, the assumption apparently being that anyone who was here knew how to handle the traffic, they walked to the nearest bay doors. With a sickly hiss, the doors opened onto a grey corridor.

The dim passage spilled them out into the commercial space-port. To get to the transports, they had to go through customs, which made Anaea edgy, glancing over her shoulder, but they passed without incident.

A melee of sound assaulted them as they entered the rotunda. At every counter, every gate, the snarls of haggling scorched the air. Lists of prices hovered in holograms above each station, only suggestions.

"Money's going to be tricky," Gwydion murmured. "We don't have much without linking into the public systems."

"The bracelet should be enough to help," she said.

He blinked in surprise. "But it's dead, isn't it?"

"A good Tweaker can fix it." She surprised herself by the confidence in her voice. "And it fulfils one of their greatest needs: privacy."

She guided them towards an exchange merchant on the edge of the plaza. Someone stepped on Penelope's tail. The kearl squalled her indignation.

Two people waited for the merchant to finish his current transaction, so Anaea dropped onto a bench. She had spent the last few days in idleness, and yet her bones longed to be still.

"Anaea!"

Her eyes snapped open. She felt more than saw Gwydion pivot above her, and, after the first crack of her heart faded, she squeezed his arm in reassurance.

The broadly-set figure ducked through the crowd and skidded to a halt. "Figured you would be back, but never thought it would be so soon," he said.

"Neither did I," she said, "but it's good to see you. Gwydion, this is Richard. Rip, that is. Friend of Fl—"

The Tweaker raised his eyebrows, affecting a hurt look.

"—friend of mine," she amended. "Rip, this is Gwydion."

She wanted to say more, but the words tangled on her tongue and left her blushing. "How did you know I was here?"

"Was at the port for a consult when I got a message from Flick. He's got the information net tapped for references to several subjects, including you. Caught a call from a captain and asked me to investigate."

"Is that legal?" Gwydion asked.

Rip blinked. "Any reason it should be? Come on, I'm done for the day. I'll take you to the Cauldron."

The decision, Anaea reflected, had been made for them. She glanced at Gwydion. Would he take this as a sign of divine intervention?

"We need to stay low," she said. "I don't think the warlord would take kindly to my return."

"No problem. Do you still have my stunner?" he asked, leading the way out of the rotunda.

"They confiscated it," she said. "I bought a commercial model."

He clapped a hand to his forehead. "We're going to have to do something about that."

"Is there something you can do for me?" Gwydion asked. "I hope not to use it, but after the way we left Serendipity, it's needful."

"Sure," Rip said lightly. "Any special requests? You're the hypermental, aren't you?"

Anaea trailed behind with Penelope. Just shy of the spaceport exit, she called out, "Wait." When they turned, she said, "Can you lend me enough to send a small package off-planet?"

"Let me get my hands on that pedestrian zinger and we'll call it even," Rip said.

"What are you thinking?" Gwydion asked.

Anaea pulled the data stick out and flipped it over in her fingers. "I'm going to send this to Phailin. All of it. She'll know what it means."

"Are you two trying to drive me mad?" Rip asked. "All these

cryptic remarks. What happened on Serendipity? Is Phailin a name I'm supposed to know? Bet Flick does." He added the last in a mutter.

"I'll explain when we get settled," Anaea said. "I promise."

He rolled his eyes. "Fine. I've got you."

The shipping system was automated. She watched the data stick vanish into the machine and let out a long breath.

Outside, in the darkening crimson air, Rip led them towards a low-slung hovercar, an anonymous grey beast with impact-marks studding its flanks.

"My own sweetheart," Rip said with a sweep of his hand. "Souped up, patched up, just back on her feet."

Anaea swallowed. "Oh."

What's wrong? Gwydion's thoughts pulsed concern.

You didn't ride much when you were here, did you, she replied.

Rip paused with one hand on the door. "You two all right? I promise she's safe. She does what she's told."

"We're fine," Anaea said, climbing in the back. Penelope hopped onto her lap.

"No worries. I'll get you out of sight in no time flat."

The cab rides Anaea had taken had been harrowing, but presumably, commercial drivers had legal restrictions in regards to endangering their passengers' lives. Rip had no such compunctions. The hovercar leapt off its mark and zigzagged into the traffic flow, rebounding off air and spinning to take advantage of a tiny opening. Then they hit a straightway of open air and plunged forward.

The city blurred past. Gwydion stifled a groan, clutching the handhold. Penelope hissed, her talons digging into the much-battered gown Anaea still wore. Rip tossed back a conversational question; Anaea shook her head to indicate she couldn't hear, and immediately wished she hadn't as the world spun.

Police sirens wailed inside the hollow of her ears. She jumped, jerking in the seat. The metal ground into her back.

Gwydion lurched forward and grabbed Rip's shoulder. "What

are you doing bringing their attention on us?"

"I'm driving normally!" Rip protested. "This is an open stretch and I'm a notch above the speed limit." He hesitated, his hand slithering across the control panel. "They're signalling us to pull over. But I wasn't breaking any laws."

He reached the conclusion at the same time Anaea did; she could see it in his eyes. "I've done some pretty fancy flying in my time," he said softly. "We could—"

The hovercar grunted and oozed to a halt. Rip scowled and smacked the console. "What? No."

"Mechanical problem?" Gwydion asked.

Rip shook his head. "No, it has to be a control pulse, but I have this thing shelled from that. Blast." He shrugged, adding, "I guess if every program were foolproof, Flick would be out of a job. And he'd have to sleep on my couch."

The other vehicle pulled up alongside them, a black capsule. An officer stood in the open door, regarding them flatlye.

"We only have orders concerning your passengers, boy," he said to Rip. "Sit back quiet and we'll overlook the half dozen regulations this trash-heap is breaking."

Rip puffed up with indignation, then looked back at Anaea. She shook her head; he deflated. With a sigh, he put his hands behind his head.

"Come, then," the officer said impatiently. "Unless you're thinking of plunging over the side. You might only break a few bones."

Gwydion's eyes narrowed, as if he was considering trying to escape, but he stood, offering a hand to Anaea to steady her. She felt queasy stepping over the brink onto the other vehicle, but the knot in her stomach held it down.

Penelope eyed the distance between the two vehicles, then vaulted, scampering into the hovercar so fast she wrenched Anaea forward onto the seat. One of the officers snickered, but was cut off by the glares of his fellows.

"Tell Flick we'll be fine," Anaea called, forcing what she hoped was confidence into her voice. Rip's face screwed up in doubt as the police hovercar folded shut and steered away.

"Why are we being detained?" Gwydion asked.

The driver never looked back. "You'll find out."

"I'll need to speak to the warlord," Anaea said, her tongue sticking to the roof of her mouth at the audacity. "He'll want to hear I have to say."

"Not my department." His voice was hard to read: scoffing? Or did he believe her? The hovercar arrowed towards the warlord's fortress. Other vehicles cleared out of its path with dangerous haste. Anaea stared at the fortress and tried to force herself to think it looked smaller than it had before.

They landed into the care of four officers, blank-faced and aggressive, a violence that lurked under every touch and look, waiting for an excuse. Gwydion stepped closer to her, his body taut. Penelope scrambled between them, tail snapping.

Anaea asked for Avidan, but one stare from the lead officer convinced her not to ask again. The officers searched them and confiscated the stunner. Anaea wondered how many more she would go through and hoped this wouldn't be the last. They descended into the depths of the fortress. The guards thrust she and Gwydion into the searing glow of a double cell.

"What do you think the odds are he's not going to give us a chance to explain?" Gwydion asked softly.

"What will he do instead?" Anaea slid down, relieved the cell allowed more freedom of motion than her last berth here, though she still could have crossed it in two paces. "Can he execute us? That seems like an extreme reaction." Her throat tightened, conflicting necessities chasing themselves around her mind and trampling her.

"He can do anything." Gwydion mirrored her position on the other side, hands on his knees. "You spoke with him. What was your impression?"

She shook her head. "I don't know. It was a short conversation. That didn't seem to be his style, but to maintain power in a place like this – maybe." She didn't want to tell Gwydion what Avidan had said. She was almost sure he hadn't meant it.

"We won't make it easy for them," Gwydion said.

She didn't respond. If it came to that, what difference would it make?

*

AFTER A FEW hours of dull silence, only Penelope's chitters to break it, the pair had a visitor.

Anaea scrambled to her feet, upsetting the kearl. "Dezba!"

"You shouldn't have come back," the trainer said. "If anything, you look less impressive than the last time I saw you."

Anaea flushed, feeling foolish for her initial relief. "I had no choice," she said. "If I can explain—"

"You can explain anything you want," Dezba said, "if you can survive the next twenty-four hours."

"Survive?" Gwydion asked. "We're not in the same position we were when we left. Anaea and I are appointed representatives of—"

She held up a hand. "Doesn't matter," she said. "You're below any level where matriarch authority reaches. I'm here to warn you."

Anaea bit her lip. "Warn us about what?"

"Blake is dropping you into a raptorhound run. Three beasts, three miles." Dezba spoke briskly. "Reach the end of the stretch, and you walk away. Or," she added with a lift of one brow, "whatever you're here to do."

"That's madness," Gwydion said. "You can't mean it."

But Avidan had threatened just that.

Anaea willed the dizziness out of her system. "We don't have the luxury of a game," she protested, surprised by the phrase that came to her lips. "I've learned something about the matriarchs and a mission they've planned. Avidan needs to hear it."

"I believe you," Dezba said. "So do this and succeed."

"You can't expect this of us," Gwydion said. "This isn't the way things are done."

Dezba snorted. "That's how it is here."

Anaea's fears rushed out over her. "We can't do this."

"You will." Dezba spoke with assurance; then her lips turned up. "Or you won't. You'll find a rock pile fifty feet up the starting mark. There will be weapons under it. Hand to hand. Anything more would skew the game, and Blake would halt it."

Anaea bit her lip. "I don't know how to—"

"Point and thrust." The advisor's eyes swung to Gwydion. "You may also find something of use."

"You can't talk Avidan out of this?" he asked.

"I've done everything I can because I like Anaea. Take it or leave it." Without waiting for an answer, she swept out.

Anaea darted after, but jarred into the force wall. She expelled a shuddery sigh. "We don't have any other choice, do we?"

*

THEY DISCUSSED STRATEGY until there was nothing more to say. Keep moving, keep low, fight only if they had to; what more was there?

Anaea knew a little about raptorhounds from conversations with Flick, and Gwydion remembered only a bit more from history lessons. They had been the apex predator on Independence long before colonization, never learned to fear humans, who had little use for them outside of pit fights and runs. Apparently impossible to domesticate, risky to hunt, they offered no viable product worth the hassle of obtaining it, except their viciousness.

Their hides were tough, but scale-like plating further protected the throat. A dog might show its neck in submission; a creature with a weak spot might avoid exposing it in a leap from above. Raptorhounds had neither compunction.

Anaea was surprised by the chill and darkness when the officers dragged them back to ground level. One took charge of

Penelope. The kearl twisted, spit and swiped out with her claws, but he was too fast for her.

"She had better be unharmed," Anaea shouted over her shoulder. Someone grabbed her arm and shoved her into the maw of a vehicle.

The compartment was a cage, with only a bar of window along the top. Anaea pressed her nose to it and watched the fortress, then the city, shrivel. The nausea of motion sickness brought her back to her knees

Gwydion winced, his hands hovering. "I can't touch anything in here," he said. "It shouts fear and fury."

The vehicle blurred over the terrain and dipped low. Anaea felt it decelerate and tensed. "We're almost there," she said. "We'd better—"

The floor dropped out. For an instant, she was more confused than anything else, too disoriented to realize what was going on. The sensation of falling kicked in, latched onto fear, and she hauled in air for a shriek . . .

She landed with a bone-jarring thud on a pad. The world spun around her. She pulled herself up, coughing, then sputtering as the vehicle sprayed a viscous fluid over them. "Gwydion?"

"Here," he said from behind her. "Ow."

"Are you all right?" She rolled up into a crouch. Before her stretched a jumble of jutting stone, masked with jungle foliage and a wet, oppressive grassy scent.

"Nothing worth than bruises." He crawled up next to her. "Where are we?"

Her eyes settled on the streak of red at the edge of the pad. "The beginning of the run."

36

GWYDION TWISTED TO LOOK BEHIND THEM. "WE could—"

"Welcome to the starting line." Avidan's voice wafted down from above. "Your destination is three miles to the east. The raptorhounds are also on the trail. You've been doused with one of their favorite scents. I'll be interested in seeing who makes it, as will the rest of your audience."

So they were entertainment now. Anaea remembered Flick's stories, but she had never imagined she would be in one. She craned her neck. "We need to talk to you, Avidan!" she shouted, straining to be heard. It sounded like a projection coming from the vehicle, but if the system was two-way . . . "I wouldn't have come back if it wasn't important—"

The announcement concluded, "Get running."

The hairs on the back of Anaea's neck prickled. She didn't have to ask to know that was more than dramatics. She jumped off the edge of the mat.

She spotted the stone pile Dezba had indicated and tipped her chin. Gwydion headed in that direction. She scampered forward, trying not to hunch to the ground.

"How do we find east?" she asked.

"Look for the blue star." He crouched in the dirt.

She peered up at the black expanse, forever without a reigning body in its night. The stars seemed to blur and dance together. She squinted, forcing them to diminish to tiny points, and finally made out a faint speck of blue on the low horizon. A small phalanx of drones hovered overhead, presumably recording the drama.

The jungle crackled. She whirled, lifting her arms in a warding gesture. Her foot slipped off the rock, twisting her leg.

Nothing burst out of cover, and she huffed out an embarrassed breath. The marsh had to be home to other creatures.

"Found something!" Gwydion did a credible job of sounding surprised; maybe he was, unsure if Dezba had meant her offer.

Anaea hurried over. "What?"

He handed her a long-bladed knife, pale fingers trembling on the hilt. A second weapon rested under his knee. *And a stimulant patch with three bursts.*

She threw herself into a hug and kissed his cheek. "Let's do our best not to use them," she whispered.

He pulled to his feet and led the way. The stones were slick, occluded with moss and hidden beneath low-hanging branches. One of the drones broke off and swooped after them. Anaea winced as a jagged leaf cut her ankle. Her captors hadn't let her change. Fleetingly, she mourned the dress as it had been, a dream in a shop in the Sanctum. Then she planted her hand on her thigh and ripped herself a longer stride.

The stone strip narrowed, petering off into pebbles. It bent to the north. A wall of shrubs blocked the eastern route.

"What do you think?" she asked. "Does the path lead back the right way?"

Gwydion hesitated. "If we run into a barrier we can't cross—"

A piercing call, half shriek, half growl, rang through the jungle, echoed once, twice by matched voices. Her heart hammered; her lips locked on the next logical question, and she plunged forward, shoving through the branches into the underbrush.

The ground sloped up, eroded by rain and roots. She tried to use the knife to hack away the worst cover, but branches eluded her only to spring back in her face.

The call came again, much closer and from another direction. Anaea shivered, halting in place.

Gwydion bumped into her. He clutched her arm, the shiver passing through his skin. "We're better off here," he said. "We can hear them coming."

"Right," she whispered. She made herself walk, pushing through the dense underbrush. The ground rolled, pitching downwards. She ducked under a dead tree, bark scraping her back.

She lost her footing and dropped, sliding on her knees in the muck. She imagined the squelch hiding other sounds. Through a shroud of fluorescent green, she saw the shallow walls of a riverbed. She pulled herself into the tepid water, wincing at the splash.

"River runs due east," Gwydion said.

"Do you think we can wash off this scent?" she asked.

He shook his head. "I don't think it will be that easy."

Anaea didn't respond. It had been a foolish thought, spurred by dread. She waded in deeper where the water didn't echo her every step. The scratches on her legs stung.

The raptorhounds sounded off again, much, much closer.

The river bent around twice, turning them away from their goal. Anaea bit down her panic. Keep moving. The treeline fell away, a dusting of shrubs for another hundred yards, but then the only cover was thrusting rocks and stone pillars. Open terrain.

Gwydion glanced at the sky. "Still our best bet."

She clambered out of the water, shoes heavy, legs aching. She wished she had spent more time in athletics. "Can we take it at a jog?" she asked.

They headed out across the silent plain, the drones wafting

after. The night air rushed down, whistling over her skin, kissing her cold. She strained for another hunting cry or the sight of movement, but she could only turn her head so many times before the world started to spin.

The darkness of a heavy cloud blocked her view, then plunged down. Struck stupid, she realized it wasn't nature, but some impossible shape leaping from a pillar. She dropped, falling, her arm trapping the blade underneath her.

It missed her, landed, skidded on the stone. A hulking grey shape, marred with old scars and the pressed definition of muscles, vaguely canid, but only because there was no other comparison in human experience. It was too broad, too square, hairless and leather skinned, heavily armored beneath the throat with scales. It snarled, fangs flashing.

Fangs longer than her knife.

"Hey!" Gwydion circled into view, dropped into a combative crouch. "Over here, you mangy mutt."

The raptorhound's head swung in his direction. Anaea shoved an arm under her, struggling for the knife hilt, wondering how it would make any difference. "Behind you!" she shouted.

He whirled as a second raptorhound charged out of the shadows. He jerked, weaving out of the way. The hound pivoted, spinning after him. Starlight flashed off its armored throat.

Anaea lurched to her feet, tightening her grip on the blade. The first raptorhound snapped about, attracted by the motion. It snarled, jaws distending to reveal more teeth under the fangs, and she stumbled. As if relishing her fear, it strained after. She wanted desperately to keep an eye on Gwydion, but she was powerless to look away from the beast.

The raptorhound lunged. She held her ground for what seemed like eternity – long, too long – and lashed out with the knife. It caught flesh, bumped, dragged, scuttled free. The hound's head whipped around. She screamed at the sudden pressure, then realized in a confused flash it had ripped her dress, not her thigh.

She had wounded it on the shoulder, a thin score. It thrashed, wrenching the fabric. Her heels slipped, tipping her on the edge of free fall. The other beast released a shrill yelp.

The raptorhound tore its mouthful free and spat it out. Before it could come back at her, she stabbed at its head, not expecting to hit, just trying to stay on the offensive. Its neck swung, slamming into her arm. Her hand went numb; the knife slid to the tip of her fingers. She gasped and tightened her grip, wobbling.

A heavy claw connected with her backside. She toppled, landing hard. The sting of the blow shot fire up her spine. She rolled, landing on her side in time to have the world turn into a surge of bared teeth and open maw.

On the edge of her vision, she saw the red streak of its injury. She stabbed out as hard as she could. The knife squelched into flesh. The raptorhound howled and jerked aside, ripping the blade out of her hand. She let out a cry.

The other raptorhound tumbled into the nearest rock, pushed by more than its natural momentum. "Anaea," Gwydion shouted. "We're clear. Run."

She shoved upright and bolted. Porous stone drummed against her feet, as if the earth itself protested her flight. She fought the instinct to turn and check where the raptorhounds were, if they were still gathering themselves from their injuries or breathing hot on her neck. Fear pounded her.

Gwydion's shape flickered at the corner of her eye. *If we can make it to the treeline, we can climb.*

Anaea shook her head, trying to pin down the warning that clamored in the back of her thoughts. She kept running, unable to escape the feeling they were running into—

Third hound. She shoved the thought in Gwydion's direction, heart in her throat. *They travel in threes.*

He wavered, straightening. She started to turn, but the two raptorhounds lurked behind. The treeline was still their best bet.

A low growl, and the third raptorhound slunk into view, sliding out from the shadows of a rock. Its tail lashed, and the baring of fangs looked like a grin of anticipation.

Anaea skidded to a halt, wobbling. Gwydion dropped into a crouch, rubbing the patch on his arm. She was relieved to see he still had his knife.

A high-pitched snarl sounded as if in her ear. She flinched, snaking a look behind her. The two raptorhounds moved stiffly, but closed fast.

"Anaea!"

She jerked as the third hound lunged. Gwydion dove into its path. The beast slammed into him. They toppled to the rocky ground. He pressed up with his arm to bar the clamping jaws, but the lower fangs ripped into his skin.

Anaea's stomach clutched. She grabbed the first rock that came to hand. She had no plan, swiping out blindly and catching the raptorhound on the flank.

The creature's head snapped up. It howled, more surprise than pain. Its tail whipped against her arm. Gasping for breath, Gwydion stabbed with the blade. It skittered off the scales under the raptorhound's throat.

Hurry, hurry . . . the words pounded inside Anaea's head, reminding her of the other two hounds. Not properly braced, but desperately hoping, she aimed her next blow at the thrashing hound's head.

The raptorhound arched sideways and buried its teeth into her arm. Agony flashed her world black. Dimly, she saw Gwydion surge in again, and this time, the creature had left softer skin exposed.

It seemed to take forever before the jaws loosened in death. Her body released shuddering tension in sympathy. In slow motion, she rocked to her feet and thrust down a hand for him. He clasped it and dragged himself upright, the blade shaky in his hand.

Growling brought her head around. The two raptorhounds circled, bodies hunched low. The one she had injured limped; the other sported a patch of bloodied white fur under its jaw.

They weren't closing, she realized. They held off, wary now.

Anaea took one step back, then another. Gwydion stayed in front of her, breathing hard. For the first time, she saw the shallow rake of claws down his chest.

The raptorhounds advanced. Anaea swallowed hard. Relief flared through her as her back hit a tree. She felt around for a handhold.

"Can you hold them off with a thought?" she asked.

He tightened a quivering hand on the blade hilt. "Might be able to."

"You go first and cover me from there," she said.

Gwydion looked disturbed, but swallowed it and vaulted into the lower branches. He turned as he did, tossing the blade to her. She clung to it.

His foot swung over her head. The tree crackled. The white-jawed raptorhound inched closer, head snaked low. She swept the blade sideways, praying her fingers wouldn't drop it. The hound jerked aside.

The other gathered itself – and hit an invisible wall with a startled yelp.

"Anaea," Gwydion called.

A half-second debate over the knife – through her belt and be unable to use it? In her hand and risk losing it? – and she scrambled for the lowest branch, shoving herself up until she could brace her foot against it. She compromised with the blade, tucking it in her hand with the point down her wrist. Her other hand grabbed the next branch up. Leaves stripped through her fingers.

The raptorhounds circled, closing the distance on each circuit. Climbing without taking her eyes off them forced Anaea to move by feel, her heart stopping when the branch in her hand shuddered. A body length and a half above the ground. Almost out of reach . . .

The limping hound charged, limbs gathering for a spring. She could see the height in the launch and froze, fumbling for the weapon. It twisted in mid-air as if struck and hit the tree.

Claws raked against the bark. They slashed inches from her leg. She screamed inside her head, too panicked to let it out.

The raptorhound lost purchase and slid, but not before a final lunge. Anaea kicked up and away, bracing herself when her foot impacted, but what she hit was a fleshy snout, not the wetness of an open maw. Her heart stopped and started again in the same instant. She dragged, pulled, wrenched herself higher up.

"Hand," Gwydion said. She reached towards his voice, felt his fingers close over hers. She braced her feet against the trunk and pushed into the upper branches.

A fork in the trunk formed the only perch. She slid into it, finding herself nose to nose with him. They both breathed heavily, close enough that they panted in chorus. Every part of her ached.

His face was grey, pinched. "You all right?" he asked.

She twisted to watch the raptorhounds. They were out of range of even the most powerful leap. "Will be," she said. "You don't look well."

He mopped at his brow. "Not meant to be pushing like this," he said. "Feeling it."

Carefully, Anaea planted a foot in the next fork over and levered herself upwards. She could see through the treeline and where it broke again, a line of artificial red in the stone. "I can see the end mark from here," she said, wondering why she didn't feel relieved.

Gwydion put it into words for her. "Can we climb that far from tree to tree? It could take hours."

She glanced up at the drones, wondering how the spectators would react to such a lull and what might be done to renew the action. She bit her lip, lowering her gaze back to the circling hounds. "Do you have another boost?"

"One." He rubbed his arm. "I don't think I can get much out of it. What are you thinking?"

"We wait." She studied the flayed marks of red on her arm, wincing as the wind touched them. "When they start to lose interest, you rustle the trees back the way we came. Loudly."

"And hope that catches their attention." Gwydion nodded. "It's worth a try."

She handed him the blade without a word. She ripped off another layer of her skirt and motioned for his arm. The two deep scores there were worse than the shallow wound on his chest and easier to bind.

He held his arm out. She worked, fingers shaking. These were not conditions she had ever imagined, safe on Themiscyra. Just enough to slow the bleeding and hope that medical care would be available if they finished this maze. No – when they finished this maze.

The raptorhounds prowled around the tree in a lashing, lathered fury. They slowed to casual circles. Finally, the limping hound laid down under the tree, head on its paws and peering dolefully upwards. If it weren't for her stinging injuries and the taste of her heart in her mouth, Anaea might have laughed.

The cold and the pain blurred together. Her eyes teared up from the wind. Briefly, the sight of the two hounds minding their wounds rather than their trapped prey, seemed a mirage.

Gwydion, she thought, not wanting to draw attention with speech.

Now?

She extended one foot and slid it towards the lower branch. The raptorhounds did not react. *Now.*

The sudden skittering and rustling from the jungle startled her, even though she had been expecting it. The white-furred hound's head snapped up. The other barked, as if to ask a question. The first rose, tail swinging, but with no purpose.

Gwydion frowned, his brow furrowing. Something cracked loudly. This time, the raptorhound spun, baying. It plunged into the underbrush. Anaea held her breath, fingers clenched in the branch. The other hound gathered itself and sprang after.

She started to swing forward, reaching for the limb below her. Gwydion grabbed her arm. *Wait.*

Protests bounced off the inside her thoughts. They only had

until the raptorhounds reached the source of the sound, found nothing, then circled around, but it would be less time than that if the descent drew them back. Frustrated, she ground her teeth.

Dark shapes streaking across the stone under starlight, further away, and ever closer to their return . . .

Now. His thoughts tightened around hers.

She nearly leapt, dropping, scrambling, with only a second's presence of mind to avoid rattling the branches too hard. She landed with a thump, sending a shudder through every open wound.

He settled next to her with a suppressed hiss of pain. *Run.*

She sprinted over the light ground cover, her limbs dragging in protest. She hopped over treacherous patches of moss, wincing every time her feet landed. So loud. But there was no sound of pursuit, and the distance lengthened.

They were going to make it, and with that realization, she had space to be furious. It shot adrenaline through her. She had to slow as the trees shrank together, casting out vines in binding ties. The underbrush thickened, setting off a small riot under her feet.

She wasn't surprised when she heard the raptorhounds howl.

Faster. Her urgency poured into the thought. She had no idea how far they had come, how close they were, and she strained through endless trees. They grasped her greedily, branches snatching, limbs thrust up to trip and tangle.

Labored breath, drowning out the sounds of the jungle. Another baying cry, closer this time. She sensed Gwydion lose a pace, then another . . .

She broke through the trees and saw the red line ahead. She wanted to shout, but had no air in her lungs. The downward slope sent her tumbling towards it. The underbrush exploded with rustling, the raptorhounds now only seconds behind.

Maybe fifty feet off, then thirty. Ten—

Gwydion fell, landing hard on one knee. The impact drove a hoarse cry out of him. Anaea pivoted, saw the raptorhounds streak out of concealment, joyous now their prey was frightened and running. She grabbed his arm, pulled him halfway upright and eeled her weight under his. She stumbled, half-carrying him across the line.

She toppled, landing in thin, sticky grass. He dropped next to her, gasping. She rolled into a crouch and knew from the shaking of her arms she couldn't make it to her feet, not before the raptorhounds were upon them.

37

ANAEA CRAWLED, STRAINING TO PUT DISTANCE BETWEEN herself and the raptorhounds. She dove, and a surge of electricity lanced through her body. A wall of force followed, blocking the way even as the creatures cringed back, whimpering.

Relief pounded through her veins and made room for anger again. This silly game, when so much was at stake! The wasted time, the blood lost, and for what? Gwydion's face was pallid. He might still be in danger, if there was a cost to pushing too hard under the influence of stimulants.

The dim bulk of a hover vehicle filled her vision. The guards materialized, this time impersonal rather than brutal. They escorted the pair into the hold.

Gwydion moaned and lurched away from the walls. She steadied him, helping him balance. The journey passed in a blur. The guards walked them to a medical facility, where doctors took over.

Anaea dozed; when she awoke, the window in her room told her it was dawn. She poked at the dividing curtain and checked on Gwydion. He was still asleep. Pleasantly groggy, she lolled back and refused to let herself think.

Some time later, she looked up to find the lean, dark figure of Blake Avidan resting against the door frame. His pale eyes wandered Anaea's face what seemed to be casually, but she felt the intensity.

"That was quite a run," he said.

"We didn't do it to be entertaining." She was surprised how soft her voice came out, when she wanted to scream. She had no breath.

He shrugged. "But you were. That's worth something. Enough to forget I asked you never to return."

"It wasn't my choice," Anaea said. "The ship – we—" She locked her lips on the words. She didn't want to tell him they had stowed away.

Though a flicker of curiosity crossed his features, he did not pursue the unfinished sentence. "It doesn't matter. Had you intended to stay at distance, you would have found a way to do so."

Astonished, she pushed up and gathered energy to argue, but in this place, strength and will were the only things that mattered.

Anaea took a deep breath, let it out. "There's something more important I need to talk to you about." Was this man the right one to turn to? His quirks could be lethal, but what warlord would be better? She had respected him at their first meeting, felt he answered honesty in kind; now, she was less certain.

"There is little more important than the right game," Avidan said in a low voice. "But what have you to say?"

She had mulled over different ways to ease into the speech and finally decided on directness, but that didn't slow the pounding of her heart. "The matriarchs are about to make a unique discovery: a previously unknown space station. A place that has technologies beyond what either side of the Bridge has discovered."

Avidan made a sound of appreciation, but he was quick on the next point. "And how do you know all this?"

"I was born there. It's my home." She felt a quiver of ambivalence as she said it, and yet nowhere else could claim the role.

"Ah." His expression lightened, but held no surprise. "That makes a good deal clear."

Anaea fought a flush. It wasn't an insult, she told herself. "I never claimed to be anything other than a stranger here."

"No, you didn't. I assume you're telling me about this because you expect me to try and beat the matriarchs to this place, to dispute their claim?" He arched a brow.

"Close," Anaea said. "I don't want anyone to claim them." She looked at her hands, not wanting to see his reaction. "Instead of the matriarchs alone profiting from the association, you can, as well." She looked up and added, "I'll speak for you." Not the time to mention she had left a fugitive.

Avidan snorted. "Better an even playing field than no battle at all. I'll make inquiries. You didn't expect me to take your word for it, I hope?"

"There isn't much time," she said. "The expedition has already launched."

"Then perhaps I shoot them out of the sky?" He laughed. "Your expression, Anaea, is worth gold. No, I would not do that. Perhaps some convenient bureaucracy, to cradle them in the red tape they love so well? That will give time for preparations. I believe you—" he pierced her with a sharp gaze "—but I need confirmation."

"I understand." Part of her screamed at the delay, but it was how government moved, and it might give Phailin time to respond.

"You will be there, whatever I find," Avidan said. "In the meantime, you two are my guests and have free range of the fortress, within reason."

Anaea shuddered, not anxious to spend time in this place that held so many unpleasant memories. "I want to see my friends in the city," she said. "We left Ri . . . Richard quite abruptly."

He nodded. "Once the doctors discharge you, one of you

may go. Thank you for this opportunity, Anaea, if opportunity it turns out to be." He stepped out.

"That was a very polite way of keeping us under his control," Gwydion remarked.

She pulled the curtain back. "How long have you been listening?"

"Long enough to think we made the right choice, even if it was made for us." His voice was soft.

She jerked in surprise. "But he—"

"He can outmatch Morgan," he said, "and he's hard, but he's fair. We won't find better."

"I hope you're right," she said.

*

"I KNEW ALL along," Flick declared.

Anaea had been released by the doctors shortly after her conversation with Avidan, though her throbbing arm protested that decision. They provided her with a spare set of clothing and returned her other belongings. She went straight to the Cauldron and Rip's workroom, where she found the Tweakers in conference.

"Of course you didn't, idiot," Rip said. "When would you have figured it out? When she rejected your advances?"

Flick made a face. "Unlike you, I don't assume that just because a woman isn't interested in me, she must be from a colony of indoctrinated lesbians."

"True." Rip smirked, leaning back. "I'd assume I could convert her."

Anaea cleared her throat. "Is there anything you want to know?"

"Why'd you leave?" Flick asked.

"It just happened," she said. "I thought I wanted a lot of things. What I found was a lot different than my teachers led me to believe, and different than what I expected from Gwydion's descriptions."

Rip leaned forward. "So they told you we'd descended into anarchy?"

"Well . . . yes." She felt embarrassed, as if she had to explain. "It was an attempt to protect us from wanting to explore."

"Protect." He snorted.

She agreed, and felt slightly sick for it. "They had their reasons."

"Hey, why are you defending them?" Flick asked. "Fact you're here says you don't agree. Hasn't the bad outweighed the good?"

"It has," she admitted. "For me. For an entire colony . . . I don't know. But the decision is out of anyone's hands now."

The silence had leaden weight. Rip rumbled, "So you really produce everything in an artificial environment? Totally self-sustained?"

The pair asked her more questions, which she answered with a sense of relief. Explaining her life was strange, but it was something she knew and did not need to analyze. When she rose to leave, Flick handed her a pouch.

"What's this?" she asked.

"From my grandmum." He looked sheepish. "Treats for Penelope. I know, but she insisted, huh? Come back and tell us how it went."

Anaea smiled ruefully. "I'll try."

She returned to the fortress reluctantly. Halfway to her room, Dezba Moon intercepted her.

"How are you doing?" she asked, rapping out the question.

"Stiff and sore, but I'll be fine." Anaea glanced over her shoulder, then added, "We wouldn't have been, without the patches and knives. Thank you."

"Maybe, maybe not. Avidan didn't say anything to me about the addition, but I'm sure he knew where it came from." The woman shrugged, though a hint of a smile played at her lips. "He asked me about you, though."

Anaea tensed. "What about me?"

"If I thought you were telling the truth." Dezba chuckled, a raspy sound. "I told him I doubted you would do anything else."

Anaea blushed. "I try to be honest."

"Yes." This clearly amused the woman, but she didn't linger on mockery. She gestured for Anaea to follow her. "You made the right decision, Anaea. I'm biased, yes, but I've seen other warlords, the ones too weak to take chances and have underlings simmering to undo their work, and the ones who will make any bargain only to destroy it at the next convenient moment. And I'm a woman: I have no desire to see us marginalized, reduced and forced into corners."

"The matriarchs—" Anaea hurried to keep up.

"Would squeeze your friends into the embrace of consensus." Dezba shook her head. "I told Blake to send me. I know his mind, and I think your people would deal better with my face."

"I think you're right," Anaea said in a soft voice, feeling somehow relieved. With no firm basis for it, she still trusted the trainer more than she did the warlord. She went on, "You offered me instruction in self-defense. Does that offer stand?"

Dezba nodded, businesslike. "It does."

*

FIVE DAYS PASSED. The self-defense lessons didn't provide much distraction: the first day, Anaea could only manage an hour, and not more than two the following days before she found herself dizzy with exertion.

Dezba restrained her amusement at her pupil, but not enough to hide it. "You'll be fine," she said. "Just don't pick a lot of fights."

"I'm not planning on picking any," Anaea said.

"Now that's just poor strategy," the trainer replied.

Gwydion slept most of the first three days, recovering. There was no word from Phailin. Anaea kept telling herself it was too soon for the message to have made it through.

Penelope was rattled and hissy, but unharmed. Anaea visited Marianna with the kearl in tow and even attended a rowdy game night with Flick, but found the routine of the Cauldron only intensified her restlessness. She replaced her ruined dress with more practical clothes, making the necessary purchases in a perfunctory fog.

Avidan called her into his study in the afternoon of the fifth day. "The information I can glean supports your claim," he said. His expression was neutral: neither surprise nor pleasure. He essayed a tiny smile, as if to look less robotic. "You depart in three days."

"How far ahead of the matriarchs?" she asked.

He needed no prompting to grimace. "I sent word to Centurion to delay the matriarchs, but the district warlord ignored my request. Three days will put you out just behind them. It's the best that can be done."

Anaea surpressed a quiver of relief. Right behind, no time for either to take the advantage; it was what she had hoped for.

"Make sure you and your boy are prepared." By Avidan's tone, that was a dismissal.

Anaea sought Gwydion out with the news. He hugged her and planted a gentle kiss on her lips. "You're brilliant, you know," he said.

In the haze of the kiss, she was perfectly willing to agree, but she shook her head. "Say that when this is over."

"No matter what happens, I—" he stumbled, stuttered to a halt. The link fluctuated in her thoughts.

She placed a finger on his lips. "That sounds like finality," she said. "Don't. Let's just think one step ahead. Please?"

"Will do," he said. "Promise."

She visited Rip that night and received a pair of custom stunners from him. "As promised," he said.

"You've done more work than that bracelet will pay for," she protested.

He shook his head. "Take it. Sounds like you might need it."

The departure, for all its build-up, was underwhelming. Two liveried officers showed up to escort them and haul luggage. A sleek, cobweb grey vessel awaited them on the fortress' private landing pad. Faint flashes of light whipped across its surface.

Dezba met them on board and introduced them to the crew and specialists – trained to discern the physical value of the technology and planetary surroundings. "I'm handling negotiations," she said as she guided them into the central corridor. "I would appreciate anything you can tell me of the internal intricacies."

Anaea swallowed. "I don't know most of Asteria's advisors," she said. "I can't tell you much."

"Then I'll manage," she said. "Settle in. Strap down. We leave in ten minutes."

She and Gwydion had a shared room with a webbing system. Anaea shoved her bag under the bed and secured Penelope in the net before she pulled herself in. He grabbed her hand and squeezed until she thought he would cut off the blood-flow, and she didn't mind.

The ascent was as smooth as a whisper. The overhead announced when they were out of the atmosphere and it was safe to unstrap. The journey had begun.

As they raced towards the hyperspace corridor, Dezba quizzed her about Themiscyra. At first, she tried to be vague, but then she realized she genuinely knew very little about what defenses the station had and let her answers ramble.

Back in her quarters, Anaea felt the extent of her nervousness only when she went to sit on her bed and dropped the last few inches, shaking.

Gwydion settled next to her and pressed her to him. She was beginning to be used to the puzzle piece of opposition of their bodies, but this time it felt heightened, new. "Are you all right?"

She smiled weakly. "All she did was ask questions. I was just so frightened of saying the wrong thing . . ."

"Never."

She laughed at the vehemence in his voice. "You know what I mean." She pressed her cheek to his. The shelter of his presence comforted her.

"Do you want to talk it through?" he said. *We can plan for Dezba and Avidan.* His thoughts were a fire around her.

She shook her head. Without knowing what the warlord intended, and whether Dezba would carry out his agenda or her own, she could see no point in circling the same tired thoughts. "No. Please. I don't want to talk. My home could be destroyed, and it's out of my hands now."

She had fretted, worried, planned, second-guessed and waited for hours and days without tears. Now the tears surged out of her, buried against his neck. His thoughts touched hers, soothing, but most not matched to words.

Anaea pulled back, breath pounding in her chest. He stroked the tear off her cheek, gently.

"You did everything you could," he said.

She kissed him fiercely for answer, tasting the smoke as a bittersweet warmth in his mouth. His hands pressed against her back, melding them together. It seemed to her they were made to match, so perfectly crafted she fitted to him in every detail . . . until fabric interfered. His hands slipped under her shirt, a gentle imprint on her body. She twisted onto his lap, fingers clutching into his hips. No need to interpret the sensations surging down the link, slamming against rational thought.

Anaea broke the kiss, her mind pounding with questions. All her experience with the men of either side of the Bridge was a mote and a moment. She had learned a lot with Gwydion, but only scratched the surface – literally. Anatomical differences she knew, but that was medicine, and there was no science to this moment.

"You're here, and I'm here," she said softly, "and that might not happen again."

"Maybe," he whispered. He kissed her cheek, her jaw, her neck, as if marking each spot.

The cabin jarred with the transition into hyperspace. Her body floated without elevation, humming with the sensations of otherness. Each touch seemed to flare like starlight against her skin. A surprised gasp escaped him, the change vibrating down the telepathic link between them.

Man or not, she knew him, trusted him . . . wanted him. His uncertainty bumped up against hers; they jostled, laughed, awkward even in passion. That subtle mindlink helped them navigate where she had mostly theory and he would have treated her like glass; in the surreal softness of hyperspace, she felt as transparent and light.

It could have been frightening, but in that moment, she was home. She let herself forget every discovery but the one beside her.

38

The ship had not dropped from hyperspace when Anaea awoke, though she might have felt weightless even so. The warmth of his body held her still. They were, in more ways than one, in another universe, and she had no desire to move.

His breath, slow with sleep, tickled between her shoulder blades. Now she had trouble not moving; she tensed against a squirm. His head turned, hand sliding off her hip.

Practical need intruded, and she shifted. One foot edged out of the bed. It hadn't been constructed for two: a jostle would probably knock him off the side.

"Anaea?" he mumbled.

She turned her head to smile apologetically. "Didn't mean to wake you."

Gwydion's eyes focused on her, and with clarity, his face turned grey. He pushed up. "Oh, God," he said, "we . . ."

The fog burned away, revealing she stood on the edge of a cliff. Now stillness was necessity, as she fought the desire to latch onto him. "What?"

He read her face or felt a quiver in the link. He reached out to cup her chin. "No," he said. "It's not you. It's never you. You're perfect."

As her heart sounded off, she asked, "Then what?"

"According to my beliefs, how we spent the last few hours is reserved for married couples." He flushed faintly, but his eyes didn't leave her face. "Anything else is wrong."

Relief filled Anaea at the same time that despair drained it away. It was not personal, just a matter of religion, but that religion meant a lot to him. She wanted to laugh off his concern, but she had no right to do so. Yet how could she smile, nod and accept it? If she had been a religious scholar, she could have argued about the changes in belief over the centuries, the different ways it was interpreted, but none of that was the point.

"I can't believe that," she said. "We're standing on the edge of something neither of us can predict, needing something to hold onto as we fall. That you've been here for me has been . . ." She hadn't realized her throat tightened until it forced her to swallow. "We're in a place where there are no rules: hyperspace. Why must it be a sin?"

"It's all right because it didn't happen in the universe as we know it?" Gwydion asked, a trace of humor sneaking into his voice. He looked embarrassed; his hand slipped from her chin. "I can't change what I believe because it's inconvenient."

She looked away, her heart shuddering. "I didn't ask you to." She had no right to ask anything of him. "I want . . ." What did she want? After a flash of irrational longing, she knew that it wasn't to matter so much to him that his beliefs didn't. But she couldn't accept that what they'd done was wrong. "Please don't make this sordid. It isn't."

"Anaea." He slid about to face her. "You're right about one thing: we don't know what will happen next. You . . ."

The tension in his features astonished her, then made her cold. He thought there was a possibility this mission could kill her? How? Would Dezba abandon her if she became inconvenient?

But that wasn't it. It was the memory removal the station had perfected: death of another kind. She could lose everything, a story that had happened to someone else, and Gwydion with it.

"Nothing is going to happen," she said, voice quavering. "To either of us."

"I hope you're right," he said. "But if it turns out otherwise, I'm glad I spent this time with someone I love."

Her head snapped up. She swallowed the words and felt them expand inside her. "Gwydion," she whispered, "did you just—"

Raw fear flashed through his eyes, came through hard enough the link echoed with it. He'd loved before, she remembered, known it was doomed without having to say a word. Trying to soothe that hurt had brought her lips to his the first time. The memory rushed over her and chained into others, so sweet she knew there was only one response.

"No," she said. "Stop. I love you, too."

The embrace of it made her feel safe again, made her want to sing. She leaned forward and devoured whatever he might have said with a kiss.

Perhaps she only imagined it tasted different. That jealous claim she had resisted earlier now seemed right. Neither of them could be sure enough to make promises, but that didn't matter.

He placed a light hand on her shoulder, breaking the kiss. "I hate doing this," he said, "but—"

But he had his convictions and that strange religious conscience speaking in his ear. For now, with the unknown so close and the future obscured, she was all right with that, though her body hummed.

"I understand," she said, forcing herself to pull away. "Back in a moment." She gathered her clothes and went to the bathroom alcove. She paused with her hand on the door and studied him, imprinting his stillstunned face in her mind. Then she ducked inside and started her morning routine in a serene haze.

She reached for her shirt to pull it on, and the haze shattered as the ceiling panel clattered free and hit the floor.

"Ah . . . err . . . wow," said the figure framed in the opening. "I apparently have really bad timing. Sorry?"

"Well, stop looking," Anaea yelped, surprised by the embarrassment that surged through her.

"Oh. Right. I'd avert my eyes, but—"

"Flick!" She grabbed the shirt again and strung it across her front.

He clapped a hand over his eyes and peeked out through one finger. "You know, Rip was wondering about . . ."

"Anaea, is everything all right in there?" Gwydion called.

Flick craned his neck from the door to her and back again. She hadn't thought she was blushing, but a smirk flashed across his features. "Oh, wow, finally?"

"Give me two minutes and come in," Anaea called out, using the towel for a shield as she wriggled into the shirt. "What are you doing here?"

"It was the only human-sized opening I could find into this cabin," he said.

"I mean what are you doing on the ship." She pushed her arms through the sleeves. "How did you get here?"

He made a derisive sound. "That's like asking a master chef how he boils water. Simplicity in itself."

Gwydion knocked once and opened the door. He tried twice to say something, then gave up.

"I came to see this station of yours," Flick said. "A boy from the Cauldron gets the first glimpse at undiscovered territory? How could I miss that? Oh, and I came to help you, too," he added. "Good to see you again, Gwydion. How are you feeling?"

Anaea was vaguely gratified to discover Gwydion could blush just as readily as she. "If Dezba catches you on the ship . . ." she said.

"Pfft." Flick waggled a shoulder. "She came from the Cauldron. She'll understand." Anaea wasn't quite sure how true that was, and she didn't want to test it.

"How did you—" Gwydion started.

Flick held up a hand. "Please. No more."

"Come inside and talk," Gwydion said.

Anaea backed out as Flick flipped down from the ceiling. Penelope peeked out from under the unused bed and vanished again.

"Where are you stowed?" Gwydion asked. "This isn't a big ship."

"Spent a few hours in the vents before I discovered two of the crew are shacking up and one doesn't use his room," Flick said, plopping down on the floor. "So what have I missed?"

Anaea summarized as she perched on her bed. "Dezba seemed to be looking for an advantage over the matriarchs," she said, "but I don't think I told her anything she won't see in a few glances."

"I bet you kept everything zipped up," Flick swiveled to face Gwydion. "Can't you read her mind, see what he's planning?"

Gwydion sucked a breath in through his teeth. "If it comes to that," he said, "but the ethics of it—"

"Ethics." Flick lolled, head craned at an unlikely angle. "Seriously? In the middle of all this, you're worried about ethics? Winning the right way?"

"It's not as easy as turning them off," Gwydion said.

Anaea could feel the argument brewing, mostly from the Tweaker, but if pushed Gwydion would push back. She cleared her throat. "There's no other hypermental on board to watch us," she said. "I think she's either not planning something—"

"Or planning something that knowing won't stop," Flick said. "Or she's got sedatives packed, did you think of that? Counting on your politeness and waiting for the moment when it's too late."

Gwydion frowned. "You've spoken to her more than I," he said to Anaea. "Does that seem likely?"

She hesitated, thought it through. "Not likely," she said, "but possible. Flick, can you find out?"

The boy stared, his mouth moving like a fish. Then, he grinned. "I think I might be able to," he said. "We make a good team, don't we? I do what has to be to done, and you two make sure there's still a reason for doing it."

Gwydion chuckled. "I'd say that's about it."

The tension between the two evaporated, though the context of the conversation hinged on great insult. It was as if, the words never being spoken, both could simply will away the implications.

Anaea reached out, grabbing Gwydion's hand and squeezing Flick's shoulder. "Thank you," she said. "You both will be invaluable."

Penelope stuck her head out from under the bed and chittered.

"Ahh, she feels left out," Flick said with a snicker.

*

"Moon says to come at once," the guard at the door said.

Heart pounding, Anaea followed, Gwydion a pace behind. He squeezed her elbow and sent a pulse of thought that didn't quite reach reassurance.

A massive viewscreen dominated the bridge, backlit by stars. Asteroid detritus whirled in the foreground. The sight of the space station slammed into Anaea's stomach. This was real, not a dream, not a mistake. She scarcely noticed the other ship, a flashy bulk splashed gold and green.

It was not the first time she had seen Themiscyra from a distance, but it seemed new. The station looked like a puzzle grid, each piece different from the last; ancient salvage fused together for use, not aesthetics.

"We're not far behind the matriarchs," Dezba said from next to the viewscreen. "Engines are still hot. Not much to look at, your home."

Anaea wrenched her eyes away from the view. "It's beautiful," she said softly.

"Hmm?"

She lifted her voice. "Don't judge on appearances."

"I won't." She turned to face her. "Stay. If calculations are correct, we should be almost in sensor range."

Gwydion murmured to her, "The Hound was so close. Couldn't have been more than a few light-minutes away."

She nodded and said nothing. She slid her hand into her pocket and activated the listening device Flick had given her. She hoped wryly it would only be used for his entertainment, not intervention.

"Incoming signal," a crewman reported. Dezba nodded.

"Unidentified vessel," a cold soprano poured onto the bridge, "you will remain at distance as your sister ship has done. We do not appreciate the show of force."

Dezba flicked a questioning look to Anaea. She shook her head, feeling numb. It was no one she recognized.

"We are not sisters, or kin, to anyone on that ship," Dezba said. "We come from a different quarter."

The silence had weight to it, and edge. It extended to the point of pain. Finally, the voice returned. "Then who are you, and what do you represent?"

"Dezba Moon, dispatched by the warlord of Nissyen, voice of the Pinnacle Empire," she replied briskly. "I wish to meet with your people on equal terms."

"We have not yet accepted guests." The woman's voice lost none of its bite. "Wait here."

"Connection has been cut, master trainer," the crewman reported.

Dezba nodded, still at attention. Anaea clutched her unease and took a seat without waiting for invitation. Gwydion remained standing, hand on her shoulder.

It seemed forever before the crewman announced, "New transmission."

"You are invited," the soprano voice said, "to send a small, unarmed party to meet with us. Please leave your ships in orbit around the station."

"Thank you," Dezba said, crisp. "I look forward to it." Once the arrangements were completed and the connection severed, she turned her attention to Anaea and Gwydion.

"You're both coming," she said, then addressed Gwydion. "If she notices anything of value, I want you to relay it."

Gwydion started, the slightest widening to his eyes. "If Anaea thinks she sees something you need to know, I will pass it along," he said. *She's not afraid of intrusion.* The thought-touch was pensive.

No, she's not. Flick had assured them Dezba had no supplies for drugging the hypermental, but this was a new wrinkle.

Dezba's eyes cut sideways, perhaps betraying she saw the nuance, but she did not call it out. She ordered the technology specialist and two crewmen, outfitted as guards, to the shuttle.

"I should change," Anaea said. She had purchased one formal outfit. If she looked the part, she might feel less vulnerable. Something she had learned from the matriarchs, she supposed.

"No." Dezba snorted. "We are what we are. Come."

The shuttle was an escape pod not meant for six. Anaea found her elbow jammed up against the wall. In darkness, they surged towards the station.

A bump as the shuttle touched down in the landing bay. Dezba commandeered the airlock door.

The scent hit her first, crisp and sterile: a familiar aroma she had never noticed before, almost sweet beneath the metallic edge. She assumed it must be a product of the engineering choices unique to Themiscyra. Tears pricked at her eyes; she blinked them back.

The bay had been cleared for their arrival, but they were not alone: the matriarch group decamped from a larger shuttle on the other side. The group had come in their finery, with two ceremonial female guards and a tiny doll of a woman whose sole purpose seemed to be to serve as Morgan's satellite.

Morgan was in her element, gold hair swept back in a labyrinth of braids. One curl dashed across her brow, gemlike on pale skin. She wore a gown of variegated green, each hue bleeding into the next and turning her into a living representation of Serendipity.

Dezba advanced to meet her, and matched her without

adornment or flourish other than the confidence of her step.

"Morgan Dennison," she said. "Your reputation precedes you."

Her chin came up, a haughty tilt. "You have the advantage of me," she said. Her eyes slid past him and narrowed, the expression venomous. "And I see why. You have vermin in your employ. Take care they do not bite." Her voice hissed like dry ice.

Gwydion bowed his head. "I hope *I* have not given offense, miss Dennison."

Anaea shot him a startled look. By the subtle rumble in his tone, he was enjoying the moment.

"Your upstart Petrarchs—" Morgan began.

Dezba cut off her tirade with a lifted hand. "Our hosts are watching," she said. "Our best faces, please."

She bared her teeth, but subsided. "Of course."

The docking bay doors opened, and an older woman with bronze skin entered. "Welcome to Themiscyra," she said, in the distinctive soprano they'd heard over the comms. "If you will follow me?"

The main corridor lay silent. Their guide commanded four transport cars, and the rapid flight through the halls took the most direct route to the administration hub and showed as little of the station's secrets as possible. It was deserted;probably the corridors had been sealed off, though that wouldn't stop anyone with a rebel streak and knowledge of the quickways.

They halted in a corridor. The only thing to distinguish it was a subtle scent to the double doors: real cherry of Earth origins, preserved in its natural state. A pair of younger women stood guard, while a third sat to the side with a datapad. It was Orithia.

Gwydion's hand was vise-like on her arm. *You said they would erase her memory.* He sounded as panicked as she felt, and his reaction sent her spinning further.

Sickness swam up through her veins. *Not if they recruited her,* she responded. *The way Valasca tried to recruit me.* Somehow, her reluctance mixed her up and pushed her forward: she was first out of the car and fighting to keep her balance. Gwydion caught her arm.

Orithia studied her datapad. The nearest guard nudged her, and she looked up. Her features slackened and lost color. She stared at Anaea; then her eyes darted past to Gwydion, and her cheeks caught fire.

She felt him flinch. *Which means the last thing she remembers about us . . .*

The false memories Gwydion had created. It had been a cruel scenario, that the pair had forced Orithia to aid their escape, but the only way to keep her from taking blame. Apparently, it had worked too well, and what should have been erased . . .

Morgan floated out of her car and blocked Anaea's view. The woman was occupied with ignoring Dezba and never looked back.

"Problems?" the warlord inquired.

Anaea jumped. "Nothing." She started forward and heard a crackle from her pocket. Surreptitiously, she slid her hand in and found the listening device cold. That explained Orithia's presence, and meant Flick would not be able to eavesdrop.

The double doors swung inwards, revealing a rotunda conference room. It surprised Anaea that her feet didn't drag, so much of her will tried to hold them back. Dezba quickened her pace to match Morgan's, leaving both entourages in a disordered pack behind.

"You," Orithia whispered. "Is this because of you and your toy man?"

Anaea stumbled to a halt. "No," she said. "This was going to happen without me. He's not – you're not—" Where could she start? Answer the betrayal, the jealousy, the fear? Beg for forgiveness, cry out the truth in the vain hope it would be heard? She thought she would break under the pressure of the words. She opened her mouth to try again.

The imperial guard grabbed her arm and pulled her into the chamber, beyond reply.

39

THE DOORS GLIDED SHUT AS THEIR ESCORT SLIPPED AROUND the table and stood next to the room's only occupant. The figure rose, spreading smooth brown hands in greeting. "Welcome to Themiscyra, whatever strange chance has brought you here," she said in a voice like liquid starlight. "This is my First of Security, Toxaris Liu, and I am—"

Anaea had no doubt who she was, and she stared, taking in the woman's russet hair, kissed with silver, and green eyes. She had a face that suggested age without surrendering to it, lean, balanced and tranquil. Though Anaea still ached from seeing Orithia, wonder overwhelmed her.

"—Asteria Cole, leader of this community," the woman finished.

Asteria: queen by acclaim, founder, legend, ageless. Anaea felt the urge to grovel or gape, and even Gwydion's nudge couldn't shake her out of it. Out of the corner of her eye, she noticed Dezba twitch. Perhaps she recognized the name from a history archive. It occurred to her that Asteria was the only person here, perhaps anywhere, who might remember the time before civilization had split into empire and collective. What must she think of it?

Dezba advanced. "My name is Dezba Moon, advisor to the warlord of Nissyen," she said. "I speak on behalf of Annwyn for the Pinnacle Empire. My companions—" She made introductions down the line.

Asteria's eyes caught Anaea's. Anaea swallowed, her throat parched, but the station leader waited until Dezba fell silent. She lifted a hand.

"I know miss Carlisle," she said, "and would be most curious to hear about the circumstances of her homecoming."

Morgan whipped about with an exclamation so high-pitched it was almost inaudible. She tried again, "What do you mean, homecoming?" She glared at Dezba, then faced Asteria. She couldn't hold the ferocity of her expression, and lowered her eyes. "If you've already made a deal with the warlords, we have wasted—"

"Please don't make assumptions." Asteria's voice refrained from amusement. "I would speak with you later, miss Carlisle."

Anaea nodded by instinct. "It would be my honor," she said, voice faint. Only then did she think to glance at Dezba, who seemed undisturbed.

Careful, Anaea. Gwydion's thought was soft, worried. *You left a fugitive, and came back—*

I didn't betray them. Her thought shoved against him, hurt by the reminder. No coming home, even if she wanted to. Orithia had made that clearer than she had ever wanted, even if she still desperately hoped there was some way to explain.

With another smouldering look flashed beneath long lashes, Morgan performed her introductions. "My crew was selected by committee amongst our best and brightest," she said.

"Really now." Dezba's voice was flat.

Anaea bit her lip on laughter. Gwydion coughed.

"Please be seated," Asteria invited, "and explain what has brought you so far into the distance of space."

Anaea dropped into her chair with a sense of relief. A muffled chirp came from the listening device. Was Flick trying to restore the connection?

"We live in the shadow of a once-great civilization," Morgan said smoothly, laying her hands on the table. "We have lost much. In some cases, we have lost those who were once our brothers and sisters."

Gwydion shot Anaea a look. *She hasn't figured it out yet.*

No one has said anything. And though other residents of the station might have been openly shocked seeing the menfolk, Toxaris' expression never flickered. She was cool as glass, watching the proceedings with analytical interest.

"We offer you the patronage and protection of the Galactic Collective," she said. "We would be honored to shelter you."

"At what price?" Asteria's voice was neutral.

"I'm sure we have much of mutual benefit to offer each other," the matriarch's scientist spoke. "I would love to see your labs."

"Those details can be worked out as we go," Morgan said. "Perhaps a few concessions to ensure we can adequately oversee your defense from more brutal parties—" she tossed Dezba a significant look "—and to help you smoothly interface with our protocol."

Dezba hardly reacted, other than a slight twitch to her lips. Anaea thought she seemed amused at how the matriarch had couched her offer.

Asteria tipped her head to Dezba. "And – do I call you warlord?"

"Emissary will do," Dezba said, neutral. "Anaea told us we had a chance to make first contact with a faction that had new technology and different takes on the old. We'll trade for it, top price, not take it by force, as some might suggest." Her eyes flicked briefly to Morgan.

Anaea let out a breath, only aware she had been holding it from the way her chest hurt. It was working the way she had anticipated. One more verbal step could have the two civilizations at each other's throats. It would have gone quicker with Avidan, but Dezba was a little more subtle, more difficult to rattle . . . and still a woman in a realm of women, for all that that made her a traitor in Morgan's eyes.

"What do you have to offer?" If Asteria noticed the tension, she did not react, her posture relaxed.

"What do you want?" Dezba countered. "Planetfall? We have the resources. Better enforcement?" She glanced towards the security chief.

Anaea watched the set of Asteria's lips. *One hit, one miss.* It seemed harmless enough; she added, *Pass it on, Gwydion?*

Dezba finished, "I'm sure we can find something."

"Indeed." Asteria folded her hands.

"What happens if we align with your opposite?" Toxaris asked.

Both factions leaned forward, words spilling over each other caution, advice, protests, and then tumbling into silence when it became clear no one had gotten anything in edgewise.

"We would not hold that against you, of course," Morgan simpered, "but we would do everything in our power to dissuade you."

"You sign with them, we don't deal." Dezba never raised her voice, but her words were iron. "We have things they can't offer, and you won't get them any other way."

"Interesting." Asteria seemed intrigued. *Do you understand why I had to see it for myself?* Anaea wondered. "I know so little of your respective factions. Tell me more."

Anaea's mind wandered as both halves bandied words across the table. She brooded on Orithia, the listening device, the private conversation she had promised the station leader. The respective scientists praised advancements of medicine, surveillance and hyperspace conduits. Anaea shook her head, remembering that the shuttle she and Gwydion had stolen moved faster than anything either side had produced. The factions praised the memory of Earth and came just shy of implying that Themiscyra must be culturally bankrupt for being out of touch.

"Of course, we can't offer the same masculine pursuits as our opposites," Morgan added disdainfully at one juncture.

"We have no one in need of masculine pursuits," Asteria said.

It took Morgan a moment; then she gasped. "Truly?"

Her notekeeper, silent until then, popped her head up. "We've heard of you," she said, "but we thought it was an urban legend."

"Then I hardly see why you would consider the other offer," Morgan said. "When the matriarchs are the ones who give women their proper place."

"That may be, or it may not," Asteria said calmly. "But this meeting is over. I have much to consider. I would speak with each of you privately, but first, I wish to meet with the daughter of my home. The guards will guide you to the docking bay."

Anaea wanted to melt into the chair. It surprised her when both sides agreed without protest – but then, there was no missing the stalemate.

Gwydion kissed her cheek. "Good luck," he said. Out of the corner of her eye, Anaea saw Asteria arch a surprised eyebrow. She flushed. *Love you,* he added silently . . . and after that, he could have pinned her to the table with a passionate kiss and she wouldn't have felt any shame.

Love you, too.

Morgan snatched at her shoulder, fingers digging in. "I don't know what game you're playing," she said, "but it's going to destroy you." Before Anaea could reply, she strode out in a billow of green.

The doors whispered shut, and Anaea was alone with Asteria, founder of the station, a woman who would have been a saint or goddess if the beliefs of her home allowed. Or not quite alone: Toxaris remained, but sat so still she might have been a fixture.

"There is a question I must ask you, Anaea," Asteria said. "I do not like to, but I expect you will answer honestly."

Anaea swallowed. She knew what was coming, and it burned.

"Is this your doing? Are they here because of you?" She raised one hand in a looping gesture, indicating both sides of the table.

"They all seem to know you and the young man who escaped here with you."

"I didn't cause this." Her voice sounded petulant in her own ears. "The matriarchs have been assembling data for years. I found out they had plans to come here because I was in the right place at the right time." She wanted to break down and gasp out the story, justify her decisions, look for approval. She kept her voice steady and her explanation simple. "I informed the warlords. I hoped they would concentrate their energies on each other."

"Very shrewd. And they have, though it may not last." Asteria sighed. "If nothing else, we have a choice. Scylla and Charybdis."

Anaea frowned. "What?"

"Greek mythology. Two monsters positioned on either side of an ocean strait. One a woman with vicious hounds' heads for a torso, and the other a mysterious thing that spewed out treacherous whirlpools. The passage between them was so narrow that one had to choose between perils."

"Which is which?" Anaea asked wryly.

"You have more first hand experience with them than I," the station leader pointed out with a hint of a smile.

That set Anaea back with an almost physical shock. It made sense, of course: the departure for Themiscyra had been before the two societies rose from the chaos of Y-Poisoning. But even in jest, the words made her world spin.

"What about the boy?" Toxaris asked. "Could he have made a report to the matriarchs? He doesn't share your loyalties."

"No." Anaea met the security chief's gaze. She spoke in a whisper, but did not look away. "He understands how much your people value their sanctuary. Even if he didn't, he would trust me. And I trust him." She felt the outrage flushing her cheeks. After everything he had been through . . .

It was only after she fell silent that she realized she had said "your people," not "our people."

"A child's judgement." Toxaris spoke with neither censure nor warmth. "Perhaps accurate, perhaps not."

"There is nothing to indicate that Anaea is wrong in supporting her young man," Asteria said. Her expression softened, betraying maternal sympathy.

Her young man . . . well, Anaea supposed she had made it obvious. She felt a creeping guilt, as if she had somehow betrayed the station by falling for him.

"What should I know about these individuals, since you seem familiar with them?" Asteria asked. "How much power do they have?"

Anaea took a breath to steady herself and explained what she knew: Morgan's allegiance to Traviata; the regina's influence; Avidan's confident hold upon Nissyen, but also how tentative it might be; Dezba's rare position as a woman in warlord society.

Of her own part in events, she kept silent. She feared a full account would show she had been unprincipled, a coward, counting friendship above the big picture.

Toxaris arched a brow. Her unwavering gaze left Anaea with the feeling she had been condemned despite her omissions.

"Would it be accurate to say that much of the influence they claim to have depends on our agreement to work with them?" Asteria asked.

Anaea blinked, considering. "That . . . makes sense. If they succeeded, it would gain a lot of recognition. On either side of the Bridge."

"So they gamble with cards they are not yet holding." The station leader smiled slightly. "That is useful to know. Yet we must let them aboard to view the labs." The expression shifted, tensing as she thought out loud. "It will be hard to keep the women out of the way."

"Why?" Anaea asked.

"It would mean shutting things down with a plausible excuse," Toxaris said, "and of those in the know, few belong to the research division. There hasn't been a need."

"No." Anaea took a steadying breath. "Why hide it? Once an arrangement is made, and I'm assuming the factions won't leave until they have one, the residents will need to know, won't they? Why not now, give them time to adjust?" She thought of Orithia, clinging to denial, embracing the thought of a mind-wipe . . . she couldn't even give her friend that peace.

"We have not considered," Asteria measured the words with care, "whether or not this will become public knowledge on Themiscyra."

Anaea stared. "How is it a question?" she asked. "Didn't you tell everyone that civilization had collapsed into anarchy to prevent someone from leading the factions to the station? It's happened. It can't be changed."

"Do you really want them to know the universe you're describing to me?" Asteria's voice was weary. "Is it that much better than anarchy?"

"Yes. It isn't your choice to make. You can prepare them. You can warn them. But you can't force them to stay." Anaea felt light-headed. Only once the words were out did she realize what she had said, and without hesitation or doubt or the thought it was not her opinion to offer. Though still in awe of Asteria, she would say it again if she needed to.

Asteria did not respond right away, and the room seemed to grow very cold. Anaea clenched her fingers on her lap, her nerves singing.

"Can't is a strong word," Asteria said finally, mulling as if she tasted it between her lips. "Because of your firsthand experience, I will consider your opinion, but the decision is complex and must be explored before we do anything hasty."

Wrong, Anaea thought, a little dazed. Everything seemed crystalline, a sensation frightening in its intensity.

"I understand," she said, bowing her head.

"I know a decision to maintain secrecy also closes the station to you, and I am sorry for that," Asteria added. "But your return would raise too many questions."

Anaea wanted to rub her ears at the implication behind that statement. "You mean there's any hope of my coming home?"

Why had she used that phrase? It swirled around her like an icestorm, cutting with its brilliance. She had no desire to shrink back into Themiscyra's shell. If she had wanted a cocoon, she would have stayed in the Sanctum. Yet the thought made her want to weep, to hold on with a strength she didn't understand. Hiraeth. She knew it after all.

Asteria tipped her head. "Of course. You were born of Themiscyra."

"But the way I left the station . . ." she trailed off.

"That can be resolved," Asteria said. Anaea almost missed the disapproval that flickered across Toxaris' bronze face. "But for now, your warlord acquaintance would miss you, am I right?"

The point of no return had never existed. Numb, Anaea nodded.

"Then you should ease her fears." Asteria rose and offered a hand. "Thank you, Anaea, for all your efforts."

Anaea clasped the hand and was surprised when it wasn't pearl, but human flesh. She smiled sheepishly. "I am honored."

"The car will be programmed to take you to the docking bay, and nowhere else," Toxaris said. "Your faction can pick you up there."

As she stepped out of the conference chamber, Anaea released an enormous breath and the weight of a hundred whirling thoughts. Just when she thought she had come to terms with the situation, it twisted under her feet . . . but this time, she thought it was for the better.

"Why did you come back?"

Her head jerked up at the raw voice. Orithia stood there, datapad clenched hard enough to break it. Cold dread sluiced Anaea. She had assumed her once-friend would have departed once the meeting had ended.

"I didn't—" Anaea bit her tongue. "It was the only thing I could do to help."

"You could have helped by staying away. Or never leaving." Orithia's muscles wound so tight it seemed impossible she could be able to speak. Hazel eyes blazed, locked on Anaea's face and inescapable. "By not bashing your way out with brute force."

Anaea wanted to shout they had worked together, but that memory was buried. Even if Orithia could have trusted her as she once had, no amount of persuasion would be enough to cast doubt on the false recollection that had taken its place.

Strong, terrible images. Gwydion had done his work well.

"I'm sorry," Anaea said. "They would have killed him and imprisoned me. I was frightened. I shouldn't have dragged you into it."

Orithia hissed in a breath. "Killed him," she echoed. "You know how long it took me to accept what this was really about? I kept telling myself that no, the Ann I knew would never do something like that. But it was about him. It was always about him, and not because you didn't want to see someone die. You lusted after him the whole time, and then you just had to involve your old girlfriend. Had to rub it in my face."

Shock ripped through Anaea. The pain battered up against her throat, preventing words. She took a step away, fighting for distance. This was how Orithia had viewed the encounter? The hatred clawed at her.

Anaea?

It was the last voice she wanted to hear, even with its concern. She shoved his thoughts away, hard.

"Ori, I swear to you that never crossed my mind," she said. "I grew closer to him later – much later."

"Not unless you went back in time, you didn't," Orithia said, her voice like acid.

"I turned to you because you were my friend." But that wasn't right, didn't fit the story the programmer knew. Anaea shook her head in confusion. "I never lied. Not then. Not now."

"I'm sure that comforts you. You may have broken every other rule, but you didn't lie." The rage faded, and Orithia's face scrunched up, braced against tears. "You even went and stole my pet. Who does that?"

Anaea went still. If she reacted now, it would be with un-healthy laughter. The idea she had stolen Penelope was so absurd it hurt, but what other conclusion could Orithia have reached? She had to get away from this; couldn't face the accusations and think of the hours and days her once-friend had gone around and around the same points, twisted up in the agony of disbelief.

And she and Gwydion had caused it.

"I'm so sorry," she whispered. "If there's any way I can make things right—"

Orithia bit her lip, expression quivering. "Ann," she said. "You know you used to mean the world to me. Lover or not."

"Ori." Anaea was afraid to speak further or even to breathe.

"The fact you think can make amends means you don't understand what you've done." Orithia whirled on her heel, fleeing down the corridor and out of sight.

Anaea wrapped her arms around herself to hold in the over-load of emotions. She stumbled to the car, afraid if she didn't move, she would lose all will to do so. She dropped onto the seat and tuned out as the car glided away, not even looking up at her home. Her former home. There really was no going back.

40

T HE WARLORD FACTION SENT THE SHUTTLE FOR HER. SHE tried to arrange her thoughts for Dezba, but her mind fixed on Orithia's face.

Once aboard, she stumbled in a haze to the trainer's quarters, hardly hearing her questions. She told Dezba she had given Asteria general information about the two civilizations and her opinion of their strength. She was surprised when Dezba didn't press. Then she said the station leader had discussed homecoming, and in the other's expression, she had her answer. She wasn't pushing because he thought it might destroy her relationship with Themiscyra.

Dazed by this new power, she excused herself and went to see Gwydion. She collapsed in his arms.

He stroked her hair, hand trembling. "I worried when you shut me out," he said. "I knew you weren't in physical danger, but . . ."

"Orithia." It surprised Anaea when the whole story didn't tumble out on the name. It was full of nuance, regret and confusion, but the words stopped on her lips. One note of fear came through the rest. She had to say it first, or she would never say it at all. "Gwydion, she accused me of throwing her life into confusion and doing everything I did . . . because I wanted you."

"That's not true," he said. "You had reason to be fascinated with me, but not—" He paused, colored.

Anaea frowned, chased by her anxieties. How could she look back and be sure? "What if it was? What if, underneath everything . . ."

"Are you the kind of person who saves someone only because you're attracted to them?" His voice was soft.

"I don't think so." Her doubt knotted around her.

"I know so. It's not the way you are." Gwydion sighed. "We need to see her," he said. "I can remove the block, if I'm close enough."

That hadn't occurred to Anaea in the tumult of the confrontation. She hadn't even realized it was possible.

"Should we do that?" she asked. "Right now, she's certain she has the high ground. If we break that barrier and she realizes the hate she's been holding, everything she's thought against us . . ."

Gwydion stared. "Should we? The truth is always the best option, Anaea. I have a hard time dealing with the thought of her censure when she means so much to you, but we owe her, too."

She hated the idea of causing her friend more pain, but there was no avoiding that. Neither could she face Asteria and claim the women of Themiscyra had a right to know their circumstances while keeping Orithia ignorant. She bit her lip and nodded.

"How much did Flick get?" she asked. "I think—"

"More than they wanted me to," replied a voice from the grate above. It popped free, and the Tweaker dangled into view. "Your girls are aces at jamming, Anaea."

"How long have you been listening?" Anaea felt the color grow on her face.

"Not really listening," Flick said, "just keeping an ear out for my name." He shimmied down and landed with a thunk. "Will take me some time," he said, "but I think I can adjust to the frequency. I'm going to upgrade to an earpiece. I want to be able to talk if something comes up. I thought I might try to create another, so you both have them. Just in case you get separated for some – oh."

"I can speak to Gwydion mind to mind," Anaea said, finishing his train of thought. "It shouldn't be necessary, and the more you pilfer—"

"Ahem. Acquire," Flick corrected.

"—borrow from the ship, the more chance there is someone will notice."

He shrugged. "Fair enough. I'm itching to get off and see this for myself, but in the meantime, I've got a battle to fight."

"Do you think you can bypass the jamming?" Anaea asked.

"Do I? Of course. Easily? No." Flick grinned. She had never seen him so excited, cheeks pinked, eyes bright.

"I'm glad someone is enjoying this," she said wryly.

*

WORD CAME FROM Themiscyra the next day, morning by station time, inviting the warlord party to view the medical facilities. Remembering her encounters there, Anaea shuddered.

"I would like to send a message," she said to Dezba as they stood on the bridge. "Personal business."

Dezba arched an eyebrow. "What about?"

Anaea considered, decided to trust her. "I need to speak to an old lover," she said. "I burned some bridges I shouldn't have." She kept her voice pitched low.

"Record it and I'll have it sent over."

Would Dezba review it before it was sent? It didn't matter: Anaea had nothing to hide. In the quiet of her quarters, she took a deep breath. "Orithia, it's Anaea. Can we meet? I promise I can explain everything, and if I can't, then . . . I won't ask anything else of you."

She tried twice more and came up with nothing better.

It would have to do. She had learned her way around words, somehow, but not with such an old friend and such pain.

There had been no response by the time they departed. The technology specialist burbled about what they might see. Three security officers met them at the docking bay: Toxaris and two younger women. She halted Gwydion with an extended hand.

"I have concerns about your abilities," she said. "You can submit to a sedative patch, or return to your ship."

Gwydion glanced over and caught Anaea's eyes. She shrugged helplessly, then nodded. *You have to be on the station to see Orithia.*

He started to offer his arm, then hesitated. "I would feel better if Anaea could apply the patch," he said. "No offense."

She blinked, then realized what he was doing. "I can," she said. "I had some medical training here."

Toxaris lifted a brow, then offered Anaea the patch. Anaea ran her finger over the marking. *It's one of the rarer sedatives,* she thought. *The counter-agent won't be in the public labs.*

I'm sorry. He caught her other hand and squeezed as she applied the patch.

She shook her head, thinking. Toxaris performed a curt welcome to both parties and gestured for them to follow.

The route through Themiscyra was sealed off from the daily passage of residents. They entered the infirmary through a back entrance Anaea had not known existed. She strained her brain trying to figure out if it might have made a difference in their escape.

She forgot that consideration when their tour guide approached. It was Thalestris, smooth and ageless as she had ever been, and betraying not a blink at the sight of Anaea. Toxaris made introductions, a swirl of names and acknowledgement. Anaea could not take her gaze off the obstetrician, the surety and ease she had once envied. It now seemed it was the gift of having a closed sphere, one whose opposite boundaries could almost be touched.

"Anaea," the raspy voice said. "The universe always seems to bring us back to the start."

Anaea's first urge was a bubbling of words, defending the places she had explored, argument against the way Thalestris had portrayed them. It was not her companions or discretion that made those words vanish, but realization of how much Thalestris must have known, from salvaged ships, from quarantined men.

"It was a greater journey than I had ever expected," she said quietly.

Thalestris remained as mild as ever, but the expression that flashed across her features was one of pity. "Perhaps you are relieved to return." She turned back to the visitors, clearly expecting no reply.

"No," Anaea said. She had wrestled with many emotions, but relief was not one of them.

Thalestris did not answer, and Anaea felt the gap between them widen. She did not regret it; too much had changed.

Anaea lingered at the back of the tour, not able to focus on the banal description of things she had grown up with. To her bemusement, the scientists asked frequent questions and gazed bright-eyed upon the answers. Even Morgan lifted her fluting voice at intervals. Gwydion seemed normal, but the occasional stumbled step or slurred word showed the effects of the sedative.

After the third stop, Toxaris gestured Anaea aside. "You have a message from Miss Roslin," she said.

Anaea's heart squeezed. "What is it?"

"She says she'll meet you in the Preserve in an hour." The security officer managed to convey disapproval without shift in expression or tone. "Detours will not be tolerated."

"Thank you." Anaea felt a quiver in her stomach. Now she had no choice: she had to find the counter-agent for Gwydion's sedative.

Once out of Toxaris' watchful eye, she rubbed her ear. "Did you hear that, Flick?"

"Sure did. Give her my compliments on a scrambling job extremely well done. I think I'm in love."

Anaea smiled, bemused. Clearly, he hadn't heard the conversation between she and Gwydion. "There's a problem, though."

"The sedative, right? What do you need?"

The group disappeared into a lab. Anaea quickened her pace, not too much, and kept her head down.

"I need to get into the Section C supply room," she murmured.

"Working. Hang tight."

She glided past Toxaris, trying to look natural. To her relief, the security chief never glanced her way.

She stepped up to Gwydion's side and kissed his cheek. The tech in the lab stared openly at the display of affection, and Morgan shot them an annoyed look. Under that cover, Anaea murmured, "I'm going to get the counter-agent."

"But—" he started. She shook her head. She had no choice if they were to fix things with Orithia.

His expression tightened; he obviously regretted the sedative and the things he couldn't say around curious ears. He glared in the direction of her earpiece hard enough she worried someone would squint twice.

"He's making faces at me, isn't he," Flick commented.

Anaea bit her lip to stop a giggle. She mouthed, "Trust me," to Gwydion. She didn't need to feign interest: everyone knew this place was an open book to her, so they would hardly expect her to pay close attention. A faint smile crossed her lips at the analogy.

The leaders of the warlord and matriarch parties stood in tense courtesy; the scientists, oblivious to the sour vibrations, took notes and asked questions. En route to the next lab, Flick spoke again. "Got it. You're going to want to drop back and hang a left."

She fell back a step, then another, heart in her throat. Three paces, four. The door was at her left. She darted into the food preparation area for the infirmary, ducking down to counter level. The door whirred shut.

"Now what?" Her whisper seemed like thunder rumbling.

"Out the back. You'll have to take the long way around."

She edged forward, finding the door in the semi-dark. He

must have turned off the light sensors.

"Crap on a stick."

She tensed with her hand on the pad. "Flick?"

"Just go," he said. "Hurry."

Anaea pressed on the plate and edged into the hall. She froze when she heard voices. Her heart shuddered as she listened, but the voices never moved. She crept forward.

The voices belonged to two doctors chatting in a break room. Neither looked her direction as she snuck past, her nerves jangling.

She followed the corridor's curve, alert for motion, but the halls lay quiet. Toxaris must have cleared out all non-essential personnel. The corridor bent back around towards a series of doors.

"Which?" she whispered.

"You mean you don't know?"

Fear sparked down her spine. "Flick, I—"

"No, I've got it," he said hastily. "I'm just surprised, you know."

"I don't remember everything," she said, cotton-mouthed and feeling the desire to shove his head into something hard.

"Second door, right."

She palmed in and scanned the cabinets. She had never been in this supply room, but the layout was logical and the counter-agent came quickly to hand. She put it in her pocket and turned.

"Stay there. Don't breathe."

"Flick—" she started, then heard the patter of steps. She dropped into a crouch, dizzy. She reminded herself the worst they could do to her was throw her off the station.

Then she would never make things right with Orithia. The thought squeezed her so hard she felt sick.

The steps paused outside the door. "Are you coming?"

A second set of footsteps approached. Scolding, then footsteps retreating. Anaea sagged.

"Go," Flick said. "I've got two tricks left. Not to mention your Toxaris seems like a sharp eagle."

Anaea sprinted for the door and almost toppled when it opened. She gathered herself with a shaky laugh, skidding in an attempt to be silent. She waited for Flick to tell her she was out of time.

Silence. A faint crackle. Had she been disconnected? The kitchenette door opened under her hand. She eased forward, wincing when her hand struck something. The clang echoed.

"You almost there?"

She puffed out a breath. "At the door," she said.

"Go. Returning to normal security in three, two—"

She slipped out into the main corridor and saw the group clustered in the hall. She took one step, then another. Hurrying, but not too much.

". . . will discuss our methods, but not in extensive detail," the guide was saying.

Toxaris turned, her eyes raking Anaea's face. "Where have you been?" she inquired.

Anaea smiled weakly. "I just . . . got homesick, lingered to look around, and lost track of time. I'm sorry?"

The security chief remained motionless for long enough Anaea felt sweat gather at the back of her neck. Behind her, Gwydion stiffened. Dezba laid a hand on his shoulder.

Toxaris spun away. "Don't let it happen again. You have twenty minutes before your meeting."

It was the longest twenty minutes of her life. She slid up to Gwydion and gave his hand a reassuring squeeze, but there was no luxury for conversation. Even Flick was silent. Hard at work, she hoped, not shut out by the station systems.

A legal officer arrived to escort Anaea and Gwydion by hovercar. Her eyes never left the pair, which meant no opportunity to pass him the counter-agent patch.

"You want I should give her a jolt and knock her out of the car?" Flick asked.

"No," Anaea hissed so sharply the office shot her a look.

"Okay! Try to do a girl a favor . . ."

She met Gwydion's eyes. One look at the quirk of his lip, and it was all she could do not to burst out laughing. Her anxiety only made her more giddy.

The hovercar halted in front of the Preserve. The guard stepped down and regarded them with a hint of wariness. "I'll be here," she said.

"Thank you," Anaea answered, turning. Her feet grew leaden. She had no idea how her friend would react to Gwydion's presence.

"If I could turn invisible right now, I would," he said, as if for reassurance.

"Anaea?" Flick's voice cut through. "I'm getting rammed hard. I'm about to lose the—"

She stopped still, waiting. She let out a slow breath. "We're on our own," she said softly.

Gwydion squeezed her arm, then retreated a pace. She slipped her hand into her pocket, fingering the patch. They walked under the arch into the Preserve. Once past the weeping willow near the entrance, they would have enough cover to apply the patch.

"You brought him."

Orithia's voice trembled, more scared than outraged. The girl stood with fists clenched, her cheeks as bright as if they had been splashed with blood.

Anaea's hand tightened on the patch. "I can explain," she said. "Please hear me out—"

Orithia whirled and darted up the avenue between exhibits. Anaea rushed after, heart squirming in her throat. "Ori!"

"Anaea!" Gwydion called after her. "The patch . . ."

She hesitated, pivoting on her heel. She turned just as someone struck him from behind. He staggered under the blow and whirled to face a second attacker.

Her instincts surged to run to his defense, even though she could do nothing, had left her stunner on the ship ship. The hand with the patch came up – no, she couldn't throw it to him.

The faint whine of a weapon charging brought her to a jerked halt. "You can't help him, Anaea."

She recognized the voice and spun, confusion crashing into dismay. Valasca Braun, in charge of the weapon, with a junior security officer at her elbow and Orithia behind them now, her eyes wet but stance determined.

"What do you want?" Anaea asked. Her eyes went past the doctor, locking on Orithia's face.

"Answers," Valasca said shortly. "The real ones, not the tripe you've fed Asteria. I've seen thorugh you as she has not, miss Carlisle, and you—" She jerked her head in negation. "Enough talk."

"There aren't other answers," Anaea said. "Orithia, you—"

For an instant, she had forgotten Orithia no longer knew. She wavered, fighting to think up some defense.

"I said enough," Valasca said.

The blast caught Anaea and sent her toppling into darkness.

41

As soon as Anaea recovered from the stun blast, which was less like waking up and more an explosion of light and stinging nerves, she reached out her thoughts for Gwydion. She felt nothing through the link, and a wave of nausea rushed through her. No, she told herself, no reason to fear. He was still drugged, so she wouldn't feel him.

Questions punched her in the gut as she rocked upright on the cot. Where was she? What did Valasca want with her – answers, but about what? What did she expect to hear? Why was Orithia involved? Could the girl she knew have done this, even to someone she hated?

To try and explain now would be impossible, would risk exposing Orithia to the chief doctor's wrath. Anaea remembered the last time she had faced Valasca, during the escape from the infirmary. So much had happened there, and now it all seemed that it could have happened no other way.

The resting room was featureless, even smaller than quarters for trainees. She stretched, studying the ceiling corner opposite the pillow. No numbers there to tell her what section she was in, even if she could remember the codes.

She had to try the door. She slid to her feet, surprised to find herself wishing for the stunner. As her hand approached the palm plate, the door slid open. She jerked back, startled.

"Sit down, Anaea." Valasca's words were a command.

She stayed where she was. "Where are we?" she asked. "What did you do to Gwydion?"

A burly security officer advanced and shoved Anaea back on the bed. Anaea's brain buzzed, putting pieces together. Valasca, Orithia, at least two security personnel – for she was sure this wasn't the same woman who had stood behind the doctor in the Preserve – how many people were involved?

"He will be fine," the doctor said. "He might have been the catalyst to your betrayal, but I have no interest in him."

Anaea swallowed, tasting relief for a dizzy second. "I didn't betray anyone."

"You know that's not true."

The shaky voice brought her head up. Orithia appeared lost and drained; Anaea couldn't look away.

"If I needed any proof you were lying," Valasca said, "your actions towards Orithia would be enough."

Did she believe that, or was it justification to keep Orithia on her side? Anaea opened her mouth, the words singing against her throat. She closed her mouth. No. Her protests would be seen as an attempt to drag Orithia with her, or worse, cast suspicion on the programmer.

"I thought our lives were in danger," she said, instead. "I did what had to be done. Everything else, you already know."

"Those are the lies you poured out to Asteria." Valasca spoke evenly. "I think I can do without that."

Anaea's mind chased around itself. Where was the way out of this? Could she make up something to please Valasca? But then what consequence?

"I have nothing else to give you," she said.

She watched Orithia's face, knowing she wasn't Gwydion and

couldn't sense the thoughts turning beneath the frozen, lonely eyes. Yet she felt the programmer was somehow as frightened as she.

"Then I suggest you find more inside yourself," Valasca said. "Come."

The guard pulled her upright. Anaea didn't protest, numb. "At least tell me where I am," she said. "It's not as if I can get out."

"If you think someone is listening," Orithia lifted her voice, "then you might want to see this." She extended her hand with an attempt at dramatic flourish and opened it, revealing a tangle of disassembled parts. "Your friend can't listen now."

"Enough of that," Valasca said. The guard pulled Anaea into the next room. Its only fixtures were a restraint chair, a medical cart and an electronics panel. Valasca's hand lingered over the last. "Confess now, and I will have it broadcast to Asteria and the station leaders. They will perhaps show more understanding towards a willing confession."

Anaea swallowed hard. "I have nothing to confess."

Valasca turned from the panel, eyes hard. "And you persist." She gestured to the guard.

The woman pushed Anaea into the restraint chair and fastened the straps. The urge to laugh beat against her chest. Were they afraid of her melting through the floor and so escaping? Had her departure from Themiscyra been that remarkable?

The doctor's eyes locked on hers. The laughter drained away, leaving her ears thick with silence.

"I'm injecting you with a medium dose of a truth stimulant," Valasca continued. "I will increase it until I see results."

There was a fine line between the highest useful dosage and enough to risk brain damage. Anaea knew the dosage levels. Why could she remember that so clearly and not the location codes? Valasca could calculate precisely how much to give her. Anaea closed her eyes, felt the coldness in her veins.

"How did you meet Gwydion?"

Anaea hesitated, feeling the words surge up within her. "On

a salvage mission. The White Hound. It was myself, Marpe, Kyme—" Somehow, she found she could remember the whole crew. Details she was not sure she consciously noticed the first time fell off her tongue. The effects of the drug, not to force truth but to enhance recall and decrease the barrier between mouth and brain.

She had never realized just how strange it would feel. The floating detachment muted her emotions to a whisper. She would have otherwise been embarrassed to reveal Gwydion's first cryptic remarks, the conversation in the infirmary. Orithia dimmed to a blur at the corner of her vision. As much as she strained, fearing the impact of her words, she could not focus.

Valasca pushed onwards. The interrogation skimmed past subjects that strobed in her thoughts; she took light, rapid breaths and thought of Justin's books, the imprint of letters, the heady aroma . . . anything to keep from blurting out the steps in between, where Orithia had helped her spy on the operation and then creep onto the White Hound to check the records—

"I didn't mean to drag you so deep, Ori," she said. "I could have—"

Valasca gestured. The guard slapped her. That knocked Anaea straight, and she grasped at coherence before it eluded her again.

She tumbled into the next stream of thought, how they had escaped the infirmary, the false threat Gwydion had made. She sank back, worn through by the recitation.

But Valasca had only now reached her purpose. "When you arrived at your destination, who did you inform about Themiscyra? How much did they pay you?"

The laughter didn't sound like her own, brittle and childish. "They paid me with your protection," Anaea said. "I had nothing, gained nothing . . . Phailin knew without needing to be told. I asked her to leave you alone. I thought it would be that simple." Was that really the truth? Anaea doubted the power of the stimulant and felt free, for how could she ever have believed that?

Valasca hissed in. "Who else?"

"Only Avidan, after I knew the matriarchs were on their way." Anaea tasted the bitterness of that decision and succumbed to the urge to justify it. "When I learned from Upala—"

"Stop." The chief doctor moved behind her. "I'm sure you had plenty of time to rehearse your story en route. It surprises me you can overcome the stimulant, but once I increase the dose . . ." Her next words came near Anaea's ear. "I remember the dull, obedient child you were."

"I'm not lying," Anaea insisted.

"Tell me what the matriarchs offered you."

Mincing dialogues with Traviata flashed through her memory. "They offered me my life," she said, "and I wouldn't take it. Not even when my silence hurt the Petrarchs."

"Did you tell them?"

"No!" She was surprised when it didn't come out as a shout.

Valasca sighed as if she were dealing with a child. "If I have to keep elevating the dose like this – but as you will."

She hadn't quoted numbers, had given no indication how close the coldness that flooded Anaea's veins was to the maximum dose. Even knowing it had to be deliberate, an attempt to scare her, Anaea trembled and couldn't stop as her hands jerked against the restraints.

The scuff of a foot on the floor seemed like thunder. "Dr. Braun," Orithia's voice said timidly, "I'm not sure . . ."

"Oh? The time for being unsure has passed." Valasca straightened to level a significant look on the programmer.

Anaea felt a flash of hope. Was Orithia having second thoughts?

"I don't mean that." Orithia shook her head, vanishing behind curls. "I mean if you increase it so fast, might it destroy what you're looking for?" She spoke as if their captive were an object, and Anaea railed at herself for trying to imagine her freedom out of nothing.

"You have a point," Valasca said. "This will be the highest dose, for today. But I'm not through asking questions."

Not done, perhaps, but none of the questions were new. The chief doctor repeated the same inquiries in different words, as if expecting the change would defeat some defense which, with the way the stimulant was supposed to work, Anaea couldn't have created.

Apparently tired of the lack of answers and the flood of information Anaea couldn't stop and ached to hear on her lips, Valasca relented. She dropped her hands and strode out of the room in silence.

Orithia had disappeared sometime during the questioning. That left the guard to remove the restraints and thrust Anaea back into the room. She didn't try to resist. The floor pitched up and welcomed her. She crawled to the bed and closed her eyes. She didn't dare rest for long . . .

*

Anaea?

Gwydion's thought prodded her out of numb slumber. *Gwydion! You're all right.*

Me? I'm fine. Have you been hurt?

She rubbed her eyes, sat up, tried to ignore the sour taste in her mouth. *Knocked around a little, but no.*

What happened? I thought I saw Valasca, but no one believes me. He might have been trying to rein in his emotions, but he was still muzzy, and anxiety bled through, sharpening the stab of her heart.

You did. Anaea closed her eyes, composing herself so the story came out in straight lines instead of a single burst.

When she had finished, his anger spiked down the link. *You're obviously telling the truth. What more does she want from you? Another hypermental could—*

He stopped, and she understood his frustration. He was the only person within light-years who could prove she was telling the truth, and no one would accept the explanation from him. She knotted her fingers in the thin blanket. *Your turn,* she thought.

The guard who took us to the Preserve doesn't seem to be part of . . . this, he replied. *Took them a while to get me on my feet, longer to sort everything out. Toxaris still doesn't believe it, and Dezba is quiet as a waiting volcano. I guess as far as she's concerned, we're her people right now.*

Anaea pondered what that meant. Was she anyone's person? Her efforts to find a place she belonged had only resulted in temporary alliances. She wanted to believe it was hope of rescue, but Dezba had already stuck her neck out more than once. There were limits.

Asteria calmed things down. Gwydion's thoughts held a trace of awe, and she wondered if it was genuinely his or rubbed off from her. *She thought the easiest way to confirm you hadn't simply suffered some mishaps was to allow me to reach you, so she gave me an antidote patch. She sent for Valasca, but—*

But she can lie, and no one can disprove her, Anaea finished the thought with despair, or rather, the two thoughts blended, overlapping in her head as he finished a similar sentence. *Now that you can sense the link do you know where I am?*

No. It doesn't work like that. He had considered lying, she sensed, felt that queer note of falsehood quivering between them. *I could scan the entire station, slowly, but Toxaris won't allow me to stay here, unsedated, for that long.*

She's worried about the risk of the women learning the truth. Anaea remembered her conversation with Asteria, her insistence the people she had grown up with had a right to choose. Her current predicament, so twined with the question of discovery, had not changed her mind. *They want to continue the way things were.*

I won't allow this. His determination tightened around her. *We're being forced to return to the ship. Toxaris doesn't trust me to remain here. Flick and I will be back, I promise.*

She wrapped herself around the words and the glimmer they represented. *I'll hold you to that.*

I can't reach the station from the ship. Once I leave Themiscyra, we'll be out of touch. His thoughts warmed. *I love you.*

The words made her giddy-hot, an intensity that flushed her body despite her fears. *I love you, too. It's going to be . . .*

Would it be fine? Or would Valasca do her permanent harm, either in anger or in pursuit of what she wanted to know? Anaea's attempt to finish that sentence was interrupted as the door opened. Her eyes widened.

Good luck, she sent the last thought, then scrambled to her feet to face Orithia. She wouldn't let herself feel relief or hope.

"She will push you past the maximum safe dose if she has to," Orithia said. "Why do you risk it?"

Why do you care? Anaea wondered, too afraid to ask the question. "Because I'm telling her the truth," she said. "And I'm trying to protect you."

The programmer stiffened. "Don't try," she said, her anger coming out faint and wavery.

"Why else would I seek you out?" Anaea asked.

Orithia pressed her lips tight. "To gloat?"

She hadn't meant to say it, hadn't meant to invoke the past at all, but the statement astonished her. "Does that sound like me?"

They stared at each other in silence, Orithia trembling, eyes hard. Anaea hurried on, "You're in danger here. If station security finds us and Valasca hasn't learned what she wants, you'll be arrested with her. Dezba may demand they make an example of you."

"Unless you tell her who you sold us to." Orithia's gaze pierced.

"I can't," Anaea said. "I can't give her details that don't exist. Even if I made something up, what would happen?" Confinement, or worse, if Valasca's temper overcame her? She shuddered. "And what about the negotiations?"

Orithia turned, chuckling hoarsely. 'You say you want to protect me, but you cling to that story. I don't know how you do it."

Anaea could insist; she could beat her head against a truth

that could not be proven, speaking to a person who should have believed her without proof. It would be no more effective than Valasca's interrogation, trying to create an answer from nothing.

She took her heart in her hands before she spoke, calm, measured. "Do you want me to lie, to make something up for Valasca? Because I can. If you think that's the way this has to be, I will."

The words were no strategy, she discovered, spiraling into them. She had wondered whose person she was, and it had nothing to do with factions or alliance. She threw her lot in with friends, even when they no longer felt the friendship.

She could claim it was the warlords she had sold information to. Done correctly, that admission should alienate Dezba.

She could do this. She could confess and walk into whatever pain awaited. Maybe Gwydion and Flick would find a way to prevent it, and they would flee as fugitives. They'd had so much practice in doing that!

When Orithia turned back, surprised, Anaea held her gaze with a steadiness that felt impossible. Her fears rushed and halted in her throat. For a moment, the hazel eyes that met hers held warmth and depth. Then it disappeared, obscured behind a fierce blinking of lashes.

Orithia retreated. "This is about the truth," she said. "Not about how you treated me or anything else."

Anaea felt their connection slip away. She lifted one hand as if to grab for it, though it wasn't physical, couldn't be held. "Then I can't do anything," she said. "I've told the truth. I wish there was a way I could make you believe me."

"You'd have to . . ." Orithia hesitated, her lips wavering as she pressed them together. "I should go. There's nothing more to say."

Nothing, Anaea thought, that would change anything. "Orithia, I'm sorry."

"I'll make sure she doesn't kill you." On those words, the programmer stepped out.

Anaea stared after, numb as those words lit the fear hovering within her. If Valasca were convinced enough, threatened enough, angry enough . . . she could already lose her place in the station for conducting the abduction. Would any risk dissuade her?

Anaea sent a silent thought to the young men who could not hear her now. *Hurry.*

42

A THOROUGH EXAMINATION OF ANAEA'S PRISON FOUND no distinguishing marks, and no way out. She considered breaking off a weapon, but couldn't find a panel loose enough to pry free. In any case, she doubted it would do much good. The techniques she had learned from Dezba might work against Valasca, but against a trained officer?

The towering officer returned with a horse-faced blonde woman, also armed. Anaea thought she recognized her as one of Gwydion's attackers, though it was difficult to be sure.

The blonde led the same interrogation Valasca had. No restraints or truth stimulants this time, only hostile eyes. Anaea realized if even one detail varied from the account she had given before, they would hammer on that point, and take it as proof she had somehow managed to lie through the drug.

She was sweating and shivering by the time the blonde finished. Her eyes were shuttered, unreadable. Anaea hoped her consistency had planted some doubt in the woman's mind.

"Valasca told me to inform you that when she returns, her next step will be the use of force," the blonde concluded as she stepped to the door. "I suggest you think about that."

Anaea's mind leapt in two directions at those words. Force – torture? A turn back almost a thousand years to a time when people had believed it worked. Valasca might have that medieval mindset. And . . . when she returned. The summons Gwydion had mentioned. If Valasca couldn't maintain her composure in front of Toxaris and the others, might rescue be on its way even now?

What would happen to Orithia?

Anaea dropped back onto the cot, exhausted, wracked with fears, wishing she didn't have to feel any of it. Without thought, she scrabbled at the cot leg, but it wouldn't come free.

It wasn't much later when the door opened. Orithia, clear-eyed now, though still cold and unmoving in the doorway.

Anaea rested her hands on her knees. "What's on your mind?" No clock, she realized suddenly. She flashed back to the old-fashioned timepiece on the mantel of Eastwood's inn and felt bizarrely homesick.

Orithia looked past her. "What's it like out there?"

Anaea started in surprise. "I thought you didn't—"

"What is it like." There was no inflection.

Anaea knew she had to make the words count. "It's different than I imagined," she said. "The things we learned about the universe are there, but it's as if the colors are different. It's big, chaotic and ruthless, but people enjoy every moment. The bustling pulse of millions of people. The singing clarity of open air. You can't describe it, you can't make a hologram of it."

"Is that why you gave us away?" Orithia asked.

Anaea's fingers dug into her knees. No, she told herself. Don't protest. "I can see why the station leaders wanted to hide it from us, but I think it's beautiful, and I think we deserve the choice. I found something out there . . ."

"What, *yourself?*" From anyone else, it would have been nasty. Orithia tried to sneer, but it came out flat and plaintive.

"Maybe," Anaea said. "I found an occupation – an art – to pursue. I know that might not seem like much to you. You always knew you wanted to be a programmer—" She stopped, for the girl had drawn away.

"Thousands of people on Themiscyra find their life's work here."

"I know." Anaea tried to smile. "Maybe I'm just broken. Or maybe there are others here who don't realize what they've missed."

Orithia frowned. "I suppose that boy of yours helped you find it."

The bitterness rocked Anaea backwards. "No," she said, "though I have to give a man – a friend – credit for helping. Books, Orithia," she rushed out the words before the other shut her out, "archaic and mysterious and tactile. Stories that don't change with fashion and times. You can immerse yourself in the same tale that captivated someone three centuries ago. There's so little room for that nostalgia here, but out there . . . the universe is so wide anything can exist. And does."

"There's a reason those things don't exist here," Orithia said. "They serve no purpose." She took a breath, forcing out the last words. "And focusing on them makes you a relic, too."

"No." Anaea shook her head. "I don't believe—"

"Enough, Anaea. It doesn't matter. And I hope, I have to hope, things will go back to normal after your friends leave." Her voice quavered.

Once again, though instinct cried at her to respond, Anaea remained silent. She thought she heard a trickle of doubt in the programmer's voice. The glimmer that maybe things wouldn't be better back to normal. She feared she would smother that if she pushed.

"I just hope—" Anaea stopped herself. Too late to believe Orithia wouldn't be hurt.

"Maybe that's your problem. I—" Orithia ducked her head. "Goodbye, Anaea." She fled as if pursued by raptorhounds.

Drained anew, Anaea let the tension out of her body in one dizzy rush. There would be an instant when she would have to decide whether to make a false confession or accept the consequences of silence, and either way, once she made that decision, a rescue party wouldn't change the outcome.

*

ENOUGH TIME PASSED that Anaea wondered if Valasca had been detained. What would her captors do? She was spared coming up with more than seven scenarios by the return of the burly officer.

"Doctor wants to see you," she said.

Anaea's fingers lingered on the leg of the cot, taking obscure comfort from the weapon that wasn't, then rose and followed. Valasca stood in the next room, vibrating impatience. The other two security officers and Orithia waited there. The whole group?

Anaea studied Valasca, straining for some indication of how the conversation with Asteria had gone. The tautness of anger shrouded the doctor's face. The heavyset officer nudged Anaea into the restraint chair.

Valasca moved behind her. The cold hiss of the drug entered her system.

"You were informed of the consequences of withholding, I trust." The doctor's voice was soft, monotone.

"I can't tell you anything more than I already have." Her heart pondered so high in her throat she was afraid of swallowing it.

"Who did you sell us to?"

"No one," she said.

Orithia shifted uncomfortably. Anaea's gaze snapped to her, breath held. She had made a promise and would keep it. The programmer started back a step, eyes wide. One of the officers glanced at her; she flattened her features. Anaea felt her heart lurch with relief. Orithia might be starting to believe.

"Why, if not for profit?" the blonde asked.

Anaea explained again she needed to even the score between the two civilizations. "Avidan wouldn't even see us without risking both our lives in a race against raptorhounds," she said. "We could have died. We lost Justin and his workshop, the beautiful books—"

Valasca interrupted. "I don't care what pathetic tragedies you faced," she said. "I don't care what other crimes you and your pet hypermental committed. And I don't have time for fencing with shadows." The doctor stepped back. "Hook up the projection node." As the blonde advanced, securing the disc to the back of Anaea's neck, Valasca continued, "This is the last chance I give you, Anaea. I will destroy you. Don't doubt me."

The words forced a shiver through her. "I believe you."

"And?"

Was this the moment? Her thoughts tried to reach out and came whirling back to nothing in the thickness of the drug. "I believe in my friends."

Valasca hissed in a breath. "You believe in people who can purchase you. I should have seen it from the first. Well – no matter." In that dismissal, she consigned Anaea to nothing.

Anaea gulped in a breath to steel herself, but the burst from the node came first. Everything turned brighter, glowing. Enhanced by the stimulant, it burned the back of her eyes. She flinched and closed them, only to find the auras dancing inside her lids like fire.

A jab from the burly officer brought her eyes open, startled, and she cried out as color assaulted her. She would have said before the room was grey, monotone, her interrogators a blur of brown and pale yellow; now it blazed ivory, amber and gold. It reminded her of her experience with the mindfire worms, but there was nothing pleasant about this attack on the senses.

"Talk to me." The node distorted the sounds, driving them into Anaea's temples.

She shook her head. "You know everything there is to know."

It was the first time, she thought absurdly, images dancing around her brain, that she had lied. Everything there was to know? Even she didn't understand the whole story.

"So stubborn."

The colors flared, incandescent needles in her eyes. Anaea

started to cry out, but the sound of her own voice made it worse. She bit her lip. It hurt as well, but gave her somewhere to focus in the surge of sensations.

"When did you inform the matriarchs of our existence?"

"I didn't," she said; after the first syllables, it was a whisper. "We all did. Starting before I was born. It had to happen."

"No," Valasca said harshly, "this place was designed too well. A perfect sanctuary, to shut out the rest of the universe as it stumbled along in its death-throes."

The words pounded into Anaea's head. "It's not dying."

The doctor's fingers dug into Anaea's skin. The feeling flared up her arm. "Scalpel," she said. "It will die, in the end."

And so will we, Anaea thought, but couldn't brave the words. She thought she felt a touch at the back of her mind and strained towards it, but the effort caused her senses to burst into shuddering rainbows. She winced, gave it up as a trick of the imagination.

"What did this Avidan offer you?"

She shook her head. The thin blade pressed into her arm. Her world narrowed to the electric hiss of pain flashing up the wound. It pressed on her senses, heard and seen and smelt. She felt her lips part, but had no air.

"What did he offer you?"

The pressure increased, until it seemed to drive into her bones. She was too aware of her body to believe it even as her mind screamed. The stimulant crashed in her system, the words boiling inside her. They were as futile as the gasp.

"Lights! Valasca." Which one of her captors was speaking? The blonde? "She can't even talk. Let up."

Blessed release, almost as overwhelming as the pain. Anaea would have slumped, but the restraints prevented her. She started to heave in air, then regretted it as her chest ached.

Her helplessness frustrated her. Through all this, she had been weak. Where was her courage? Had it ever been there, or had she simply stumbled from one desperation to another?

She gradually became accustomed to the silence. Her captors

were still. She looked up, swallowing, and hit the flint wall of Valasca's eyes.

"The truth, Carlisle," the doctor said. "Now."

Anaea looked past her, saw the scarlet whorls of Orithia's hair, and focused on her face amongst the bleeding color. Slowly, Orithia shook her head.

She took a steadying breath, needing a hundred more, and told the truth.

*

It didn't take long for Valasca to decide the scalpel was at fault for Anaea's continued silence and change methods. What seemed eternity later, the doctor halted the interrogation. The burly officer dragged Anaea back to her room.

Exhausted, shivering, she curled under the covers. Coherence fought her. She didn't want to think clearly, wanted to melt into haze to escape the pain, and the remnant drugs made it far too easy. If Gwydion was back on the station, how much of this would he feel?

She enjoyed worrying about someone else. It made her feel as if her own situation were less dire. Thoughts chased to the surface. A perfect sanctuary, Valasca had called Themiscyra. Was that the ultimate goal? Paint her as a villain and get people to turn away from what that villain represented? Anaea represented escape, exploration. Even she wasn't sure her discoveries were worth it.

She had told Orithia she would confess if asked. Now she realized she couldn't. Admit she had sold Themiscyra, and she was branding all outsiders with that brush: traitors, schemers, with ethics for sale.

She pushed off the covers, ignoring the spasms of pain that shot through her. She had told Asteria; she had told Valasca. She would scream it if she had to, even there was no one to hear.

She bent for the cot limb, rattling it. Her fingers slipped, almost crushed beneath the bar. She winced and drew her hand to her lips.

No waiting to be rescued. Could she surprise the burly blonde? Maybe—

The door opened. She jumped, startled, and felt a hysterical laugh gathering at the back of her throat. The surprise was on her.

Her visitor was Orithia, wound tight, holding herself as if she could project a wall between them, but staring past it.

"The books," she said in a thick voice. "You really believe in them."

Anaea nodded, confused. "I know it won't save lives or even matter to any but a handful of people," she said, "but I touched something special."

"That's the Anaea I knew," Orithia said slowly, "but that woman wouldn't have forced me against my will. For anything."

Anaea tensed, sensing the door open, but knowing it would slam if she ran at it. "I want to explain myself," she said, "but the truth will make trouble for you with Valasca." No need to point out what the doctor was willing to do to defend her beliefs.

"You think you did the right thing, somehow," Orithia said. "But you won't tell me what that is."

"It will put you in danger, and I can't do that." Anaea's heart shuddered. She hoped the programmer would believe her, against the evidence planted in her mind. Could years of friendship, and their halting conversations here, overcome the invented betrayal? Had she said enough? Had she said too much?

Orithia watched her, face awash with emotions too quick to read. Finally, she spoke. "It's too late to stop that," she said. She turned and palmed open the door. "Go. I'll stall if they ask me to close the corridors. That's all I can do."

Warmth rushed into Anaea's limbs along with relief. "Come with me," she said.

"I—" Orithia gulped down the words she might have said. "I can't."

"I'm sorry." Anaea stepped into the hall, aching at the distance she put between them. "Thank you. I'll tell—"

"Just go." Orithia closed her eyes.

Words, too many words, stinging like the cut of the scalpel. Anaea started walking. Five paces. Ten. The room where she had been interrogated, the restraint chair with one armrest still blood-spackled. The electronics panel, but if she called for help, it wouldn't come in time.

Past the next door, she spotted marks on the corridor molding and knew where she was. There were a few residential sectors of Themiscyra that had never been opened, planned for population growth. It meant she had a lot of ground to cover to make her escape, and she was flush and shaking. She pressed her body against the wall to steady herself.

"How did you get out?"

Anaea oozed to face the blonde officer, blood hissing in her ears. She tried to keep her eyes level, not stare too hard at the fact the woman hadn't reached for her stunner yet.

She played muddled – not hard to do. "What? You didn't do it on purpose?" She wobbled into the center of the corridor, hands spread.

The blonde's eyes narrowed in suspicion. "Why would I do that?" She moved closer, as one might do to a wounded animal.

Anaea thought she would choke on her breath. "To show me even if I can't get out, there's nowhere to go."

"There is nowhere to go," the blonde said. "And you're going back there."

She reached for Anaea's elbow. Anaea sidestepped, jamming her shoulder into the other woman's chest. Shove and step past, Dezba had directed, enough to get room to run. But instead of running, she grabbed for the stunner.

Startled, the officer wrenched about. Anaea's fingers brushed the hilt of the weapon and slid free. What should have been a neat charge turned into a slip and a stumble. But the advisor's voice snapped in her head, waking her body when she would have frozen.

The blonde grabbed her right arm and twisted it behind her. Anaea kept turning with the motion and jammed her other palm up into the woman's nose.

She had no expectation it would work, and was stunned when the officer reeled backwards, releasing her. Rather than freeze and gibber, her first instinct, she snatched for the stunner. Loosened from its holster by her earlier attempt, it tumbled free. She grasped it and backstepped.

The blonde straightened, groaning, and glared. Now shes recognized she had an opponent, not a frightened child. She advanced, eyes giving away nothing.

Anaea's hands shook on the stunner. She took a step back, desperate for distance between them, but the officer moved with her. Her fingers curled around the unfamiliar device, feeling how fragile it was compared to the souped-up creation Rip had given her. Unfamiliar? This was her world and should have been natural to her.

"Put it down, Anaea," the blonde said. "This can get a lot worse."

"How?" she asked. Her mind carried her through the aim, the lift of her arm . . .

The woman hesitated – still thinking she wouldn't shoot? – then lunged.

The stunner blast haloed the air. The blonde's head jerked back. Anaea gasped as the fringes touched her. Her world spun, and a feather touch would have dropped her, but she had hit the security officer squarely enough the woman fell and did not move.

Anaea panted. She closed her eyes, trying to force the stunner halo away from her blistered senses.

Alarms shrilled down the corridor.

43

THE BLAST LANCED THROUGH ANAEA LIKE AURAL LIGHT-ning, even without the projection disc. She winced, knees locking. She shoved herself upright, forcing her hand to tighten on the stunner.

She sprinted up the corridor, trying to remember how many rooms to a region. Why was it so difficult when she had grown up in a space identical to this one? She heard a door whine behind her and dropped her shoulders. Should she weave? Not enough span in the corridor to prevent herself from being an easy target.

The door at the juncture ahead opened. The burly officer stepped out, weapon in hand. Anaea tensed, swinging up her hand to fire.

Then she realized the woman wasn't facing her, but scanning the hall towards the exit.

Before she could take advantage of the distraction, Valasca's voice rang out from behind. "Stay where you are, Anaea, or—"

"Or what?" Anaea turned to face her, bone weary, but hands as steady as rock. "What else could you possibly do?"

The other officer appeared at her elbow, looking to Valasca for instruction.

"There's nowhere to go," Valasca said. Her eyes slid to the fallen blonde, impassive. "You may have gotten lucky once, but you won't again."

Anaea put her back to the wall. The burly officer first, she thought, heart pounding. If the woman closed with her, there was no resisting. But what chance was there even if she did everything right? Something else in the sequence of events nagged at her, but she couldn't pin it down.

The lights went out, plunging the corridor into darkness.

Anaea yelped and ducked instinctively. The air above her flared with the nimbus of a stunner – whose? She slid low, holding her breath and counting her steps.

"Anaea!" Valasca shouted.

She jerked up, whirled, and fired. By the cut-off cry in the darkness, she had hit someone, but there was no way of knowing who. Her eyes soaked in the lack of light and started to adjust, in enough time to be paralyzed by the massive figure looming over her.

The officer lunged. Anaea pulled back, looking for a opening to strike even though she couldn't remember a word of Dezba's teachings. It startled her when the woman crashed to the floor.

Anaea!

The voice burst into her consciousness despite the lingering drugs, despite the instincts that pounded higher thought out of her, despite the distance – no, that wasn't right. *You're here,* she thought an instant before her eyes made out the two figures at the end of the hall. The smaller of the two lowered his stunner. Relief sang through her.

"Orithia," Valasca snapped, "get the lights back!"

Had she put them out in the first place, or merely not stopped Flick from doing it? Anaea pushed away from the wall, weaving around the fallen woman.

Flick's voice cut through sharply, "Ann, watch—"

She saw the shape out of the corner of her eye and tried to jerk out of the way. Valasca grabbed her shoulder. The woman's fingers drove in, raw strength born of desperation. Anaea felt the scalpel skim her ribs. Her world stopped.

"Sometimes, a thing has to be done personally," the chief doctor said in a low, soft voice. "Drop the stunners and hold still."

The lights returned, a vicious strobe in Anaea's eyes. She cried out, squeezing them shut. The stunner tumbled out of her hand by reflex.

"You can't hurt her," Gwydion said. "The security forces will find this place, and soon. They'll want answers for everything that happened here."

"What if I tell them a traitor died? Who is to know the difference?" Valasca addressed him, but the words hissed in Anaea's ears.

"Hey, lady," Flick said softly, "we don't have to leave this to the law to sort out. We can all walk away and no one has to know."

Gwydion flicked him a stunned look, but then nodded agreement. Surprise rushed over Anaea, that Gwydion, so honorable, would break on that point.

But that willingness wouldn't save her. She could feel the taut fury vibrating through Valasca and knew there was no compromise in the doctor. Trying not to hold her breath, she turned her free arm, angling it inwards.

"Then I have no recourse, do I?" Valasca would have sounded calm, but the flatness in her voice allowed no emotion. The hand on Anaea's shoulder pulled her backwards. "Either way, you intend to see your own justice. It seems only fitting that I finish mine."

Anaea reacted what she instantly knew she was too soon, jabbing her elbow into Valasca's abdomen. The doctor jerked. The scalpel twisted into Anaea's side; it grated against a rib. She heard herself cry out, but resisted the impulse to cringe away, throwing her momentum into the blow instead.

Combined with Valasca's stumble and the loosening grip, she

dropped free. She lunged for the stunner; she never needed it. The two men acted before she could.

She collapsed, cheek against the floor. Their footsteps sounded like a thundering horde as they hurried to hover over her.

"Anaea?" Gwydion pulled her up, or started to. When she winced and curled on herself, he halted, though one hand gently cradled on her shoulder. "What happened?"

"Should I start kicking them while they're down?" Flick wondered, but the levity was harsh.

She shook her head. "Find Orithia," she said.

"Uh, Anaea?" Flick said, his hand wavering. "These people aren't going to stay out long."

"You can shoot them again," Gwydion pointed out, voice calm, though she could hear the underlying anger and worry.

"Err, right." Flick shifted his stance. "Did she just twitch?"

Gwydion helped Anaea to her feet. They wobbled down the hall into the interrogation chamber. He hissed in air, painfully fast. "What did . . ."

"Not now," she said.

Orithia had stationed herself in the next room. She hunched over her equipment and snapped up when the door opened. Her eyes raked over their faces. "Why are you here?"

"We owe you an explanation," Anaea said. "May he touch your mind?"

Orithia shrank back. "So you're going to make me believe whatever you want?" Yet her tone was more anxious than combative.

"I can't make you believe anything you don't want to," Gwydion said.

"Do it," the programmer said, voice flat.

Anaea didn't know what she was expecting: a swirl of light, a pained shudder from Gwydion, a scream from her friend. Nothing happened until Orithia's eyes widened, her lips parting. "Oh . . . oh! When you left the infirmary . . ."

She dove forward and grabbed Anaea in a bone-rattling hug.

It set off all the pain in Anaea's body, and she didn't care. She returned the hug, crying with relief.

Orithia pulled back reluctantly and fixed Gwydion with a fierce look. "Your job was to protect her," she said.

"Uh, guys?" Flick's voice floated down the hall. "Can we go? Toxaris and her people noticed the commotion. They're on their way."

Gwydion grimaced. "I was afraid of that," he said.

Anaea blinked in confusion. "Why is that a problem?"

"Toxaris wouldn't let us use our respective talents to find you," Gwydion said quietly. "We snuck out. We aren't going anywhere, Flick," he continued, gesturing for the women to follow him into the hall. "Nothing to do but stay and face the music."

"Aww, seriously?"

"What about you?" Anaea asked, studying her friend. "I can tell Toxaris that you—"

Orithia shook her head. "Tell the truth," she said. "There's been enough trouble from concealment and false impressions."

"In the interests of that," Flick said brightly, "I should tell you I've never had a better matching of wits."

Orithia looked nonplussed, but smiled, a tentative curl of her lips. "Thank you," she said.

Anaea wobbled out into the interrogation room. The sight of the restraint chair made her ill, but her thoughts swirled fast and fierce. She remembered Asteria's intimations they would continue the deception even though the need for it had ended. She thought of Valasca, defending their perfect sanctuary. Thought of the rescue she had found beyond its borders.

She looked over at Orithia to ask her how the broadcast system worked. She was stopped by the weariness and pain on her friend's face, so recently soothed.

This had begun with Orithia. It had never been a choice for Anaea: she knew from the beginning she would follow the mystery wherever it led. Her first decision had been what to tell the programmer about the truth she had learned. Could she make that same choice for the whole station?

"Orithia," she said, "how widely can this broadcast?"

"It can broadcast to any single region," the programmer said.

One fact, one revelation, one question. Not forcing the information on them, but an invitation. Anaea had a duty not to cause panic as much as she had a duty to the truth. Was this what the station leaders felt? "Region 11," she said. It was where she had lived with other interns.

"Anaea," Gwydion said, "are you sure?"

She smiled; it hurt the muscles of her face. "I'm sure."

"Wait," Flick said, "are you . . ." He caught the tension in the air and clamped his mouth shut.

Orithia palmed the panel. She nodded to Anaea.

Anaea would have closed her eyes, but she was afraid she would fall. "My name is Anaea Carlisle," she said. "I'm one of you. I know some of you. I've been beyond Themiscyra, and there's more out there than you know." She glanced over at her companions and only then knew what she would say. The words flowed, a talent she now believed in.

"A place where Tweakers put two devices together and come up with something greater than the pieces. A place where the Hypermental Chamber teaches its people to live around the secrets of others. A place where no good deed goes unrecognized and its worth is like coin."

She wanted to say more, but that was enough. Enough to challenge Themiscyra's version of reality without shattering it.

"It's a place I believe in."

She exhaled a long, slow breath and gestured to Orithia. The programmer closed the connection.

She had given the station denizens the possibility of more. Had it been the best decision? She might never know, but it felt right.

"Just so we make it perfectly clear to the authorities," Flick said, "that was not my idea."

*

Station security arrived and took everyone into custody. Toxaris treated them as criminals. The officers went around and around the story until Anaea began to feel as if she were back in Valasca's care, asserting truths that would never be believed.

It ended with Asteria's arrival. She swept Anaea away. Unsure what Orithia had confessed, and how she could tell the story so as to absolve the programmer of her mired involvement, Anaea emphasized only how her friend had helped her escape.

"That indicates she was part of Valasca's plans," Asteria said.

"She felt hurt and betrayed," Anaea said. "I can't blame her."

"It is not a question of blame." Asteria's voice remained mild. "It is a question of legality."

Anaea tried to control her plummeting heart. She felt as if she had descended through the station to drift in space. "The others used her," she said. "You can't—"

Asteria held up a hand. "Allow me to finish," she said. "I can make personal exceptions. No harm will come to her, and your companions will be released back to the warlord party." She chuckled. "As is for the better, for Toxaris would like to roast them."

"If they hadn't acted, I would be worse off."

"I know." The station's leader looked at her keenly. "You were ready to sacrifice all to protect your honor. Why?"

"It's not solely my honor," Anaea said. "Right now, I stand for the outside world. If I confessed to Valasca's accusations, it would make warlords and matriarchs alike look like thieves and schemers."

"And they aren't?" Asteria arched an eyebrow.

Anaea blushed, but refused to lower her eyes. "Not all of them. I still believe what I said before, and I will put my life on the line to stand by it."

"So you've shown." Asteria shook her head. "I just heard

about your stunt in Region 11. I am dismayed, but impressed. It cannot have the effect you intended. How can I open the way to some without destroying the hermetic safety of this place?"

Anaea hesitated. "I'm not sure," she admitted, "but—"

"There is no but. If I cannot ensure our way of life for some, I will not give it up for all." The station leader frowned, but the expression was gentle. "You have done well to bring your friends here. I will bargain with them, and I will send them away."

Anaea had no great plan to keep Themiscyra safe, no assurances or experience to guide her. "You can't keep the secret forever," she said.

"I never asked for forever," Asteria said. "But this is not the time."

Now Anaea regretted not shouting every piece of evidence, making herself hoarse in defense of the truth, but people would ask questions. People would wonder. It was a beginning, if not the one she had hoped for.

Her companions joined her outside. "Is your friend going to be all right?" Flick asked. "She's amazing, and I want her to teach me that trick she used to hide the system outputs. I could use a routine like that."

"Come," Toxaris said, appearing at the head of the corridor. "The sooner I have you three off my station, the happier I'll be." Her eyes narrowed on Anaea. "If you were still a citizen, I would see you never left confinement, after that stunt you pulled."

Anaea wanted to shrivel under that gaze, but she stood firm and said nothing. She would not apologize.

Toxaris led them to the conference room, where Dezba prowled with the look of a caged animal. She rounded towards the door as it opened.

"Glad to see you're all right," she said. Though her eyes lingered on Flick, they moved away without comment. She gave Toxaris no consideration other than a nod; the woman returned neither explanation nor courtesy. The tension sang between them.

"Let's go," Dezba said. The trio followed her to the docking bay. Flick looked uncertain, but didn't bolt.

"You're Marianna's grandson, aren't you?" Dezba fixed her attention on Flick as they entered the bay, steel gaze. "Did you stow away on my ship?"

Flick stood square and sure. "Yes. Had to be done."

Anaea tensed, looking over at Gwydion. *He can probably find some place to hide on the station . . .*

An ominous moment of silence as Dezba regarded the stowaway . . . and then laughed, a short, quiet burst. "And managed to launch a rescue expedition from hiding. Clever. You've made yourself useful; thank you. Step out of line and you won't have berth home."

"Understood," Flick said hastily, even as his face split into a grin.

Back on the ship, Dezba queried her for details. She explained Valasca's intentions, even as her stomach knotted up. She fought down the desire to be ill.

"If I had faked a confession," she said, "I think it would have ruined any chance at alliance."

"You did well. Falsehood serves no one." Dezba shook her head. "If your women don't punish her, I will intervene. No one can assault my people in that fashion."

Her people? Anaea restrained her protests, suspecting it was a matter of saving face, not sentiment. She shuddered, wondering what sufficient punishment was to a warlord who dropped people into a raptorhound run.

Anaea tried to rest, but her mind caught in endless loops, repeating thoughts in the same way she had faced her interrogators. Valasca, the security officers, Orithia, Justin, whirling together in a morass that refused to make sense.

She rubbed Penelope's neck as she curled up on her bed. "We'll get you home," she said. "Soon."

The kearl chittered, nudged her, and wound up under her

arm. Methodically, she licked at the cuts on Anaea's arm, a small, determined nursemaid.

*

Negotiations resumed the next day. Toxaris informed them that Valasca had been stripped of her position pending judgment. Asteria asked Anaea how she was recovering. And Orithia was there, smiling shyly, her presence in the outer room enough to reassure Anaea the programmer would be fine.

The negotiations were a disaster. Asteria, Toxaris, and another blonde tried to wring answers from both sides, with little result. Dezba's cold anger prompted even more sweetness and softness from Morgan. Briefly, Anaea feared Themiscyra would slide into Dennison's arms, unilaterally, but Asteria was too canny for that.

Morgan took offense. "Why are you indecisive, when she's so obviously against you?" she asked.

"She's being honest," Asteria said. "She's angry one of her allies was in such danger, and rightly so."

"Allies, or pets?" Morgan asked. "Best be sure what a warlord means."

A few hours after they had begun, Orithia entered. "There's a new message for us." She didn't seem to have the courage to look at Asteria directly, her awe leaking up with sideways flits of her eyes.

"Is there something wrong on my ship?" Morgan inquired.

Dezba started to speak, then shrugged. "It's not on my end."

"No, no. It's not from either of the ships. Someone new." Orithia glanced hastily at Anaea. "I thought there were only two empires out there."

"Yes," Dezba said curtly.

No, Anaea thought, her puzzlement evaporating as she remembered the message she had sent. Was it really only days ago? She pushed to her feet. "Two empires, but more than two factions," she said, surprised at the clarity of her voice. "Asteria, may I speak to you?"

Asteria nodded, gesturing them into the corridor. "What is this about?" she asked.

"If I'm right," Anaea said, "the person who sent that message is the answer to your question."

"Hmm." Asteria lifted a brow. "Come with me." She strode up the hall to an office adjoining and activated the projection console. The incoming message revealed a hearteningly familiar face, blonde hair pulled back in a ponytail.

"My greetings to the people of this station," she said. Her tone was formal, but it strained like children anxious to run.

"I would greet you in turn," Asteria replied, "but I do not know you. I am Asteria Cole, the leader of Themiscyra."

"Themiscyra . . ." Phailin tasted the word, then grinned. "Dr. Phailin Anders of the Sanctum. I came here on the invitation of a denizen of yours, I believe."

"Hello, Phailin." Anaea surprised herself with her own words. "I see you got my message." Awkwardly, she stepped into the range of the projector.

Phailin laughed. "Good to see you, Anaea. Yes, loud and clear. You know, I asked you to find facts for me, not to completely disrupt a legislative movement."

Asteria arched a brow, inquisitive, but then her expression darkened. "Dr. Anders," she said, "when did you learn of this place?"

Anaea caught her breath, hearing the doubt and anger in the station leader's voice and able to guess her line of thought. If Asteria had detained Valasca and trusted Anaea, only to find the chief doctor's accusations were true, what then?

"Almost too late," Phailin replied amiably. "After your visitors got their start, for sure." She sobered. "When I told your girl I would never harm a place like this, if it existed, she gave me back nothing more than hypotheticals. I was impressed enough with her behavior, then and later, to ask her to serve as my ears in Serendipity.

"We've been looking for you for a long time," she continued. "Possibly longer than anyone else. We've had the rumors of history to encourage us."

"Why?" Asteria spoke bluntly, but without hostility.

"Because my enclave aspires to the same thing yours does. A shield against the outside world. A place where the polarized rule of matriarchs or warlords doesn't apply."

"I see." Asteria's face lay like glass, still, serene, but obviously deep in thought. "We shall have to talk."

Anaea took a step back, hearing the thrum of her heart quiet, and aware only then how fast it had been pounding. The two had met, as she had hoped, and seemed to understand each other. It was a good beginning, the best she could ask for.

She felt a tightness in her chest ease. It was a sense of finality, that she had done everything she could.

Phailin quirked a brow, noticing her retreat. "Where do you think you're going?"

Anaea spread her hands. "This is all above my head—"

"We may need a translator, a cultural one, and I can't think of better." The doctor's image glanced to her opposite. "If you have no objections?"

"None," Asteria said.

44

THE TWO WOMEN, WITH ANAEA AS THEIR MIDDLE GROUND, talked for hours. Phailin described the Sanctum and her philosophy. Asteria responded warily, couching her responses in vagueness and partial information, but warmed as the conversation continued. Soon, they spoke as equals.

At Phailin's urging, Anaea told the story of what had happened with Traviata. The Sanctum's leader growled at the regina's schemes.

"You did this as much for us, I think," Asteria said mildly.

"I did the best I could," Anaea replied.

"You did enough that the Sanctum is secure, more than it was, even," Phailin said. "And enough that I can make an offer."

Asteria listened attentively and nodded. "That seems ideal," she said. "Your assistance will—"

"There's something else we need," Anaea interrupted.

Both women turned startled looks on her. "Well, go on," Phailin said.

"Offer escort to any woman of Themiscyra who wants to leave the station," Anaea said. "I'm not asking you to babysit them or guide them forever, only to enable their first steps." She turned to Asteria. "And I'm asking you to give them the option."

She held her breath, feeling her audacity vibrate against her chest. But she had negotiated with warlords, spoken before Council in Serendipity. She felt sure in her voice, and this was exactly what Asteria had asked for: if the Sanctum served as an intermediary, they could open the door to some without endangering everyone.

Asteria nodded slowly. "So be it," she said.

"You won't regret it," Phailin said. "I think offering an orientation program is only fair, under the circumstances."

Anaea felt the strings in her heart snap, relief, joy. She would be the station's first and last fugitive.

The two women clasped hands on the deal, then summoned the respective factions to the conference room. Morgan recognized Phailin, her eyes narrowing. Anaea tried to look inconspicuous.

"The station of Themiscyra has forged a trade agreement," Asteria said, "with the enclave of the Sanctum. We have promised them exclusive access to technology and goods."

Dezba launched out of her chair. Morgan went white and summoned breath for an imperious speech. The other faction members shouted over each other.

"And we," Phailin said, her voice cutting through the din, "will be happy to bargain with both sides."

The scientists gabbled questions en masse. Morgan launched into her speech, but there was no wind in her voice. Dezba turned his gaze to Anaea.

"This is your game, then," she said softly. "Your plan from the beginning, if you could achieve it."

She swallowed, feeling her throat twist and knowing her two friends were aboard the shuttle. But the warlords valued directness and honesty. She had to trust that.

"Yes," she said. "I never made you any promises. I only showed you the way."

Dezba's silence seemed to absorb every other sound in the

room. "That's true," she said. "I don't know if Avidan will feel the same way."

"He's not here," Anaea pointed out.

For an instant, fleeting, the advisor smiled. "That," she said, "is also true."

Anaea slumped in her chair, dizzy with relief. Dialogue continued without her. The rest of the meeting passed in a blur, dissolving into promises of individual negotiations. She rose to leave, her ankles quivering.

"Anaea!" Morgan's voice halted her.

She wanted to keep walking, but made herself turn. "What is it?"

"You're still with Gwydion?" Despite the inflection, it was not a question.

Anaea folded her arms above her stomach. "Yes, I am."

Morgan studied her with cool scrutiny, then smiled slowly. She laid a hand on Anaea's arm. "When this began, I hated you," she said. "With what I've seen recently – better you than I. I so hope" – her tone turned saccharine – "you can make the best of such a sticky situation without embarrassing yourself more than you already have. Get in touch with me if you need assistance, hmm?" She sailed out of the room.

Anaea stared after, trying to process the offer couched in venom, the admiration wrapped in insult. "What was that about?"

She also realized she would never get an answer.

*

SHE MET GWYDION later in a prayer alcove. The dim gold light wreathed them in a blanket of shadow.

"It's official," she said. "You can stay as long as you want. Phailin vouched for you, and so did I." Peculiar as it felt, that was beginning to mean something.

"I appreciate it," he said. "Does that mean you'll be staying? I—" he flushed. "I want to be where you are. But I understand if my religious – if that's a problem." He glanced about, a man hunting for meaning.

Anaea focused on the question. "I don't think so," she said. "At least, not more than a couple of weeks until this is sorted out and I can finish patching things with Orithia. If I can."

Gwydion frowned, confused. "I removed the memory alteration."

"It's not about betrayal or lost love any more," she said. "It's about the fact that I went and she stayed. That I can feel this new reality singing in my bones, and she still prefers the old one. May always prefer it."

"I wouldn't count her isolation as destiny yet," Gwydion said. "She seems extremely interested in the programming infrastructure and techniques Flick is showing her. Could be she just enjoys bumping heads with him, too, I'm not sure."

"I'm happy to hear that," Anaea said, "but that won't bring us closer. Though Penelope seems none the worse for wear and has taken up as if nothing happened." She perched on a bench, trying to sort her feelings into a forward direction. "But after that, I'm going to leave. I have to leave. This place feels so small, so simple, so . . . known. Do you understand what I mean?

"Phailin wants me to come back with her, work on the orientation program – give anyone who leaves Themiscyra a smoother ride than I had. She says it's necessary not only for us, but for the people we meet." Anaea smiled wryly. "I'm not sure about that, but she is a psychologist."

"Well, look at what you did to society," Gwydion said. His voice was teasing, but she couldn't miss the anxiety in his face.

"After that, I don't know," she continued. "All this, and I still have no home, but I think that's all right. I have so many places to look, I don't want to stop just because I can. I would love you to come with me . . ."

She took a deep breath to steady herself, which was a mistake. Gwydion pushed into the silence. "If you're going to tell me I can't for my own good, don't," he said. "I can fight my own battles.

And whatever happens, I can't sit still. You've helped me realize I'm not home yet, either."

"No." It reminded Anaea that a man who could read minds didn't always know how to read people. "I'm not trying to push you away, but I know some things have been awkward for us."

Gwydion blushed. "I can't apologize for that."

"I'm not asking you to." Anaea drew strength from the serenity of the alcove. "I told you in my belief system, there isn't such a thing as marriage, but there is a life-tie." Her heart squeezed, and she hurried on, "Those who are life-tied are the only ones who can contribute genetic material to a child, so . . ." She spread her hands. "It's the closest we have. I can't look ahead, I can't know the future, but I know I want you to be there, without guilt muddling us." Anaea held his eyes. "Would you form a life-tie with me, for a year, for two? Would that be an answer?"

"A hundred theologians," he said, "would have a hundred different replies." He reached out, pulling her close. "My heart says no just God, or any divine force, would frown on this compromise." A soft chuckle. "Loophole."

Joy filled her, banished every dark space. "If it's a loophole," she said, tipping her head up, "it was meant to be there."

"Maybe," he said, "but . . ."

She quieted him by kissing him, and quickly forgot that had been her original intention.

He broke the kiss. "Two years," he said. "We'll give it two, and then . . ."

It wasn't a surrender or an admission that this might not be forever. Instead, it was a step on a journey where it was too soon to know the destination. Anaea knew her answer was out there, and she would know it when she reached it.

503

About the Author

Lindsey Duncan is a chef/pastry chef in the catering field. She is also a professional performer and teacher on the traditional lever harp, also referred to as the Celtic harp. She has been writing since her fingers first touched the keys at the age of eight, and has short fiction and poetry in numerous speculative fiction publications. Her contemporary fantasy novel, Flow, is available from Double Dragon Publishing.

She lives in the United States near Cincinnati, Ohio, with two Bichon Frise dogs, Peri and Lexi. She can be found on the web at LindseyDuncan.com